Roisin MEANEY

The Birthday Party

HACHETTE
BOOKS
IRELAND

First published in Ireland in 2019 by
HACHETTE BOOKS IRELAND

First published in paperback in 2020

2

Cataloguing in Publication Data is available from the British Library

Paperback ISBN 9781473643079
Ebook ISBN 9781473643055
Audio ISBN 9781529368222

Typeset in Bembo Book Std by Bookends Publishing Services

Printed and bound in Great Britain by Clays Ltd, Elcograf S.p.A.

Bunting image: © PixMarket/shutterstock.com

Hachette Books Ireland policy is to use papers that are natural, renewable
and recyclable products and made from wood grown in sustainable forests.
The logging and manufacturing processes are expected to conform to the
environmental regulations of the country of origin.

Hachette Books Ireland
8 Castlecourt Centre
Castleknock
Dublin 15, Ireland

A division of Hachette UK Ltd
Carmelite House, 50 Victoria Embankment, EC4Y 0DZ
www.hachettebooksireland.ie

For Rory Barnes, one of life's gentlemen,
remembered fondly

HENRY MANNING, PROPRIETOR OF ROONE'S only hotel, was making plans. Weeks to go yet, tomorrow only the first of June, but half the fun was in the planning.

A marquee set up in the grounds, because a summer garden party sounded wonderful, but everyone knew you couldn't depend on the weather in Ireland, even in August. Lots of canapés, trays and trays of them. His chefs would be busy.

Flutes of champagne to greet everyone on arrival. Real champagne, none of your Prosecco or Cava nonsense. Wine and beer on offer too – he might steer clear of spirits – and tumblers of Mrs Bickerton's sparkling lemonade (named after the long-departed hotel guest who had shared her recipe with Henry) for the children in attendance, and the wise older souls on the island who kept their distance from alcohol. Tea and coffee put out later, when the cake appeared.

Music, of course. He pictured a string quartet out on the lawn – or in the gazebo if the rain came. Henry was partial to a little Vivaldi in the summertime, and was casting about among his musical connections for a suitable ensemble that would fancy a night on the island.

The cake would be five tiers at least, on a scale big enough so everyone who wanted it got a taste, and ordered from the mainland so he didn't offend any of Roone's bakers by choosing one over another. Candles to be lit and blown out: wasn't Henry as entitled to a wish as anyone?

No fireworks, much as he enjoyed a bit of airborne fizzle: too bright in August, the days still too long, the nights not yet cloaked in enough darkness. Fireworks, he felt, were better suited to New Year's Eve, when he unleashed a modest number of rockets and Catherine wheels at midnight for the benefit of those who had chosen to see out the old and herald the arrival of the new at Manning's.

A speech. He felt one should be made. Not long: the latest version had run to approximately three minutes and forty seconds when he'd tried it out before his bedroom mirror. A few words of thanks, a few amusing anecdotes pulled from his thirty-seven years at the helm of Manning's.

A mention of his grandparents, Charles and Dolores, who had built the hotel eighty-two years ago this October – and his parents, Jerry and Tess, who'd taken it over in due course and extended it to cater for the increasing number of tourists to the island. And Victor, Henry's older and only sibling, who'd set sail for America as a young man, in search of somewhere more adventurous than twenty-eight square miles of island set on the westernmost edge of Europe.

Victor had left Roone, but not hotels. He'd ended up with a chain of them along the American east coast, had made quite a packet before he'd jumped, aged sixty-two, from his penthouse window to escape the fire that raged below – started, it was discovered, by a carelessly wired refrigerator. No mention would be made of that sorry episode, of course. Poor Victor – dead, they'd been assured, from a heart attack before he'd hit the concrete, thirty-three floors later.

Bunting, lots of bunting. Henry had a thing for bunting. The very sight of the colourful little triangles fluttering above the lawn, any lawn, brought an answering flutter beneath his waistcoat, and made him feel instantly more festive. Even in the rain, bunting lifted the spirits – and after the recent sudden death of a much-loved island resident, spirits needed very badly to be lifted.

As to invitations, none were to be issued. Over the next few days Henry would simply put out the word that everyone was welcome, and it would pass among the islanders quicker than Fergus Masterson in his postal van. Not everyone would turn up, of course: there were those on Roone who wouldn't be seen dead inside the hotel. Uncomfortable with a hotelier who had never produced a wife, whose interests clearly lay elsewhere – although Henry had never flaunted his status, never made any declaration, or paraded a male companion about. No matter: let them condemn him if they must. Let them stay away, and Henry would enjoy himself with guests who didn't judge him for his preferences.

August the second he'd chosen for the party.

Six days before his actual birthday, which he was planning to mark more privately, and more quietly, in Paris – but he wanted the public celebration too. He wanted the congratulations and the gifts and the toasts, surrounded by friends he'd known since boyhood, and their children and their children's children.

Not every day a man turned seventy. Not every man batted away death for all those years. Henry intended to make the most of it, and give Roone a night it wouldn't forget.

JUNE

Eve

FOR THE PAST SIX WEEKS THERE HAD BEEN A simmering in her head. That was the only way she could put it. A slow, steady simmering, a quiet bubbling that now and again rose up and threatened to – what? Spill over and drown her. Send her screaming into the nuthouse. Cause her to do something terrible and unforgivable and irreparable.

It was a miracle she'd been able to keep afloat, to go back to work after the week off she'd been granted following Hugh's death. It had taken everything she had not to snap at her little charges, or raise a hand and let them have it. If the parents had known how close she'd come to it once or twice, they'd have taken their children away and never allowed her within a mile of them again.

But the parents were being so gentle with her. So caring, so kind. *How are you?* they asked, in hushed voices. *How are you coping, dear?* Bringing her batches of cookies, or paper bags of apples from their trees, or pots of homemade jam. As if food, any food, could help, even if she'd been able to stomach it. As if anything could make her feel even a tiny bit less dire. She wanted to scream at them to go away, to leave her be, but of course she couldn't do that either.

It was Hugh. It was all down to Hugh, all his fault. She couldn't think about him, couldn't stop thinking about him. How could he have *left* her? It was unconscionable that he wasn't there any more, that she couldn't pick up the phone and hear his voice, or meet him for one of their beach walks, or arrive at his house – his and Imelda's house – and watch him light up with pleasure at the sight of her. That had been worth anything, the smile she'd brought to his face. *Hello, minx*, he'd say to her, gathering her into him with his good arm. *What have you to say for yourself? Account for your movements.*

It was unbearable that he would never be there again, that his chair at the top of the table was now empty, and would stay empty. She felt ragged from the loss of him, and tightly wound as a bow string, and the simmering never let up for a minute.

In the week immediately following his death, the crèche having been temporarily handed back to her predecessor Avril, Eve had spent most of her time with Imelda. Both of them too dazed to think straight, too shocked to do more than sit in silence a lot of the time, Imelda eventually getting up to reheat someone's donated casserole that they would then push around their plates until it grew cold.

Even after she resumed work, Eve had continued

to spend as much time as she could with Imelda – and every night, except for one, she'd returned to the apartment above the crèche that had been her home since January, and tried to catch even a couple of hours' sleep.

But one night, she hadn't. One night, only nine days after Hugh's death, she'd sought refuge from her grief and loneliness – and now, a month later, when she'd thought things couldn't possibly get any worse, they had. Now everything had changed again. Now, along with missing Hugh, along with wanting, every now and again, to throw something fragile against a wall, she had a new situation to grapple with, and she had no idea how she would cope. If she would cope.

'Eve, love, you must try to eat.'

She lifted her head and looked at Imelda. *If only you knew.* 'I can't.'

'Just take a small –'

And then it happened. Out of nowhere – only of course it wasn't out of nowhere: it was out of the simmering of six weeks – she finally bubbled up and spilt over.

'I *can't* eat!' she cried, shoving away her bowl of soup, causing it to shoot across the table and go flying over the edge, landing with a clatter and a reddish-brown splash on the kitchen tiles, spattering cooker and cupboard doors, and Imelda's slippers that sat on the floor by the fridge. 'I *can't* eat – stop *nagging* me! You're not my *mother!*' Her voice high and shrill and not sounding at all familiar, and Imelda's mouth dropping open, her face full of bewilderment, and Scooter appearing from under the table to lap up the spill, apparently unaware that Eve had finally taken leave of her senses, had gone over the edge as surely as the soup.

'I can't *stand* this!' she shouted, pushing back her chair with a screech. 'I can't *bear* it! I'm going home!'

'Eve, it's alright, I understand you're —'

'You *don't* understand!' she shot back, snatching up the jacket she'd dropped in a heap on the worktop. 'You have no *idea*!' Wrenching open the back door and slamming it behind her, running from the garden to the road, blood singing in her ears, praying to God she met nobody on the way home – and for once, God listened.

In the apartment she sat with her head in her hands, trying to blot out the fact that she'd shouted at Imelda, who'd done nothing to deserve it. Still on fire inside, her breath coming short and fast, her fingertips tingling. Her phone rang, more than once: she ignored it. She sat, dry-eyed, throat hurting, wanting it all to stop. Needing it all to go away, but it wasn't going away. It was going nowhere.

And then, as darkness crept into the room, blurring outlines, leaching colours, as her breath slowed and softened, she thought, *Imelda would have left me anyway. Imelda would have left like everyone else, once word got out.* So it didn't matter that she'd blown up in the kitchen: in fact, it was probably for the best. Cut the tie, be the one to end it.

As she was undressing for bed, her phone rang again. She picked it up and saw Imelda's name, and shut it off.

Laura

'I'D PREFER,' HE SAID, 'IF YOU TOLD NOBODY about this.'

She regarded her fingers, resting on the steering wheel. There was a small blue bruise on a knuckle that she didn't remember getting. 'I really think you should tell Susan.' When he didn't respond she turned to face him. 'Why won't you?'

He met her gaze. 'Because I choose not to,' he replied, the words carrying little emotion – she never remembered him raising his voice in anger – but she could see in the tiny narrowing of his eyes the irritation the question had caused. You didn't question him.

She looked away. She lowered her hands to rest them in her lap. Through the windscreen she watched the approach of the ferry that would take him from the island, an hour after it had dropped him here.

The surprise of seeing him on the doorstep, completely out of the blue. She'd been in the middle of cleaning up after the breakfasts – at least he hadn't arrived in the middle of the full Irish but no tomato, and the extra toast just lightly browned, and the soft-boiled egg but make sure the white was set. At least he'd waited until all that palaver was over.

You weren't expecting me, he'd said, which had to be the understatement of the century. He must have left Dublin at cockcrow to arrive on Roone by eleven. She wondered what he'd told Susan to explain his absence, but she knew better than to ask him that. Susan came often to Roone, but his last appearance on the island had been for Laura and Gavin's wedding, coming on for three years ago – or was it four? They'd married in October, three months after Marian and Evie were born, which made it four years. Time flew, whether you were having fun or not.

There's something, he'd said, *I need to talk to you about* – so she'd left Gav and the boys finishing off things in the house and she'd brought him out to the field, and he'd told her as they walked the perimeter what he'd come to tell her, and she'd tried to take it in, but she still hadn't done that, not really. And then he'd asked her to drive him back to the ferry, so she'd returned to the house and got the van keys from Gav, and here they were.

'I appreciate this,' he said. 'I know it's asking a lot.'

In all her recollections he'd never asked anything of her, never looked for her help in any way before this. But this wasn't just any old request, any old favour: this was a big one. This was about as big as it got. And to have to keep it from everyone, even Gav, even Susan, was asking a hell of a lot. She'd have to make up a tale for Gav, who'd be dying to know what had prompted the visit – and Susan could never even be told that the encounter had taken place.

She turned again to look at him, and again he met her gaze steadily. He'd never been one for looking away, she'd give him that. He met a situation head on, like he was meeting this one. He'd got older looking since their last encounter in Dublin, a year and a half earlier. The skin on his cheeks was beginning to descend, the first hint of jowls forming. The bags beneath his eyes were more pronounced, the brilliant turquoise of the irises fading, but the face was as arresting, as commanding of attention, as it had always been. Sixty-five, wasn't he? Not old these days – and by all accounts, working as much as ever.

'I wish ...' she began, and came to a halt. She wished so much. She wished he was different. She wished their story was different. She wished she'd held her tongue on that last encounter instead of telling him, in a fit of anger, that he would die alone. She wished they loved one another, and depended on one another, and missed each other when they were apart.

Some minuscule shift occurred in his face then, some blurring of the edges happened. 'What do you wish?' he asked mildly, eyes holding hers, an almost-smile on his mouth – but her courage didn't equal his, and she shook her head.

'So many things, I wouldn't know where to start. We'd better get going,' she said, reaching for the door handle.

'Stay,' he said, 'there's no need for you to come out,' so she remained where she was, and echoed his goodbye – no embrace, never an embrace. She turned the van around while he was still walking across the pier, not thinking about the conversation they'd had in the field, because God alone knew where that might bring her. Best to put it from her, to pack it away where nobody would find it, to never dwell on it.

On the way back to Walter's Place she thought up a story for Gav. *An insurance thing*, she'd say. *Some official arrangement he wants to set up. To be honest, it was so boring I didn't pay it too much attention. Some form he needs me to fill in.* It wasn't great, it wasn't even particularly believable, but it would have to do. She hated lying, only ever did it when she knew the truth would hurt, but he'd left her with little choice.

She pulled up by the five-bar gate and got out. She left the van unlocked – this was Roone: only tourists locked their vehicles – and made her way into the field, because she felt a sudden need to talk to George.

'What do you make of that?' she asked him, running a hand along the rough hair of his neck. 'Is that not the weirdest—' And then she had to stop, because the lump in her throat was making it difficult to carry on. She lifted her face to the sky, palm resting against George's comforting warmth, and drank in the fresh air with the taste of the sea on it until it steadied her.

'He comes here,' she resumed, stroking the soft ear, scratching along the length of the nose, 'no warning,

George. Not a phone call, not even a text. We could have been gone away.' Although he'd known they wouldn't be gone anywhere, not with the season in full swing, and the island bursting at the seams, like it always was in the summer months.

'Why me, George? Why did he have to –' She broke off again, blinking and swallowing, pulling more sea air into her. God, this was ridiculous. She'd have to hold it together when she went inside, or Gav would see right through her. 'OK,' she said then, patting the donkey's flank. 'OK. Thanks, George. Always good talking to you.'

He meant nothing to her. They had no bond, like a normal father and child would have. All her life he'd failed her. She'd resolved to sever ties with him that last time, sworn never to let him get to her again. And now here he was, dragging her back.

Get a grip, she told herself, crossing the field to the house. You've agreed to his request, nothing more to be done. It's his problem, not yours. Let it go, let it off, don't think about him any more.

She entered the house, setting her face to meet Gav and the kids. Becoming once more Laura the wife, Laura the mother, Laura the one who sorted things out. Laura the sister in a few weeks, when Tilly flew over from Australia to spend her third summer on Roone.

Little imagining, as she pushed open the scullery door, smile in place, that letting it go, letting it off, was going to prove completely out of the question.

JULY

Imelda

HIS TIES. HIS TIES TORE HER HEART IN TWO.
Every one of them drawing her back, every one of
them throwing up a memory that made the loss of
him a thousand times worse.

His narrow dark green tie in a fine wool. Their
first dinner together in Manning's Hotel. The salmon
mousse she'd eaten in tiny morsels, terrified he'd ask
her something when her mouth was full. His smile
when she'd told him about the ballet classes she'd
taken up the previous year, nervousness causing
her to blurt it out. Kicking herself the minute she
had it said, in case he thought her a fool to be doing
something like that at her age. His fingers touching
hers briefly when they'd both reached for the salt: the
skip it had caused inside her, like a foolish smitten
girl.

His navy tie with little red and grey boats stamped
on it. The night he'd leant towards her as the credits
were rolling after a film in Tralee – a spy thing she
hadn't been able to make an ounce of sense of – and

asked her in a whisper, his breath warm on her ear, if she'd ever consider marrying him. Not three months since they'd first laid eyes on one another on Roone's smallest pebbly beach, a day into her holiday on the island. She'd returned to Mayo less than a fortnight later, and after that the two of them had met up on Sundays only, in Tralee or Galway. Really, when you thought about it, it was no time at all to be thinking about marriage, but both of them had been certain by the time he'd asked the question. They'd reached an understanding, was how people would have put it.

His striped tie, rust and maroon and white, which had always put her in mind of a school uniform. His visit to Mayo so they could break the news together to her sister Marian and her brother-in-law Vernon. Marian's mouth dropping open when they'd told her, for once rendered speechless. Vernon beaming like someone who'd just won the Lotto, pumping Hugh's good arm, welcoming him to the family, telling him he was most welcome, most welcome indeed.

His wedding tie, the most heartbreaking of all. A beautiful dove grey, embossed with tiny repeated triangles in a shinier finish. His face at the top of the church, pale and tremulously smiling as she'd walked towards him on legs she couldn't feel, hanging on tight to Vernon's arm. Sick with nerves, but also knowing that she was entering the happiest time of her life. Wanting, despite her shakiness, to break away from Vernon and run up the aisle to him, hardly able to wait to become Mrs Hugh Fitzpatrick at the ripe old age of fifty-four. Little dreaming that before her sixtieth birthday she'd be his widow.

Was it too soon to be doing this, to be packing up his clothes? She had no template, no timetable for grief. Should she have waited longer? Probably – but she'd woken up needing to be around his things, needing to touch and sort and fold them, even if it killed her. She rolled the ties into neat rounds and secured them with straight pins. She placed them on top of the folded shirts, her heart broken clean in two with pain and loneliness and white-hot rage.

Not six years together, after waiting her whole life for him. The unfairness of it, the unbearable, unforgivable cruelty of it sent the anger raising a pulse in her temple, threatening to eat her up in its dreadful ferocity. Not even six years, when others got decades and decades, and children and grandchildren, and anniversary after anniversary after anniversary, before Death decided it was time to call a halt.

Denied his future, since losing him she'd hungered for his past. In the days that followed the funeral, when her grief had been bedding in, fierce and frightening, she'd ambushed his niece Nell, born and bred on Roone like Hugh, for what she could remember about him as a younger man, and poor Nell, full of her own loss, had battled tears as she'd reached into her memories and pulled them out.

He made a scarecrow once for some farmer who was looking for it. The head was a burst football, and he carved a bit of driftwood in the shape of the farmer's moustache and painted it to match, and stuck it on. I remember my mother giving out to him, in case the farmer took offence, but Hugh only laughed at her.

He found a wall clock for my birthday. I would have been nine or ten. It was in the shape of a yacht, and it had an anchor for a pendulum. I thought it was the most wonderful thing I'd ever seen. It's still around somewhere, I'm sure. I'll have a look for it and show you.

He helped me to paint Jupiter, *after Grandpa Will died, Hugh's dad. I was seventeen, and I missed him terribly. He'd left me his little rowboat, and I got it into my head that I wanted to paint it, as a sort of tribute to him or something, I don't know, and Hugh came with me to get the paint – I wanted something bright so we picked out yellow – and we painted it together.*

I remember when his bid on Considine's pub was accepted, and he renamed it Fitz's and made it his own. He was so happy then, and we were all delighted for him. There was a huge session in the pub on the opening night. Nobody had planned it, but every musician on the island turned up with an instrument – and I'd swear the music never sounded better. I remember the sun coming up as I walked home with Dad.

Imelda had listened to all the silly precious recollections. She'd added them to her own pathetic few, and held them close and kept them safe. She unfolded them in the darkness of her sleepless nights and walked through his early life with him, acquainting herself with the young man she'd never known. It kept her from falling completely apart.

She closed the box that held his shirts and ties,

mouth pressed tight, squeezing back the tears that wanted to fall all the time, all the time. The crying she'd done in the past seven weeks, rivers and rivers of heart-scalding tears – but there seemed to be no end to them.

Seven weeks. An eternity, an instant. Seven weeks since she'd woken and turned to him, and seen immediately that something wasn't right. A peculiar purplish tinge to his skin, his eyes almost but not quite closed, a slackness to his features that was more than sleep, that was beyond sleep. *Hugh*, she'd said, thinking stroke, thinking brain bleed, not thinking worse, not yet, *Hugh, wake up*, reaching towards him, putting a palm to his cheek – and the horrible clammy iciness of it had made her recoil, as if he'd burnt her.

She'd risen to her knees, feeling a tumble of her insides, *No, no*, feeling everything in her turn to water, feeling the breath go from her, placing trembling fingers to the side of his neck, and then to his wrist, praying for a pulse, however weak, *no*, praying for a sign of life, *no, no, no, no, no, no*, gathering him up, what was left of him, pressing the coldness, the stiffness of him to her, *no, no, no*, howling it out, *How could you? No, no*, and nobody at all to hear her, with Eve moved out and Keith in Galway and God not giving a damn. While she slept beside him he'd taken his last breath and gone away from her, a month before his fifty-seventh birthday, his present of a navy sweater already bought and wrapped and sitting in the boot of her car, the only place he wouldn't find it.

Heart, Dr Jack had said. *A massive heart attack. He wouldn't have suffered*, he'd told her, and she'd clung, she was clinging, to that. Let him not have felt a thing. Let his life have come to a gentle and painless end. Let *her* suffer – let all the suffering be hers.

The immediate aftermath, the days following his death, she remembered only in disjointed, unrelated fragments – somewhat, she imagined, like the recollections of an Alzheimer's patient, whose lived life could only be recalled, if at all, in haphazard, misaligned episodes.

The hands, all the hands of Roone reaching out to shake hers, not a soul on the island, young or old, who hadn't known Hugh. *Sorry for your trouble, sorry for your trouble*, like a litany, like a Taizé chant, a poem learnt off by heart, the words affording some tiny solace by their very monotony. People calling her lovey and darling and pet, calling her all the names he'd called her.

The wobble in Henry Manning's chin, his eyes swimming as he told her that Hugh's first job had been washing up in the hotel kitchen at weekends as a schoolboy, a missing forearm no hindrance at all to him. *As fast as anyone*, Henry had told her, *my father often said there was nobody like him to work*, trembling mouth downturned in a way Imelda might have found comical, once upon a time.

The ham sandwich cut into four little squares that she'd forced herself to eat at someone's urging. Too much butter in it, a smear of the English mustard that she hated, but she'd chewed and swallowed and washed it down with warm tea so that she'd be left alone.

The smell of wet clothes during the endless night of his wake, when people sat in relays by his coffin through the darkness, as island custom demanded. Rain pelting down outside, a fitting soundtrack it felt like.

Isolated images too. A bunch of big white and yellow daisies, tied with a green ribbon. Someone's green quilted jacket draped over the back of a chair. Someone else's silver drop earrings in the shape of flying birds. A biscuit sitting ignored on a saucer that had beautiful pink roses painted on it. Whose saucer? She had no idea, part of the paraphernalia of crockery and glasses that someone – Nell? – had rounded up for the wake.

The dreadful coldness of the lips she kissed as she told him goodbye, the day of the funeral. The taste of the blood she drew from her cheek, biting hard into it as the coffin lid was lowered. Trying to distract herself from the other pain, but there was no escape from it.

The feel of her sister's arm about her waist as they stood at the open grave, her brother-in-law on her other side, propping her up between them. Nell standing across the way, similarly flanked by her husband and stepson, weeping quietly as her beloved uncle was put in the ground.

His wellingtons, side by side in the shed some

days later, when Imelda had gone in search of a vase for flowers someone had brought. His dark green wellingtons, patched with stiffened earth, the sight of them bringing a wave of such desolation that she literally sank beneath it, dropped to her knees on the musty wooden floor, wrapped her arms about herself and rocked in anguish, her errand forgotten.

Enough. Enough. She crossed to the wardrobe and lifted out his everyday jacket, the donkey-brown herringbone with the worn leather elbow patches that he'd had forever, that he'd refused to let her replace. She undid the pinned-up right sleeve and let it fall to match its comrade.

She pressed the worn nubby cloth to her face and drew in the scent of him that still clung to it. She closed her eyes and imagined it growing solid and warm again, with the heft of his body inside it. She pictured her cheek resting against his chest, remembered them dancing in the back garden on warm summery nights with nobody to see them, the kitchen window open so they could hear the radio, the stars keeping vigil overhead.

Thank God he'd resisted her efforts to bin it. This she wouldn't give to charity. This she would never be separated from, not to her dying day. She'd wear it: she'd settle it across her shoulders when she sat on the patio on chilly autumn afternoons with her book and a mug of camomile tea. It would be her comfort blanket, as it had been his.

She checked the clock radio: time to get moving if

she was to make ten o'clock Mass. Still going every Sunday, despite her hatred of God these days. Still compelled, for some unknown reason, to sit and kneel and stand with the rest of the congregation. But she hadn't taken communion in seven weeks. It was her single small protest, and it afforded a tiny satisfaction.

She returned the jacket to the wardrobe and moved the cardboard box to the chair by his side of the bed. She'd bring it to Tralee next time she was going. She'd drop it into a charity shop and come away quickly, before she could change her mind about parting with anything of his.

She picked up her phone and pressed Eve's number, and listened to the rings that were still going unanswered. 'It's me,' she said when she heard the beep. 'It's Imelda. Please give me a ring.' The same message she'd left half a dozen times now, and no response to any of them.

Eve was hurting, she knew that. Hugh had become the father she'd never known. They'd formed a deep bond – Imelda, to her shame, had been almost jealous to see it – and his death had shaken the girl immensely. Imelda had to remember that, and make allowances. But *she* was hurting too, and this wasn't helping. She'd just have to let it take its course, and wait for Eve to come back to her.

She smoothed down her skirt. She ran a hand through her hair, for all the good it did. She pushed down the rage that still threatened, every second of every day, to get the better of her. She opened the door and walked out to face the life that had to be faced, wishing for the thousandth time that she, not he, had died.

Tilly

TEN MORE DAYS TILL SHE BOARDED THE first plane. They might as well be ten centuries. How was she to get through them without dying of anticipation, and endure the endless hours of travel that followed? Four flights in total to get her from Brisbane to Kerry. Over an entire day in the air, the in-between hours spent walking around airports, trailing through Duty Free shops, sniffing perfumes till she couldn't tell one from another, sleep-deprived but terrified to sit for any length of time in case she fell asleep.

And even though there were still ten days to go, she'd already packed and unpacked her case half a dozen times. She'd also tried on every stitch in her wardrobe, searching for the best thing to wear when Andy set eyes on her – saw her in the flesh, as opposed to on a screen – for the first time in ten months and twenty-five days.

She'd almost settled on the turquoise dress he'd said matched her eyes – except that it was a little worn at the seams now, a little faded. Maybe the jade green tunic top she'd got from her best friend Lien for her last birthday – he had yet to see it, and Tilly loved it teamed with her navy cropped pants – but did the colour really flatter her pale freckly skin, her nondescript brown hair?

How about the terracotta sweater in a fine wool that she'd found on a sale rail after Christmas – or was it a bit too dressy, with its rows of tiny beads running around the neckline? Maybe her black sundress then – but it was linen and would crease horribly in transit. Oh, it was impossible to choose, but trying them all on, debating and rejecting and deliberating, passed the time before her shift at the restaurant started at five.

Kerry airport was where they were to meet. *I bought a car*, he'd told her. *Well, my dad mostly bought it. Eight hundred and twenty euro, bargain.* He'd turned his phone so she could view it, and Tilly had seen a small blue hatchback – a Fiat, she thought he'd said. It looked a bit dented, and the paint had flaked off in patches, but it had a working engine, and it was bringing him to the airport on Tuesday, and then it was taking both of them back to Roone, where Tilly was staying for three and a half glorious weeks.

She couldn't wait.

I've got a summer job, he'd told her. *I had to, to pay Dad back for the car. I'm working in an ice-cream van at the pier.* An ice-cream van: how perfect was that?

Show me, she'd said, and he'd shown her a van that was painted bright yellow with a big window at the side, above which was written *Soft Whip* and *Cold Drinks* in coloured cartoon letters. She imagined the two of them there, he passing out the orders, she taking the money and making change. This would be her fourth visit to Ireland: she was well used to euros and cents by now.

She thought back to her first trip, two and a half years earlier. So afraid she'd been, so desperate as she'd flown halfway across the world, pregnant and heartbroken. Abandoned by the man she'd fancied herself in love with, and who'd professed to love her, until he'd taken what he wanted and vanished.

On discovering she was pregnant she'd fled from her adoptive parents to the only place she could think of, on a mission to find a sister she'd never met, knowing just her name and that she lived on a tiny island, located off the coast of another tiny island. Clinging to the faintest of hopes that this complete stranger would help her, would somehow make everything right.

It hadn't begun well. Her money had been stolen in Heathrow airport as she'd slept, a disastrous start to the whole hastily planned endeavour. But the kindness of various strangers on her onward journey had eventually enabled her to make her way to Roone, and to her sister Laura.

And things *had* sorted themselves out on the island, but not in the way she'd imagined. Her pregnancy had come to an end of its own accord, the life that had begun a few weeks before her trip slipping out of her one evening, the miscarriage leaving her unaccountably bereft – her head told her it was a good thing, her heart disagreed – but ultimately grateful.

And of course, not only had she tracked down Laura, and been welcomed into Walter's Place Bed & Breakfast, and made the acquaintance of Laura's husband Gavin and her delightful children, she'd also been introduced to Andy Baker, the boy who lived next door to them all.

She remembered her first sight of him like it was last week: shovelling snow from the path outside his front door, bundled into a padded jacket and a woolly hat, nose pink from the cold. Not exactly eye-catching, not particularly arresting – but all the same that first encounter, the first time their eyes had met, the brief greeting they'd exchanged, had caused a delicious swoosh in her heart, had sent a warm rush of blood to her cheeks.

Love at first sight, no other explanation for it – and miracle of miracles, he'd been drawn to her too. Not as dramatically as she'd been to him, but before her far too short stay on the island had ended they'd formed a connection and agreed to keep in touch, and they had.

Their relationship had been carefully nurtured through daily emails, and FaceTime chats that involved juggling time differences and schedules, and occasional actual letters in actual envelopes with stamps on them. Their feelings for one another had survived and grown, and with each of her subsequent visits to Roone she'd fallen more deeply in love with him.

And now she was preparing to meet him for the fourth time. A week on Tuesday, at ten minutes to seven in the evening Irish time, her plane was due to land in the quaint little airport at Farranfore, County Kerry. She would walk down the steps and cross the tarmac. She would collect her luggage and enter the tiny arrivals hall, her insides turning somersaults every step of the way, and he would be waiting for her with the keys of his dented blue car. She closed her eyes and imagined their embrace on meeting. She could almost feel his arms tight around her, the wonderful warmth of him as she nestled in. They belonged together – anyone could tell you that.

And before her time in Ireland was up, she was going to ask him to marry her.

It had come to her some weeks earlier when she was sitting at the hairdresser's, waiting for her usual trim. Flicking through a magazine, she'd come upon a feature on various celebrity weddings – and as she'd turned the pages and regarded the smiling faces of the alarmingly thin but impeccably dressed brides, she'd thought, *I want to do that. I want to get married.*

The thought had sat in her head for the rest of the day. She'd looked at it from every angle, and there was nothing she didn't like about it. She ticked off the reasons it made sense. After two and a half years of thousands of miles between them, and only brief periods of actually being together, their love and commitment was a given. They were in perfect sync, so at ease with one another, both inclined more to the quiet than the vivacious. She got on well with his family, particularly with his stepmother Nell, who seemed to approve of her. She adored his accent, and the funny way he worded things sometimes. She loved their differences every bit as much as the things they had in common.

Their physical attraction was undeniable. They'd come pretty close, last summer, to going all the way: she'd been the one to call a halt, whispering that maybe they should wait. She'd regretted it afterwards; on the plane that was carrying her away from him she'd called herself every name she could think of. But when she'd given it more thought, she'd understood that it was a legacy from the disastrous outcome of her encounter with John Smith, the man who'd used her so badly. Not that she didn't trust Andy absolutely, but crossing that threshold again with anyone was always going to be momentous.

And really, what was their hurry, now that she'd decided to take matters into her own hands and make things permanent? They had their whole lives to enjoy one another – and there was something utterly romantic, she felt, about waiting until their wedding night. Some might say they were too young to marry – she'd be twenty in December; he'd passed that milestone in March – but as far as she was concerned they were plenty old enough to know what they wanted.

She'd move to Ireland, of course: she was only dying for a reason to do it. She'd hand in her notice at the Indonesian restaurant where she'd worked part time since her mid-teens, and full time since leaving school. Initially she'd relocate to Limerick, where he was studying computer science. He currently lived on campus, so she probably wouldn't be able to move in with him, but they could find a place together, be it ever so humble. She'd hunt down a job, it didn't matter what. She'd scrub floors, clean toilets, if it meant making enough to pay rent and buy food, and be together.

But Limerick would only be temporary: when Andy graduated in two years they'd return to Roone. The beauty of computer programming was that it could be done remotely, so he could live anywhere, and they both loved the island, despite neither of them having come from there. Andy had spent the first eleven years of his life in Dublin, and Tilly, of course, hadn't laid eyes on Roone until she was seventeen – but she couldn't imagine them living anywhere else once he qualified.

And on Roone, she would finally realise her other dream.

For as long as she could remember, she'd wanted to be a writer. She'd kept a diary as a young girl, and written short stories as a teen, and dabbled in poetry here and there, but her heart was set on writing a novel. She hadn't got round to starting it, hadn't yet come up with a big enough idea, but on Roone she would. Once she became a permanent resident of the island she'd be inspired: she was certain of it.

It was perfectly feasible, all of it. It was what she wanted, and she knew he wanted it too. And in the twenty-first century, the second millennium, she didn't have to wait for him to pop the question. She'd pick her time carefully, wait for the perfect moment. And he'd say yes. He had to say yes.

She'd return from Roone engaged. The thought, whenever she allowed it in, sent a thrill shooting through her. For the umpteenth time she slipped off the ring that Laura had given her on her first visit to the island, and moved it to the third finger of her left hand. It was too loose for that finger but it didn't matter. She could still imagine that the small blue stone was a diamond, and that it had been placed there by Andy.

The wedding would be on Roone. With him having so many more people to invite than her, it made sense. No way would Ma and Pa make the trip – she didn't have to ask them to know that. They'd never left Australia, never flown anywhere at all: the long trek to Ireland would be out of the question. This would also rule out Robbie and Jemima, at ten and five far too young to travel such a distance alone – so apart from Lien, who would definitely jump at the chance to visit Ireland, Tilly would have nobody at all from her side.

Or rather, she'd have nobody from Australia. Laura and her family would be there – and Susan, the stepmother Tilly had acquired along with a sister, would come from Dublin with Tilly's little half brother Harry, who would make an adorable pageboy. And it was certainly not a given, but Luke Potter might just show up too.

Tilly had yet to meet him in person, the famous artist whose face looked out sternly from so many sites on the internet – but what father would refuse to give his daughter away on her wedding day? It was true he'd shown scant interest in her up to this, but she'd live in hope.

Laura would be supportive, Tilly was certain of it. Just nineteen herself when she'd married for the first time, Laura knew about love, how it caught you up, how it couldn't be ignored or put on pause. Laura would be happy for her.

The news might not go down so well in Australia. Tilly could already hear the reaction when she returned home and told them she was engaged. *You're too young, you hardly know him, it's too soon.* Even Lien, she suspected, didn't rate her chances of anything lasting with Andy. A holiday romance was how they all looked on it, even though it had survived this far. But she'd show them: she'd prove to everyone that it was more than a fling, more than puppy love.

She'd miss home, of course she would. She'd miss Ma and Pa, and Robbie and Jemima. She'd miss Lien, her closest friend since early childhood – but Australia wasn't the moon. She'd go back every now and again, and Robbie and Jemima could make the trip the other way when they were older, and Lien would be a frequent visitor.

She pulled open the drawer in her locker and retrieved her sister's last letter. Laura was one of the few people she knew who didn't have an email address – Tilly's emails had to go via Gavin – and who still wrote letters. The handwriting was erratic, with a hurried look about it, and the pages often featured smudges and marks of unknown origins, but Tilly looked forward to their arrival once a month or so. She'd picture Laura scribbling down the news at the big kitchen table, tucking the finished pages into an envelope, sealing it and addressing it to Tilly. Pressing her face to it when it arrived, Tilly would swear she could smell the sea.

Tilly –
Won't feel it now till you're here. I've lost track of the number of pictures Evie and Marian have drawn for you: they're all stuck up on the bedroom wall for your viewing pleasure. It's been raining away for the past week, bring the wet gear – although the postman in Donegal who usually gets it right says we're in for a sunny July, so fingers crossed. And Gav pulled up a twin carrot yesterday, which he says is another good weather omen. Can't say I ever heard of that one, but you never know. Andy got his hair cut lately, I presume in your honour. He looks mighty fine, and just about deserving of you. He'll have told you about his summer job –

we're all expecting lots of free ice-creams, with our connection. And you'll have been told that he has a car, so you won't know yourselves, swanning around like royalty.

Con Maher, I don't think you've met him, he used to run the creamery, has just become a grandfather to triplets, so he's Roone's current celebrity. Henry in the hotel is having a giant party for his seventieth, the day after my birthday, so you'll be here for both. I told Henry as long as he was splashing out we might as well do a joint one so he'd get value from it, but he only laughed at me, so it looks like I'll have to buy my own cake and candles. What's new?

Ben and Seamus are counting the days to the summer holidays – can't get my head around the fact that they'll be starting secondary school in September. My little men. Evie lost a tooth the other morning; Marian was raging when the tooth fairy didn't leave anything for her. I'd swear she's been pulling at one of hers since. Poppy is finally out of nappies, can you believe it? Certainly took her time.

Just to prepare you, poor Nell is still very upset over Hugh. Those two were very close, more so since Nell's mam died a few years back. Never know what's coming, do we?

Well, I think that's all my blather. It's after ten here and I'm cross-eyed with tiredness and I have nine guests to feed in the morning, so I'll sign off and see you soon, safe trip,
love Laur, and the rest of the gang xxx

She folded the pages and slipped them back into the envelope. She reached for the rattan bag that held the presents she'd bought, and spread them out on the bed. A necklace threaded with amber beads for Laura, more boomerangs for Ben and Seamus – how they managed to keep losing them was a complete mystery. A peg doll each for Evie and Marian, a sweet little furry koala for Poppy, and a book on Australian animals for Gavin, who'd been working in Dublin Zoo when he'd met Laura.

Chocolates for Andy's parents, picture books for their two small children, his half-siblings. And for Andy, a leather wristband with his initials engraved on the small silver disc that hung from it.

AB. Andy Baker.

TB. Tilly Baker.

It was only a matter of time.

Laura

SHE PICKED UP THE PHONE AND PRESSED THE answer key. 'Susan – everything OK?' Twenty to ten, late for her stepmother to be ringing.

'Hi, Laura. I'm just letting you know that Harry and I are coming to Roone on Saturday for a little while.'

'What? This Saturday?' Unheard of for her to visit them in the summer. Spring and autumn were her times, when the B&B was closed and Laura had plenty of spare rooms. 'Susan, you know I'd love to see you both, but I'm completely full, and Tilly is due—'

'Don't worry, I knew you'd be busy. I've booked a room for us in the hotel.'

And then it hit her. Susan knew. Laura's father had told her what he'd told Laura, and she was trying to process it. She needed the space from him to figure out what lay ahead for them.

'Well, it'll be wonderful to see you.' Laura would make no mention of it, not until Susan did, but it loomed like an elephant in her head. 'How long will you stay?'

'Two weeks.'

Longer, much longer than her usual visits to Roone. 'We'll see you Saturday then.' Odd, was it, that she'd be happy to be away from him for that length of time? 'Give a shout from the ferry so I'll know you're on the way.'

'I will. It'll probably be late afternoon.'

After hanging up, Laura resumed her scone making. It was a relief that Susan knew; now there need be nothing unsaid between them. Presumably he'd also told her that Laura already knew: if not, it would come out soon enough.

In the week or so that had passed since his unexpected appearance, Laura had been unable to keep him from her thoughts. In idle moments – changing sheets on a bed, filling little dishes with marmalade, mopping a bathroom floor – he'd drift into her head, prompting a wash of the mixed feelings she'd always had about him. His coming here, and what he'd told her, had unsettled things, had stirred up emotions that she'd patted down and tidied away.

Gav had seemed to believe her clumsily concocted reason for the visit – or at any rate, he hadn't brought it up again. Perversely, Laura had found herself slightly annoyed by this: why hadn't he seen through her, and pestered her until she'd told him the truth? This wasn't a secret anyone should be asked to keep.

A sudden sharp rap on the back door startled her. Who could that be? Her guests all had keys for the front door. Nell used the back way, but she never knocked.

Laura set down her rolling pin and wiped floury hands on her apron. She glanced across the room at Charlie, fast asleep in the bed that Gav had fashioned from driftwood. Some guard dog; just as well Roone was as safe as it was. 'Come in,' she called.

Let it not be Michael Brown, their farming neighbour who showed up every so often, claiming to have run out of sugar or milk or whatever when what he was really looking for was someone to talk to. Poor Michael was lonely, God love him, stuck in that rambling farmhouse with nothing to keep him company but memories of a dead wife, and a son who seldom bothered to come over from Killarney – but Laura's alarm was set for half six, as it was every night she had paying guests under her roof, and she was most definitely not in the mood to be neighbourly.

It wasn't Michael Brown.

'Sorry,' Eve said. 'I know it's late.' Twin pink spots in her cheeks. Hovering in the doorway, a hand gripping closed the collar of her jacket from the evening chill. 'Can I come in? Just for a few minutes.'

'Of course you can.' Poor love, still so shook after Hugh. 'Is anything wrong?'

'Is Gavin here?' she asked, sweeping the kitchen with a look, as if he might materialise from the fridge, or come crawling out from beneath the dresser. 'Are you on your own?'

'For the moment. Gav's gone to collect the boys, but they won't be long. What's up?'

'I ... wanted to tell you something. At least, I have to tell *someone*, and you were the only person I could think of.'

Tension written all over her face, her whole body rigid with it. Oh dear, this didn't look good. 'Sit down,' Laura said – but Eve made no move, just went on standing in the doorway.

'Eve, what is it, love? Are you sick?'

'I – no.'

'Is it Imelda?'

A shake of her head, hair tumbling.

'Look, I'm just making scones for the morning – let me get them into the oven and we can talk. You want to boil the kettle for tea?'

'No ... thanks.' Stepping into the room then, pulling off her jacket, folding it over a chair back.

'Grab that cutter,' Laura said, 'and we'll go faster.'

In silence they worked, Eve's head lowered, her face hidden as she pressed the cutter into the soft dough. Whatever was to come wasn't good. Good didn't keep quiet; good didn't have you afraid to tell it.

At length the baking trays went sliding into the preheated oven. A dozen attempts at least it had taken under Nell's tutelage for Laura to produce a scone she could expect anyone to pay for – and even now it was a gamble each time, some batches decidedly more successful than others. Happily, her own family never minded eating the rejects.

'Sit,' she ordered again, shutting the oven door – and this time Eve pulled out a chair and perched on its edge, looking tense as a rabbit in headlights.

'OK,' Laura said, untying her apron strings, shaking it out. 'We haven't got a lot of –'

'I'm pregnant,' Eve said. Loudly, almost defiantly – and instantly, Laura thought, *Of course you are*. She should have known the minute the girl had shown up. What else would have her in such a pickle?

She sat and put a hand on Eve's knee, trying to frame the right response. Was there even a boyfriend? If there was, Laura had yet to hear of him. No serious romance, as far as she was aware, not since Eve and Andy Baker had finished – when? Must be well over two years ago now.

'Right,' she said. 'OK. First things first. Are you absolutely sure about this?'

'Yes.'

'You've missed a period? Or more than one?'

'One – and I've been … feeling sick.'

'OK … and I presume you've done a test?'

A nod. Hardly obtained in Roone's one and only chemist: she'd have gone to Tralee for it if she wanted to keep this quiet – and by the look of her, she did. Laura was pulled back to her own first pregnancy test, just a couple of months after marrying Aaron, and their wild excitement at the positive result. Yet to learn she was carrying not one but a brace of babies; in blessed ignorance too of the horror that awaited her, the obscenity of his suicide a week before his sons were born. *Don't think about it.* Even now, years later, the loss of him could stop her in her tracks.

She returned to the business in hand. 'Eve, you don't have to tell me if you don't want to, but I'm guessing this was a one-off – since I don't think you're with anyone at the moment, are you?'

Another shake of the head. Just gone twenty, her birthday a couple of weeks ago. No party for her this year, with Hugh's death still so fresh, but Laura had brought chocolates to the crèche when she'd gone to pick up Evie and Marian. *From all of us*, she'd said, and Eve had given a ghost of a smile and thanked her.

She must have known by then, or suspected. She might have been counting days, and thinking about getting herself a test.

'I had to tell someone,' she repeated. Still in shock, still getting her head around it. This, on top of Hugh. The last thing she needed.

'It's good to tell someone,' Laura agreed. The girl wasn't what anyone would call a great beauty but she had a pretty enough face, and the same curvy figure as Laura, and of course that glorious hair. Ripe for the picking, if a man had a mind to.

A thought struck Laura then. Awful, unthinkable on Roone, but needing to be voiced. 'Eve, did someone … force himself on you?' She couldn't give voice to the word, not in this quiet, ordinary kitchen where her children ate and played and laughed every day.

'No,' Eve said. '*No.*'

Quickly, definitively. An act of consent at least then, even if the goose, and whatever gander was involved, hadn't thought to take precautions. Another unsettling thought occurred. 'Is he married, Eve? Or in a relationship with someone else?'

Eve's eyes slid away to focus on Laura's hand, still resting on her knee. 'No.'

Less vehement than her last response. Sounded like he was taken, and she didn't want to admit it. Laura considered the possibilities. The year-round population of Roone was in the region of three hundred and fifty, with slightly over half of those being boys and men. In theory, any post-pubescent male could have done the business, but assuming she hadn't dilly-dallied with anyone under eighteen, or over forty, the unmarried suspects probably numbered no more than twenty or thirty. Add in the married ones, and the total went considerably higher.

Laura regarded the girl's bowed head, watched the hands that were unable to stay still, fingers squeezing and twining about one another. She hadn't had much of a life before Roone, by all accounts. A father she'd never known, a drug-addled mother who was still battling to kick the habit. Eve and her half-brother taken into care when Eve had been no more than nine or ten, the two of them separated when no foster family could be found to accommodate both.

And to make matters worse, the teenage son of her foster parents had abused her for years, a fact she'd eventually admitted when she'd come to spend a summer on Roone with Hugh and Imelda, who'd offered respite fostering. And now Hugh, the closest she'd come to a dad, had been snatched from her without warning. A rough deal by anyone's standard.

Had it left its mark on her, all this trauma? How could it not? Laura vaguely remembered some talk of Hugh and Imelda looking for counselling for her, after they'd learnt of the abuse. Had it gone ahead and if so, had it proved effective in unravelling the girl's misfortunes? She had no idea.

'Eve, is there anything more you want to tell me?' Like whose it is. Like why you were so careless. Like what you're planning to do next.

Eve didn't lift her head. 'It's nobody you know, if that's what you're wondering. He's not from here.'

Not from here. Well, that was a relief, Laura supposed. Some tourist then, or a visiting relative of one of the islanders.

'Have you told him?'

'No.' Pause. 'I can't. I just can't.'

Laura let it go. 'So you're – what? About six weeks gone?'

Another nod.

Six weeks would put it not long after Hugh's death. A whole other consideration, best set aside now. Six weeks, all her options still open. Laura thought suddenly of Imelda, who wouldn't be the most liberal. She'd disapproved of Laura and Gavin living together before they'd tied the knot. Oh, nothing had been said, Imelda had never pointed the finger, never condemned Laura to anyone else, as far as Laura knew, but the older woman's censure had been there in the tiny drawing back that Laura had noted whenever they'd encountered one another. Judgement had been made, without a doubt.

All behind them now, and Laura wasn't one to hold a grudge. The two of them cut from different cloth, which was fine: a dull world they'd have if everyone thought the same – but the fact remained that Imelda held conservative views, and an unmarried and pregnant Eve would be extremely difficult for her to come to terms with, especially now. Better for all, maybe, if the problem was made to go away quietly.

Eve looked up. 'I know,' she said. 'I know I've messed up. You don't have to tell me.' Winding and pulling a strand of hair. 'I ... I'd had a bit to drink – well, a lot. I know it still shouldn't have happened, I *know* that.'

'I see.'

A lot to drink, which would explain the lack of precautions. Drowning her sorrows maybe, after Hugh. Defences lowered, inhibitions gone. She wasn't the first to be caught – and not the first on Roone either. More than one island household with a baby being raised by grandparents – and that girl of the McCarthys last year, absent for four or five months. Looking after a sick relative overseas was what had been said, but there'd been whispers.

Laura darted a look at the clock on the wall. Any

time now Gav and the boys would show up. Mad about one another Eve and Andy had been, eyes for no one else. Were they sixteen at the time? Not much more than that. Nell watching them like a hawk, terrified they were going to run off together and come back married. The fire, the thrill, the butterflies of teenage love: oh, Laura knew all about that.

Hadn't lasted, though. Eve had been the one to call a halt after a year or so, and Nell had worried all over again when she'd seen how badly Andy had taken it. First love for him – for both of them, Laura guessed.

The girl had her own quarters now. A couple of poky little rooms above the crèche that she'd been running since January, when Avril McGuinness had finally decided to call it a day after forty-odd years of giving the youngsters of Roone their first taste of organised education.

Imelda will miss her, Nell had said, when word went round that Eve was moving out, but Laura had thought that Imelda wouldn't be too disappointed. With Eve's departure, she and Hugh would have the place to themselves again – and it wasn't as if Eve was moving further than about ten minutes down the road. They'd have waved her off happily enough, Laura thought, little realising how short a time they had left together.

So what now? As a dedicated and devoted mother of five, Laura loathed the idea of abortion, but undoubtedly there were times when it made life a whole lot easier.

'So nobody else knows about this?'

'No.'

Laura supposed she should be flattered. Of course they had history, the two of them. Eve had helped out in the B&B her first summer on Roone. Laura's idea, doing what she could to help the situation, despite Imelda's disapproval of her living-in-sin status. Anyone could see that she and Hugh were floundering, not a clue how to handle the silent, sullen teenager they'd been landed with. Eve had agreed to do a few morning hours at Walter's Place and she'd managed fine, and she and Laura had got on, as much as anyone could get on with her in those early days.

And there was the other bond too, of course. A couple of weeks after Eve had started at the B&B, Laura's twin girls had decided to put in an appearance before their due date, and nobody had been around to help with the delivery but Eve and a sister of Imelda's, who happened to be staying there with her husband at the time.

Somehow they'd muddled through the delivery, and the girls had been named after the two proxy midwives in gratitude, and Eve was godmother to Laura's Evie.

All very fine and good – but, Lord, why couldn't she have chosen one of her friends to confide in? Why on earth bring it to Laura's door? She didn't have the energy, not with her father's news determined to take up so much of her headspace. Still, here they were, and she had to deal with it.

'So there's no way you can get in touch with the guy?'

'No.'

'You can't – or you won't?' Gently said, but it needed saying.

'Can't. I just *can't*. It's … complicated.'

'Complicated? In what way?'

'… I can't tell you.'

Silence. He was taken, definitely.

'I made a mistake,' Eve said. 'I thought you'd understand.' A trace of defiance in the words.

'I *do* understand, Eve – Lord knows I've made my share of mistakes. I'm not judging you, or accusing you, just trying to figure it out. Look, I'll do what I can for you, you know that, but I can't give you money – we just don't have it to spare.'

'I *know* that. I'm not looking for money – I didn't come here for that. I just wanted to *tell* someone.'

'And that's fine, you can always talk to me. I'll try to help you, whatever you decide.'

A beat passed.

'I've already decided,' Eve said steadily. 'I know what I'm going to do. I'm keeping it.'

The decision made, just like that. 'Eve, it's still early days—'

'I've made up my mind.'

'Are you absolutely sure? You've thought it through, and you're prepared to raise a child without a partner?'

A second passed. 'Yes, I'm sure. I know it'll be hard on my own, I *know* that, but it's what I want.'

Laura thought of Imelda again, and her likely reaction to this. 'Eve, have you considered the implications – for everyone, I mean?'

Eve's mouth twisted. 'You mean for Imelda.'

'Well, Imelda for one. She's been like a mother to you, Eve—'

'She's *not* my mother.' Sharply said, the colour deepening a little in her cheeks. 'She doesn't get to decide this.'

'I know. It's your decision, I know that – it's just, it's such a huge one, Eve. It's a life-changing one. You need to be absolutely sure you can handle it, that's all.'

'I *am* sure.'

'You could also lose your job at the crèche – has that occurred to you? They might take exception to an unmarried mother running it. Look, I'm not telling you what to do—'

'I don't *want* you to.' Her anger flaring again, her voice rising with it. 'I don't want *anyone* telling me what to do – Jesus, I've had enough of that! And I don't *care* about the job – let them take it if they want to!'

'Ssh, Eve, you'll wake the girls.' Poor foolish creature, blind to the obstacles, the many pitfalls on the path she seemed bent on. 'Look, just keep me posted, OK? You can pick up the phone anytime, or call around again. And remember, you can always change your mind about this. You mightn't think you will, but I'm just saying you can. Your options are still open for another few weeks.'

Eve rose to her feet, took her jacket from the chair back. 'Promise you won't tell anyone,' she said, pushing arms into sleeves. 'Not Nell, or Imelda, or anyone.'

Laura's heart sank. Just when she was getting rid of one secret, along came another. 'Eve, you'll have to tell Imelda. She can't hear it from someone else.'

'I will tell her, but not yet. Promise you'll say nothing.'

'I promise.' What choice did she have? She couldn't betray the girl's trust. Just then, to her vast relief, she heard the faint clang of the field gate being opened. 'They're here – I'll let you out the front.'

When she opened the door she saw the rain. Not falling hard enough to make noise against a window, but heavy enough to wet you if you were out in it for any length, and Eve had a twenty-minute walk home, with no hood. 'Take this,' Laura said, lifting an umbrella from the stand – but Eve produced a green fleece beanie from her pocket and pulled it on. Doing it her way, as ever.

On impulse, Laura put her arms around her. 'Mind yourself,' she whispered, and Eve submitted briefly to the embrace before pulling away. Not one for displays of affection, never having experienced much of it. Laura watched her hurrying down the path, full of romantic notions, no doubt, of raising her child alone. Pictured herself breast-feeding the perfect little cherub in a rocking chair. No clue about colic and croup and the dozens of other infant ailments, the teething and the nappy rash and the endless feeds, the days and nights of little or no sleep, the terror of being completely responsible for keeping another human alive, with no training course to ensure that you knew what you were doing.

She returned to the kitchen to find Gav and the boys there ahead of her.

'What's burning?' Seamus asked.

Susan

'I CAN'T DO THIS ANY MORE.'

'Can't do what?'

'I can't live with you. I'm leaving.'

That got his attention. That made him turn from his canvas and regard her with the intensity she'd found so thrilling when they first met. He hadn't needed to lay a finger on her: that searching gaze, as if he could see into the core of her, was all it had taken to set her ablaze for him. That look, or his slow, lazy smile with half-closed eyes – those had been his weapons. Those she had never been able to resist, had never wanted to.

He wasn't smiling now.

'You can't live with me?' he repeated. His voice mild but his gaze like ice, like flint. Boring into her.

'You've changed,' she said. 'You've … gone away from me.'

'I'm right here. I'm here every day.'

'Luke, you know what I mean. We've been through this. I can't reach you any more. It's like you've shut us out, me and Harry, and it's hurtful and unfair, since I can't think of anything I might have done to deserve it, and you won't explain, or even try to. I can't take it. I give you everything, and I get so little in return.'

A tiny narrowing of the eyes that she didn't miss. 'You live in the lap of luxury, and you don't have to earn a penny.'

The accusation stung. 'You were the one who was all for me giving up work when we got married. Anyway, I'm not talking about money. You know that's not what this is about. I don't care about money.'

'Easy not to care when it's there for the taking.'

'Luke, don't do this. Don't keep pretending you don't understand. You've become so … distant. It's like Harry and I don't exist for you.'

A beat passed. A horn hooted, one short peremptory note, below on the road. 'You knew,' he said, 'before you married me. You knew what I was like.'

'You weren't like this.'

He'd always been focused on his work; that much was true. Always so intensely driven, and she couldn't say this hadn't impressed her, his complete commitment to his art. It was frustrating too, certainly, when she felt he'd set her aside – but she'd weathered those times when he was lost in a painting, and waited for him to come back, and he'd always come back.

But not any more. Even in bed now he wasn't hers: he was there physically, but his heart, his soul, were somewhere else.

'I need you to be with me,' she said. 'I need you to want to be with Harry and me. Really with us.'

A beat passed. He didn't look away. 'I am the way I am,' he said. 'I can't change that.'

'Then you'll have to let me go, because I can't deal with it.'

He tipped his head an inch to the side, a movement so slight she almost missed it. Say something, she begged silently. Argue with me, fight for me – but instead he turned away to fold his arms and regard his canvas.

The painting, almost completed, was of a young woman wrapped in a tangerine bath towel, sitting on a low stool and bent at the waist as she painted her toenails scarlet. The skin of her bare shoulders rosy and glowing, her hair caught up in a white turban, a few damp brown curls escaping. A gathering of small creases in the skin where her leg met her turned-up foot. Intent on her task, lower lip slightly pursed, a tiny glisten of saliva at its centre. Eyes masked by heavy lashes.

War Paint, he was calling it. It was about eighteen inches by two feet. It would fetch thousands – tens of thousands, maybe more – at whatever auction it was put into. Like all his works, it was technically brilliant – but was it lacking, she wondered, in soul?

Maybe nobody else saw it. Maybe it was just because she knew him so well. Seventeen years since they'd met, over fifteen as his wife. Mother to his third child for the past two years.

Harry had been all her doing. She'd hungered for a baby, long before she'd met Luke. She knew he didn't want another child, he'd always been open about that, so she'd tried to quell her yearning, but the hunger hadn't gone away, had grown instead until she'd taken a chance at the age of forty and thrown her pills away.

He hadn't been pleased, of course, when she'd told him she was pregnant, but she'd remained steadfast and eventually, reluctantly, he'd had to accept it. A son, she'd thought, since daughters hadn't done the trick. A son he wouldn't be able to resist: a son would shift his priorities, make him want to put them first – and the Fates had smiled on her, and a son she'd had.

And for a while, it had seemed like things were changing. Oh, he still painted, and his focus at times could be as fierce as it had ever been – he'd missed Harry's Roone christening, preoccupied with an important commission – but overall he was spending more time with his little family, he was making an effort to be a father. The balance, she'd felt, was shifting in their favour.

Until a few months ago, when there was no more balance, no more Luke Potter the husband and father. He'd reverted fully to Luke Potter the artist, Luke Potter the household name, and she had no idea what had caused it.

He turned back to her. 'It's not what I want, your leaving,' he said. 'You must know that.'

'How can I know, when you never show me? When have you last talked, really talked, to me?'

He scratched at a point above his elbow. 'There are—' He broke off. 'I have things,' he said, 'on my mind.'

'What things? Tell me. Let me in, Luke.'

He gave an impatient little toss of his head. He picked up a brush, pushed his fingers through its bristles. 'Are you taking Harry with you?'

She felt like weeping. Did they mean so little to him that he'd let them walk out of his life with such little protest? 'Yes, of course I'm taking Harry.'

'Where will you go?'

'Why do you care?' she shot back, and immediately regretted it. She mustn't lose her temper. She mustn't turn this into a war of words.

But he didn't retaliate. He said nothing more. He dipped his brush into paint and worked in silence for what felt like a long time, as she stood in the doorway, still waiting, still clinging to a foolish, naïve hope that he'd suddenly become the man she desperately needed him to be.

The studio air was heady with the sludgy smell of oil paint. It permeated the house, drifted into each room, seeped into every cupboard. It was on her skin and her hair and her clothes, it flavoured her dreams – but here, in this space where he created it, you could hardly breathe for it. Did he even notice?

Eventually she spoke. 'I'll arrange for someone to collect our things later. I'll be in touch when we find somewhere to live, so we can sort things out.'

'Go if you must,' he replied, without turning. 'Just remember it's your choice, not mine.'

Her choice, when everything in her was screaming to stay. Not her choice, far from it, but the only option she could see.

She was going to Roone, to her stepdaughter Laura, who knew Luke as well as Susan did, who would understand why Susan was leaving. Her journey wouldn't end on the island, but it would begin there. It would begin with two weeks of having to do nothing but let the dust of this departure settle and figure out what came next, to consider her options and pick the most promising – or the least intimidating.

She needn't go as far as Roone, on the other side of the country. She could go to Trish, or Rachel, or several other friends who'd known her before she married Luke, and who never criticised him to her face, but who had plenty to say about him, she imagined, among themselves. She could go to her friends, but she had to get out of Dublin, and she wanted Laura.

For the time being she would avoid her mother, who'd never hit it off with Luke, the much older man who'd already been married and divorced – and who made her feel inferior, Susan suspected, purely because of his renown. Attractive, confident, used to attention, her mother resented it being focused instead on Luke whenever they were out together. Over the years, dinner invitations and the like had been dutifully issued, but more often than not her mother had found reasons to turn them down – and Luke, proud Luke, had never tried to win her over.

Nothing would be said if Susan turned up on the doorstep announcing that her marriage had ended, but she would sense her mother's quiet satisfaction, her poorly disguised relief, and she wasn't having it.

What would her father, she wondered, have made of her choice of husband? He'd died when Susan was sixteen, so his opinion of Luke would be forever unknown. Perhaps just as well.

'Won't you look at me?' she asked, and he did, and hope flared in her. Now he'd speak, now he'd make promises – but he remained silent.

They stood there, separated by just a few metres. It might as well, she thought, be an ocean that flowed between them, so far apart from one another they'd become.

'Goodbye,' she said, and left him, already brimming over with loss.

In their bedroom, one floor below, she picked up the bag she'd already packed and brought it downstairs. There wasn't much in it: a few changes of clothes for her and Harry, a few of pairs of shoes, cosmetics and toothbrushes. She wasn't thinking beyond a fortnight. She stored it in the boot of her car and climbed the stairs again to her son's room. She crossed to his bed and nudged him gently awake.

'Come on, lovey, time to get up. We're going in the car.'

He opened his eyes – his father's eyes, somewhere between blue and green – and regarded her sleepily. She lifted him out and dressed him. She slipped his feet into shoes and brought him yawning to the bathroom. Afterwards she fed him a banana and poured milk into his blue cup. He never ate much first thing in the morning.

They left the house. She strapped him into his child seat and placed Toby, his beloved blue elephant, in his arms. She closed his door and slipped into the driver's seat. 'Daddy is staying here,' she said, watching his placid little face in the rear-view mirror. Daddy, not Luke. He'd always been Luke to Laura, and he'd suggested the same when Harry had come along, but Susan wasn't having that for her son. 'Daddy is busy with his painting.'

She turned to look at him, her precious only child. 'We're going to see Laura,' she said. 'And Evie and Marian and Poppy and Ben and Seamus.' Cousins, she and Laura called the relationship between their children, although technically Harry was their step-uncle, if such a role existed. 'That'll be good, won't it? You'll like that, won't you?'

He nodded. His second birthday last month, and he had yet to utter a single word. Not a mama or a dada, no baby babbling. Nothing that could be considered an attempt at communication.

He wasn't deaf: he turned his head at sound. There was no physical impediment that his paediatrician could identify, nothing to explain his lack of speech.

His vocal cords were in order: he laughed and cried like any another child, if maybe a little less frequently. He understood what was being said to him, or asked of him. *He's just a late developer*, Susan was told. *Give it time. Keep speaking to him, but try not to dwell on it. Try not to put pressure on him.*

The doctor's eyes said different things though. *Don't fuss, leave him be*, the eyes said. *Stop wasting my time. Stop wasting your money.* Was it Luke, she wondered, was it down to him? For all his earlier efforts with his son, Harry had received little physical affection from him. He wasn't a natural hugger, an easy cuddler, a kisser of bruises. Had Harry sensed this? Had it trapped the words inside him, made him fearful of letting them out?

She looked through the car window at the beautiful red-brick house that was, that had been, her marital home. Luke's studio, a replacement a few years earlier for the one at the bottom of the garden, took up the entire top floor and was lit by windows front and back in addition to two huge skylights. She pictured him there where she'd left him, painting alone, nobody to bother him now. He'd get someone in, she thought, to cook his meals and make his bed, like the woman he'd employed in the period between his marriages. He'd replace Susan with someone who demanded nothing of him but a weekly envelope with money in it.

His love had taken her completely by surprise. She couldn't believe that such a commanding figure, so important and self-assured, could possibly be interested in her. He'd pursued her with a single-mindedness that had amazed and thrilled her. He'd told her that he needed her, that he couldn't function without her. He'd said things she'd loved to hear; he'd whispered them to her and they'd made her giddy with happiness, made her feel like she could raise her arms and the rest of her would follow, that she could float all the way to the moon.

And of course his fame had appealed to her, though she knew how shallow it made her sound to admit it. She was aware of people watching them when they were out together; she sensed the envy of other women, and was gratified by it. She'd feel his palm resting lightly in the small of her back as they followed a waiter to a restaurant table. Heads would invariably turn when he was recognised, and she'd marvel that she was the one he'd chosen, when he could have had anyone, or almost anyone.

Where had it all gone? Where had *they* gone? Try as she might to find a cause, no cause presented itself. Why had he changed from the sometimes distant but ultimately loving man she'd married? What had moved him out of her reach? Did he still love her? Was it there somewhere, buried beneath, smothered by his obsession for work, or had it flown for good?

She felt a heat behind her eyes, but she refused to give in to it. She opened the handbag she'd bought last Christmas with Luke's money – *Get what you want*, he'd said, like he always did – and checked for their passports. Ready for every eventuality. 'Right then,' she said aloud, stowing the bag in front of the passenger seat. 'Let's go.'

She reached for the small remote control that lived in the pocket of her driver's door. She pressed a button and the big metal gate slid slowly to one side with a low rumble. She started the engine and left the driveway, and heard the gate sliding back into place behind her. Shutting her out, shutting him in.

She drove through the streets to the motorway, the traffic thankfully light in her direction, everyone coming into the city at this still early hour. Rain fell; wipers swished it away. She left the radio off, preferring the silence. She crossed the country as clouds grew dense above her, pulling down the sky, as the rain fell more solidly the further west she travelled.

Shortly after noon she exited the motorway. In a village café she ordered an omelette for Harry and mushroom soup for herself. 'Your brown bread is delicious,' she told the woman who'd served it to accompany the soup, and the woman thanked her. 'My daughter's the baker,' she said. 'I leave it to her' – and Susan wished for a normal family, with a daughter who baked bread.

By the time they reached the pier it was heading for four o'clock, and Harry had had an hour's nap. As the Roone ferry approached, Susan phoned Laura. 'We should be at the hotel by half four. Don't come if you're busy.'

'Of course I'll come. Gav is on dinner duty: he's doing his special meatballs, so I'm free as a bird. See you soon.'

They remained in the car for the twenty-minute crossing, Susan's only interaction a brief exchange with the ferryman, who probably recognised her face but maybe wasn't aware of her connection with Laura because she'd never made it known to him. 'Have a nice trip,' he said, and she promised him she would.

The hotel façade had had a fresh coat of paint since her last visit to the island, just before Easter. The apricot it had worn for as long as she'd known it was gone, replaced by a rather nice aquamarine. She parked as close to the main door as she could and got out, stretching her cramped muscles. She opened the rear door and unbuckled Harry, and collected their joint bag from the boot. They made their way inside and booked in, and were shown to their first floor room.

She was hanging the few items of clothing she'd brought, and Harry was sitting on a cushion on the floor watching cartoons, when Laura arrived. 'How's my main man?' she asked him, crouching to ruffle his hair. 'Can I have a hug?' He submitted to her embrace, and returned to his programme when it was over.

'Good to see you,' Susan said, kissing her cheek, and being kissed in return. They sat side by side on the room's small navy couch, fingers intertwined. Susan eased her shoes off one by one and let her weight sink into the couch. She felt drained, as if the leaving had sucked all the vitality out of her, as if her energy had remained behind in the big house in Dublin.

'I think I know why you're here,' Laura murmured, squeezing Susan's hand.

She'd guessed. Of course she had. Susan studied the beautiful back of her son's head, the shock of dark hair above the pale slender neck. 'I hate that it's come to this, but he's left me with no choice.'

Laura made no reply.

'I hope you don't mind that we've come here – I mean, with him being your father. I'd hate for you to feel caught in the middle.'

'Caught in the middle?'

Something in her voice made Susan turn. Laura's face was full of puzzlement, a crimp in the skin between her eyes.

'What do you mean?' she asked. 'Why would I be caught in the middle?'

'Well, with us splitting up –'

'Splitting *up*? You've *left* him?'

Clearly not what she was expecting after all. 'Yes, I've left him,' Susan said, darting a glance at Harry. 'What did you think this was about?'

Laura's frown didn't shift. 'I – I don't know. I don't know what I thought.'

'But you just said –'

'Well, I just thought you might need a break, that was all. I didn't expect *this*.'

It sounded to Susan like an accusation. She let the words sit in the air between them, feeling utterly disheartened. She'd thought her stepdaughter of all people would understand, would accept Susan's decision without question. Would even show some sympathy. Then again, however she might feel about him, he *was* her father.

'Sorry,' Laura said, giving her hand another squeeze. 'Sorry, I didn't meant to – it was just … a surprise. Do you want to talk about it? Can you tell me what happened?'

Susan pulled a hand through her hair, feeling again the weariness in every muscle, every move. 'Nothing happened. I mean, nothing specific. It's just lately – well, you know what he's like, so focused on his work—'

'I know. I *do* know – but that's just Luke.'

Susan shook her head. 'It's different now. It's as if he's not even living with us any more, you know? As if he's put a giant wall between us. I can't connect with him. I can't find him.'

'He might have things on his mind.'

'Well, of course he—'

'Have you tried talking to him? Have you asked him if anything is wrong?'

'Of *course* I have,' she replied, a little more tartly than she'd intended. 'I've tried all I can, and I can't get through.'

'So—' Laura began, and stopped. And began again. 'Maybe you just need to persevere, Susan. I mean, splitting up is so final, isn't it? Maybe he just needs more time to open up to you.'

All the times Laura had moaned about him to Susan, all the times she'd voiced her resentment of how absent he'd been as a parent – and now here she was telling Susan to have more patience. It would seem, when it came down to it, that blood really was thicker than water.

'Sorry,' Laura said again. 'It's between you and Luke, and none of my business. I just hate to see you separating, that's all. He never deserved you, but he was so lucky to have you.'

Susan gave a bitter smile. 'Pity he can't see that.'

'I think he can,' Laura replied, nodding slowly. 'I'm sure he loves you, Susan. I know he does.'

The remarks only served to irritate Susan. 'How can you possibly know that? You haven't seen him in well over a year. How can you have the smallest idea how he feels?'

'I just know,' Laura insisted. 'I can't explain it, but I do. Lord knows I've no illusions about him, but I just … I wish …'

She trailed off. Silence stretched between them. Susan watched a cartoon man being chased by a big yellow animal that could have been a dog or a dinosaur.

'So what will you do now?' Laura asked eventually.

'I'll get a job, and I'll find a place to live.'

'Where?'

Where indeed? Dublin made the most sense, with practically all of her friends there, and Harry enrolled in a local school – but Luke was in Dublin too, and she would need to stay well out of his ambit.

'I don't know where,' she admitted. 'I haven't decided yet.'

'You could stay here. I'd love it, and so would the kids and Gav. We could find you a place to rent till you got sorted.'

Susan summoned a smile. 'Thanks, darling. It's lovely of you to suggest it, but I'm not sure Roone is for me. You know I love my visits, but long term ...'

Long term, Roone would drive her out of her mind. She'd miss the shops, and her regular manicures and facials, and her twice-weekly yoga class. She wasn't much of a walker, and hadn't cycled for years. She didn't swim or sail. She wasn't interested in the Roone activities.

And anyway, what job could she hope to get on the island? She'd been working as a school secretary when she'd met Luke, but Roone's one and only school was surely all sorted on that front, and she didn't imagine secretaries were in big demand elsewhere on the island. She might pick up something seasonal – waitress, bar worker, the hotel might need a chambermaid – but come the autumn, when the tourists packed up and went home, she'd in all probability be surplus to requirements.

'I'm just catching my breath here,' she said. 'I'm gathering my strength, trying to figure out what's next.'

The room was tasteful and anonymous and blessedly quiet, although the receptionist had told her that the hotel was almost full. The rest of the residents might make their presence felt later on, but for now they were keeping it down.

'It mightn't be forever,' Laura said. 'He might come after you.'

Susan couldn't imagine it – and neither, she was sure, could Laura – but she said nothing.

'How will he find you, if he wants to?' Laura persisted. 'You'll need to let him know, just in case.'

'I will,' Susan said shortly, smothering another bolt of frustration. Surely she couldn't have forgotten what he was like. The idea of him coming to reclaim Susan, like some rom-com leading man, was as likely as him throwing up his painting and going to work in a donkey sanctuary.

The cartoons ended and Harry climbed silently onto her lap, his small heft warm and heavy against her as he ran his thumb across the soft fur of Toby's blue ear and looked steadily at his half-sister. Sunlight ran down the cream walls and splashed onto the pale grey carpet.

'So when does Tilly arrive?' Susan's other stepdaughter, the one she hadn't known existed till a few years ago.

'Four more days. The girls are that excited, you'd swear the Queen was coming.'

'Isn't that sweet? I must meet her for a chat when she's settled in.'

'She'd love that.' Pause. 'Susan, what'll I tell people?'

'Tell them the truth,' Susan replied, conscious

of her little son sitting silently in her lap. Listening, maybe. Understanding, maybe. 'Tell them what I've told you.'

'But, well, would it be wiser to say you're just taking a break or something? In case anything changes, I mean. You never know, do you?'

'Laura, please listen to me,' Susan said quietly. 'I know it might be hard for you to hear, but it's happened. It's over, and nothing is going to change that. You know and I know that he's not going to come after me.'

Laura reached across and patted Harry's knee, and smiled at him.

'I know it's not what you want to hear,' Susan went on. 'I know you're disappointed. I'm disappointed too.' Putting it mildly.

Laura made as if to speak, and checked herself.

'What is it?'

'Can I ask you something?'

'Anything.'

'Do you still ... love him?'

Susan shifted slightly, adjusting Harry's weight. 'Yes,' she whispered.

She wondered what he was doing right now, right this minute. Was he thinking about her? Had it sunk in that his wife and son were gone from him? And what would Harry make of it, the longer his daddy didn't reappear?

Sooner or later she'd have to tell him what she'd done. She'd have to put it into words he'd understand,

and try to ensure that he didn't hold it against her. She was sure he loved Luke, in the unquestioning way of children – and now she'd separated them, and there was every chance that they'd never again live under the same roof.

'Hey,' Laura said, 'are you OK?'

'I'm fine,' Susan said, but she wasn't.

Laura put out her arms. 'Harry,' she said, 'come with me to the window. Let's look at the sea and find some boats' – and off they went, leaving his mother to escape to the hotel bathroom, where she ran the tap so he wouldn't hear her letting out her loneliness.

Despite what Laura said, Luke mustn't love her. That was the ugly truth of it. She loved him, but he mustn't love her back. He couldn't, or he wouldn't have let her walk out just like that. It hurt like hell that he'd chosen painting over her.

After a bit she sluiced her face with water and patted it dry, her eyeliner leaving black marks on the soft white towel. She and Harry would move on. She'd find a new home and a new job and she'd get over this, she'd recover. And in time her marriage would arrive at the same quiet ending as his first marriage to Laura and Tilly's mother.

And Luke, in all likelihood, would not look for custody of his only son. He might not even want occasional contact. If this happened, if he and Harry became completely estranged, Harry might want to know about him one day. *What was he like?* he might ask, curiosity getting the better of him, and Susan would tell him the truth as kindly as she could. She'd explain that his father had an immense talent that had left little room for anything else. She'd say he'd loved her and Harry in his own way, but that it hadn't been enough to keep them all together, and she'd have to hope that Harry would be content with that.

Life would go on. And in time, she might even learn how to be happy again.

Eve

SHE SHOULDN'T HAVE LIED TO LAURA. SHE shouldn't have done that. But how could she have told her the truth, when Laura was so friendly with Nell? There was no way she could have risked it. Nell would hit the roof if she knew – and probably James too.

And Imelda. Every time she thought of the row they'd had – no, not a row, just Eve lashing out – it made her want to cry. She'd hurt Imelda, when Imelda was already hurting so badly. She was still hurting her by ignoring the phone calls – but how could she answer? How could she trust herself not to blurt it out, and destroy Imelda completely?

She opened her spiral-bound notebook and found a pen that worked. She sat at the rickety little table she'd pulled over to the window, and began.

Dear Mam,
I hope you're feeling OK, and they're treating you
well. I just wanted to drop you a line and let you know

She paused, pen in the air. And let you know.

that something happened a few weeks ago. Well,
two things happened. Hugh died in his sleep on the
fifteenth of May, that was the first thing.

She stopped again to blot her eyes with a sleeve.
Come on.

It was very hard. It was a big shock. Hugh was like a
dad. He was there for me like my own dad never was.

She reread it, tapping the end of the pen against her
teeth.

That's not a dig at you. I don't blame you for that.
Anyway, a week or so after, I heard that a friend was
having a house party for his twenty-first. I wasn't
going to go. I didn't feel like a party, I was still in
bits over Hugh, but a few pals said it might help to
take my mind off it for a few hours, so in the end I
went.

She set down her pen. She got up and walked to the
sink. She filled a cup with water and drank it.

Andy Baker was at the party. I told you about Andy.
We went out for over a year. I was the one to finish
with him, and I can't explain why. He begged me not
to, he said I was killing him, but something made me
break it off. I think it was to do with Derek Garvey,
and my head being all over the place. He was the one
in the foster home who abused me. I told you about
him too.

Again she set down her pen. She propped her elbows on the table and rested her chin in her hands as she read over what she'd written. It was so stilted, she'd never been any good at writing, but she felt compelled to get it all out of her – and this way she could tell the complete truth.

It was hard, though. It was reminding her of things she'd rather forget. *The first time I saw you*, Andy had told her – when they were solid together, when they were unafraid to say those things to one another – *I knew there was something there. Every time I saw you I felt it more.* And she'd wanted to hear it. She'd lapped it up, and said the same back to him.

And then, the Christmas after she'd ended it, when they'd been six months apart, Tilly had arrived on Roone, and word had flown around the island within days that Laura Connolly had a sister she'd known nothing about. Eve had seen her around the place; tall, pale freckly skin, wishy-washy hair. Could have passed for Irish until you heard her talk.

Eve had never cared for the Australian accent.

And the following summer Tilly returned to Roone, and word got out that she and Andy had become an item. When she heard it, Eve hadn't known how to feel. She'd told herself she was glad for him, that he must have recovered from the hurt she'd caused him, but there was a small bit of jealousy too, if she was perfectly honest.

Would they have got back together if Tilly hadn't arrived on the scene? Maybe, maybe not. After Andy,

Eve had gone out a few times with Gary O'Donnell. She'd never fancied him, but he'd been coming on to her for a while, and she was lonely. It hadn't lasted beyond a month though. Her heart wasn't in it: there was no spark, no point to it, and his kisses left her unmoved. In the end she'd told him she still wasn't ready for a new relationship. *It's not you*, she'd said, that hackneyed old line, but it was all she had.

Relationships were tricky, living on a small island. For one thing, your options were seriously limited. And with boyfriends and exes all knowing one another, who could tell what information was being passed around? Avoiding anyone you'd rather not meet was difficult too. Best to stay single, she'd decided, until someone she couldn't resist came along, so she'd kept her distance from anyone who looked like he might be working his way up to asking her out.

Two summers had come and gone, and Tilly with them, and she and Andy were still together, despite living on opposite sides of the world. Eve told herself she was happy for them, and she almost believed it. Didn't stop her feeling lonely every now and again. Didn't stop her being nostalgic for what they'd had, the magic they'd made when they were together.

And then, just a few weeks ago, Frog Hackett, one of Andy's best buddies, had thrown a party for his twenty-first, and Eve had been invited along with everyone else. Despite her misgivings, she'd let herself be persuaded by her friends, and she'd gone.

But within minutes of arriving she'd known it was a mistake. Everyone was happy, everyone was laughing. A few were dancing. What was she doing there? She'd felt alienated from them, and disloyal to Hugh's memory. She had no business enjoying herself. She'd made up her mind to leave – but before she could, someone had put a paper cup of wine into her hand. She'd knocked it back too quickly, anxious to be on her way, but it had floated into her head and made her want another.

She picked up her pen again.

I had too much to drink at the party. I think I was trying to drown my sorrows or something. Anyway, I remember crying at one stage, and Andy putting an arm around me. We left the party with a few others, but by the time we got to my apartment, it was just the two of us.

Now. The hard part.

I don't remember a lot of what happened after that. We made coffee – well, one of us did, because I found the mugs in the sink the next morning. And then

She scrubbed her face with her free hand. Write it. Write it.

And then we slept together.

She crossed it out, and wrote,

And then we had sex.

There had been no sign of him when she'd woken early with a thumping head and a raging thirst – thank God it was Saturday, and no crèche. She wished she could remember it. Her clothes were in a tumble on the floor: had they undressed one another? Had it been hurried and exciting, or slow and sweet? Had he spoken? Had either of them? It killed her that she had no memory of it, none – but it must have happened.

It wasn't the first time they'd gone all the way. Despite being mad about him, despite really wanting him, it had taken months, seven or eight months, before she was comfortable with that level of intimacy. He hadn't pestered her, hadn't pushed her in any way, but she knew he was dying for it too. In the end she'd been the one to initiate it, to make it plain that she was ready.

And they'd been careful, of course they had. They'd gone to Tralee on the ferry and bought condoms in a big chemist where nobody knew them. They'd giggled about how many they'd need, and what kind they should get. She hadn't been able to look at the checkout girl as Andy had paid: she'd pretended to be really interested in the perfume display by the till.

It had taken them a while to get the hang of them – he was as clueless as she was – but they'd never been stupid. They'd been careful in the other sense too, careful to hunt out places where nobody would find them. No mean feat on Roone, but by then she knew the island almost as well as he did. They found their spots.

No condoms the night of the party, though.

She picked up the pen again.

And now I'm pregnant. Imagine that, Mam. Your daughter is pregnant.

Since the night of the party, she'd encountered Andy a few times, but they'd never been on their own. They'd had no proper conversation, not a single one. She guessed he hadn't confided in any of the others about what had happened between them. Why would he, with Tilly on the way?

God, Tilly.

I feel bad that it happened, since Andy has a steady girlfriend. It wasn't planned by either of us, but I know he'll be feeling bad too that he was unfaithful. They only meet once a year, she lives in Australia and comes over for the summer, but they must be serious if they can keep it going like that. I haven't decided yet whether to tell him I'm pregnant. I don't know what to do about that.

She shouldn't have said anything to Laura. She should have kept the whole thing to herself. She'd felt so completely on her own though: she'd needed someone to share it with, and Laura was the only person she could think of. She couldn't tell any of her friends that she was pregnant, with them all having been at the party, and knowing that Andy had walked her home. They'd put two and two together in no time, they'd know it was his, and they couldn't know, not yet. So she'd turned to Laura.

And telling her had helped. Saying it aloud, saying what she'd decided to do about it, had convinced her that it was the right thing. Of course she'd been shocked at first, when she'd realised she was pregnant – who wouldn't have been, in her situation? But as the shock was abating, as the implications of what had happened were sinking in, she could see that it wasn't the end of the world. In fact, the more she turned it over in her head, the more she could look on it as a positive development.

I'm keeping it, Mam. You're going to be a granny. I don't know how you'll feel about that, but I hope you'll be happy for me.

For as long as she could remember, she'd looked forward to being someone's mam, maybe because her own mother had made such a mess of it. Maybe Eve wanted to redress the balance, give someone a loving mam, a mam who cared, and didn't spend money on whatever drug she could get her hands on instead of buying food for her children.

Hadn't she already been a mother to Keith, in everything but name? Hadn't she practically brought him up while they were still living with Mam, before they'd both been taken out of the house and handed over to strangers? She'd stolen food for him:

she'd lifted packs of cooked ham from shops, she'd swiped bottles of milk from doorsteps, gone through supermarket bins to find stuff that wasn't too much out of date.

She knew how to look after someone smaller than her, and she was determined to look after this baby as if her life depended on it. It shouldn't have happened like this but it had, and she'd accepted it. Even if it meant everyone turning against her, even if it meant having to leave the island she'd come to love, she was having this baby – and she was going to keep it. She was giving it up for nobody.

Didn't mean she wasn't terrified at the thought of the labour. Being there for the birth of Laura's twin girls four years earlier had stunned her: she'd known having a baby was painful, everyone knew that, but she hadn't realised there was such a *brutality* about the business of giving birth, hadn't known how it stripped away every ounce of – humanity, or whatever you'd call it. It ripped it all apart, it reduced the woman to a grunting, sweating, roaring mess. But Eve would get through it, like Laura had, like so many other women did.

What if Andy denied everything, if she decided to tell him? What then? It was only her word that it had happened. He could say he'd left her at the apartment door and gone straight home, and who would everyone believe? He'd been living here a lot longer than she had; his father had married an islander.

She didn't think he'd deny it: he was too decent a person. But Tilly was about to arrive for another summer, and Eve couldn't very well drop the bombshell before that. If she did decide to tell him, it would have to be after Tilly's departure, sometime in August. She supposed it could wait, provided Laura kept her word and told nobody.

There's another thing. I had a row with Imelda. I shouted at her, for no good reason. I feel really bad about it, but I think I needed to create a bit of space between us. I need to not be around her just now, until I make some decisions.

What of Hugh, she wondered, what would he have made of this? She remembered how proud he'd been when she'd got the job at the crèche. *You've done well for yourself, love*, he'd said. *I knew you would.* He'd had such faith in her, one of the few people who'd really believed in her. She couldn't bear the thought that he might be disappointed now, that he might feel she'd let him down.

Oh, there was so much to sort out, so much tossing about in her simmering head as she lay chasing sleep each night. Thank God the crèche was closed for the summer.

Anyway, I just wanted to let you know how things were. Don't worry about me, I'll figure it out, and I'll come to see you soon. I'll bring the little oranges you like.
love Eve xx

She read it through from the beginning. It covered two pages of her notebook, back and front. She detached them carefully from their spiral binding, and read the letter through again. Then she ripped the pages in half, and in half again, and again, and dropped the little pieces into the plastic bin under the sink.

Mam didn't read letters. Mam had no interest in letters, or in Eve. For the past several months Mam had been living in the psychiatric wing of a Dublin hospital, her mind destroyed by drugs, her body ruined by the lifestyle they'd dictated.

The last time Eve had seen her, a few days before Easter, they'd sat in a room that smelt of someone else's feet, and her mother had replied to Eve's questions in a low, defeated voice. She'd shown no curiosity about her daughter – Eve hadn't been entirely sure that she'd even recognised her. It felt like nothing remained of their connection, and she'd been so sad and confused on leaving that she'd thought she might not return.

But she could still talk to her – she could still open up and let out whatever was inside, even if it was only words on paper, even if Mam never got to read them. Better that she never got to read them. Better if she didn't know the half of what was going on.

She looked out at the rain. Some summer this was turning out to be.

Imelda

IT STOOD ON THE DOORSTEP, ALL ON ITS OWN. It was big and bright green and made, she thought, of rigid plastic. There were little black wheels, four of them, on its underside.

Imelda hitched her bag onto her shoulder and examined the suitcase more closely. No identifying tag or sticker, no indication as to who might own it, or who might have left it there. She nudged it with her foot: it didn't budge. She took hold of the handle and gave it a small tug, and the resistance she met told her it was full, presumably with the things that people usually put into suitcases. But whose was it, and what on earth was it doing here?

Could it possibly belong to Eve? Imelda had never seen it before, but Eve could have picked it up in a charity shop. She might be regretting her recent outburst. She might want to move home again, to be with Imelda while they mourned. But there was no sign of Eve – and anyway, she'd hardly arrive with bag and baggage before talking to Imelda about it.

She glanced around the small front yard. All was as it should be, the various pots and tubs still in their usual places, no sign of any other foreign object. She walked around the house and found the back garden similarly undisturbed – and there was Scooter, asleep in the corner she always chose for her naps. Had the dog witnessed the arrival of the suitcase? Had she heard the sound of its approach, and padded out to investigate?

'Who was it?' Imelda asked, and Scooter lifted her head briefly before settling back, not caring who it was.

Imelda let herself into the house and stood for a moment in the kitchen, listening to the silence. Would she ever get used to it? Not that Hugh had been loud – she could hardly remember him raising his voice: even his laughter had been gentle – but he'd been there, and he'd had plenty to say for himself.

When Eve and her brother Keith had shared the house with them, there was noise. Two teenagers – how could there not be noise? Sometimes the siblings would bicker, but it rarely lasted. *Leave them at it*, Hugh would tell her. *They'll sort it out*, and they always did.

But now everyone was gone. Now it was just her and Scooter. Nobody to chat with, no sound when she ate but her own chewing and swallowing, and the occasional soft judder from the fridge, or shriek of gulls if the window was open. There was the radio, of course, but sometimes it annoyed her, and she had to switch it off.

She dropped her bag onto the kitchen floor and

crossed to a chair. She sat and placed her forearms on the table and lowered her head onto them. She was dreadfully tired, more exhausted than she could ever remember. She'd never realised before how grief could suck everything, everything out of you except the awful, endless longing for what was gone.

And then there were all the stepping-stones that had to be negotiated, all the milestones to pass on her journey without him. Her first night alone, a week after the funeral, when her sister had packed up and gone home. Her first unaccompanied visit to his grave, when she'd stood by the turned earth, still covered with flowers, and torn strips off him for dying. The first time she'd put out the bins, always his job. Every first driving the pain deeper into her.

And the month's mind Mass, falling cruelly on what would have been his birthday: how horribly it had stirred everything up. The little church as full as it had been for the funeral, everyone there, she knew, to show their ongoing sympathy – and it had been appreciated, she'd been glad of it.

But all through the Mass she'd relived the full dreadfulness of his death. All through the prayers and the hymns and the kneeling and the sitting, the pain had come at her in waves. Several times she'd felt the near-uncontrollable urge to burst into hysterical tears, to let her anguish out unchecked, and only the knowledge that any display of high emotion would alarm and upset Nell on one side of her, and Eve on the other, had enabled her to keep her composure.

After Mass she'd been surrounded, everyone shaking her hand again or pressing her shoulder again or gathering her into an embrace again, till she wanted to scream at them all to let her be, to allow her to mourn him undisturbed. The month's mind had been hard.

And two weeks after that, she'd said the wrong thing to Eve, and the girl had shouted at her and left in anger, and still hadn't reappeared, or been in touch. The silence of that, the hurtfulness of that – but she'd come back. She'd have to.

She lifted her head. Food. She should eat: nothing since a lunchtime apple and a small wedge of Cheddar. She crossed to the fridge and looked without enthusiasm at eggs and yogurt and sausages. She pulled out the vegetable drawer and saw carrots that should have been eaten a week ago, and left them there.

She cut bread from a loaf and toasted it. She spread butter and lemon curd and had it standing at the window, unable to eat alone at the table.

She'd have an early night, even if it wasn't yet eight o'clock, even if daylight still streamed into the room. Even if, despite her exhaustion, sleep would undoubtedly prove fitful at best.

But then she thought, no, she wouldn't go up just yet. There was something too defeatist, something too slippery-slope, about getting into bed so early. She'd lie on the couch instead, close her eyes there for an hour or so.

She went upstairs and took the eiderdown and

Hugh's pillow from their bed. In the sitting room she turned on the television, the volume set so low she could barely hear it. It was company she craved, but the kind that didn't require any interaction. The kind that ignored her, and allowed her to ignore it.

She slipped off her shoes and her cardigan. She should brush her teeth – they still felt coated with lemon curd – but her toothbrush was upstairs and she couldn't face the return trip.

She lay back and pulled up the eiderdown and looked at the ceiling while she listened to the small voice of a newscaster telling of a drugs seizure in Kildare, and a landslide in the Philippines, and accusations of more crooked elections in Africa. She closed her eyes and gradually the voice became a soft wash of sound, and she drifted to sleep.

She woke with a start. What? She blinked, disoriented, too hot. She pushed aside the eiderdown and turned her head and saw the fireplace, the mantelpiece, armchairs. The sitting room, yes, and the day returned slowly to her, and with it the knowledge that Hugh was gone, the fresh cruel blow that waited for her on each awakening, bringing with it the same blackness.

The mantel clock read twenty past eight; she'd slept for little more than half an hour. The doorbell rang – and she realised it must be for the second time, the first having surely been what had wakened her. Someone with an apple tart or a fruitcake, some well-meaning neighbour who would need tea made for them, and who would sit and talk for an hour, and tell Imelda how brave she was being, and how Hugh would have wanted her to carry on.

She closed her eyes again. Not tonight. She couldn't take it. She'd lie quietly, and whoever it was would go away. She waited for the sound of retreating footsteps, and for a time heard nothing. She imagined them standing undecided, maybe peering through the sitting room window. She didn't budge, didn't open her eyes – and then the letterbox snapped, making her heart skip. She imagined a note hastily scribbled, *Sorry I missed you, hope you're feeling OK.* Now they would go. She heard a clatter, a roll of wheels on concrete – and abruptly she remembered the green suitcase, greeting her on her return earlier.

She opened her eyes. She sat up and pushed her feet into shoes, and ran a hand through her hair. The sound of the wheels was growing fainter. She grabbed her cardigan and shoved her arms into the sleeves. She went out to the hall and stooped to pick up the folded torn-edged page, still pulling her cardigan into place. She scanned the brief message, written in pencil, the lettering shaky:

Dear Mr and Mrs Fitzpatrick
Here is Gualtiero Conti. I come to stay in your house.
I come two time but you are not here. I go now to
hotel. Please come. I wait for you in hotel.
GC

Gualtiero Conti.

Mr Conti.

She'd forgotten him.

God Almighty. She had completely and utterly forgotten Mr Conti.

She couldn't let him go without an explanation. She had to stop him. She opened the front door and saw nothing. She strode to the gate and there he was, short and straw-hatted, retreating in the direction of the village at a fairly rapid trot, pulling his case after him.

'Stop!' she called. 'Wait!'

He halted. He turned. He was already fifty yards, maybe more, from her. She lifted an arm, gave a ridiculous little wave. 'Mr Conti!' she called, and back he came. Plump, dressed in a beautiful navy pinstripe suit. Glasses, ruddy-cheeked. Smiling.

'I'm so sorry,' Imelda said, as he approached. 'I was asleep, I ... didn't hear you. And earlier I was ... out. I'm sorry. I'm Imelda Fitzpatrick,' she added. She hoped to God she looked halfway decent, but she doubted it.

He was shorter than her by a couple of inches. His skin was tanned. Behind the glasses his eyes were toffee brown. He raised his hat, exposing closely cropped grey hair. He gave a little bow from the waist. 'Mrs Fitzpatrick,' he said, his voice unexpectedly deep, '*incantata*. Please to meet you.'

Imelda's mind raced. She'd have to come clean. She'd have to admit she'd forgotten about him. She'd explain about Hugh; he'd understand, and go away.

He'd have to find somewhere else to stay until he could return to Italy.

But before she could open her mouth, he spoke again. 'Please, Mrs Fitzpatrick, you 'ave the toilet?'

'I – beg your pardon?'

'You 'ave the toilet for me, please?'

The toilet, the least she could do. 'Yes, yes, of course. Follow me, I'll show you.'

She led him up the path and back into the house, the green suitcase bumping along in his wake, hopping over the threshold. 'You can leave it here,' she told him. 'The bathroom is upstairs, first door on the left.'

'Left?'

'This one,' she said, touching her left shoulder. 'First door.'

'Ah – *sinistra*. Thank you, Mrs Fitzpatrick.' Another little bow. He climbed the stairs, his tread light, the straw hat still perched on his head. He left a faint scent in his wake that put her in mind of freshly sawn wood.

She stood in the hall, eyeing the suitcase, trying to marshal her thoughts. March, was it, or April? A lifetime ago, it felt like. Eve gone since January to the apartment above the crèche, Keith's hotel management course already under way in Galway. The house hers and Hugh's again, after nearly four years of sharing it with others.

Like to earn a bit of pocket money this summer? Nell had asked over a morning coffee. *Laura has had an enquiry from an Italian couple who stayed with her last year – the husband is looking for accommodation for his uncle in the summer. He wants to come for about a month and do some painting.*

Couldn't Laura put him up? Imelda had enquired, not sure she fancied the idea of taking in a stranger for an entire month.

She doesn't want him. Long-term stays don't really pay her – and, anyway she doesn't have a single room, so he'd be taking up a double. I said I'd ask around. Don't worry if you'd prefer not to.

But the more she'd thought about it, the more the idea had appealed to Imelda. An older man, presumably quiet in his habits – and they'd still have Keith's room free, if he fancied coming back for a weekend now and again. *Would I have to cook for him, or could I just give him the room?*

Well, he'd probably expect breakfast, but you wouldn't be obliged to do more than that. You could always ask him – Laura has an email address.

I'll talk to Hugh – and Hugh, when she'd brought it up, had had no objection. *Why not? It's only for a month – and it would give us a taste, see if we wanted to do more in the future.* So Imelda had sent an email, and Mr Conti had replied, and after a bit of back-and-forth – he'd always addressed her as Mrs Fitzpatrick, despite her signing off as Imelda, so she'd felt obliged to stick to Mr Conti for him – they'd settled on the ninth of July for his arrival date.

The ninth of July, which was today – and here he

was. And Hugh was gone and Imelda was falling apart, and keeping Mr Conti now was out of the question. She'd have to let him stay the night though – her heart sank at the thought, but evening was drawing in, and she didn't have the energy to try and find him somewhere else before dark.

God – was the room even ready? Eve's old bedroom she'd earmarked for him, the one her sister had stayed in after the funeral. Imelda was fairly sure she'd changed the sheets after her departure, but she hadn't set foot in it since then, no dusting or vacuuming, no windows opened to let in the fresh air.

Oh, what did it matter if the room was clean? What did any of it matter now? He'd be in it for a night, one night. He'd survive.

The toilet flushed. She checked herself in the hallstand mirror – God, her hair, all over the place. A tap ran – at least he washed his hands. The lock slid back, the door opened and out he came onto the landing, hat held to his chest as he descended the stairs. She'd break it to him now: she'd just say it out.

Or she'd offer him some refreshment first, to soften the blow. 'Mr Conti, please come into the kitchen. I'll make some tea – or perhaps you'd like coffee?'

He raised a palm. 'No, no, *grazie*, Mrs Fitzpatrick. No tea or coffee for me. Only some water, please – and after, you show me my room? I am little bit tired.'

God, his room. She was going to have to dive in.

'Mr Conti,' she began, and stopped. She looked down at his shoes, which were black and shiny. She swallowed, and tried again. 'Mr Conti—' She came to another halt. 'You see,' she said, 'it's – well, my husband—'

She stopped again. No, it was beyond her. The words refused to come. She lifted her gaze and took in the man's polite half-smile.

Tell him. You can't stand here like a dummy. Out with it.

'I – my – the thing is, Mr Conti—' breathe, breathe '—this is a very … bad time for me.'

Something softened in his face. The little smile dimmed. He tilted his head a fraction to the left, and waited for more.

'My husband died,' she blurted, 'nearly two months ago. Very suddenly. It was a – a – it was—' She clamped her trembling mouth shut, blinked furiously to keep the tears from falling.

For a moment he didn't speak, just held her gaze with those brown eyes while she went on doing her very best not to break down. 'Mrs Fitzpatrick,' he said then, softly, gently, 'I am so sorry to hear this terrible thing.' Such sympathy in his tone, such concern in his voice, it was all she could do not to let out an anguished howl. A sound escaped her, somewhere between a sob and a moan. He placed a hand on her arm, the lightest of touches, so light she barely felt it.

'Mrs Fitzpatrick,' he repeated, in the same gentle way, 'your 'eart, 'e is very sad. I can see this, yes.'

She nodded, speech still beyond her. *Your heart,*

he is very sad. Don't make a fool of yourself. Finish what you have to say. She cleared her throat. 'Mr Conti, I'm so sorry, but I can't keep you here. I just … can't – but of course you can stay tonight, and I will help you, I will try my best, to find another place for you tomorrow.' The words stuttering out, shaky and disjointed and too fast. 'I'm sorry,' she repeated. 'Really sorry.'

He lifted a palm in the way he had done before. 'No, no sorry,' he said. 'No say sorry. Come,' he said, propping his hat on the end of the banister. 'I make the tea for you, Mrs Fitzpatrick.'

'No – honestly, there's no need—' but already he was moving down the hall, sensing the geography of the house, turning to look back questioningly, so Imelda followed him. What else could she do?

In the kitchen he located the kettle and held it under the tap – God, her plate and cup still sitting in the sink, toast crumbs on the worktop – while she silently dropped a teabag into a mug. She didn't want tea, tea was the last thing she wanted, but she hadn't the energy to protest. Did he understand, she wondered, that she'd given him his marching orders? Maybe he understood perfectly. Maybe this was an attempt to ingratiate himself, to get her to change her mind and let him stay.

Immediately she felt ashamed. He'd come twice to the house, and twice nobody had answered his ring of the bell. He must have thought goodness knows what. He hadn't been angry when they'd finally met, like another person might have been. He was simply being kind now – he was showing sympathy. How could she suspect an ulterior motive?

'You sit, Mrs Fitzpatrick,' he said, crossing to the fridge as if he'd been here for weeks instead of minutes. Peering in. 'You like the milk or the lemon for the tea?'

'Milk, please,' she murmured, dropping onto a chair. There wasn't a lemon in the house. 'My name is Imelda,' she added, her weariness returning, an enormous yawn escaping before she could stop it. God, how rude.

'You like also the sugar?' he enquired, depositing the milk jug on the table. Maybe he hadn't caught the yawn.

'No sugar, thank you. Mr Conti, this is really not necessary –' but there he was, bustling about, taking two glasses from a press.

'Is possible to drink the water from the –?' he asked, indicating the tap, and she nodded, so he filled the glasses and set one before her. 'Take a little, please,' he said, and she sipped obediently. He opened drawers and found a spoon. The kettle boiled and he made tea. He stirred, he fished out the teabag and dropped it onto the draining board. He placed the mug in front of her. '*Ecco*,' he said, accompanying the word with a smile of such warmth that Imelda summoned an answering smile for him.

'Thank you.'

He took the chair beside her, set his glass on the table. 'You are welcome, Mrs Fitzpatrick.'

'Imelda,' she repeated. 'Please call me Imelda.' She had no stomach, right now, for Mrs Fitzpatrick.

'Ee-mel-da,' he said, stretching out the *l* in the middle, giving the name a musicality it didn't deserve. 'And I am Gualtiero.' Swallowing the *g* so it came out more like a *w*. 'Please to meet you,' he said, the smile filling his face again. Extending a hand so she had no choice but to take it.

Hard to put an age on him. She thought over sixty. Teeth sound, and looked like his own. Hand warm, and softer than she'd expected.

'Eemelda,' he said again, 'I go tomorrow, no problem. You no worry about me, OK?'

He had understood, and he wasn't upset. 'Yes,' she said. 'Thank you.' Another yawn came without warning. 'Sorry,' she said around it, reclaiming her hand to clamp it over her traitorous mouth. 'I'm afraid I'm very tired.'

He got immediately to his feet. 'You must go to the bed,' he said. 'You take the tea and you go. I go too, you show room for me.'

She brought him upstairs and opened the door of his room, and stood back to let him enter. She gave the place a quick scan and decided it would do. Towels: he needed towels. She took two yellow ones from the hotpress and handed them to him. 'There's just one bathroom, I'm afraid,' she said, 'but there's plenty of hot water' – and he waved a hand and assured her one bathroom was no problem.

'What time would you like breakfast?' she asked,

trying to remember what there was in the fridge. Eggs, she thought. And yogurt. Was that enough?

He lifted his shoulders, pursed his mouth. 'Nine o'clock?'

'Nine is fine.' She'd be awake well before it, and nine gave her time to scoot to the supermarket, which opened at eight, for supplies. Maybe she could make a few phone calls too, before he appeared, try to get him sorted. 'Anything in particular you'd like?'

Another shrug. 'Perhaps eggs,' he told her. 'Any way cooking eggs. I can do, if you like.'

'No, no, I'll do it.' She could at least scramble his eggs before turfing him out. 'Well, goodnight then.' She'd forgotten his first name, unless it was Garibaldi, which she was fairly sure it wasn't.

'*Buona notte*, Eemelda. I wish you the good sleep.'

In the bathroom she hastily used the toilet and brushed her teeth and washed her face. She hurried downstairs and bundled up her bedding and returned it to her room. She closed the door and leant against it. What a thing to happen, what a state of affairs to find herself in.

Would she be able to get him somewhere else though? It would be terribly difficult, with the island full of tourists. Even the hotel might be full – not that she could really suggest the hotel to him, when it would surely be far more expensive than her modest charge.

And the fact that he wanted to stay for an entire month, four whole weeks, made her task all the harder.

Even if she managed to get him a bed somewhere, chances were they wouldn't be able to keep him for so long, which meant he'd have to be moved around. God, what was to be done?

She'd ring Nell first thing, she decided. Nell would help. If it came to it, there might be someone like herself who didn't normally take in people, but who had a spare room and wouldn't mind a bit of extra cash. It was awful to do it to him, especially after the confusion surrounding his arrival. Poor man was probably regretting his decision to come to Ireland.

Nell must have forgotten about him too, and Laura. *Eggs for breakfast*, she remembered Laura saying. *Whatever else you have, they always expect an egg. Remind me nearer the time and Gav can put you on his delivery list.*

She took off her clothes and slipped her nightdress over her head. She rummaged in the wardrobe for her dressing gown and hung it on the back of the door. Better be prepared in case she encountered him on her way to the loo in the middle of the night.

She climbed into bed. She hugged Hugh's pillow to her chest. The pillowcase was unchanged: she couldn't bring herself to take it off, with its lingering, heartbreaking scent of his aftershave.

She could hear the man splashing about in the bathroom. She'd forgotten to show him how to work the shower, or to point out that the water could be cloudy at times.

She didn't think he'd have been much bother as a lodger. She thought he'd be good about leaving the bathroom presentable. From what she'd seen, he was mannerly and kind; really, the ideal lodger.

He'd come to paint, she recalled. Maybe he was a professional artist, like Laura's father. The weather hadn't been great so far, apart from one good week in early May, but it had picked up a bit in the last couple of days, and the forecast was for a settled period. If he did end up staying for the month, in whatever accommodation he found himself, she hoped he'd see a good deal of sunshine.

She had to admit that there was something … reassuring about having another person in the house. It mightn't be the end of the world if she didn't get him sorted somewhere else right away. Putting him up for another night or two wouldn't kill her.

He was a complete stranger, it was true – but maybe a stranger was better than someone she knew. She'd have to make an effort in his presence to be more cheerful than she felt – it wasn't his fault that he'd arrived in the middle of this nightmare – but their interactions wouldn't stray into the personal. He'd probably be out much of the day too, if the weather behaved itself.

Your 'eart, 'e is very sad. Such warmth in his voice, as if he could really see her sorrow, and really cared about it.

She closed her eyes – and for the first time in a month she fell asleep almost immediately, and slept right through till morning.

Laura

'I'D COMPLETELY FORGOTTEN ABOUT HIM.'

'So had I, and so had Imelda. He just turned up on her doorstep.'

'God, she needed that like a hole in the head. So what did she do?'

'Nothing much she *could* do. It was getting late, she couldn't see him without a bed for the night, so she brought him in.'

'Oh, the poor creature – although you'd have to feel a bit sorry for him too, landing in to her like that. So has he found somewhere else?'

'Not as yet. I've asked around – I knew you were full – and everyone is booked up for the moment. I even rang Henry at the hotel, I know he'd have given him a special deal, under the circumstances, but he doesn't have a room free all this week, so Imelda is hanging on to him for the time being. I'm trying to think of anyone I might have forgotten.'

'Gosh, that's tricky. I'll keep an ear open.'

'Do. He's offered to go back to Italy – the poor man must feel totally in the way – but she says she couldn't have him do that. Will I stop now, or do you want more off?'

Laura studied her damp head in the salon mirror. 'Go another inch. I'm not sure when I'll have time to come back to you.'

Nell resumed her cutting. 'You're as busy as ever.'

'Up to my eyes.'

'Keeps you young.'

'Hah – don't know about that. Sometimes I feel like a hundred.'

'Well, you don't look it. Tip your head down.' She worked along the back of Laura's neck. 'So Tilly arrives tomorrow.'

'Yes, we're all set.' Laura watched tiny snippets of hair landing silently on the wooden floor. 'Andy must be excited about seeing her again.'

Nell gave a laugh. 'Andy, excited? Have you met my stepson?'

'Well, I know he's never been the most demonstrative, but I thought he might open up a bit to you.'

'Not really. I have to drag things out of him – and his father doesn't fare much better. I'm sure he's looking forward to seeing her again though.'

'It's tough on them, isn't it? Getting together so rarely. I don't think I could do it.'

'Me neither.'

'I mean, Skype is all very well, or FaceTime or whatever they use, but it can only do so much. It can't keep you warm in the winter. It can't make you a cuppa when you're gagging for one, or give you a foot massage, or show up with a bunch of flowers after a row.'

'I wouldn't say they ever have rows.' Nell met her eye briefly in the mirror. 'Imagine if they got married, Laur – in about ten years' time, I mean. That'd make us some class of in-laws.'

'Wouldn't that be hilarious. I hope he knows he'd have to ask Gav's permission first, before he popped the question.'

'Gav? He's not her father. He'd have to ask Luke.'

Silence.

'I'm joking,' Nell said.

'I know you are. So was I.' But with the mention of her father, the levity had gone out of the exchange for her. The thoughts she'd managed to banish as soon as she'd stepped into the salon came hurrying back. Time for a change of subject.

'By the way,' she said, 'Susan is here, with Harry. I meant to tell you.'

Nell looked at her in surprise, her scissors stilled. 'Here? On the island? When did they come?'

'Saturday.'

'They can't be staying with you.'

'No – they're at Manning's.'

'... Everything OK?'

'Nell, she's left him.'

'Oh, no. Oh Laur, that's too bad. I'm so sorry to hear that, for both their sakes – and for Harry.'

She'd left him. She'd walked out on him. He hadn't told her, he'd simply withdrawn from her, and it had driven her away. The land Laura had got in the hotel room when Susan had said it; the scrambling she'd had to do to conceal the truth. So now he was alone, and his wife and child were at the other side of the country. He needed Susan more than ever, but she wasn't there. She'd taken Harry and fled, leaving Laura still holding a secret of enormous proportions. What a mess. What a God almighty mess.

'So what now?' Nell asked.

'She's trying to figure that out. I suggested she stay here on the island, but she's more of a city person. I'm hoping it's just temporary.'

Nell made no response. She knew what Luke was like: Laura had told her often enough how distant and infuriating he could be. She wouldn't be too surprised at Susan's departure. She might be wondering, as Susan herself had no doubt wondered in the hotel the other day, why Laura seemed against the split.

'How's Harry?' Nell asked.

'As adorable as ever, but still not a word out of him. I'm kind of worried about that, although I wouldn't say it to Susan.'

'He's what, two now?'

'Just gone, last month.'

'I wouldn't lose any sleep over it. Boys are slower. Tommy was nearly two before he started making sense – and I bet you found your girls caught on quicker than Ben and Seamus.'

'I suppose they did.' But Laura remembered Nell's Tommy starting on the baby gibberish a long time before his second birthday, her boys too. Harry was such a silent, solemn little thing. No surprise maybe, given his male role model.

She flicked the pages of the magazine on her lap, looking without interest at the celebrities whose images gazed back at her. The impossible buffed perfection of them. The magnificent houses, not a cushion out of place. The adorable children in immaculate designer clothes that didn't have a speck of dried-up tomato sauce or chocolate ice-cream on them. No snotty noses, no soggy-looking nappies, not even a scabby knee. Fantasy lives, nothing like the messy reality.

'Penny for them,' Nell said, tilting Laura's head to the side.

'Hardly worth a penny. Just looking at the beautiful people and thinking what a load of rot the whole celebrity thing is.'

'Nice to have their money though.'

But Luke and Susan had money, lots of it, piles of it, and look how happy it had made them. Money fed you and clothed you and housed you. It had its uses, but it sure as hell didn't buy happiness.

'Seen any sign of Eve lately?' she asked. Casual as you like.

Nell caught her eye in the mirror. Those two weren't exactly the best of buddies, not since Eve had had the nerve to break up with Andy. 'I've passed her in the street a few times. Why do you ask?'

'No reason, just wondered how she was doing. After Hugh, I mean.'

A week – or was it more? – since she'd turned up at Walter's Place and broken her news to Laura. Nothing else had happened, no text, no call, no further visits. Not up to Laura: she'd made it plain that her door was open if Eve needed help. And still the girl hovered in her head, jostling for space with Luke. *Promise you won't tell anyone*, she'd said that evening – but Laura was already struggling to keep the other secret: would the world implode if she shared Eve's with Nell, who could be counted on not to let it go further?

She decided it wouldn't.

'Can I tell you something?'

Nell set down her scissors, lifted the damp towel from Laura's shoulders. 'Of course you can.'

'You have to swear you'll say nothing to anyone, not even James.'

'This sounds big.'

'Seriously, I'd be shot if it got out.'

Nell caught her eye in the mirror. 'Are you sure you want to tell me?'

'No, but I'll burst if I don't say it to someone, and you're far more discreet than I am.'

'Go on so.'

Laura listened for a tread on the stairs outside, and heard none. 'It's Eve. She's pregnant. She told me last week.'

Nell stared at her. 'Eve? You can't be serious. I didn't even know she had a boyfriend.'

'She doesn't. She didn't say who it was, just that it was nobody I know, and that she's not in a relationship with him.'

Nell's mouth tightened. 'A one-night stand.'

'By the sound of it.'

'Has she told Imelda?'

'No, absolutely not. Can you imagine how Imelda would take it, especially now? Nobody knows, apart from me – and now you. I haven't even told Gav.'

Nell took a hairdryer from a shelf. 'When? I mean, when did it happen?'

'Few weeks ago.'

'After Hugh?' The question asked lightly, Nell unwinding the hairdryer cord.

'I don't know.' Yes, in all likelihood after Hugh, but nothing to be gained by admitting it.

'So what's she going to do?'

'She says she wants to keep it.'

'That'll go down really well,' Nell said grimly. 'Wait till Imelda hears.'

'You won't tell her, Nell? Promise?'

'Of course I won't. I wouldn't dream of it.'

'Sorry. I know I have a cheek to ask, after just

blabbing it to you, but she'd be in right trouble if Imelda found out.'

'Trouble of her own making.'

'I know. You're right.'

She should have kept her mouth shut. Then again, Nell certainly wouldn't want to cause Imelda further trauma. Laura closed her magazine, returned it to the bundle on the counter. 'I do feel a bit sorry for her though. I mean, she's had a lot to cope with.'

'We all have stuff to cope with – and she's caused her share of trouble too. Remember her and Andy.'

'I do.'

'She really messed him up.'

'Nell, that was ages ago.'

'Doesn't matter.'

'Don't be too hard on her. We all broke hearts in our day. I remember one fellow, can't think of his name, Terry somebody, asked me to go to his debs. I said no, because I fancied someone else like mad and I was hoping he'd ask me. He didn't, he asked Julie McDonald. I was in bits. Anyway, I ran into Terry's mother a while later and she gave out stink to me, said how could I hurt him like that. Imagine telling your mother someone wouldn't go to your debs with you. Mind you, Terry went on to make a packet in IT – I missed out big time there.'

But Nell had stopped listening. She was pushing the dryer plug into the socket, her face set.

'Let it go, Nell. It wasn't meant to be, or she

wouldn't have finished with Andy. Anyway, isn't he happy now with Tilly?'

'He is,' she said, and switched on the dryer, which mercifully made further conversation difficult. It was touching how protective she was of Andy. James's son by his first wife, Nell only inheriting him in his mid teens, but having taken him well under her wing before then. Doing what she could for him when he'd moved as a troubled eleven-year-old with James to the island, still grieving for his mother.

Watching Nell drying her hair, Laura felt bad. She'd betrayed Eve, broken her word. She'd send her a text later, let her know she was thinking of her. She could do that much, at least.

By the time Laura's hair was dry, Maisie Kiely had arrived for her weekly wash and set. 'Isn't it a grand day, ladies? About time that old rain dried up for itself – am I right or am I right?' she demanded, looking fiercely from one to the other.

'You're right, Maisie,' Laura told her, wondering if anyone had ever had the temerity to suggest that she might be wrong, about anything at all. Maisie might be coming dangerously close to eighty, but you didn't mess with her.

Nell hung her jacket. 'Have a seat at the basin, Maisie, and I'll be right with you.' She took Laura's money, gave change. 'Talk soon. Tell Tilly I'm looking forward to seeing her.'

'Will do.'

Maisie was right; it was a dream of a day. A bare

hint of a breeze, the sky at last showing blue again, sunlight pouring onto faces and buildings, bringing everything into sharp relief. Maybe they were finally getting a summer, just in time for Tilly's visit.

On her way home, following an impulse she could hardly understand, Laura detoured onto the pier and made for the yellow ice-cream van.

'Hey,' Andy said, setting aside his phone. 'Your hair is nice.'

'Just out from Nell,' she told him. 'Looking forward to seeing Tilly?'

He grinned, tucking hands into armpits. 'Yeah.'

She let a few seconds pass, waiting for more, but no more came. 'Everything OK with you?' she asked. 'Summer going well so far?'

'Yeah, it's fine.'

'How were the exams?'

'Not too bad.'

'When will you know?'

'Middle of August.'

Laura didn't see much of him in the normal run of things, despite them being next-door neighbours. When she dropped over to Nell on the weekends he was home from college, he was usually out with friends, or studying in his room.

Two and a half years with Tilly, and still going strong.

Apparently.

'Seen Eve lately?' she asked. Just for the hell of it.

He coloured slightly, a pale pink washing onto his

face. A hand came up to scratch an ear. 'Not much, but she's around. Why do you ask?'

Why did she ask indeed? 'I was just thinking I've hardly seen her since the crèche finished up. Hope she's coping alright since Hugh died, that's all. Thought you might have some news of her.'

'Not really.'

There was no reason to suspect him, no reason in the wide world. Eve had said it wasn't anyone Laura knew – why would she say it if it wasn't true?

But people didn't always tell the truth, did they? People lied when they didn't think the truth would be well received.

It was just a notion she had, one that had crept into her head sometimes when she wasn't paying attention. She hoped he was innocent. She liked him, always had – and of course Tilly was mad about him. She hoped to God he wasn't involved.

'You want an ice-cream?' he asked.

'Go on then,' she said. 'A small cone.'

Stop seeing a problem where there isn't one. He's with Tilly, and Eve is pregnant by someone else.

A little boy in green shorts and a mustard-coloured T-shirt, four or five, scampered across to the van, a man following some distance behind with a buggy. *Canary Islands*, the T-shirt said, above a red and yellow parrot. 'Conor!' the man called, but the lad ignored him.

'I want a ice-cream,' he said, watching Laura's order being created.

'What's the magic word?' Laura asked – ever the mother – but the boy made no response. No magic words in his house.

Andy handed Laura her cone, took her euro fifty. 'Will we wait for your dad?' he asked the boy, who shook his head firmly. A tuft of his blond hair stuck up in front, reminding Laura of Ben and Seamus at that age. Impossible hair the two of them had had as kiddies, nothing to be done but let it go its own way. It hadn't improved much in the meantime, but she felt its management wasn't really her responsibility any more, now that they were heading for twelve in November.

'Do you have any money?' Laura asked the boy. 'You need money for ice-cream.'

'My *dad* has money' – and here came the harried father to rescue the situation. Laura took her leave and headed home, relishing the cold sweet creaminess of the cone – she should really treat herself more often – and the feel of the sun on her bare arms, and the occasional pleasant citrus waft from her newly washed hair.

Had he looked guilty – or was the blush simply a natural reaction to a mention of his old love?

She remembered the two of them together in the early days, just after the girls were born, and Eve was still helping her out at the B&B. She remembered him calling there a few times to collect Eve, and the way she'd light up when she saw him. Love's young dream, a right Romeo and Juliet they'd been. No wonder Nell had fretted they'd elope. Imelda too, probably, not that she'd have confided in Laura the Jezebel.

She found herself wishing that Walter, the previous owner of her house, was still around. 'I need you,' she told him. 'I could do with someone to listen to my rubbish, and tell me to cop on.' But nobody was listening. Walter had finally made his departure: she didn't feel him about the place any more. And maybe she'd imagined him all along. Maybe he'd buggered off after dying, like most people did.

Active imagination, one of her teachers had written on a long-ago report card. Trying to think of something positive to put down, no doubt. *Good student* had never featured, or *attentive in class*. But hadn't she done alright for herself, even with her lack of study, her paltry academic achievements? Hadn't she created a happy home for her children, despite her own childhood home being far from a happy place most of the time?

She walked past the hotel, waving in the driveway at Henry, who stood at the bottom of a ladder by the gable wall. A man halfway up was trailing a string of bunting. The party, she remembered. Not for another few weeks, but the birthday boy would be anxious to set the scene. Must get him a nice present. Something flashy: Henry liked his bling. Shame he had no boyfriend to celebrate with on his big night.

Further on, just across from the church, a low-sized, rather heavyset man stood by an easel, looking out to sea. He wore a white shirt with sleeves rolled to the elbows, and loose navy overalls. On his head was a straw hat, by his side a little folding table that was covered with a muddle of tubes and jars. An enormous lime green suitcase on wheels sat behind the table, presumably to cart all his stuff about.

He turned at the sound of Laura's footsteps and lifted his hat a fraction, like Walter used to do – the memory caused a pang – and smiled at her very sweetly. Nice-looking for his age; somewhere in the late sixties, she guessed. Wasn't Irish, not with that tan. Following another impulse, she crossed the road.

'Hello,' she said. 'Lovely day for painting.'

He gave a little bow of acknowledgement. '*Sì, signora*, a beautiful day.'

This was Imelda's man: it had to be. 'Mind if I look?' she asked, and he stepped aside to allow her to stand before the easel.

'Golly,' she said. 'Gosh.'

It was the sea, and it was certainly colourful, every shade of blue and green imaginable, with dashes of white and purple and yellow and black and pink and orange thrown in. The water moved, or seemed to, beneath a sky that was also vibrant with great colour and energy. 'That's wonderful. Really wonderful.'

'*Grazie, signora*,' he murmured with another little bow. 'The sea, she is very ...' he turned a hand, searching for the word '... alive.'

'Yes, indeed.'

She wondered what he'd say if she told him her father was the great Luke Potter – as a painter himself, he would undoubtedly be familiar with the name, although Luke's meticulously executed paintings were a million miles away from this gloriously chaotic creation.

'I'm Laura,' she told him instead. 'I live just up the road, another five minutes or so.'

He wiped his hand on his overalls before offering it to her to shake. He said a name she didn't quite catch, and told her he was pleased to meet her.

'Can you say your name again?' she asked, and this time she heard it, and wondered.

'In English,' he added, 'is Walter.'

Yes. In English he was Walter. He was so like him, in manner and gesture. She told him about the other Walter, who had lived where she lived now. She told him about her and Gav buying the house after his death and turning it into a B&B and calling it after him, to keep his memory alive.

'Is good story,' he said. 'Roone is special place, I think. I feel, here.' Tapping his chest with fingertips.

He got it. Not everyone got the island but he did, after only a few days. 'I used to think,' she said slowly, 'after Walter died, that I could still – that he was still around, still here. I would feel him nearby, now and again. I know that probably sounds very … silly, but I really thought he wasn't gone. Roone makes you believe that things like that can happen.'

She waited for him to laugh, but he didn't. 'Is not always easy,' he said in his halting English, 'to see what is real and what is not. Sometime the 'ead is playing tricks, but perhaps not always. I think we cannot know for sure.'

'I agree.'

Look at them, going all philosophical in the middle of a sunny day, within a minute of meeting. She found him endearing, found herself wanting to delay her departure, even though there were plenty of jobs awaiting her. 'You're staying with Imelda,' she said, 'Mrs Fitzpatrick,' and his face changed.

'You know this,' he said, 'because I think Eemelda ask if you have place for me. She tell me she ask everybody, but all is full.'

Poor man, landing into such a fraught situation. 'I wish I could help – in fact, your nephew and his wife stayed with me last year – but I have no vacancy until the end of the month.'

'Yes. This is problem. I know this is bad time for Eemelda.'

Nice the way he said her name, made it sound almost Italian. 'You know, maybe it's a good thing that you're here,' Laura told him. 'Maybe she needs to have someone in the house with her now.' Clutching at straws, but she wanted to offer some comfort.

He gave another smile, although she got the impression that she hadn't convinced him. She bade him goodbye and kept going, sorry she couldn't have been of more practical help to him. Maybe she'd invite him to dinner, if their paths crossed again – and they surely would. She could do that much for Walter's Italian counterpart.

She reached home and let herself in by the front door. She admired her hair in the hall mirror before making her way to the kitchen.

'You look gorgeous,' Gavin said, surrounded by his three small daughters. Toys and games and books pretty much covered the kitchen table and spilt onto the floor. It always amazed Laura how quickly they could make such an impressive mess. 'Doesn't Mum look gorgeous?'

'No,' Marian said, and tittered.

'No!' Evie shouted, darting a defiant look at their father. 'She looks howwible!' Erupting in giggles along with her sister.

'*Not!*' Poppy cried, lifting her arms towards her mother. Faithful old Poppy, not yet old enough to recognise a bit of nonsense. Laura gathered her up and kissed her loudly on her soft plump cheek. 'Thank you, darling. Don't listen to those two witches.' She turned to Gavin. 'Did the boys walk Charlie?'

'They did, they're back. They're boxing up the eggs outside.'

Good. All her chicks accounted for. 'Any arrivals?' Two new parties she was expecting today, from England and from Germany.

'Nobody yet.'

'Any hope of a coffee?' Her taste for it had finally returned last year, nineteen months after her last chemo session.

'Coming up,' he said, pushing back his chair. 'You want me to heat a scone?'

She shouldn't, not after the ice-cream. On the other hand, the scales had been kind when she'd stepped up this morning. 'Go on.'

Her hair was newly cut. The sun was shining. Her husband and children were healthy. Bookings were solid, pretty much, right up to the middle of August, and coffee and a scone were on the way. All was well.

She deposited Poppy in a chair and gathered the fallen items from the floor. She took blackberry jam from the press and searched in the fridge for the whipped cream that they'd almost, but not quite, finished off the night before. If she was going to have a scone, she might as well do it right.

She turned from the fridge, the bowl of cream in her hand, and felt, for an instant only, a cold dark rush of something – what? Before she could define it, it was gone. She stood where she was, trying to puzzle out what might have caused it, or what it might mean. A premonition of some kind, a portent of oncoming trouble?

Before she'd come to live on the island, she'd have dismissed it without a thought, called it a goose walking over her grave and forgotten about it the minute it had passed. Now, having experienced for herself Roone's inexplicable magic – mushrooms that cured arthritis, a signpost erected by nobody, an apple tree that fruited three times in a year – she was more inclined to attach some significance to it.

'Coffee,' Gavin said, clearing a space for the mug on the table.

'Thanks …'

The microwave pinged. Her scone was presented to her. She looked down at it, still a little thrown.

'What's up? What did I forget?'

'Sorry,' she said, taking her seat. 'Miles away.'

She spread jam, topped it with cream. She was being silly. It was a half-digested bit of breakfast sausage making its presence felt. Or it was her father and Susan and Eve, or it was all the concerns that went along with being a working mother of five young children.

She ate the scone and chatted with her family, and resolved to believe that nothing bad was headed their way.

Tilly

'G'DAY, SHEILA,' HE SAID. 'YOU TOOK YOUR time.'

His Australian accent was atrocious, but the sight of him was truly wonderful. He was there, he was right in front of her, after her long wait to see him. She abandoned her case and threw herself into his arms. Unwashed, largely unfed, hair a complete fiasco, no sleep for the past thirty-one hours, not a *wink*. Deodorant and blusher and lipstick applied hurriedly, for all the good they'd done, in the Ladies at the airport while she'd waited for her luggage.

'Don't look at me,' she commanded, face pressed to his jacket. She breathed him in, relishing the feel of him, the solidity of him. 'I look a fright. Keep your eyes closed all the way back to Roone.' Roone!

She felt the bubble of his laughter. 'Might be tricky, what with me driving and all.'

She inhaled him again. He smelt of the outdoors – and something sweet, like fairground candyfloss. 'It's so good to see you,' she murmured. 'Missed you so much.'

'Me too, Sheila.'

Without moving from his embrace she thumped his arm. 'I've *told* you to cut out the Sheila – and your accent is awful.'

Another laugh. 'Well, so's your Irish accent – and you're supposed to *be* Irish.'

When I move over here, I'll pick it up. The comment stayed in her head. Not yet, not yet. She was already listening to Irish singers on YouTube, Lisa Hannigan and Ham Sandwich and Damien Rice and Imelda May. She'd sound like a native in no time – or at least she'd sing like one.

'Right,' he said, drawing back, 'we need to get a move on.' Her flight from Dublin had been delayed, causing two hours longer of a wait. The frustration of it, when she'd been so close to seeing him. He stooped to reclaim her case, slung an arm through hers as they made their way across the small arrivals hall to the exit doors that slid apart at their approach.

She drew in a breath as they walked out. The air here was different. Not just cooler and fresher, but different in a way she couldn't define. The scent of Ireland. Maybe all countries had their own aromas. She wished she could bottle it, bring it back to Australia and draw it deep into her lungs in the middle of a muggy summer's afternoon.

It was dry, had been all day by the look of the ground, and beautifully mild. And how wonderful that at twenty past nine in the evening the sky had yet to lose all of its colour. She marvelled at the generous daylight hours of Ireland in the summertime.

But best of all, they were together again. It felt unreal. She was light-headed with happiness, beside him where she belonged. Singing on the inside.

The car looked worse in real life than it had on FaceTime. Spotted with rust, some of the larger patches painted over in the wrong shade of blue. Various dents on the wings, a series of long scrapes running the length of the driver's side. She was careful not to laugh. 'It's great.'

'It's a heap,' he said, shoving her case into the boot, 'but it goes. It's fine for Roone.' He slammed down the lid. 'Get in, or we'll miss the last ferry.'

If only. She yearned for something, anything, that would prevent them from making the crossing to the island. A flat tyre, a sudden storm that forced the cancellation of the ferry, too many cars waiting to board ahead of them. She willed them to be stranded, obliged to find a place for the night, just the two of them. Of course she was eager to see Laura and the children – but Roone, and all it held, would still be there in the morning.

He drove carefully, like she remembered, not showing off the way other guys might do with a girlfriend in the passenger seat.

Girlfriend. Fiancée. Another thing she had to hug to herself.

'So how's the ice-cream business?'

'Good, plenty of customers. Even on the rainy days it's not bad. Lots of visitors around right now. You'll see it when we get to the pier. You can help me out if you like.'

'I like,' she said, reaching over to rest her hand lightly on his thigh. 'What are your hours?'

'I just do afternoons, and they're pretty flexible. Pádraig said roughly lunchtime to teatime.'

'Pádraig?' Her mouth exploring the unfamiliar name. 'Do I know him?'

'Lelia's husband, Lelia in the café. Pádraig owns the ice-cream van.'

'I remember Lelia, but not him.'

'He runs a drive-in movie place too, started it last month in the yard behind the creamery. It's just a lorry with a screen on the back of it.'

'Wow – a cinema for Roone. Have you given it a go?'

'Yeah, been there a few times. It's still a work in progress. There's no cover, so when it rains everyone has to turn on their engines and put the wipers on, and the sound quality isn't great either, but it's good for a laugh. Pádraig says he's ordered a canopy: I'll believe it when I see it.'

She was jealous of his friends, able to see him whenever they wanted. Male and female friends, which made it a tiny bit harder again. 'So you start work, what, around noon?'

'Yeah, around then.'

While she stayed with Laura and Gavin she helped

out with the guest breakfasts, and the cleaning of the rooms afterwards. A noon start would suit her beautifully. 'And finish around six?'

'Or maybe a bit later, depending on the weather, and the demand. I can play it by ear, Pádraig said.'

She smiled. 'Play it by ear.' She loved the Irish expressions. 'What about days off?'

He shrugged. 'Haven't really been taking them, wasn't bothered. But if I want one, Pádraig says he'll fill in, as long as I don't do the dog on it.'

'Do the dog on it.' She had no clue what it meant, but it made her sigh happily.

He shot her a look. 'There is one thing. I've been helping Dad out a bit too in the pub, in the evenings. Now that Hugh's gone …'

'Oh.' She'd forgotten that the pub his father managed had belonged to Hugh, the man who'd died. All the interlinkings on Roone, everyone connected to everyone else, it felt like. 'So the pub is still open then.'

'It is, so far anyway. I suppose Imelda will sell it eventually.'

'Hugh's wife?'

'Yeah – well, widow now.'

Imelda. The name rang a bell but she couldn't place her, couldn't find a face for her.

'You would have met her at my house,' he said. 'She'd often visit with Hugh. They were the ones who fostered Eve.' Keeping his eyes on the road.

Eve. That name definitely rang a bell. Tilly saw the long red hair, the generous curves of the girlfriend who had preceded her. Eve still lived on Roone, still presumably hung around in the same loose group as Andy. She and Tilly had encountered one another on occasion, and Tilly always thought she sensed a kind of wariness in Eve, and she felt a little awkward too. It was silly, she knew that. He and Eve were history, well over by the time Andy and Tilly had met. Maybe it was inevitable though, that they'd never be entirely comfortable in one another's company.

'So I'm filling in two or three nights a week in the pub, for the moment anyway. You're welcome to come and sit at the counter, but it mightn't be much fun for you.'

'Not to worry.' Nothing was going to bring her down today. She had three and a half weeks – she could stand not being with him every evening. 'How are Nell and James?'

'Good. Fine. Well, Nell is still very upset about Hugh, of course, but other than that, they're OK.'

'And the kids?' His two little step-siblings.

He groaned. 'Wrecking my head. Berry never stops talking.'

'Berry is talking? Can't wait to hear her.'

'Well, a lot of what she says is nonsense, but she loves the sound of her own voice, like most women I know.'

'Cheek.'

Tilly recalled a dark-eyed, mop-headed scamp from the previous summer, just learning to toddle about, full of mischief and bubbling laughter. Called

Bernadette after Nell's maternal grandmother, the name shortened to Berry for the benefit of her brother Tommy, too young then to manage the full thing, and now she was Berry to everyone. 'Is she two yet? I forget which day her birthday is.'

'It's tomorrow.'

'Great – I haven't missed it. And Laura's Evie and Marian are four on Saturday, and Laura's own birthday is August first. We'll be all partied out.'

'Hey,' he said, 'what's with the we? You can go to all those girly parties if you want – I'll be busy in the van.'

She slapped his thigh lightly. 'Andy Baker – you have to go to your own sister's, at least.'

'Um, no I don't. Not if it involves a gang of small female people. I might go to Laura's – her nights are usually good craic. But there's a different party coming up that you'll probably want to come along to. I know Nell and Laura will be going.'

'Are you talking about the beach barbecue?'

'No – there's that too, but the owner of the hotel, you mightn't remember him, he's throwing a party for his seventieth at the beginning of August, the night after Laura's, I think.'

'Oh, yes – Laura mentioned something about it in her last letter.'

'Right, and everyone's invited.'

'Everyone? You mean all his friends?'

'I mean everyone on the island. Literally everyone, kids and all.'

'Wow.'

'It probably won't be that exciting, not with all the oldies around – and the kids – but there'll be plenty of grub and booze. Henry will throw a good party, I'd say. Could be a laugh. The gang is going anyway.'

She'd been to the hotel once; she'd met the owner. It was the summer following her first trip to Roone, and her little half-brother Harry was being christened there. He'd had his official christening in Dublin, but his mother Susan, Tilly's stepmother, had wanted another on the island, and she'd asked Tilly to be his Roone godmother. And apart from her delight at returning to the island – and to Andy – Tilly had been looking forward to meeting her father, who was Harry's father too.

But it wasn't to be. He hadn't accompanied his wife and child to Roone. Susan had told everyone he was busy with a new commission, but could he not have taken just a couple of days off?

Don't worry about it, Laura had said. *It's typical of him*. Tilly had tried not to be hurt that her father didn't seem interested in meeting her. He'd sent her a cheque, when Laura had told him of her existence. It was sizeable: it had enabled her to make her return trips to Roone, and she was grateful for that, but money was a poor substitute for the man himself.

So she'd written him a letter. *I want to thank him for the money*, she'd said to Laura, who'd passed on his address and warned Tilly not to expect a reply. Tilly had spent a lot of time, and far too many pages, trying to find the right words, wanting to say much more than thanks for the cheque. The end result still didn't feel exactly right, but it was the best she could do.

> *Dear Luke,*
> [she'd written – because Dad, or any variation of it, had sounded presumptuous]
> *I'm just back in Australia after my first visit to Ireland, and I want to thank you very much for your generous gift to me. I only discovered I was adopted a few years ago, and since then I've wanted to come and find my Irish family. I really enjoyed getting to know Laura and Gavin and their children, and even though I was only on Roone for a few days, I loved it. I'm still in school, but I graduate next year, and I hope to return to Ireland for a longer visit next winter – your summer. I would really love if we could meet up then. I know how busy you are, but maybe you could find the time. I could travel to Dublin if it made it easier for you.*
> *Your daughter,*
> *Tilly Walker*

She'd made no mention of meeting his ex-wife, the woman who'd given birth to her a few months after leaving Ireland and settling in Australia. It hadn't gone well: there had been no tearful reunion, no arrangement to meet again – but even if it had, she thought he mightn't appreciate the reminder of his first failed marriage. She'd posted the letter and she'd waited for his reply, but it hadn't come.

So much for parents loving their children unconditionally: Tilly hadn't experienced it from either of hers. Thank goodness for Ma and Pa, who'd brought her up with generosity and kindness – and love too, even if they weren't the type to be comfortable putting it into words.

The christening in Roone's church had been enjoyable. The little room they were given in the hotel for the party afterwards had been decked out in flowers and baby blue bunting.

I've never been to Australia, the owner had told her, *but I'd love to go some day.*

If I'd been born on Roone, I don't think I'd ever want to travel anywhere else, Tilly had replied. He'd laughed, thinking it a joke, but she'd meant it, and it was still how she felt. Despite her limited experience of life on the island, Roone felt like home. It was in her bones, in every drop of blood that raced through her. Crazy, given that none of her family came from the island, but the truth nonetheless.

'I wish I lived there,' she said. 'On Roone, I mean.'

Andy threw her a glance. 'Would you not miss Australia?'

Not the *Me too* response she'd hoped for. She didn't dwell on it – men could be tactless. 'I suppose I'd be bound to miss it a bit, but I really love Roone. It's got under my skin.'

'What about your folks – and your brother and sister?'

She shifted in her seat, removed her hand from his

leg. 'They're not really my family though, are they?'
Saying the words, she felt a stab of disloyalty – Ma
and Pa had never once made her feel like she didn't
belong, even when the children they'd never expected
to have had come along, years after they'd adopted
Tilly – but it was the truth. 'Laura's my full sister, and
her children are my nieces and nephews. They're my
family. And,' she added lightly, 'you live there too.'

'I do indeed.'

'How d'you like Limerick?'

He shrugged. 'It's fine. It'll do.'

'You wouldn't settle there though, would you? I
mean long term.'

'Probably not. Dublin maybe, for a while. For the
experience.'

Dublin hadn't featured in her plans. She'd never
been there, but she imagined it was much like Brisbane.
Big, noisy, full of people and cars, and tall buildings
lined up in rows. She'd never been drawn to cities,
always preferred the feel of a smaller community. She
could put up with it though, as long as she was with
him. And her father was in Dublin – maybe it was
meant to happen. Maybe if she lived there, it would
be impossible for him to go on ignoring her.

They drove in silence for a while. She looked out
at the passing countryside, at the fields dotted with
cattle and sheep and bordered by trees and hedges,
or by those funny walls with stones that seemed
to balance magically on each other. She loved the
magnificent purple and green mountains rearing up

behind it all. *Kerry is known as The Kingdom*, he'd told her, and she could see why.

They drove along the main street of a small town, and shortly after that she saw a sign for the pier. Not far now.

'By the way,' he said, 'your stepmother's on the island.'

She looked at him in surprise. 'Susan's on Roone?' Laura had made no mention of an impending visit. 'How long has she been there?'

'Few days, I think. I heard Nell saying it to Dad.'

She remembered Susan telling her that she usually avoided the island in the summer. *I come off-season*, she'd said, *when Laura isn't busy* – and sure enough, there'd been no sign of her the previous summer. So what was she doing on Roone now? 'Is anything the matter?'

He hesitated. 'I'm not sure I should be the one to tell you. I probably shouldn't have said anything.'

'Well, you did say something, so you must tell me. What's going on?'

He glanced her way again. 'Look,' he said, 'Susan and your father have split up. That's really all I know.'

She digested this in silence. She knew little about their relationship: neither Susan nor Laura had made much mention of it. But from what she knew of her father, and from his apparent dismissal of her, she guessed that he might not be the easiest to live with. Still, it must be tough to walk away from a marriage, whatever had caused it to end.

'Is Harry with her?'

'I've got no idea.'

He must be. She wouldn't have left him. 'How long is she staying on Roone?'

'I really don't know anything else. You'll have to ask Laura.'

She was glad she'd get to meet Susan again, and presumably Harry too, but sorry it was under such circumstances. Hopefully Susan wasn't too upset; hopefully this move was one that brought her more relief than sadness.

Staying awake was becoming an effort, with weariness ambushing her in waves. She fought against the urge to close her eyes and drift off, determined not to fall asleep on him. She yawned repeatedly, conscious of how stale her breath must be. Why hadn't she thought to brush her teeth in the airport?

'You'll sleep tonight,' he remarked.

'I certainly will – you got any gum?'

'Try the glove compartment' – and there, hidden under a sheaf of receipts and wrappers and balled-up leaflets, she found half a roll of hard mints, which did the job.

The ferry was just pulling in when they drew up at the pier. They followed a cream camper van onto the deck. The van's registration plate didn't look Irish, but she wasn't practised enough to identify the nationality. She checked out the occupants of surrounding vehicles, and recognised nobody.

The ferryman remembered her. 'Back with us again, all the way from Australia.'

'Back again,' she agreed, scrabbling about in her head for his name. Ken, or maybe Joe. Something short, three letters.

'Staying long?'

'Three and a half weeks.' Not long enough. Never long enough.

He turned to Andy. 'I hope you've hidden your other women away,' he said with a wink, and Andy laughed and told him they were all well hidden.

Other women. She knew it was a joke, but it caused an unpleasant twist in her. They were so far apart for so much of the time – was it realistic to expect his thoughts never to stray elsewhere? Cut that out, she told herself. It's Andy, who'd never hurt her. When the man had moved on to the next car she enquired about his name.

'Leo.'

Leo. She should have remembered. 'He didn't charge me,' she said, 'the first time I took this ferry.'

'Didn't he? Why not?'

'I suppose because he'd heard about me, like everyone had. Laura's sister who'd shown up out of the blue.'

'So you're talking about when you left Roone. Not when you arrived.'

'Yes.'

'But that wasn't your first time on the ferry, it was your second.'

'No, it wasn't. I didn't come by ferry. It was cancelled on Christmas Eve because of the storm, remember? A fisherman brought me and your gran over on Christmas Day.'

'Oh yeah, I remember Gran showing unexpectedly. I'd forgotten that.'

She smothered a rush of dismay. Had he also forgotten their first encounter, so momentous for her? And what about their first goodbye, when he'd driven her to the pier from Walter's Place? Their relationship barely begun, no kisses yet, nothing said on either part, but an understanding there. Feelings stirring – well, more than that on her side. Sparks flying between them, ready to ignite.

Not sure how this goes, he'd said, having wheeled her case onto the ferry, and she'd replied, *We should probably hug.* She could vividly remember the thrill of being physically close to him, the pure happiness of her arms around him, the feel of his embrace, their bodies pressed together. She remembered how cold his cheek had been against hers, how her nose had tingled with the chill. Had he forgotten all that too?

She opened her car door. 'Come on,' she said, 'let's get moving, or I'll definitely fall asleep.'

They climbed the metal steps and stood by the rail. It was colder out here on the water, and her jacket was in the boot along with her case, but she didn't care. The sea was amazing to her, and such a novelty, living so far from it at home. The air here was a whole new level of glorious too; sharp and salty and clean, like something you could almost taste. And there was Roone on the horizon, the long, dark hump of it gladdening her soul.

She turned to watch the other travellers emerging from their vehicles. Three little boys erupted from the rear of a blue estate car, hopping about in identical red raincoats. Further down a woman opened her boot and withdrew a wheelchair, which she unfolded before depositing a young girl in it. From a silver hatchback came a trio of middle-aged females whom Tilly decided were holidaying nuns, based on nothing more than their collective sensible shoes.

She shifted her gaze once more to the island, its features becoming slowly more defined as they drew closer. There was the narrow finger of the lighthouse at its southernmost tip, there the hill that reared up on its way to the cliffs on the far side. Soon she'd be able to pick out the larger buildings, the supermarket and petrol station at the start of the village street, the church and the hotel and the old creamery on the coast road.

She wondered if she'd have the courage to do what had seemed so natural a prospect when she was back in Queensland. Now that she was here, it had taken on a new and alarming significance. Just a question, she told herself. Just asking him to spend the rest of his life with her, the cowardly part of her shot back. She'd gather her courage and just do it, when the perfect moment presented itself.

She took his arm and placed it around her shoulders. She held on to his hand and squeezed it, and leant across to kiss his cheek. 'I can't believe I'm here,' she said. 'I think I'm dreaming. I'm going to wake up any minute in Australia.'

He smiled. They were almost the same height, her eyes just an inch or two below his. 'Want me to pinch you?'

'No thanks.'

As they stood there, a heavy shower descended out of nowhere, forcing them to retreat to the car. She watched the water streaming down the windscreen, blurring everything beyond it. 'I hope it won't be like this all the time.'

'The past few days have been fine,' he replied. 'I think the forecast is good for the next while.'

'Laura said that too. Some farmer in Donegal.'

'Yeah. Sounds mad, but he's usually spot on.'

She regarded his profile as he fiddled with the radio. The short brown hair, the pale skin, the blue dark-lashed eye. The nose slightly bigger than it needed to be, tiny freckles scattered across its bridge. Pinpricks of dark stubble on his chin and jaw. The white scar, thin as a pen line, that zigzagged down from beneath his eye – a legacy, he'd told her, from a car accident on Roone, sometime before they'd met.

She looked at the whorls of his ear, the fair hairs and faint network of veins on the back of the hand that turned the radio dial, the bitten nails, the thin silver ring she'd brought him from Australia last summer. Oh, she loved him. She loved every bit of him.

He looked up. 'Radio's on the blink. Could be the ferry.'

'Doesn't matter,' she said, although she loved the informality, the chattiness of Irish radio talk shows. It didn't matter – nothing mattered now that she was finally here.

It would be alright. Everything would turn out right. It had to.

Eve

EVEN AT THIS EARLY HOUR, THE SUN WAS TOO bright. It irritated her, made her skin prickle. She'd slept badly, Derek Garvey pushing into her dreams like he often did, telling her he wasn't finished with her, promising he'd find her. She knew this couldn't happen in reality: he'd been sent to jail, was still in jail for what he'd done to her.

Ironic, given his constant threat, his way of keeping her silent for so long. *If you tell, they won't believe you,* he'd said. *I'll say you're making it up, and they'll take you out of here and put you into a loony bin for the rest of your life.* So she'd held her tongue and endured his abuse until Roone had given her the courage to speak.

She'd told the police everything she could remember. She'd emptied it all out of her while a machine had recorded it silently, and she'd signed the transcript when they'd typed it up and handed it to her.

The trial in Dublin had lasted just a week, with Hugh and Imelda accompanying Eve on the day she was called on to give evidence. *There's no need for you to come,* the social worker had told them. *I'll be with her all the time*, but Hugh had stood his ground. *We'd like to be there too*, he'd said, in a voice that didn't encourage contradiction. Eve had loved how quietly stubborn he could be, how he would brook no argument when he'd set his mind on something.

In the courtroom Eve had sat behind a screen, flanked by Hugh and Imelda, with the social worker relegated politely to a more distant seat. Visible to the jury but to nobody else, Eve had nonetheless felt horribly exposed, her stomach twisted into a tight knot as she'd imagined Derek in the dock, maybe only a few feet from her, and his family sitting close by.

She'd pictured each of them in her mind's eye: Mr Garvey, who hadn't once, in all the years she'd lived in his house, addressed her by name; Mrs Garvey, who'd fed her and clothed her and left it at that; and Valerie Garvey, who'd told Eve not to talk to her at school, who'd sniggered with her friends whenever Eve was within earshot.

She'd visualised the faces of his family as she described what their precious son and brother had done to her, with Imelda never letting go of her hand the whole time. She was sure Mrs Garvey would want to kill her: she'd probably convinced herself that it was all lies. But Eve had kept going, like the social worker had told her she must do – and with each word, with every disclosure, she could feel a small loosening inside her.

The jury had needed only a day of deliberation for

the twelve of them to decide that Derek Garvey was guilty, although he'd sworn he wasn't. He'd been given six years, with the last two suspended, which meant he'd be set free in the next few months. Eve was certain he wouldn't come looking for her, even if he knew where she was, which she doubted. If he did, if he set foot on Roone, he'd be in danger of being locked up again.

But that didn't stop him invading her dreams every so often. She'd wake up sweating, heart pounding, sure he was there in the dark bedroom with her. They'd wanted her to have counselling, Hugh and Imelda. They'd pleaded with her to talk to someone, so to keep them happy she'd gone along with it, but it hadn't helped. The woman they'd brought her to in Tralee kept asking her about Mam, and the men she'd brought back to the house while Eve and Keith had still been living with her. What was the point in going back to all that? What did any of it have to do with Derek Garvey?

Eve had endured two sessions, just so Hugh and Imelda would see she'd tried, and then she'd told them she didn't want to go back any more, and they hadn't pushed her. She was perfectly fine, she said; she was over all that. She made no mention of the continuing dreams: they'd stop eventually.

And Mam – well, it was sad about Mam, but there was nothing to be done. Mam had chosen a path and it had destroyed her, and Eve just had to come to terms with it.

And now she was to be a mam herself. Now she was moving on, putting the past well and truly behind her. Oh, she was still missing Hugh like mad, still anxious and apprehensive about what was ahead. None of that had changed. The simmering was still there, just under her surface – she suspected it would remain with her for several months, until her life returned to something resembling normality. Nothing to be done but to live with it, and to deal with her changing circumstances as best she could.

She'd made a few decisions too, since confiding in Laura. She'd resolved to leave Roone before her pregnancy became apparent. It would never work, she'd realised, staying on the island and raising Andy's baby – because it would inevitably come out, the identity of the father. People would do the sums; people would remember the party, and Eve having too much to drink, and Andy Baker walking her home.

And even if he wanted to be a part of it, which she doubted, his family would never accept it. Nell, and probably his father too, would hate her for what they would see as the trap Eve had set for him. Laura would hate her as well, for coming between him and Tilly. The entire island of Roone, or most of it, might well shun her.

And Imelda – well, Imelda.

Eve couldn't tell her. She couldn't stand in front of the woman who'd saved her, and tell her what she'd done, and watch her face crumble. It would be unfair to expect her to be OK with it, knowing how she felt about that kind of thing, so Eve would go away.

Nine weeks today since Frog's party, which meant that the baby was due in the second half of February. She figured she might be able to remain on the island until the end of October, so that she could continue to earn her salary. The committee who'd appointed her as manager of the crèche in January wouldn't be pleased when she left them in the middle of the school year, but they'd get over it.

She'd tell Imelda that she wanted to live in Galway with Keith. That would make sense. She'd promise to come back and see her often. And then, when she'd sorted a place in Galway, when she'd fixed herself up with a job there, she'd write Imelda a letter, and tell her the truth.

She'd say she hadn't meant for it to happen. She'd say she was sorry for letting her down. She'd tell her she didn't expect Imelda to have anything to do with her from that point on, unless she wanted to. She'd leave it up to Imelda.

She wouldn't name the father, but she'd tell Andy at some stage too. It was his baby, and he had a right to know. She'd ring him when he was back in college in Limerick and ask if she could meet him somewhere, and then she'd tell him. She'd say he didn't have to be involved if he didn't want to, but she'd appreciate some financial support. It was the least he could do.

She'd look for house-cleaning jobs, once she got to Galway. She remembered her foster mother Mrs

Garvey looking for a cleaner once, and having awful trouble getting one. Her plan was to put an ad up on a few noticeboards, or make out leaflets and post them through the letterboxes of the houses in well-off parts of the city. It would be good to have a job where she could decide her hours, especially when she got bigger, and wasn't able to do as much.

In the meantime she'd found herself a summer job at Manning's Hotel. It hadn't occurred to her to look for work while the crèche was closed, but she'd got a call from Maria Fennessy a few nights earlier. *He's looking for someone,* Maria had said. *I thought you might be at a loose end.* Maria worked behind the reception desk at the hotel. Her daughter Claire had been one of Eve's little charges for the past year.

Doing what? Eve had asked.

Mostly chambermaid stuff, cleaning the rooms, but he might want you to help out with the food and drink orders too, room service and lobby service and that.

It didn't sound strenuous. It would give her something to do – she was finding the days long, with her two closest friends gone to Greece for a fortnight – and the extra income would be handy. She'd called to the hotel the following day and the owner had taken her on, just like that.

Are you coping alright? he'd asked, and for one awful second Eve had thought he must have heard about the baby, but then she'd realised he meant Hugh, and she'd said she was. *Nine to two,* he'd told her, *five days a week. That sound OK?* It did. He'd mentioned a salary that sounded fair enough, and then he'd sent her to the housekeeper, Lilian, who'd asked her size and promised to find her a uniform. She was due to start tomorrow – and whatever the job was like, she'd stick it out until the crèche reopened in September, and put by the extra cash.

So she had it all sorted, more or less.

Not that pregnancy was a barrel of laughs. She felt horribly queasy a lot of the time, not just in the mornings. Why was it called morning sickness when it went on all day? She'd eaten so little over the past few weeks: dry bread or crackers – butter, for some reason, had become a no-no – a bowl of custard now and again, a mug of soup or a few spoons of yogurt when she could stomach it. The only food she actually looked forward to was bananas, which she'd never really gone for up to this. Now she was eating two a day, sometimes three. Weird.

She knew she should be building herself up, nourishing the baby with healthy food, but the thought of eating anything more substantial made her want to retch. She hadn't weighed herself since she'd moved out of Hugh and Imelda's, but she was pretty sure she was losing weight instead of gaining it. She'd just have to hope her appetite came back soon.

Her nipples had become really tender too: she could hardly bear anything, any garment, rubbing up against them. She didn't think her breasts had got any fuller, not yet anyway. She should read up about pregnancy: she knew so little about what to expect, but she was willing to learn. She wanted to do it right. She'd go online, check out websites for pregnant women: there had to be loads of them.

How are things? Laura had texted the other morning, and Eve's reply had been a brief *I'm doing OK.*

Glad to hear it, Laura had returned, and thankfully that had been it. The less contact they had from now on, the better. Hopefully Laura wasn't planning on doing anything more than sending the occasional text.

They'd have to meet though, the day after tomorrow. Laura's twin girls were turning four, and as Evie's godmother, Eve always bought gifts for both. There'd be a party, of course, but Eve had opted out of that after she and Andy had split up, telling Laura quite truthfully that she'd feel awkward with Nell there. Now she just dropped her gifts and left.

And of course Tilly would be at the party, which was another reason to give it a wide berth. Standing in a queue at the supermarket the previous afternoon, Eve had spotted her strolling past the window with Marian and Evie. The yellow dress she wore made her skin look even pastier than it was. You'd think living in Australia she'd have a bit of a tan, but she looked as Irish as the rest of them.

Eve would have liked to say hello to the girls, who'd attended the crèche for the past year. They were giddy and bubbly and scatterbrained, and she was fond of them. She could have caught up with them when she'd left the supermarket – there they were in the distance, it would have taken only a minute to go after them – but she hadn't.

She rounded a bend and Imelda's house appeared, scattering her thoughts. It could do with a fresh coat of paint: a patch was peeling under the left window, another at the edge of the gable wall. She remembered the last time it had been painted, a few months after her arrival on Roone. Hugh up on a ladder, Imelda fretting that he'd fall. *You won't get rid of me that easily,* he'd said – but in the end he hadn't needed a ladder to fall from, just a heart that had let him down.

Eve halted at the gate. She was here to apologise for her outburst, here to make her peace with Imelda. These might be the last few months they had together, if Imelda decided, on hearing the news of Eve's pregnancy, that she wanted nothing more to do with her. Eve was determined to make amends for yelling at her. She'd spend time with her: she'd come and visit every afternoon when she'd finished at the hotel.

She went around the back and let herself in by the kitchen door, which was never locked during the day. She stepped in – and stopped dead.

There was a man sitting at the table.

There was a strange man eating breakfast in Imelda's kitchen. Hugh's kitchen.

At the sight of her he rose hastily to his feet, dropping his cutlery with a clatter onto the plate before him. 'Good morning, *signorina*,' he said, dabbing at his mouth with a yellow paper serviette, giving an idiotic little bow.

Scrambled egg, it looked like, on his plate, little green flecks in it. And there, look, a second cup on the table. Eve stood where she was, her hand still on the door handle, completely unable to speak. What the hell was happening?

'You look for Eemelda,' he said – and the casual, the *familiar* way he said her name made Eve want to hit him.

The hall door opened just then and there she was, a sheaf of leaflets in her hand. 'Eve – what a lovely surprise. I never heard you coming, dear.' A lilac top, a grey skirt. A narrow grey scarf with multicoloured dots on it around her neck. No sign of discomfiture, no indication that she even remembered their row.

'Eve, this is Mr Conti,' she went on. 'He's staying here for a little while,' and the man beamed at Eve and gave another bow. 'Gualtiero, this is Eve. I've told you about her.'

They were on first name terms. She'd told him about Eve.

'Please to meet you,' he said, but Eve ignored him and went on glaring at Imelda, who appeared impervious.

'Please sit, Gualtiero, finish your food. Isn't this weather nice, Eve? Lovely to see a bit of sunshine.'

Eve remained dumbstruck. How was she acting as if nothing was wrong? *Everything* was wrong. Who was he? What was he doing here? How *dare* he be here, making himself at home in Hugh's house? The smell of coffee, allied with her spinning thoughts, was making her stomach turn over. Serve them right if she threw up.

'Will you have a cuppa with us, dear?' Imelda went on, crossing to where the mugs lived.

Us. She called them us.

'I was just getting a few leaflets about Roone for Mr Conti,' she went on, pouring coffee. Could she honestly not see that Eve was struggling here? 'He was asking me where was the Statue of Liberty sign – you know, the one on the cliffs. His nephew, who was here last year, told him about it, so Mr Conti wants to go and see it for himself. He might paint it, you never know. Did I mention he was a painter? An artist, I mean.'

She was uncomfortable, Eve realised then. Talking for the sake of it. She *had* noticed Eve's displeasure – how could she not?

His half-finished breakfast must be getting cold: despite Imelda's instruction he hadn't resumed eating, was still standing there with a half-smile on his round face.

'You look tired, Eve,' Imelda said then. 'Have a seat, won't you?' Indicating the coffee that had been poured.

Eve found her tongue at last. 'Why is he here?' she demanded, still not looking in his direction, all her hostility directed at Imelda. 'What's he *doing* here?'

There was a moment of silence. Imelda's wary smile disappeared. 'Eve,' she began – but Eve wasn't listening.

'How could you? How *could* you?' She could hardly speak, so enraged was she. 'I can't believe it!' She turned and fled, almost falling over Scooter, who'd materialised directly behind her, tail wagging.

She stormed back to the road, leaving the gate swinging wide in her wake. A *man*, installed in the house, looking perfectly at home. Where had he come from, what business did he have staying there?

And then, as she marched down the road, blood boiling, it came back to her. She recalled Hugh a few months ago telling her they'd decided to give a room to some foreigner – yes, artist had been mentioned – for a month in the summer. *We'll make a few bob out of it*, he'd said. *We'll just have to hope he's house-trained.* They'd laughed about it, she remembered. *Imelda might sit for him*, Eve had said, *make a bit of extra cash*.

And now Hugh was gone, and the artist was here. Clearly, Imelda hadn't thought to cancel his booking – but why had he stayed, once he'd been told about Hugh, which he must have been? How could he be so insensitive, expecting Imelda to wait hand and foot on him while she was grieving?

Not that she'd looked particularly put out. On the contrary, she'd seemed to have no problem at all with him being there. It was as if she'd never been widowed, as if Hugh had never even existed. How *could* she?

What was more, he was probably sleeping in Eve's room. Oh, she knew it wasn't really hers any more, but it was still maddening to think of him in there, blithely hanging his clothes in the wardrobe, arranging his things on the dressing table, getting into the bed at night.

She stomped along, full of misery and rage. Since Hugh's death, nothing had gone right. She remembered climbing the safety fence at the cliffs when she'd first come to Roone. She remembered standing at the edge, wondering what it would be like to step off. How would it feel, sailing through the air, knowing that her life was almost over, that the bad things would never hurt her again?

Serve Imelda right if she did it. Serve them all right, all the tight-knit locals in this godforsaken place. She pictured them shaking their heads at her funeral, saying what a lovely person she'd been, and how sad that it had gone this way. She pictured Imelda, full of guilt, telling Nell she should have seen that Eve was in trouble. It gave her some grim satisfaction.

At a crossroads she turned in the direction of the old fishermen's cottages, the roads and lanes of the island as familiar to her as any local. Even a complete stranger couldn't get lost on Roone, with its loop road that hugged the coast, and series of smaller ways that criss-crossed within it. Just keep going, keep moving in the same direction, and eventually you'd find yourself back where you'd started.

The route she'd chosen went past the lane that led down to the small pebble beach that Hugh used to love, the one that Eve had often visited with him. *We met on that beach*, Imelda had told her, *the morning of the first full day of my holiday*.

So much for that. So much for all the stories of her and Hugh that she'd shared with Eve. Look at her now, the merry widow.

She'd go down and fling stones into the water, she decided. It might help to burn off her anger. Might even strip off and go for a quick dip if nobody was there. It wasn't a popular spot, even at the height of the summer: most people went for the bigger sandy beaches.

She started down the rutted slope, slithering a bit when it got pebbly underfoot. She reached the end of the lane and turned onto the little beach – and spotted them immediately.

They weren't the only ones there. A pair of women, both wearing navy trousers, sat well back from the water on metal-legged folding chairs, heads bent over their books. Further along, a solitary older man lay on a brown blanket, eyes closed, palms open to the sky.

Beyond him a younger man stood by the shore beside a tousle-haired toddler in a white dress, who lifted small fistfuls of pebbles and flung them straight-armed into the water, chuckling delightedly with each series of little plops. A couple of distant heads bobbed in the sea, one topped with a red swimming cap, or enthusiastically dyed hair; at that distance Eve couldn't be sure.

And midway along the beach, between the man on the blanket and the little stone-throwing girl, Tilly stood calf-deep in the water, holding up the ends of her long red dress, hair lifting slightly in the small breeze. Andy crouched on his hunkers, a foot or so back from the water's edge, wearing cut-off jeans and a T-shirt.

As Eve watched, Tilly kicked water in Andy's direction, and he leapt to his feet. Tilly backed away, giggling, and the water rose to her knees. She lifted her dress higher, halfway up her thighs now. He stepped out of his flip-flops and waded in, and gave a sideswipe to the water, sending it flying in a wide arc towards her. She screamed and gathered her dress into one hand, and splashed him back.

Eve stood where she was, feeling trapped, exposed. The beach wasn't long: if either of them glanced in her direction, they couldn't miss her. When it happened, when Andy turned and spotted her, she felt forced to lift a hand – and after a second's hesitation he waved back. Tilly turned at that, and saw Eve, and waved too.

Damn. Damn it. What to do? Just walk away now?

No. She wouldn't do that. She wasn't in the mood to do that. She made her way along the beach, past the two readers and the supine man, some demon inside her imploring her to say it out, to scream it out: *I'm pregnant with Andy Baker's baby.*

She didn't, of course. She remained silent as she approached them. 'Hi there,' she said, eyes swivelling from one to the other. Tilly's dress was splotched with darker blue patches. They clung to her thighs, and to her flat-as-a-boy's stomach.

'Hi,' they both echoed, Andy's response coming a millisecond after Tilly's.

'Long time no see,' Eve said to Tilly.

'Sure is.'

Just that, no more. Eve dismissed her and turned to Andy. 'How've you been, stranger? Haven't been talking to you properly since Frog's party.'

Did the mention of it cause him to flinch, or did she imagine it? 'I'm OK,' he said. 'How've you been?'

'Fine. Never better. I don't think I thanked you properly for walking me home that night.' She glanced at Tilly, something fizzing around inside her like a firework. *Go on.* 'He was my knight in shining armour,' she said. 'I got horribly drunk, and he looked after me.'

'Really.' It wasn't a question. There was a silly stiff smile on her face, the kind of smile you paste on when you're trying to let on you're not bothered. 'That was nice of him.'

'Certainly was,' Eve agreed, catching his eye again. 'Like old times, wasn't it?'

'How's Imelda?' he asked, too quickly.

'She's great. She's doing amazingly well, actually. Amazingly well. I'd say she's nearly back to her old self.'

His T-shirt was grey, and wet like Tilly's dress where the water had landed. He wore a thin leather wristband she hadn't seen before. His shorts were a couple of inches too long: if she was still with him, she'd fix them.

He'd cut himself shaving, a short red line running along his left jaw. She'd kissed such cuts better, once upon a time. She'd kissed the scar on his cheek countless times. The kissing they'd done, once upon a time.

'How are you getting on in the ice-cream van?' she asked. He'd started working there shortly after Hugh's death. Eve had passed it a few times on her way to the cemetery with Imelda, but had yet to stop at it.

He shrugged. 'It's OK. It'll do for the summer.'

'What time do you start?'

'Around noon.'

'Must drop down some afternoon,' she said, 'for a sneaky cone.'

He made no response. He was dying for her to leave; they both were. It was so obvious she wanted to laugh.

'Right,' she said, wiggling her fingers at Tilly. 'Behave yourself,' she told her. 'Don't do anything I wouldn't do.'

Neither of them smiled at that. 'See you,' he said.

'Bye,' Tilly said.

Walking away, Eve could sense their eyes on her. She probably shouldn't have mentioned the party. She hadn't planned to – it had just come out. Felt good, though. Give him something to think about. Give Tilly something to question him about. Or maybe she'd say nothing, in case it made her sound jealous. Maybe she'd just wonder silently about her boyfriend walking his drunk ex home.

Like old times. That had been a good line. That had been inspired.

What would he do, she wondered, when she told him of her pregnancy in a few months' time? Would it finish things between him and Tilly, even if he didn't want to be a hands-on dad, even if he wanted nothing to do with it? Because he'd have to tell Tilly, wouldn't he? If they stayed together she'd find out eventually, one way or another, that he'd been unfaithful, that he'd fathered a child with Eve while he and Tilly were together, while Tilly was miles away in Australia.

Poor old Tilly. Eve tried to feel sorry for her, and failed.

Susan

SHE SLID THE BOLT ACROSS ON THE GATE AND pushed Harry's buggy into the field ahead of her. *A picnic*, Laura had said on the phone the evening before. *All the mess outside. With this fine weather we'd be mad not to* – and Susan had said yes, of course they would come.

A week, she and Harry had been on the island. A week of pottering from the hotel to the nearby beach and back again, and taking coffee in the garden with Tilly and Laura one afternoon, and having Tilly take Harry out another time for ice-cream with the girls while Susan went for a massage in the hotel spa. A week of early nights and morning lie-ins, and concerned phone calls from her Dublin friends, and none from Luke.

She was glad she hadn't made the acquaintance of many islanders on her previous trips to Roone. Here she and Harry were mainly anonymous, able to sit on a beach full of people without anyone coming over to chat, or paddle undisturbed at the water's edge. Here she could lie low, and give herself time to think and plan.

But today was the birthday picnic for Evie and Marian, her step-grandchildren, and there had been no avoiding it, so here they were.

It was already in full swing. An assortment of rugs and blankets had been spread out on the grass by the little orchard. Not far from this a line of children waited for a ride on the donkey's back, the operation overseen by Ben and Seamus, old hands at it by this stage.

More children were clustered around the chicken coop at the top of the field. Still more peered over the walls of the pigsty to the left of the coop, with pot-bellied Caesar no doubt eyeing them warily from within. Charlie the dog bounded happily between the various groupings.

'Let's get you out of this,' Susan said, unclipping Harry and abandoning the buggy by the hedge. As they made their way towards the house Evie and Marian came racing over, pink-cheeked and sweating in their party dresses. Susan kissed them and exclaimed at their finery and handed over their presents, a pair of musical jewellery boxes she'd found in Roone's newest craft shop.

'Where's Mum?' she asked.

'In the kitchen. Can Harry come with us?'

Susan looked down at her son. 'You want to go with the girls?' He nodded, and the three of them scampered off.

'Susan!'

She turned and saw a group of women seated

under the shade of a big umbrella by the orchard, and Nell making her way across from there in a loose green dress. Nell Baker, Laura's neighbour and closest friend on the island, whom Susan had met on every one of her visits to Roone, but whom she hadn't yet encountered on this trip. Nell, a stepmother like herself, having married a man who was already a father, like Susan had done.

Nell, whose husband James adored her. Lucky, lucky Nell.

'Laura told me,' she murmured, embracing Susan. 'I'm so sorry. How are you?'

'I'm doing fine,' Susan told her, because nobody really wanted to know how you felt. Nobody wanted to hear that you'd cried in the bath for the past six evenings while your child slept in the adjoining bedroom. Nobody wanted you to tell them how many times you'd checked your phone, or rehashed your final conversation with your husband in your head, searching for ways you might have managed it better. Nobody was really interested in how often you imagined you heard a voice that wasn't there, or fancied you caught the tang of turpentine in the air.

Two nights ago she'd rung her mother.

Luke and I have decided to separate, she'd told her. Put like that, it sounded more civilised, more of a business transaction than the collapse of a fifteen-year-old marriage.

Oh, Susan. Oh, that's too bad. Where are you, dear?

Exactly the kind of reaction she'd anticipated, the

gleeful eagerness in her mother's voice belying the sympathetic words.

I'm on Roone, she said, *with Laura and her family. I just needed to get away.* Her mother had never been to the island: she and Laura had never been introduced. *Harry and I are going to London next week. We'll be staying with Rosie and her husband till we find a place of our own. I'll be in touch from there.*

Oh, but – London? Why don't you just come home, Susan? You can –

Mum, thank you, but I've made up my mind.

Had she? Did she know, even now, if she was doing the right thing?

She'd never lived in London, but she'd been there plenty of times. She'd gone for weekends with friends before she'd married; later she'd travelled with Luke to gallery openings and exhibitions, or meetings with art dealers, or awards ceremonies. If she found herself with time on her hands, Susan would stroll through Covent Garden, or sit at a lakeside café in St James's Park, or work her way through all the departments of Harrods.

The buzz and style of London had always appealed to her – and now her friend Rosie was living there, having moved from Ireland a year previously when she'd married Ed, her Jamaican-born financier boyfriend. *Stay as long as you like*, she'd said, in response to Susan's enquiry. *Our house is one of those tall skinny ones – you and Harry can do your own thing on the top floor.*

Susan would find a job: that was the first plan.

She'd brush up on her secretarial skills – there had to be something online for that. Once she felt confident enough, she'd sign up with an employment agency. She was forty-two, not too old by anyone's reckoning – and look at all the jobs there must be in London.

She didn't need to work. Since she'd become his wife, Luke had arranged for a generous sum to be paid into her bank account each month, most of which she hadn't managed to spend, with him also insisting that she use their joint account for household expenses. After walking out on him, she'd assumed the monthly payments would cease – but upon checking her bank account the day before, she'd seen that the usual deposit had been paid in.

Money he could give. Money wasn't his problem. *He wrote Tilly a cheque for €10,000,* Laura had told her, when his second daughter had been brought to his attention. Money he had in spades, and he had no problem sharing it around, but it wasn't what any of them wanted from him.

And even if she could manage without earning a salary, she needed to find something, just part-time while Harry was in a crèche, and later in school, to keep her from going back and back and back, to stop her tormenting herself with what-ifs and why-nots. She needed a distraction. She needed a job.

'Come and I'll introduce you,' Nell said, so Susan was presented to the other women, none of whom she could remember meeting in the past. 'Laura's stepmother,' was how Nell put it, and Susan wondered if she would still be able to lay claim to that title after she and Luke made their parting official. Did you go on being a stepmother if you divorced your stepchild's parent? Not that it mattered: she and Laura would remain close, whatever their on-paper relationship. Her connection with the Connolly family on Roone would stay strong, even if her ties to the Potter family in Dublin were severed.

A space was made for Susan, a chair found. The table around which they were seated was littered with cups, teapot, milk jug and wine glasses. 'Tilly and Laura will be out in a minute to get you something,' Susan was told. In the small talk that followed, nobody mentioned Harry's father, and Susan guessed that Nell wasn't the only one who'd been made aware of the situation.

'There you are – it's bedlam!' Laura cried, emerging from the house with Tilly, both of them laden with various foodstuffs, Tilly also managing a fresh teapot – and bedlam it was, but in the open air the noise was nicely diluted, party spills would soak harmlessly into the grass, crumbs would shake easily from the blankets, and the little guests – a multitude: had Laura rounded up all the four-year-olds of Roone? – certainly looked to be having a good time.

'What would you like to drink?' Tilly asked. 'Tea? Coffee? Wine?' and Susan said she might chance a glass of white wine. Four o'clock in the afternoon, far too early for alcohol – but one glass wouldn't hurt, and it might blunt the edges of her unhappiness for an hour or two.

The children were assembled, and the picnic got under way. Baskets of cocktail sausages and chicken nuggets and chips were distributed, along with promises of ice-cream once the first course had been disposed of. Sun cream was reapplied to faces and arms of protesting youngsters; the dog in his excitement overturned a bowl of crisps, and was promptly handed over to Gavin with instructions to keep him at a safe distance.

Tilly brought portions of quiche to the adult table, and was urged to join them. 'I'll wait till the kids have finished,' she told them. 'You sit,' she added to Laura, 'I've got this,' so Laura sank into a chair and was poured a glass of wine without being asked if she'd prefer tea.

'She's a treasure, that girl,' one of the mothers observed when Tilly had moved off. 'Any sign of Andy popping the question?'

'They're too young,' Nell replied quickly, although the query had been directed at Laura. 'Tilly's only nineteen.'

'I was nineteen,' Laura murmured, and Susan remembered the wedding she and Luke hadn't attended, because he couldn't stomach the thought of his daughter marrying an unemployed bricklayer. *You should still go*, Susan had said. *You're her father –* but he'd remained adamant. *She's known him a wet week*, he'd said. *What can he offer her?* And Susan had thought, *Love*, but hadn't said it. Luke never met his daughter's first husband, never laid eyes on him until Aaron was lying in his coffin. How sad was that?

The subject was changed. Talk turned to upcoming holidays. One family was going to Portugal, another to France, a third to Mayo. Nell said she and James hoped to travel to Venice for a few days in the autumn: 'His mother has promised to come and look after the kids.'

The wine was cold, and a little sweeter than Susan went for. She watched Harry sitting silently among his chattering companions, but laughing when they laughed, and seeming perfectly content. It will come, she told herself. He'll speak when he's ready.

'There's Eve,' Nell said, and heads swung around to see her standing at the gate.

'Why doesn't she come in?' someone wondered.

'I'll go,' Laura said, and hurried across the field.

Susan had met her in the hotel the day before. It had taken her a minute to place the chambermaid with the beautiful red hair who'd tapped on her door to ask if she wanted the room cleaned – and then it had come to her.

You used to help Laura in the Bed & Breakfast. I'm Susan, her stepmother. We met a few times – and Eve had greeted her cordially, although she hadn't appeared to remember her. *I'm just doing this for the summer*, she'd said, emptying the wastepaper basket, putting fresh towels in the bathroom. *I run the crèche normally.*

Nice enough girl – and hadn't she and Tilly's young

man been going out for a while? And here came Tilly from the house, her face setting a little, Susan thought, when she spotted Eve. To be expected, maybe.

Laura returned to the table with two brightly wrapped packages. 'Isn't she kind?' she remarked, to nobody in particular. 'She never forgets them.' She set the gifts on the ground by her chair. 'I asked her to join us, but she was in a rush somewhere.'

In due course the birthday cake was produced, along with the promised ice-cream. Candles were blown out, wishes made. When she thought a decent amount of time had passed, Susan rose to her feet.

'If you don't mind,' she said, 'I'll leave the rest of you to it' – and the lack of protestations from her companions made her suspect again that they'd all been put in the picture. 'Isn't she brave?' one would say when she'd left. 'It must be so difficult, especially with a young child' – and they'd all agree, smug in their happy marriages.

Laura accompanied her and Harry to the gate. 'Fancy a bit of lunch here tomorrow, around one?'

'Why don't you come to us after lunch instead, and you can relax with coffee in the garden?' Much as she loved her step-family, the thought of a noisy lunch didn't appeal. 'And bring Tilly if she's free.'

'I will, if she's not skipping off to be with her one and only in the ice-cream van.'

'I met Eve in the hotel,' Susan told her then, waiting while Harry settled himself into the buggy. 'Did you know she has a summer job there?'

'I did – I met Henry, the owner, the other day and he mentioned it.' Laura swooped and kissed Harry's cheek. 'Did you have fun, sweetie?'

He nodded.

'Will you come and play with the girls another day?'

Another nod.

'Great.' She straightened up and hugged his mother. 'See you tomorrow then.' She stood at the gate blowing kisses to Harry as they walked away.

Back at the hotel, Susan gave him his bath and put him into pyjamas, and turned on the television. She sat on the navy couch and opened her book and tried to read it, but no matter how many times she went over a sentence the words refused to soak into her head, and eventually she gave up. She reached for the hotel phone and dialled the number for room service.

'A glass of Sauvignon Blanc,' she said, because it was Saturday evening and she was missing her husband, and it was all she could think of to do.

Imelda

HE WASN'T AN ARTIST – OR RATHER, HE DIDN'T earn a living from it. He was a chef, with his own restaurant in a hilltop village that was an hour north of Rome. His older son, Caesar, was a doctor with Médecins sans Frontières, and currently stationed in a refugee camp in Bangladesh. Paolo, his younger son and a wine producer, was managing the restaurant in his absence. This was Gualtiero's fourth trip to Ireland, his first time on Roone.

He was seventy-one. On the cusp of his fortieth birthday he had married a woman twenty years his junior. Dorotea was the daughter of Roberto, his oldest friend, and the marriage had been a happy one. To celebrate their twentieth anniversary, when Caesar was seventeen and Paolo fourteen, the family went for a holiday to Croatia. On the third day, Dorotea left their apartment for an early-morning swim – and an hour after Gualtiero and his sons reported her missing, her body was taken from the water by a fisherman, a mile down the coast. She was thirty-nine.

Following her death, Gualtiero, a keen swimmer, never entered the water again – but although it had robbed him of his wife, his love for the sea remained strong. Some months after he'd become a widower he'd begun to paint it, working solely in acrylics, and without the benefit of a single art class. His paintings were alive with such colour and energy that Imelda could almost feel the spray.

The sea in Ireland is wonderful, he told her. *Every day is different: one day angry, another sleeping, another full of 'appiness.* He told Imelda that he gave away all his paintings, mainly to friends and family members. *Some I put in my restaurant*, he said. *If person come in and say they like, I give them.*

You could sell them, Imelda protested, but this only prompted one of his soft smiles. *Eemelda, I do not want money. I 'ave enough money. If I give my painting to a person, I make the person 'appy. For me, that is better than money.*

How could she argue with that?

Eight days after his unexpected arrival, he was still with her. He'd been full of apologies when she'd failed to find alternative accommodation for him. He'd offered to leave, when two days had passed and still no other lodgings had materialised. *I am trouble for you*, he'd said. *I will change my aeroplane ticket and return to Italy* – but by then she'd got over the shock of him landing on the doorstep, and was coming around to the astonished realisation that in fact, his presence in the house was welcome.

Left alone after her sister's departure, surrounded

everywhere she looked by reminders of Hugh, she'd felt herself entering a kind of twilight zone. In between visits from Nell and Eve and various neighbours, solitary hours would pass without her being able to account for them. Mealtimes would often come and go unobserved; she'd watch a television programme and take nothing in; she'd stand in a room, wondering what had brought her there.

And then Eve had shocked her with her angry outburst, and the neighbours' visits had dwindled, and Imelda had floundered on, defeated and bereft, wondering if she would ever feel anything approximating normal again. At her lowest ebb, Gualtiero had come – and within a day of having another person in the house, another person to think of, and cater for, she'd begun to pull herself back, to begin to function again.

Is possible I make breakfast for me? he'd asked, three mornings in. *Is not necessary for you to make* – and because Imelda thought he'd feel less of a burden if she agreed, she'd put up no objection. She ate earlier than him in the morning; now she could make herself scarce afterwards. He could have the kitchen to himself, and she'd be spared the effort of making small talk as she served him.

But the following morning she'd wandered in in search of a pen, completely forgetting he was there. He'd sprung up immediately and offered her coffee, and she'd felt it would be churlish to refuse. He'd already scrambled some eggs for himself –

and supplemented them, she'd noted, with smoked salmon, which she hadn't bought.

And he must have sensed that she'd rather listen than talk, because it was then, as they'd sat across the table from one another, as she'd sipped what was really very good coffee – he'd brought it, he admitted, from home – that she'd learnt about his drowned wife, and his sons, and his restaurant.

Goodness, she'd thought, a trained chef. *You must feel free to cook an evening meal here anytime you want*, she'd said. She hadn't offered to provide dinner, although she'd felt a little guilty about leaving him for an entire month at the mercy of Roone's rather unimaginative eateries – but as long as he could cook it himself, she saw no reason not to allow him to do so.

What difference would it make to her? She was past such small concerns. She could still have her own space: they could agree on a schedule. *I generally eat around seven*, she'd told him, *so you could have the kitchen after that. Anytime from eight o'clock, if it suited.* Italians ate late, didn't they?

He'd thanked her for the invitation, and said that eight o'clock would suit him very well, and so their new routine had begun. She'd cleared a shelf for him in the fridge, and invited him to use what staples were there rather than buy his own. *Butter, milk, eggs*, she'd said, *things like that. No point in having two lots. We can both keep them topped up* – and he in his turn had urged her to help herself to anything she might find that he had provided.

So she'd caught herself dipping into his jar of olives stuffed with pimentos – Hugh hadn't cared for olives, so she'd rarely bought them – and cutting a sliver from his block of pecorino cheese – she'd never even heard of it! – and adding a little smoked salmon to her pasta.

Somewhere along the line, she'd found herself telling him about Eve. *We fostered her*, she'd said, *my husband and I. Looked after her*, she'd added, when the term had puzzled him. *Her own family – had problems.* She gave no details, seeing no need for them. *She lived with us for a few years, but now she has her own place. She's twenty, just gone.*

She'd also referred to their recent estrangement, unable to keep it to herself. *It's troubling*, she'd told him. *I know she's grieving too – she and my husband were close – but I wish she hadn't pushed me away like that.*

He was a stranger: she had no right to burden him with her concerns. He was so easy to talk to, that was the problem. When she spoke, he was silent; he really listened. He made it feel alright to tell him these things.

Don't worry, Eemelda, he'd said. *She is sad, like you say – and because she trust you, she know she can be angry, and you will forgive her. I think she come back. I think she come soon.*

He'd been right about that. Eve had shown up the very next morning – but Imelda's relief at the sight of her had been short-lived. So rude she'd been to Gualtiero; so embarrassed Imelda had felt. Doubtless she'd forgotten the arrangement to accommodate him that had been made months ago, just as Imelda herself had forgotten it – but even so, her reaction to his presence was baffling, and simply not acceptable. What right had she to dictate to Imelda, to say who should and shouldn't be allowed to stay in the house, whatever the circumstances? You'd think she'd at least have waited for an explanation before making a show of herself like that.

I'm so sorry, Imelda had said to Gualtiero after Eve had stormed off, but he'd waved away her apology. *She is sad*, he said, *is not thinking in normal way. Is not a problem for me*, but Imelda had felt bad all the same.

Oh, she didn't have the energy. Despite the distraction of Gualtiero, she was still torn apart by Hugh's death, still heartbroken at her widowed state, still unable to think of much beyond getting through the next hour, the next day, without him.

But her sleep had improved a little, which was something. And yesterday she'd picked up a book that had sat unopened by her bedside since the middle of May. She'd had to go back to the start, so completely forgotten was it – she'd begun it in another universe – and she'd managed only a page or so before losing heart, but it was another tiny step forward.

'Imelda!'

She turned, heart sinking. She'd chosen what she'd hoped was a quiet time to come and pick up a few bits and pieces in the supermarket, not wishing to meet anyone she knew – but here was Josephine

Brown, of all people, bearing down on her. Josephine, who liked nothing better than to spread a story about, regardless of its content, unconcerned as to its truth or otherwise.

She reached for Imelda's arm, gave it a squeeze. 'How are you doing, lovey?' she asked, in the sympathy-laden voice that Imelda had come to dread. She shouldn't resent it: she knew it was well-meant, in most cases – but God, how it was beginning to grate.

'I'm alright, Josephine. I'm as good as I can be.'

'Glad to hear it, that's the spirit.' Pause. 'I heard you have a visitor.'

Of course she'd heard. Josephine made it her business to hear, or overhear, just about everything that happened on the island.

'I have a tenant, if that's what you mean,' Imelda replied stiffly. 'I had no choice. It was arranged … a long time ago. He's easy, he's no trouble.'

'But, Imelda, I heard he's staying with you a whole *month* – that's the last thing you need right now. I can't imagine how hard that must be for you.' Eyes flicking to Imelda's basket as she spoke, checking out the Barry's tea and the seeded batch loaf, the washing-up liquid and the toilet rolls. 'How on earth will you manage, dear?'

'I'll manage fine,' Imelda said crisply. 'I must be getting on. Nell is expecting me.' Whisking past Josephine, not caring if the woman was put out by her abrupt departure. Such liberation grief afforded, propriety gone with the wind.

'How are you coping?' Nell asked later, when the two of them were sitting in her kitchen. 'How are you holding up?'

Mother of two young children, shadows beneath her eyes. Her hair held back from her face with a silver clip, cream sandals on her feet. An apple tart in the oven, cloves and cinnamon floating around the room.

'You shouldn't have,' she said, watching Berry unwrapping Imelda's birthday present to her, which was considerably late. The child, whose vivacious character Hugh had particularly loved, pulled yellow paper away from the crayons and drawing pad that Imelda had found in the knick-knack section of the supermarket, knowing Nell wouldn't care less what she'd spent. 'What do you say to Imelda?'

'Ta ta.'

'You're welcome, darling.'

'You want to show them to Tommy?' Nell asked, and off the child scooted to find her older brother, whom she pestered mercilessly any chance she got. Poor Tommy.

'Susan is here,' Nell said, when the patter of her feet had faded. 'You remember Laura's stepmother? She and her little boy Harry are staying in the hotel. She's left her husband.'

'Oh, that's too bad.'

But Imelda's reply was automatic, as dutiful as the little girl's thanks. How could she feel sympathy, when Susan's husband was still alive and well? She'd met the woman a few times, she'd admired her polished good looks and her warmth – but that she'd chosen to leave her husband, her living, breathing husband, whatever the circumstances, was almost offensive to a mourning Imelda.

'She's talking of moving to London, Laura says. She's got friends there.'

Imelda had been to London once. A lifetime ago, with Cathy Coleman. They'd treated themselves to two nights in a hotel, basic but clean, in Wimbledon. It was the first time Imelda had seen baked beans on a breakfast plate. They'd got tickets for *The Mousetrap*, which they'd both agreed didn't live up to its reputation. They'd visited Madame Tussaud's and the Tate, and Cathy had climbed right to the top of St Paul's Cathedral while Imelda, with her fear of cramped spaces, had turned back at the dome, and they'd taken photos of each other standing on Westminster Bridge, with Big Ben in the background.

They'd stood for over an hour with the rest of the tourists outside Buckingham Palace, hoping to catch a glimpse of the Queen – *She must be in there*, Cathy had said, *the flag is flying* – but there had been no sign of her, and no changing of the guard either, since it was the wrong time, or the wrong day, Imelda couldn't remember which. On their return to Ireland, Imelda's sister had told her about a man she'd met at a dance called Vernon McCarthy. She remembered the two of them thinking his name very unusual – and now Imelda didn't give it a second's thought, so familiar had it become.

'I saw Mr Conti a while ago,' Nell said. 'At least, I think it was him. Does he wear a straw hat and navy overalls, and is he a bit on the chubby side?'

'Yes, that sounds like him.'

'He was painting down by the pier. I sneaked a look when I was passing, but I couldn't really make it out. How are you coping with him?'

'He's no trouble. I don't see that much of him. He does his own breakfast, and he's out most of the day.' No need to mention their morning chats, which might be taken up the wrong way.

'Well, that's good. He's been lucky with the weather. Will you hang on to him, do you think, or will I keep looking?'

'I think I'll manage, thanks Nell.'

'And are you sleeping?'

'... It's improving a little.'

'Glad to hear it. Why don't you stay to dinner with us? It's just shepherd's pie, but we have plenty.'

'I would, only I have a chop taken out of the freezer.' The lie came effortlessly, she who would never have lied. She wasn't ready for the bustle of a family dinner.

Driving off, she caught sight of herself in the rear-view mirror; such a tidy-up her hair needed. On Tuesday the fifteenth of May she'd been due to visit the salon for a cut: *Nell 10.00*, she'd written on the calendar that hung on the kitchen wall. By ten o'clock her house was full, Nell and James and Dr Jack and Father William and more, and someone was crying, and someone kept boiling the kettle, and someone was holding her hand, and life as she knew it had upended and broken into smithereens two hours earlier.

As she passed the pier she spotted Gualtiero, positioned not too far from Andy's ice-cream van. Standing by his easel but not painting, just staring out to sea. Was he thinking of his dead wife who'd been swallowed by another body of water? Maybe, she thought suddenly, that was why he always painted it. Maybe it helped him to feel closer to her.

She hoped he got himself an ice-cream at some stage. Probably not a patch on the Italian stuff, but still.

Laura

'THE THING IS,' TILLY SAID, LIFTING AN EGG from the bubbling water, dropping it carefully into the yellow-spotted eggcup, 'he's not neglecting me. I mean, he's never late to pick me up – you've seen that.' She broke off as the kitchen door opened. 'Ben, here's Mrs Lindsay's egg. Ask if they need more toast.'

'And collect anything they've finished with on your way back,' Laura called after him, pushing sausages aside in the pan, dropping in discs of white and black pudding. Poppy, seated at the table, gave a sudden cry of protest: Laura swung around. 'Evie, leave your sister alone.'

'She took my crayon!'

'She's only small, let her have it. You have lots. Not on the table, Poppy, only on the page.'

'It's not fair! You *always* let her take our stuff!'

'Here,' Marian said, 'you can have one of mine, Evie.'

Laura threw her a smile. 'Thanks, sweetie.' She'd kiss her when she had a minute.

'It's just,' Tilly said, pouring away the water, 'sometimes I wish, well, I wish he'd tell his friends to get lost. Does that sound awful?'

'Pass me a plate, would you?' She really could have chosen a better time for the heart-to-heart. 'Don't you like his friends?'

'I *do* like them, they're lovely, but it's beginning to feel a bit like I'm going out with all of them.'

Laura flipped the egg in the smaller pan before remembering that Mr Lindsay had specified sunny side up. She retrieved it hastily. 'Have you said anything to Andy about this?'

'No, I'm afraid it'll sound needy. I want *him* to want to be on his own with me.'

Ben reappeared with two cereal bowls. 'The other man, not Mr Lindsay, the one with the beard, said he's still waiting for his omelette.'

'Blast – I knew I was forgetting somebody. Bring this to Mr Lindsay and tell Mr Kelly his omelette is on the way. Tilly, would you grate me some cheese?'

Tilly crossed to the fridge while Laura cracked eggs into a bowl. 'Could you get Andy to take a day off?'

'Yes, I think so.'

'Well, then. Say you fancy a picnic, just the two of you. Say you got the idea from the girls' birthday party. And while you're there, tell him how much you enjoy his friends, but you love having him to yourself sometimes too.'

'You make it sound so easy.'

'It *is* easy. Men are simple creatures, and not always that perceptive. Sometimes you have to spell things out a bit.'

But she could see that Tilly wanted more of him than a couple of hours on a picnic. She'd waited so long for her three and a half weeks, and now they were here, and they couldn't possibly live up to her expectations. She wanted the perfect boyfriend, the perfect holiday.

'Shame you don't have an Aussie fellow,' Laura said lightly.

'What?' The sudden stricken look on Tilly's face, as if she'd just been told she had a week to live.

'Just that it would make life a whole lot easier for you.'

'But I love Andy.'

'I know. I know you do.'

'And it's not as if we'll be apart forever. I'd move here in a heartbeat. He'd only have to ask.'

She would. And how would that go down with young Andy Baker, who'd grown into a lean, handsome fellow? More than a couple of Roone girls, Laura bet, would gladly take Tilly's place.

Eve flashed into her mind. *I meant to text you again*, Laura had said, the day of the birthday picnic, when Eve had appeared with the girls' presents. *Will you come in for a slice of quiche?* Knowing the likely response – and sure enough, Eve had turned down the invitation, telling Laura she was due at Imelda's.

Is everything OK? Laura had asked, and Eve had

said everything was fine, and Laura had left it at that. She seemed to want to sort it out on her own. Maybe she was sorry she'd said anything.

The grated cheese was passed over silently. 'Thanks, love,' Laura said. 'You might chop some ham, and make fresh toast.'

'Brown or white?'

'Let's go with two of each.'

Laura watched her slotting bread into the toaster, looking deflated. Poor pet. 'Look,' she said, 'I know it's tough when you're so far away from him.' She added a knob of butter to the pan. 'I don't know how you've managed to keep it going this long, to be honest. I wish I could think of a way to make it easier for you.'

Tilly chopped ham and tipped it into Laura's bowl. 'We could always get married,' she said, and laughed.

Married – after spending precisely two summers together. A double holiday romance, you could call it. 'I suspect Nell would have something to say about that,' Laura replied, smiling to take the sting out of it. 'I'd say she might think you're both a bit young.'

Tilly didn't return the smile. 'I'm nineteen,' she said. 'You were nineteen.'

Lord Almighty. It wasn't a joke. She'd been thinking about them getting married, was considering it as a viable option. Laura poured the omelette mix onto the waiting pan, wondering where to go with the conversation. 'I did marry at nineteen, but things were different with me and Aaron. For one thing we lived in the same town, and we saw one another pretty much every day while we were going out.'

Silence as Tilly ran water into the sink for the pans. Laura knew she wasn't saying what her sister wanted to hear. She cast about for something more positive.

'Maybe you could move here for a few months.'

Tilly looked at her. 'Move here? To Roone?'

'Why not? You could stay with us no problem off-season – and you'd actually have your own room. I know Andy would be in Limerick, but he could come home for weekends – or you could go there for the odd Saturday, or whatever.'

Tilly pulled on rubber gloves. 'What would I do here, though? I mean, I'd have to have some kind of a job.'

'Where do I start? You could feed the animals and collect the eggs. You could help Gav with his vegetable plot, and his deliveries. You could look after the girls and give me a bit of time off. You could paint a few rooms – they're long overdue a facelift. You wouldn't earn a mint, but you'd have bed and board.'

Tilly scrubbed at a pan. 'Or I could live in Limerick, find a proper job there.'

'Where would you stay, though? Accommodation is expensive in the cities. No, you'd be much better off basing yourself here.'

'Right.'

'Something to think about, anyway.'

'Sure is. Thanks for the offer.'

'And in the meantime, plan your picnic' – and Tilly brightened up a bit, and promised she would.

They finished the breakfasts and cleaned up. Mr Kelly of the omelette checked out with his wife, and the German mother and daughter who'd stayed two nights left too. Bed linen was replaced, towels collected, carpets vacuumed.

After lunch Tilly disappeared, having changed into her blue dress and made up her face. 'See you for dinner,' she said. 'Can I get you anything on the way back?'

She never failed to ask. 'Not a thing, love. Have fun.' And off her sister went, rushing out to be with him – and again Laura hoped fervently that no hearts were about to be broken.

So much for her supposed premonition, well over a week ago. Thankfully, nothing untoward had taken place since then. Later in the afternoon she left Gavin on duty and escaped for an hour. She'd give Susan a bit of space today, just take a walk and clear her head. She set off along the coast road, Charlie on his lead trotting beside her, delighted with his second outing of the day. The sun came and went, more clouds in the sky than in recent days. She hoped it wasn't signalling the end of the fine spell.

She ignored the turns for the various beaches, although normally she loved a paddle. Any bit of sun at all in the summer months and the beaches filled up. Give her a deserted stretch of sand, where she could let Charlie off his leash to run wild, where the salty breeze from the sea would blow the clutter from her mind. Today they'd keep to the roads, and Charlie would get his run another time.

She rounded a bend and saw him immediately, some distance ahead of her. Same straw hat, same baggy overalls – but this time he wasn't painting. No easel, no little table. His green case was there but it was unopened, propped against the low stone wall on which he sat. He faced out to sea but his head was bowed. His hands rested in his lap. She thought he might be meditating and resolved not to disturb him, to walk quietly by – but as she drew closer, she saw him dash the back of a hand to his eyes in turn.

He wasn't meditating. He was weeping. She was sure of it.

Not in a noisy way. Not in a way that would draw attention to him from the casual passer-by. If she hadn't been observing him as she'd approached, Laura might not have caught it.

But now that she had, she couldn't ignore it, couldn't walk on and pretend she hadn't seen it. Well, she could – and maybe he'd prefer it that way – but ignoring his distress seemed callous. She tried to remember his Italian name, but it had floated out of her head.

She drew Charlie closer to heel. She crossed the road while she was still a short distance from him, and came to a stop. 'Walter,' she called softly, not wanting to startle him. 'Are you ... is everything OK?'

He lifted his head. With a pang she saw the reddened swollen eyes, the shine of tears on his cheeks. '*Signora*,' he said, attempting to rise to his feet but she hurried closer, telling him no, no, he wasn't to get up.

'Has something happened?' she asked, tugging on Charlie's lead as he strained to sniff at this new person. 'Are you hurt? Injured? Do you need a doctor?' He didn't look hurt, just terribly sad. His hat hung crookedly: she resisted an impulse to reach out and straighten it.

'No,' he said, and fished a handkerchief from his overalls and blew his nose sharply. 'No,' he repeated, stowing it away. 'No doctor, *grazie*. I am not sick.' He shook his head and turned to look out to sea again. 'Today I remember,' he said simply – and immediately she understood.

'May I join you?' she asked, and he told her please, certainly, so she took her place on the wall beside him. 'Sit,' she said without hope to Charlie – and for the first time in his life, he dropped his haunches obediently, sensing the moment, maybe, in the way that animals sometimes did. 'Good boy,' she told him, giving his head a rub. 'Best boy.'

She sat with the artist and watched the sea. 'Sometimes I remember too,' she told him.

She heard the small rustling movement as he turned to regard her. 'How many year for you?' he asked.

She looked into his dark eyes. 'Twelve.'

'For me is eleven.'

She nodded, and found his hand, and held on. *In English is Walter.* Roone, in its inexplicable, magical way, had sent her another Walter.

After enough time had passed, she said, 'Can I tell you about my father?'

Tilly

TODAY WAS THE DAY. TODAY SHE WOULD do it.

Say you fancy a picnic, just the two of you, Laura had said, so Tilly had suggested it that same afternoon, and Andy had laughed and said the last time he'd been on a picnic was when he was about four, and Tilly had replied that in that case it was high time he went on another. *Let's do it soon, while the weather is good*, she'd said, so he'd asked Pádraig for a day off, and Pádraig had said Thursday would suit.

And now it was Thursday, and in less than an hour he was collecting her in the rusty blue car, and they were going to Jackson's Lookout on the far side of the island with a picnic she'd packed. And the sun was shining and everything was looking very promising, and she was going to propose and he was going to say yes.

She loved being back on Roone. Oh, she could so easily see herself spending the rest of her life here. She adored the summery buzz of the place, with long generous daylight hours, and coaches and minibuses driving off the ferry each morning with a new group of day-trippers, and the cash registers in cafés and shops ringing from morning till closing time, and music spilling from pubs each evening, and boats of all shapes and sizes bobbing in the bay. The island was bursting at the seams, and pulsing with life.

And it was so lovely to be reunited with Laura and Gavin and the kids, and to spend time next door with Nell and James, and their earnest little son and their gorgeous chattering handful of a daughter.

She loved her afternoons in the yellow ice-cream van. She got a kick out of meeting the different customers, hearing the various accents of the holidaymakers and renewing her acquaintance with the Roone residents she'd met before.

She could happily sell from a van all year round, she thought. Oh, not ice-creams in the middle of winter – but what about switching to hot food when the temperature dropped? Lelia's café only opened at weekends in the winter. Some of the pubs offered meals, and the hotel had a full restaurant – but she figured there was still room for a little competition.

She could introduce the population of Roone to *poffertjes*, the small fluffy Dutch pancakes she remembered being sold from food vans at home whenever there was a festival in town. Served warm, with a drizzle of maple syrup and a blob of vanilla cream – oh, just the memory of them was enough to make her mouth water. Or baked potatoes: they used to buy them from the vans too – and what Irish person didn't love potatoes, filled with something hot and tasty?

She could picture it, clear as anything. The hob, and the cast-iron pan to make the *poffertjes*. The stainless steel unit to keep potatoes warm, with smaller compartments for the various fillings: chilli, creamed sweetcorn, baked beans and the like. A fridge for the cold drinks. A coffee machine, and a boiler for hot water. Stacks of paper cups, cutlery bundled into serviettes.

She could position herself at the pier, where the ice-cream van was now, or maybe at the far end of the village street, near the community hall. She could open her hatch for a couple of hours at lunchtime, and again at five or six, when people were clocking off from work, and again when the pubs were closing, and drinkers had beer-fuelled appetites. The rest of the time she could concentrate on her book, the great novel that was just waiting for the right time to make its way out.

Funny that Laura had suggested her coming to live on Roone. She wouldn't like to be on the island without him though: it would feel weird with him not here. Whatever Laura said about high rents in cities, Tilly would find a way to be with him in Limerick – and if today went according to plan, she'd be taking the first step in that direction.

She'd hardly slept as she'd lain in bed last night, across the floor from Evie and Marian in their bunks. She always had to share with them in the summer, and she didn't mind in the least. The girls were invariably sound asleep when she went to bed – and their chatter in the early morning, as she hurried into her clothes to help with the breakfasts, was delightful.

What does Australia look like?

Bits of it are green and other bits are brown. You can fly on a plane when you're bigger and see it.

Is it hot or cold?

Sometimes it's hot, very hot, and other times it's cold.

Does it snow?

In some parts it does. Not the part where I live.

Is there shops?

Oh yes, plenty of shops.

And donkeys like George?

Yes, lots and lots of donkeys, just like George.

Is there ice-cream?

Oh yes. Not as nice as your ice-cream, though.

The only thing, her only small complaint, was what she'd said at breakfast the other day to Laura: she and Andy had so little time on their own. You couldn't count the snatches between customers at the van, and the evenings she spent with him invariably included at least two of his friends, unless he was helping his dad in the pub. She sometimes joined him then for an hour or so, but he was busy and couldn't chat much, and she wasn't much of a drinker, so sitting alone on a barstool with a Coke, surrounded by holidaymaking groups, didn't hold much appeal.

He'd taken her to the island's drive-in cinema, if

you could call it that, on her second evening, and they'd been alone in his car but surrounded by others, most of whose drivers he knew, so there was no sense of having him to herself.

When she thought about it, she realised that the only times she'd been alone with him for more than a few minutes were during the drive from the airport to the island on her arrival, and three days after that, when Laura had shooed her out directly after the breakfasts, saying she could take it from there, and they'd gone on a hike to the small pebbly beach he'd brought her to the previous summer, Eve thinking, hoping, they'd find it deserted.

They hadn't – but you wouldn't call it crowded either. They'd been having a lovely time, just messing around like a pair of kids, until Eve had shown up.

It had been their first time coming face to face this summer. To Tilly's private relief, Eve rarely hung around with Andy's set, or not while Tilly was there at any rate. That morning she'd seemed in a funny mood, smirking at Tilly, flirting with Andy. The things she'd said, about getting drunk, and Andy being her knight in shining armour. *Like old times*, she'd said – as if that wasn't insensitive, with Tilly right there. It was like she was deliberately trying to get to her.

Tilly had a dim memory of Andy telling her that Frog's twenty-first was coming up. Sometime in May, she thought, not that she'd paid too much attention to a party that couldn't include her. She fancied he'd complained about a hangover afterwards, and she thought she'd laughed and told him it served him right.

He'd made no mention of walking Eve home. She was pretty sure she'd have remembered that.

She hadn't asked him about it after Eve's comments on the beach, not wanting to seem jealous or possessive. She would have liked him to say something, to tell her that Eve was just up to mischief, or whatever, but he'd said nothing at all. And because he hadn't, it had burrowed under her skin and lodged there. Precisely, she suspected, where it had been aimed.

Like old times.

It was OK, she told herself. It wasn't an issue, it was nothing at all. Let Eve say what she liked: Tilly trusted Andy absolutely.

And still, it niggled.

She put it firmly from her head: time to concentrate on today. She'd dressed in her favourite printed shirt and pink skirt. 'What do you think?' she asked Evie, who could generally be relied on to give an honest opinion. 'Will I do?'

Evie scrutinised her carefully. 'Yeah,' she said eventually, and Tilly laughed and curtsied, and swept her into her arms and waltzed her around the kitchen, to the amusement of Laura, who was shelling hardboiled eggs at the sink.

'Oh, to be young again,' she said. 'To be young and in love.'

Tilly regarded her over Evie's head. 'You *are* young – and I hope you're in love too.'

'Indeed I am, on both counts,' Laura declared, depositing the shells into a plastic basin. 'Well, maybe not that young any more—'

'Oh, come on – you're thirty-one. It's hardly ancient.'

'And you're nineteen,' Laura replied lightly, 'with everything ahead of you.'

For a second, Tilly was tempted to tell her. To blurt it out, right there in the kitchen: *I'm going to propose to him today. I'm going to ask him to marry me.* She almost said it, but she didn't. Wait till it was a done deal. Wait till she and Andy could tell Laura, and everyone else, together.

She returned Evie to her seat at the table. She checked her face again in the mirror – and as she slicked on another layer of lip gloss, a horn sounded on the road outside. Her heart gave a *whump*. She took up the picnic basket – chicken wings, potato salad, apple buns, pink lemonade, sun block. She bent to kiss Evie, waggled her fingers at Laura. 'See you later,' she told them. 'Try not to miss me.'

'Enjoy,' Laura replied. 'Live for the moment.'

Live for the moment. It sounded like a sensible way to go about things. Don't worry about the future, enjoy what you have.

On the other hand, you could enjoy what you had, and plan for the future too. She walked out to the blue car, swinging her basket happily. She was a princess, and her carriage awaited, with her prince behind the wheel.

'We need to swing by Fitz's,' he said, as she climbed in. 'Dad forgot his reading glasses.'

No 'You look lovely'. No 'Nice to see you'. She turned to place the basket on the back seat, and reached across to kiss him. Princes weren't perfect, only in fairy tales. 'That's fine,' she said, rolling down her window. Nothing could ruin today: she wouldn't let it.

They drove along the village street. Andy pulled up outside Fitz's and Tilly ran in with James's glasses, and found him restocking shelves with beer bottles. 'Thanks, Tilly,' he said. 'Can I give you anything towards your picnic? Nuts, crisps, fizzy water?'

'I think we're all set,' she told him, pleased that Andy had mentioned the picnic at home. Back in the car she smoothed her skirt over her knees as they turned for the cliffs, trying to still the butterflies that insisted on fluttering madly inside her.

She'd been to Jackson's Lookout once before. It was during her first summer on Roone, when Andy had offered to show her the famous road sign that pointed out to sea, the one nobody could explain, the one that had kept reappearing each time Kerry County Council removed it. After three attempts, the council had given up, and the sign remained in place, one of Roone's more visible mysteries.

They'd puffed their way up the steep road – no car at their disposal then – which had become, after half a mile or so, a narrower path with grass running along its middle. They'd reached a turnstile and climbed it, and made their way around the edge of a field to a second turnstile, and from there along an earthy track through a small wooded area that eventually petered out and brought them to a grassy space, roughly half the size of a tennis court.

Jackson's Lookout, Andy had announced, and Tilly had walked to the safety fence at its edge and had seen the sign on the cliff side of the fence, and had read '*The Statue of Liberty 3,000 miles*'. There had been nobody there that time; she prayed it would be equally deserted today. But even if it wasn't, they'd find a spot out of earshot of whoever else was around.

The old car struggled up the hill, engine straining loudly. 'Fingers crossed,' Andy said, shifting down a gear, pressing hard on the accelerator, leaning forward in his seat as if that would make a difference. They reached the top, just about, and abandoned the car at the turnstile. No other vehicle was in sight, which Tilly took as a positive sign.

The route from the road was much as she remembered. Grazing cattle in the field – could they be the same ones as before? – lifted their heads as Tilly and Andy skirted its edge. Sunshine dappled the earthy path in the little forest. At Jackson's Lookout, the road sign stood proud, still telling anyone who cared to know how far away they were from America.

And nobody else was there. They had it completely to themselves. Good omen.

They positioned themselves on the blanket Andy had brought along. He poured lemonade into paper cups; she applied sun block and ordered herself to stay calm. They ate. They drank. They lay in the sun, fingers loosely entwined.

She told him about a couple in the B&B who'd left a porn magazine behind them in their room. 'Laura was raging: the boys could easily have found it.' She asked if he'd heard the woman being interviewed on the radio earlier that morning whose daughter had won half a million euro in the Lotto last year sometime, and been killed in a road accident the following day.

He told her about the trio of newborn pups that Bugs Deasy's sister had discovered abandoned by a roadside just outside Killarney, and the gold ring Maisie Kiely had spotted on the beach during one of her morning walks that turned out to belong to her neighbour, Bernie Madigan, who'd lost it a year earlier.

'Never,' she said.

'True as I'm here.'

She put sun block on his nose, and on the tips of his ears, and surrendered the last apple bun to him. He tried and failed to teach her how to belch at will. And every so often they fell silent, and she thought, *Now! Do it now!*

And she found that she couldn't. She found that her nerve had completely deserted her.

She wasn't sure, was the ugly naked truth.

He called her baby, and honey, and occasionally Tills, which she secretly adored. He told her he missed her, when they were on different sides of the world and he was just a face on a screen. He seemed perfectly content in her company – when they were out with his friends he would hold her hand or put an arm around her, or drop a hand casually onto her knee. He did and said all the right things – but still she wasn't sure that he was where she was.

He kissed her hello and goodbye, and hugged her often, but didn't attempt to venture further, like he'd done the previous summer. It might be a response to her pulling back: he might be showing her that he was willing to wait – and having decided that wedding night discoveries would be so romantic, she should have been happy with that, shouldn't she? But contrary creature that she was, she found his lack of urgency disconcerting.

Love was mentioned between them, often it was said. Maybe more on her part, or she would generally be the one to give it first mention, and he would echo the sentiment – but who was counting?

She was. She was counting.

She was in no doubt about her feelings for him. What she'd felt for the man who'd used her so horribly, which she'd foolishly imagined to be love, seemed so pale and pathetic now in comparison to how she felt about Andy. A schoolgirl crush the other had been, no more than that. This was different. This was the real thing.

Andy just had to catch up. He needed more time, that was all. Their brief periods together meant a slower deepening of his feelings. It was a blow, but not the end of the world. She'd learn to be patient, and wait for him. Next year it would happen, or the one after that. They were meant to be together; of that she was still certain.

They finished the picnic and packed up. He carried basket and blanket back to the car. And all the way back to Walter's Place, as he hummed along with the radio, she had to pretend to have a hay fever attack as she pressed a tissue to her nose and eyes and fought with tears that wanted so badly to fall.

Eve

THEY MET IN THE HOTEL LOBBY, AS EVE WAS heading home after her shift. Susan and her little boy were descending the stairs. 'We were just about to have a bite to eat in the garden,' she said. 'Would you care to join us? I could use some adult conversation' – so Eve went with them, having no objection to being treated to her lunch. They ordered a sharing platter of cold meats and cheeses and salads, and a little basket of chicken pieces for Harry.

'We leave tomorrow,' Susan told her. 'We've had a lovely holiday, haven't we?' and her little boy, whose nose was a bit pink from the sun, nodded.

'Are you going back to Dublin?' Eve asked.

Susan shook her head. 'Not right away,' she said. 'We're taking a little break from Dublin.' She gave a quick smile, gone as quickly as it had appeared. 'It's complicated.'

Sounded complicated. A little break, right after a two-week holiday. Eve decided to change the subject. 'I'll be helping out here with the owner's birthday party in a couple of weeks. He asked if I wanted to do an extra shift.'

Susan looked doubtful. 'Will you? Are you sure you want to work that night? Won't your friends be at the party?'

Her friends, who were also Andy's friends. The friends she'd been steering clear of lately – and who, it had to be said, were keeping their distance too, maybe thinking she needed time alone to grieve. 'They'll probably be there,' she agreed.

'And wouldn't you rather be enjoying yourself with them instead of working?'

'Not really,' Eve told her. 'I'm not in the mood for a party these days.'

Susan's face changed. 'Oh, Eve – of course you're not. I didn't think, sorry.'

Eve felt a twinge of guilt. Susan had meant because of Hugh – and it was a factor, certainly, but not the only one.

'Actually,' she said lightly, 'I'm pregnant.' Not having planned to blurt it out to someone who was little more than a passing acquaintance, but Susan was leaving tomorrow, and she didn't strike Eve as a gossip. And it wouldn't matter anyway if she said it to Laura, who knew already.

'Oh …'

Eve could see the indecision in her face. To congratulate or commiserate? 'It wasn't planned. It was – a spur of the moment thing. Nobody knows yet.' She paused. 'Not even the father.' Felt weird to say it. The father.

'I see. And … how do you feel about it?'

Eve considered. 'I feel OK, I think. I've decided to keep it.' That was enough, she thought. Any more, and she might give away too much.

'Right.' Susan gave her another fleeting smile. 'Well, I wish you good luck. Hope things work out for you.'

'Thanks.'

Susan wouldn't talk. She wasn't the type to go running around with news. Eve skewered a cube of grilled halloumi, wondering if she could chance another of the fat green olives, even though she'd had at least four already, and Susan none at all. Her appetite was back with a vengeance, which she should probably be glad about, but she didn't want to end up like one of those women who put on a ton of weight when they got pregnant and never managed to lose it again.

'How's Imelda doing?' Susan asked.

Everyone Eve met asked her that, and to everyone she gave the same response. 'She's coping.'

She'd seen Imelda in the village the day before. Eve had been emerging from the fish shop when she'd spotted Imelda crossing to her side of the street. Well within calling distance, just a few doors away, but Eve had drawn back. Her rage of the other morning had abated, but still she felt resentful of the man who was staying where he had no business to be.

Imelda had had her hair cut. It was soft around her face, the way Nell always did it. Eve watched her hitch the strap of her bag higher onto her shoulder, like she'd seen her do a million times before. She wore her grey jacket, although the sky showed no sign of rain.

When Imelda had heard what Derek Garvey had done, she hadn't asked Eve why she'd waited so long to tell someone. She hadn't asked her anything at all. *'Listen to me,'* she'd said. *'You will never have to go back to that house. Do you hear me? You will never have to set foot in that house again. I promise you that. Hugh and I will sort everything out.'* And they had. Hugh and Imelda had saved her.

Looking at her the day before, Eve realised that she'd lost weight since Hugh's death. She remembered when Imelda would eat a full slice of apple tart and follow it with another, laughing, calling herself a little piggy. *Eat away*, Hugh would tell her, *I love to see a woman who isn't afraid of her food.*

Watching her entering the supermarket with her new haircut, Eve's eyes had filled with tears. Stop it, she'd commanded. Stay strong. She doesn't need you, she's made that perfectly clear, and you certainly don't need her. Eve had seen the man too, earlier in the day, rolling his case past the hotel as she'd glanced out of a bedroom window.

In the hotel garden a pair of birds set up a sudden lively chirping. 'Sorry,' Eve said. 'I don't know why I told you all that, about me being pregnant, I mean.'

'No need to apologise. It's good to talk sometimes.'

Susan wasn't talking though. She wasn't telling Eve why she'd come to the island without her husband, and why she wasn't returning to him now. She was attractive, with large eyes and a full mouth that didn't look fake, and shiny dark hair whose cut, Eve guessed, had cost a lot more than Nell charged.

They finished eating. Dessert was offered and declined. Eve rose to her feet. 'Thanks for this,' she said. 'It was a nice treat. See you next time you're around,' and Susan smiled and wished her well again. Eve waved goodbye to the little boy, who hadn't uttered a single word all through lunch.

She walked home by the main beach. It was the day of the island's annual barbecue and she'd planned to stay away, but suddenly she was curious to see it. She could hang back by the dunes where she wouldn't be noticed.

The beach was more crowded than usual, as it always was on barbecue day. Most of the island's population turned up every year, even if it was only for an hour or two – the village street pretty much shut down from three to five – and it looked like plenty of tourists were taking advantage of the festivities too.

Men and women stood around in clusters; others sat on deckchairs or rugs. Children chased one another about on the sand, or built castles of varying complexity. Further along, a beach volleyball game was in session. Bright umbrellas were dotted about the place, beneath which babies slept and grandparents dozed.

The dark green drinks tent was there as ever: Eve

remembered Hugh helping to man it each year. The smell of roasting meat drifted on the breeze to her from the big barbecue pit, making her mouth water although she wasn't hungry after the lunch.

From her vantage point she scanned the scene, picking out familiar faces. There were Janet Brown and Nuala Considine at the water's edge, batting a small ball from one to the other, and pretending not to notice that a few tanned foreign boys standing nearby were eyeing them up.

Her boss from the hotel was there, his trousers rolled to reveal white calves as he walked by the water's edge with an old woman whose face Eve knew. Margie or Maisie, she thought. Big floppy hat on her today. Walked this beach from end to end every day of the year, pretty much, along with a few of her equally energetic buddies. People tended to live well into old age on Roone: the oldest person on the island was currently Patsy McDonagh, whose ninety-fifth birthday had been celebrated in March. Hugh had been one of the unlucky ones, taken well before he should have been.

No sign of Nell. Staying away, Eve guessed, for the same reason Imelda was. She couldn't locate Laura either, but there were Gavin and James, not too far from the drinks tent. You couldn't miss Gavin with his lanky build, and the shapeless grey hat he insisted on wearing in the sun, much to Laura's mortification. His three girls were playing in the sand at his feet, and further along his twin boys – no, Laura's boys, not his

- were kicking something around, she couldn't tell what. Getting so tall now, must be eleven or twelve.

She turned her gaze to the sea - and there was the group she'd been hunting for. They stood chest high in the water, in the formation of a rough circle, and threw an inflatable beach ball around, diving and leaping to catch it. She saw Tilly launching herself upwards in a red swimsuit, bringing an arc of water with her as she met the ball in mid-air and palm-slapped it across to Bugs.

Eve thought of her first beach barbecue, and the dark green swimsuit she'd bought a few days beforehand in Tralee, with money Imelda had given her. She remembered playing in the sea in just such a way with Andy and his friends. Early stages with him, their relationship so new that every look brought butterflies, every smile made her insides melt, every kiss was a tiny burst of joy.

She'd been on Roone for over a month, and against all her expectations she was growing attached to the island. She was also beginning to realise how lucky she'd been to end up in Imelda and Hugh's house - and to her astonishment and growing delight, she was also falling in love. The very last thing she'd anticipated when she'd been banished, as she saw it, to a place she knew nothing about, tossed aside for the entire summer while the Garveys got a break from her.

Minutes passed. She stood there, watching them. Watching him.

Their shouts and whoops carried across to her, along with the excited shrieks of little children, and spatters of laughter from others. The sun beat down, making her head hot, causing sweat to trickle slowly down her back. She gathered her hair and swept it over a shoulder. She was overdressed in a long-sleeved T-shirt and jeans. She felt like an outsider, looking on from the sidelines while everyone else had fun.

After a few more minutes she turned and walked away, the sounds of merriment following her.

Susan

'RING ME WHEN YOU LAND.'

'I will of course.'

'And don't stay away too long. London's only an hour from Kerry, and Gav can pick you up at the airport.'

'I know.'

'You might come for Christmas, you and Harry. Just a thought.'

Christmas. She couldn't imagine it in the July sunshine. Last Christmas Day the three of them had gone to a hotel for brunch with friends, an annual event that Luke tolerated and Susan enjoyed, and Harry had thrown up in the car on the way home, the start of a tummy bug that had resulted in them cancelling their dinner reservation at another hotel and eating smoked-salmon sandwiches by the fire as Harry, swaddled on the couch, watched *Elf* and ate nothing. This year, who knew where they'd be on Christmas Day?

It was almost half past noon. They stood by Susan's car, fifth in line to board the ferry, which was approaching. Harry kept a tight grip on the end of his mother's dress, a melting cone clutched in his other hand. Susan watched rivulets of ice-cream run over his fingers and drip onto the ground, narrowly missing his small canvas shoes. He always took an eternity with his food. She could have urged him to eat it faster but she said nothing. There were bigger things to worry about than sticky fingers.

'I'm sorry it's come to this,' Laura said. 'I'm sorry you're so sad. If it's any comfort, I don't doubt that he misses you.'

It's not what I want, he'd said. *Just remember it's your choice, not mine*, he'd said – and yet there had been no word from him, no call, no text, nothing at all in two weeks.

'He's a fool,' Laura said.

She couldn't deny it. And she was a bigger fool to love him, but she did.

'It's just—' Laura broke off.

Susan kept her eyes on Harry and said nothing. Don't ask me to ring him. Don't ask if he's rung.

'You know what he's like,' Laura said. 'You know how stubborn he is.'

'Of course I know that.'

'… I just hate the thought of you not being together any more. I – I don't think he'll cope, without you.'

Susan looked at her. 'Maybe he should have thought of that,' she said quietly, 'while he was pushing me away.'

Laura made no reply. The ferry arrived, its apron

running onto the slip. The familiar horn sounded, long and low, as cars on the deck started up and began to disembark. 'Finish your ice-cream, pet,' Susan said to Harry, and he handed the limp wafer wordlessly to her. She deposited it in a nearby metal bin and cleaned his hands with a wipe.

Laura's hug was tight. 'Sorry. I'm just concerned, for both of you. For the three of you. Look after yourself. Don't forget to ring when you land.'

'I won't.'

'Goodbye to my best little man,' she said to Harry, pressing her lips to his forehead. 'See you soon, sweetheart.'

They boarded the ferry, car wheels doing a double clank as they drove onto the apron. In her rear-view mirror Susan saw Laura walking back towards Walter's Place, to where Gavin and her children awaited.

Why couldn't *she* have found someone who would look at her the way Gavin looked at Laura? Why hadn't she met a man who would give her foot massages before she asked for them, and return from anywhere with chocolate for her, and always, always, put her first?

A rap on the window: she slid it down and paid the ferryman, and took her ticket. They were flying from Dublin so she could leave her car at her friend Trish's house. A car in a city the size of London, she suspected, would be more of a liability than an asset. She'd have to decide what to do with it at some stage, but for now it could stay in Dublin.

I'm sorry I won't be able to bring you to the airport, Trish had told her. *There's a meeting I can't miss at work* – but Susan was more than happy to drop the car keys through her friend's letterbox and take a taxi to the airport, with a driver who wouldn't ask how things were going, or wonder aloud whether Susan thought she and Luke would ever get back together.

The ferry got going. She turned in her seat to Harry.

'Hi sweetie,' she said.

'Hi,' he replied.

Her heart jumped.

His first word.

Had she imagined it?

'Hi,' she said again, hardly daring to breathe.

'Hi.'

He was speaking. He was communicating verbally with her. Laughter bubbled out of her. An answering beam lit his face. She clapped her hands: his miniature palms patted lightly together. Her little mirror image.

'Hi!'

'Hi!'

She made a game of it, ducking out of sight, popping up with another 'Hi!' Each of his responses, accompanied now with a gurgle of laughter, added to her delight. Back and forth they went, mother to child to mother to child. Somewhere in the middle of the bay he yawned and ran out of steam, and the game was over.

She took her phone from her bag. She had to tell Luke. She had to ring him now, before she could think too much about it, and decide it wasn't a good idea. She pressed his number and listened to the ringing tone. A quarter to one, her watch told her: he'd be having lunch, if he still did things the way they'd always done them. She imagined him reaching for the phone. He'd pick it up and see her name on his screen. He'd know it was her.

The rings stopped. She waited for him to speak, suddenly nervous, already regretting her impulse – but instead she heard a click. *Luke Potter*, his recorded voice said crisply. *Leave a message*. She disconnected – this wasn't something for an answering machine – and looked again at Harry, and saw that his eyes had closed.

Missed call, his phone would tell him, in the event that he really had missed it. He'd check to see who'd tried to contact him, and her name would pop up.

She didn't think he'd ring her back.

In a little under six hours, she and Harry would be on the plane to London. She'd debated giving herself enough time to fit in a return visit to the house to collect more things, but in the end she hadn't been able to face it, afraid of what seeing him again might do to her. She'd get someone, one of their mutual friends, to call. She might ask Denise, who was calm and steady, who'd be good in a tricky situation. Susan would give her a list, and tell her where to find things. She wouldn't look for anything they'd shared, anything they'd bought together – what would any of that do but remind her of what she'd lost?

She'd have to let him know before she sent someone to the house. He never responded to callers if he could help it. Not a problem when she'd been there, but now she'd need him to let in whoever it was, to open the gate and allow access. She'd text him, and keep it short. She'd say what had to be said, and no more.

She sat in her car as the ferry sailed on, trying to rekindle her euphoria over Harry's milestone, but it would appear, for the moment at least, that that was lost to her too.

Laura

JUST CHECKING IN, SHE TEXTED. *HOW ARE things? Give a shout if you'd like to meet up for a chat* – and within seconds, *I'm fine* floated back. Just that, nothing more. She'd dumped her pregnancy at Laura's door, she'd lumbered Laura with her secret – and ever since then, she appeared bent on shutting Laura out.

It wouldn't do. Her lack of communication, her non-committal responses to each of Laura's texts, was only causing the suspicions in Laura's head to grow stronger, and she'd had enough. There was nothing for it, she decided, but to drop by the apartment above the crèche and have it out with Eve, and get to the truth of it. She'd do it today, just as soon as she could escape.

The breakfasts were served, the rooms cleaned, the laundry bundled into the washing-machine. Guests paid up and left; Gavin arrived home from his vegetable deliveries. The boys had scampered off earlier, their morning chores dealt with. Poppy was put up for her nap, Evie and Marian settled in the orchard with their dolls and their tea sets, within earshot of the open kitchen window.

Charlie the dog was pottering nearby, cocking a leg at apple-tree trunks and nosing among the windfalls scattered around what they all called the magic tree, well accustomed by now to its multiple crops each year. Up the field, chickens scratched and clucked in the coop; in his adjacent sty, Caesar the pig finished off the breakfast leftovers.

George the donkey stood inside the five-bar gate, waiting for Michael Brown from the neighbouring farm, who came by without fail each morning with an old clothes brush for the shaggy coat, and half a carrot in the pocket of his jacket.

In the kitchen Gavin spooned coffee into three mugs while Laura grated beetroot and apples for a lunchtime salad, and Tilly filed and polished her nails.

'Cathy and Leo have a new grandchild,' Gavin told them. He always came back with some bit of news after his rounds.

'Oh, it's arrived. Boy or girl?'

'Boy.'

'Any name?'

'Not yet, not that they've been told. Annie Byrnes had a fieldmouse in her kitchen yesterday. Hopped out of the log basket at her.'

'Lord, poor Annie. She must have lost her reason.'

Lunchtime came. Children were assembled. Ben and Seamus reappeared, clamouring for food. When everyone had been fed and the boys had gone out to set up for the donkey rides, Tilly cleared the table and then vanished. Laura eyed the stack of washing-up and decided to trust that someone else would look after it. 'Gav, will you hold the fort here for a bit? I want to head out for a cycle.'

'Sure. Who are we expecting?'

'A couple and a trio, but nobody's due for another few hours. I won't be that long.'

'Take your time,' he said. 'No rush.'

She hugged him. 'See, this is why I stay with you.'

The day was another fine one. Such a run of sunshine they were getting, lovely how it put everyone in good humour. Lapping it up they were, turning their faces to the sky so they could soak it in.

Cycling through the village on the faithful old bike that had travelled with her from Dublin, Laura passed groups of brightly dressed foreign teens – on a day trip from Tralee or Killarney, more than likely, where lots of them spent a summer month learning English. Jostling each other, calling out to one another, full of youth and laughter and bravado, males and females pretending not to eye each other up. What was that song about the boys watching the girls and the girls watching the boys? Same the world over, everyone looking for someone.

At the far end of the street she turned left and cycled the hundred yards or so to the crèche, located at the rear of the community hall. A familiar place for her, a busy spot every time she'd dropped or collected the girls, children and parents milling around, Eve in the middle of them – but today it was remarkably quiet, given its proximity to the bustling village.

Wouldn't fancy it, Laura thought, living alone in such a secluded place. Peace and quiet were all very well, many times she craved it, but she'd go dotty in this absolute stillness, this constant, almost eerie silence. Not good for Eve, she thought, especially not now.

No garden to speak of either, the car park on one side and a little play area for the kiddies on the other, bordered by a wooden fence, with sandpit, swings and a slide. A small patch of green beyond it for them to run around in but no flowers anywhere, no shrubs or trees. Eve's predecessor had always filled a hanging basket in the spring and hung it on the fence, but Eve hadn't kept up the practice. Shame.

She lifted the door knocker and let it drop with a thump. She waited, and when nothing happened she did it again. With still no response, she stepped back and regarded the two sash windows overhead. One was open, three or four inches of sunshine getting in.

'Are you there, Eve? It's Laura.'

No sound, no sign of her. Laura took her phone from her pocket and placed a call, but it went straight to voicemail. *It's me*, she said when the beep sounded. *Just popped around for a chat. Sorry I missed you. Give me a call, really would like to check in with you.*

What now? She mounted her bicycle, undecided.

She could cycle by Imelda's house, five minutes further on: she might meet Eve on the road. Might as well, now that she'd come this far – but her trip proved fruitless, with no sighting of the girl. Mightn't be spending as much time there these days, with the secret she couldn't reveal.

She cycled on, deciding to return home by a circuitous route that bypassed the village. Such a pleasant day to be out and about; pity to cut it short.

On one of the back roads she approached the tiny Church of Ireland cemetery, filled mostly with Thompsons, Walter being the last of them to be laid there six years earlier. Hard to believe he was gone that long. All the changes since then.

She drew to a halt and dismounted. She propped the bike against the cemetery gate and walked in. There was a different quality to the silence here. It was, she decided, the benign silence of good, decent souls at rest. She stood before Walter's grave and remembered him.

'You've got an Italian doppelgänger,' she told him. 'He's staying here on Roone, painting the sea. He doesn't look particularly like you, but he has your way about him. I think you'd have got on.'

Back on the coast road she pulled into the verge to allow a large camper van to pass her by, a French sticker on its rear. She stood for a few moments to watch the sea, visible across a field to her left, and sparkling in today's sunshine. The immensity, the glory of it. She didn't think she'd ever again be able to live in a place without a sea view from at least one window.

She pedalled on, past a family group with a double buggy – heading for the donkey rides, hopefully – and a trio of teenage girls in frighteningly skimpy shorts, and a stern-looking couple with a pair of terriers on leads. She passed an elderly and very upright woman in a beautiful pale pink summer coat who reminded her of Nell's elegant mother-in-law. 'Fabulous day,' she called as Laura cycled past, and Laura agreed that it was.

Back home, she leant her bicycle against an apple tree. The rides were in full swing, with a healthy number of waiting children. Good old George, still earning his keep, for however long it lasted.

In the kitchen Gavin was shelling peas into a bowl with Poppy on his lap, helping herself. Evie and Marian were decorating one another's faces with the paint sticks that Nell had given them for their birthday.

'Such beautiful ladies,' Laura said. 'Maybe you could do Dad next.'

Gavin didn't return her grin. The look on his face drew her closer. 'What's up?' she asked quietly.

'Someone went over the cliff,' he murmured. 'I just got a call from James.'

And even as her heart constricted with fear at the news, even as her mother's brain was instinctively establishing her children's whereabouts – *girls here, boys outside* – she was reminded of the darkness that had passed through her a week earlier. The advance notice of some terrible badness, and now it had arrived.

And she knew it was Eve. Eve had gone over the cliff.

Imelda

IT WAS GUALTIERO WHO'D RAISED THE alarm. Abandoning everything – his easel, his canvas, his folding table, his paints, his green suitcase – to scramble from the rocks to the road and flag down a car, to communicate somehow in his inadequate English, in his profoundly shocked state, the awful plunge into the sea that he'd witnessed.

The small coastguard station at the north of the island had been quickly alerted: within minutes a lifeboat had been dispatched to the area. The news was relayed to local fishermen, who'd turned their trawlers in the same direction. As word had spread further, various other craft had begun to appear. Before long the sea was alive with activity, everyone searching, all bent on the same terrible task.

'Try to drink this,' Imelda said, placing the glass in his unsteady hands. 'It will help.'

His teeth beat a tattoo against the rim. Some of the liquid spilt on his white shirt, more splashed onto the table. She doubted that he got any at all into him before he lowered the glass. 'Sorry,' he said.

'Please don't apologise, Gualtiero.'

She wondered if he was in the kind of shock you shouldn't ignore. Did he need something stronger than brandy? Should she call Dr Jack? Hugh would have known what to do – he'd always been good in a crisis. She tended to go to pieces but that wasn't an option here, not with one of them already on the verge of falling apart.

'Would you like me to get the doctor?' she asked.

'No, no doctor, I am OK. Thank you, Eemelda. *Grazie.*'

He didn't look OK. He looked far from OK, his face still registering the awfulness of what he had witnessed. The vitality drained from it, his pupils huge, his shoulders hunched. Such a land she'd got when he and Sergeant Fox had shown up on the doorstep, the sergeant towering over him, his grip tight on Gualtiero's elbow.

Saw someone go over the cliff, he'd told Imelda. *Gave him a fair old fright.*

Saw someone go over the cliff, saw someone drop into the water pretty much right in front of him. She couldn't imagine how horrifying that sight would have been for anyone, let alone someone whose wife had been taken by the sea.

'Try some more brandy,' she urged, and he raised the glass to his lips for the second time, and managed a little better.

'I do not 'elp,' he said eventually, when he became steadier, when the life began to creep back into his face. 'I just go, very fast, with no 'elp' – and she saw the awful guilt taking over, now that the shock was receding.

'There was nothing you could have done,' she assured him. 'It would have been far too dangerous to go into the water there; you would have been risking your own life if you'd tried. It was better to do what you did, to go for help.' She saw how little difference her words were making. He might have saved a life, but instead he'd run away: that was all he could focus on.

Her phone rang, startling her, startling both of them. She saw Nell's name on the screen.

'How is he?' she asked. 'I heard he was there.'

As always, it had taken no time for word to get around. Imelda walked into the hall, pulling the kitchen door closed behind her. 'He was painting at the bottom of the cliff: it sounds like he was very close to where the poor creature went in. He's very shaken, but he doesn't want me to get the doctor. I've given him brandy.'

'If he's able to say no to the doctor he's probably OK. How are you? Do you want me to come around?'

It was Monday, her day off. 'Thanks Nell, but it's not necessary. Is there any further news? Have they found … anything?'

'Not that I've heard. I'll let you know.'

'Please do – and Nell, he left all his paints and things behind him. I wonder – could someone possibly collect them for him?'

'I'll sort it,' Nell promised. 'Tell him not to worry. Would you like to bring him over for dinner later?'

'Dinner?'

'I'd really like to meet him; Laura says he's lovely. Or tomorrow night would be good, if he's not up to tonight.'

Dinner at Nell's. The two of them driving there in Imelda's car, being observed by whoever they passed. She imagined the nudges, the whispers that would fly about: *Imelda Fitzpatrick driving around with a man, Hugh not three months in the grave.*

'I'm – not sure,' she said. 'Maybe we could leave it off for the moment, Nell.'

'Of course, whatever you think. Ring if you change your mind.'

She installed him in the sitting room with a cup of sweet tea and two biscuits on the saucer, and a rug across his knees although the day was warm. In the two weeks he'd spent in the house he hadn't once taken up her invitation to use the sitting room, opting instead to go directly upstairs following the short stroll he took each evening after dinner. Now she showed him the TV remote control, although she doubted he'd use it. 'I'll be in the kitchen if you need me.'

'Thank you, Eemelda. I am much trouble for you.'

'Not in the least, please don't think that. Try to drink the tea.'

The kitchen had never been cleaner. Each time he washed up after a meal he scrubbed the draining board and all around the sink. All her glasses shone – she suspected he cleaned things he hadn't used at all. The cutlery tray in the drawer had definitely been rinsed out, the fridge shelves wiped down. For the first time that she could remember, the wall tiles around the cooker were free of food stains. There wasn't a crumb to be seen on the worktops.

The floor was equally spotless: the mop that she pressed into service once or twice a week was now being used faithfully every night. Ingrained in him, she supposed, with his restaurant. She wasn't sure whether to be embarrassed that he was showing her up, or pleased with her pristine kitchen.

She fed Scooter, who was standing pointedly by her empty bowl. She turned on the radio and tuned it to a local station that she hardly ever listened to. When the news came on, it was the main item: a clifftop tumble shortly before noon on the island of Roone; lifeboats and trawlers, pleasure craft and a helicopter combing the area.

They featured a comment from Sergeant Fox. Everything possible being done, he said. No developments yet, everyone hoping for a positive outcome – but at this stage, hours later, it would take a miracle, she thought, for someone to be brought alive from the sea. The rough waves at that exposed end of the island were very different from the placid waters that washed in from the bay on the other side, where most of Roone's beaches were located.

Who could it be? Gualtiero's split-second sighting

hadn't been enough for him to make out the gender, or to know whether it was a child or an adult. She prayed for it to be nobody she knew. Let it be an unfortunate stranger who'd wandered too close to the edge, not realising the danger.

No, they must have realised. To get to the cliff edge they'd have had to climb the safety fence. Relishing the risk then, maybe, showing off for the benefit of others – but she dismissed that notion too. Witnesses would have come forward if they'd been at the top of the cliff; they'd have raised the alarm like Gualtiero had, but he seemed to have been the only one who'd seen anything.

So maybe there had been nobody to impress. Maybe the person had gone there alone, on a final journey. Oh, horrible, horrible thought. Walking to the edge of the cliff and not pulling back. Stepping off, dropping into the void, wanting only to put an end to a life they could no longer cope with.

A few had done it over the years, Nell had told her, but never an islander. Those born on Roone, she'd said, grew up with a respect for and an affinity with the water: it would never have been considered as a means to end it all. But there had been tortured souls from elsewhere who'd seen it as their escape route, who'd travelled to the island with no intention of leaving it alive.

Every effort was made to ensure safety at the cliffs. The fence was diligently inspected at regular intervals, and reinforced when necessary. Notices were up all over the place, warning of the dangers and forbidding trespass. Roone children were raised with threats of dire consequences if they were found anywhere near the cliffs. Accidents could be avoided – but if someone was desperate enough, they found a way.

She left the kitchen and went out to the garden. Scooter was nosing now at something under the bay shrub: at the sound of Imelda's approach, she lifted her head and pattered towards her, tail wagging. Imelda knelt and embraced her, and rested her head against the comfort of the animal's warm flank. She'd never been a dog-lover until Scooter had become part of the household, and found her way into all their hearts.

Kneeling on the grass, she recalled her own suicidal imaginings in the first unbearable days after Hugh's death. Driven nearly out of her mind with grief and shock, she couldn't say she hadn't considered the notion of following him. But that was as far as it had gone. The knowledge of the sadness she'd cause in turn for her sister and Vernon, and Hugh's family and friends who'd welcomed her to Roone, had brought her to her senses. The grief she'd be passing on to them had stopped her travelling any further down that horrendous path.

Anyway, when it came down to it, she doubted that she'd have had the courage.

She rose to her feet. She picked a dozen anemones,

pink and purple and scarlet, that Hugh had planted in the autumn. Back in the kitchen she arranged them in a small glass vase. She'd give them to Gualtiero when he emerged, and tell him to put them in his room.

And just under an hour later, while James was packing the paints and other materials into the green suitcase, while the islanders were waiting and hoping and praying, some at the scene, others in the church, or sitting silently at the bar of Fitz's pub, or huddled around radios in one another's houses, Willie Buckley, lobster fisherman, scouring the water from the deck of his boat, lifted an arm suddenly and shouted, 'Over here!'

Tilly

'I HOPE THEY CATCH THEM,' THE WOMAN IN the green skirt said. 'They should be strung up, giving us all the fright of our lives.'

'Strung up is right,' her companion in the yellow cardigan agreed, shopping basket tucked between arm and waist. 'Jail is too good for them.'

'I'd say it was those Spanish youngsters – did you see the gang of them on the street a while back? Nearly knocked me over with their pushing and shoving.'

'And that poor man who saw it, Imelda's uncle. I heard he was so shook they had to give him oxygen. It could have killed him if he had a dicky heart.'

'He's Imelda's uncle? I thought he was a foreigner. Was he here for Hugh's funeral? I don't remember him.'

The man ahead of them in the queue turned around. 'He's not her uncle. She's just putting him up for a while. He's from Russia, or Bulgaria, somewhere over that side anyway. He was stuck for a place, and she took him in.'

Both women digested this information in silence while Tilly, positioned directly behind them, wondered how much longer it would take to check out the few items Laura had asked her to pick up on her way home. In the meantime she was doing her best not to look as if she was paying the conversation any attention at all, let alone storing it up to replay for Laura and Andy later.

'He's a class of a painter anyway,' the green-skirted woman resumed. 'You've seen him around the place, Annie.'

'Would he be the low-sized stocky fellow with a straw hat?'

'That's the one. He was on the rocks above the beach the other morning when we were doing our walk. I thought he had a look of Walter Thompson about him.'

'Walter? He doesn't look one bit like him.'

'No, I know he doesn't, but there's something in him that puts me in mind of Walter all the same.'

'Maybe it's the hat.'

'The hat? I never in my life saw Walter Thompson in a straw hat.'

Her companion gave an impatient cluck. 'I *know* that. I'm just saying this fellow wears a hat too.'

The queue inched forward. Roone's only supermarket struggled to cope with the increased traffic to its premises during the summer months. The woman in the yellow cardigan shifted her weight and moved her basket from one side to the other. 'Well, I hope the sergeant finds out who did it anyway. Those boyos should be taught a lesson.'

'True for you, Annie.'

A scarecrow it had been, not a person, that had tumbled over the cliff edge the day before. Taken that morning, or possibly the previous evening, from Michael Brown's strawberry patch. Flung from the top of the cliffs to spin and somersault its way down, and land with a splash just a short distance from where Imelda's unfortunate guest had been painting.

An investigation was under way but realistically, the chance of finding the culprit, or culprits, was slim. With the island as full as it was, people coming and going daily on the ferry, there were so many opportunities for someone to enter the field at the rear of Michael's farmhouse and uproot the scarecrow.

A cruel trick though, to throw it off the cliff – and a dangerous one. A missed step, an imbalance during the throw, and the scarecrow might not have been alone in its tumble.

Tilly eventually reached the top of the queue, and her groceries were checked out in silence by the young girl at the till. She left the supermarket and headed for Walter's Place, swinging her bag. Normally she and Andy walked back together after he shut the ice-cream van – living next door to him had its advantages – but today she'd told him to go ahead, not wanting to delay him before his evening shift at Fitz's.

As she passed the hotel she saw the flapping bunting and remembered the upcoming birthday party there. It had seemed comfortably distant when

Andy had told her about it on her arrival in Ireland, but it was now just a week away. The days were flying past, just ten more till she flew home. Ten more days of trying to swallow her disappointment that she was not going to be anyone's fiancée, not this summer. Ten more days of trying to convince herself that it wasn't the end of the world.

The stop-off at the supermarket had made her late for dinner: by the time she reached Walter's Place her stomach was rumbling.

But there was no dinner, and no Laura, and no girls or Gavin. Ben and Seamus sat across from one another at the table, paler than usual, their freckles standing out starkly.

'Poppy fell down the stairs,' Ben said.

Tilly looked at him in alarm. 'What? Is she OK?'

'They brought her to the clinic. Mum and Dad brought her.'

'Where are Evie and Marian?'

'At Nell's house. Mum said we had to wait here for you.'

She set her groceries on the table and found her phone. She dialled Laura's number, but it was Gavin who answered.

'She broke her arm,' he told her, sounding frighteningly sombre. 'She's getting a cast on it now. Other than that, she's OK. Bit of bruising, but otherwise alright.'

'Thank God. How did it happen?'

'Not sure. Laura was tidying the boys' room, and

Poppy was with her, but she just ... got away from her.'

Poppy, the youngest of the five, the child who'd been born while Laura was undergoing treatment for breast cancer. Turning three in ten days, the same day that Tilly was to leave. Rushing about, like all little children, whenever she got the chance. *Down the stairs on your bottom*, Laura was constantly saying to her, but still she'd fallen.

'How's Laura?'

'She's ... OK.'

But Tilly could imagine her distress, so protective of all her kids. Beating herself up now, no doubt, for having taken her eyes off the child for a second. 'How long more do you think you'll be?'

'Not long, I'd say. Are the boys with you?'

'Yes. I'll collect the girls from Nell's and feed them.'

'Thanks, Tilly. See you soon.'

She hung up and turned to the twins. 'She'll be OK,' she said. 'She broke her arm, which is nasty, but it can be fixed. They'll be home soon.'

They looked unconvinced. Their freckles still looked darker than they should. Ben nibbled at a nail; Seamus's hands were clenched into fists on the table. A pair of softies. Underneath that big-boy bravado they were still children, not turning twelve till November.

'Did the new people arrive?'

'Yeah. Mum was here.'

Tilly wondered if any of the guests had witnessed

the fall, or its aftermath. 'Will you two go and get the girls then, and I'll do dinner?'

But the girls, when they appeared, had already been fed by Nell, who sent a dish of macaroni cheese back for the others. While the boys ate, Tilly put Evie and Marian to bed, fielding worried enquiries about their little sister.

'Her arm got broken,' she told them, 'so she's getting a special bandage on it to make it better.'

They weren't satisfied.

'Did it break *off*?'

'Did it smash in pieces?'

'How will she hold Rabbity?'

Rabbity, the tatty, adored toy rabbit that Poppy was never without. 'She can hold things with her other hand,' Tilly said, 'until the broken arm gets better. That's why we have two arms,' she added, in a burst of inspiration, 'in case one gets broken.'

They digested this. 'The old man only had one arm,' Marian said.

'What old man?'

'In Nell's house. But he died.'

Tilly puzzled it out. They were referring to Hugh, whom they would have encountered in his niece Nell's house. Hugh, who at fifty-something would have seemed old to them. Hugh, whose right arm had ended at the elbow, thanks to the thalidomide drug his pregnant mother had been prescribed for her morning sickness.

'That was different,' Tilly said, wondering how

to explain further, but thankfully they didn't pursue it. There were more questions about Poppy's status that involved hugging, and clapping, and scratching itches that couldn't be reached with the working hand. There were stories of their own mishaps, plenty of them, until finally they grew silent, and slept.

Tilly returned to the kitchen and took rashers and sausages from the big freezer for the guest breakfasts, and checked that the tables in the dining room were ready for the morning. *You heard what happened*, she texted Andy. *I won't be going to the pub tonight.* His response was immediate: *See you in a bit. Nell's making scones for Laura, I'll drop them over.*

The others returned as she and the boys were washing up. Poppy, a red bloom on one cheek, her small right arm bound from above the elbow to wrist in a pale pink cast, was asleep against her father's shoulder. Her mother was white-faced and grim.

'My fault,' she said, as Tilly had known she would. It was later, and they were alone in the kitchen. Gavin had brought Poppy upstairs; the boys were in the sitting room. 'It was my fault. I didn't keep an eye on her.'

'Laura, don't say that. It's impossible to watch small kiddies all the time. I remember when Robbie and Jemima were that age – they were always falling and bumping themselves. Ma used to say she needed eyes in the back of her head.' But she could see Laura took no comfort from it. She could see her go right on hating herself.

'Won't you try and eat something?' she asked.

'We'll need help tomorrow morning,' Laura said
– had she even heard the question? 'I want to stay in
bed with Poppy. I know it's not necessary but I want
to, just for one morning. We'll have to find someone
to give you a hand.'

'I can do it,' Tilly said. 'The boys will help' – but
again Laura pursued her own train of thought.

'We could ask Eve – she's done it before. Can you
call her? I haven't got the energy. Her number's in
my phone.'

Eve, of all people. Tilly's heart sank – but this was
no time to be awkward. She found the number and
called it. It was answered on the fourth ring, just as
she was beginning to hope it wouldn't.

'Laura.'

'It's not Laura, it's Tilly.'

Silence.

'Look,' Tilly said, 'there's been— Poppy fell down
the stairs, and we need someone to help out here
tomorrow morning. It would—'

'Is she OK?'

'She will be. She's got a broken arm and some
bruising to her face.'

More silence.

'It would only be for about an hour and a half. Just
to get the breakfasts cooked and served.'

'What time?'

'Around eight?'

'I'm working in the hotel. I start at nine.'

'Oh ...' First Tilly had heard of it, but the news came as a relief. 'Right, no worries. I'll tell Laura.'

'No, hang on – I'll see if I can go in a bit later. I'll call you back.' There was a click, and she was gone.

Tilly reported the conversation to Laura, who groaned. 'I forgot about the hotel.'

'She's ringing them. She'll call back.'

She did, not five minutes later. Laura took the call, and Tilly heard, 'You're a doll,' and 'I really appreciate it,' and it looked like she and Eve were going to be thrown together for over an hour.

They'd be busy. Breakfasts were always hectic; there wouldn't be time for awkwardness.

'How's the patient?' Andy asked later, calling by with warm scones.

'She'll live.' It was past nine, and Tilly was alone in the kitchen. The boys, unusually, had gone to bed without being asked. Gavin was watching the news in the sitting room, and Laura was upstairs with Poppy, who shared her parents' bedroom when Tilly was about.

She piled the scones onto a plate and covered it with a clean tea towel. 'You off to the pub now?'

'Yup. You need help in the morning? I could swing by.'

Of course he could: why hadn't they thought of him? 'Eve is coming,' she told him. 'Laura got me to call her.'

'Right,' he said, crossing to the dresser, taking a glass from it. 'You're sorted so.'

'She's working in the hotel,' Tilly said. 'Did you know that?'

He filled the glass at the sink and drank until it was empty. She waited, but he made no response.

'Andy?'

'Hmm?'

'Did you know Eve got a job in the hotel?'

'Nope.' He rinsed the glass and set it to drain. He took his time.

'Andy,' she said again, and stopped, not able to put words on what she wanted to ask him.

He took Nell's basket from the table. 'Better go – I'm late already. Nell's going to ring Laura in a while, when Tommy's in bed.' He put an arm around her and kissed her mouth lightly. 'See you tomorrow, sleep well.'

He left through the scullery, the way he'd come in. She stood listening to the sound of his departing steps.

She was imagining things. She was being paranoid. He had nothing to hide. She trusted him absolutely.

But he'd sure moved awfully fast once Eve's name had been mentioned.

Her phone rang. The number was unfamiliar.

'Hello?'

'Is that – Tilly?'

A woman's voice. Soft, hesitant. She tried to place it, and couldn't. 'Yes.'

'It's Imelda – Hugh's … I was married to Hugh, Nell's uncle.'

Imelda, now a widow. Tilly had seen no sign of her during her time on the island. 'Sorry for your loss,' she said, the cliché coming unbidden, sounding terribly trite to her.

'Thank you ... I got your number from Nell – she told me what happened to Poppy. I'm just ringing to know how she is, and if I can help in any way. I didn't want to disturb Laura.'

Tilly filled her in and thanked her for the call, and told her they were all sorted. Another person who could have stepped in instead of Eve. She hung up and made out a shopping list for Gavin and brought it into the sitting room, where she found him switching off the telly.

'I'm going for an early night,' he told her. 'I'm bushed. What's happening in the morning?'

She told him Eve was lined up to come at eight.

'Right. I can give you a hand till she gets here.'

'Thanks Gavin. Sleep well.'

Left alone, she flicked through the channels and found a just-begun episode of *Friends* that she'd seen more than once. She left it on, wanting the comfort of its familiarity. When it was over, she switched off the TV and wandered about the room, running a finger along the spines of the books on the shelves. Dickens and Hardy and Brontë, she read, and other names that were unknown to her. She brought her face close to them and breathed in their rich old smell. Here since the previous owner's time, Laura had told her. She and Gavin still referred to them as Walter's books.

His portrait hung in the hall, painted after his death by Nell's husband James, given as a housewarming present to Laura and Gavin when they'd moved in. Tilly had imagined she'd seen him, shortly after she'd come to the house for the first time. She'd looked out of an upstairs window and there he'd been, standing among the chickens in the coop. He'd glanced up and lifted his hat to her, and then walked out of the coop and vanished.

Except, of course, that it hadn't happened, because he'd died a few years before. Funny, the tricks the mind could play.

She tidied the magazines on the coffee table, and plucked a sock from beneath it. In the kitchen she stole one of Nell's scones and ate it with butter and blackberry jam, listening to Charlie's sleeping breaths and the steady tick of the wall clock. Eventually, having run out of things to do, she climbed the stairs and went to bed, setting her phone to wake her at a quarter to seven.

Eve

SHE WAS DEEPLY UNCOMFORTABLE: THAT much was plain. She could hardly look Eve in the eye. 'Three guests have already eaten,' she said, peeling rashers apart, laying them on a pan, 'so we have just eleven to go.'

She wore one of Laura's aprons over grey trousers and a navy top. Her hair was pulled into a short ponytail, her face free of makeup apart from pink lip gloss. She looked about sixteen.

'What do you want me to do?' Eve asked. It felt weird, just the two of them.

'Can you make porridge? I need two bowls. Laura does it in the microwave.'

'I know how she does it.' Stating a fact, not meaning anything by it, but Tilly's cheeks went pink all the same. Such a sensitive soul.

When the phone call had come last evening, Eve had felt obliged to give what help she could. She'd been feeling guilty for all but ignoring Laura's recent texts, and for letting on not to be at home when Laura had called around a few days ago: here was something she could do to make up. Her boss at the hotel had been fine when she'd explained the situation. *Try to get here as close to ten as you can*, he'd said. *The others can cover for you. Please send my best wishes.*

'Is Poppy OK?' she asked.

'I think so. Laura just wants to stay with her. Poppy sleeps in their room when I'm here.'

Eve knew the house well from her time helping out. Gavin and Laura's corner room was bright and airy, with two windows that both gave splendid views of the sea. She wondered where Tilly slept when she stayed. She couldn't have her own room, not with the place full of guests. No chance for Andy to creep from the house next door and climb through a window.

It would be funny, she thought, if he appeared now and saw his ex and his girlfriend working together.

'Handy for you,' she said, taking porridge from the microwave, setting a new bowl in its place. 'Being next door to Andy, I mean.'

Tilly didn't respond, didn't turn from the cooker. Eve regarded her rear view, her slim-as-a-boy's figure, and wondered what he saw in her. She remembered looking out at his house when she was cleaning the rooms on that side. She remembered being almost sick with excitement, counting the minutes until it was time for him to come and pick her up.

They worked mainly in silence, Tilly ferrying dishes and pots to the dining room, asking on her return for toast, a refill of a coffee pot, sliced tomatoes, beaten eggs, grated cheese. Ben and Seamus materialised and took over the fetching and carrying, which lessened the tension a bit.

In due course Evie and Marian put in an appearance, still in pyjamas, feet bare.

'Hi Eve,' they chorused, rushing to hug their crèche teacher. Someone at least was glad to see her.

'Hello there,' she said, squatting to pull them into her. 'Are you having a lovely summer?'

'Poppy fell down the stairs,' Marian announced. 'Her arm got broke.'

'I know it did. Poor old Poppy. I'll sneak up and see her when we're finished.' Because she couldn't leave, she'd decided, without showing her face upstairs. She'd keep it brief: hopefully Laura would be too preoccupied to bring up the pregnancy, or probe any deeper into it.

'Can we have sausages?'

'You can when you're dressed,' Tilly replied, lifting an egg from the pan. 'Go back upstairs and put on your same clothes as yesterday, and your sandals. Hold the banister when you're coming down.'

Bossy. Trying to sound like their mother. Eve half hoped for a note of protest, but they turned obediently and left the room.

By half nine everyone was fed, and the dishwasher

loaded. Eve turned to Gavin, back from his rounds and eating leftover toast. 'OK if I go up to see Poppy before I leave?' No way was she asking Tilly's permission.

'Sure. Bring Laura up a coffee, would you?'

She looked wretched. The skin beneath her eyes was bluish. She looked like she hadn't slept a wink, which she probably hadn't. She sat on the end of Poppy's small bed, her back against the wall. Poppy sucked placidly on a soother, a ragged little rabbit beside her on the pillow. There was a dark blotch on her cheek, like someone had pressed hard against it for a while.

The sight of her arm in a cast reminded Eve of the time when Keith, not much older, had climbed through the kitchen window at home and cracked his elbow. Questions had been asked – Mam was out; a neighbour had brought him to the hospital – but miraculously, he and Eve hadn't been taken into care. That hadn't happened for another few years.

'Gav sent this,' Eve said, handing over the coffee.

'I don't want to leave her,' Laura said, cradling the mug. 'I don't want to take my eyes off her again. I'm terrified.'

'You're her mother,' Eve said. 'It's to be expected.' Because most people had mothers who cared. 'But she's OK, isn't she?'

'She has a broken arm,' Laura replied, a little tartly. 'I'd hardly call that OK.'

A beat passed. 'Well,' Eve said, 'I'd better –'

'Sorry,' Laura said. 'Don't mind me. I'm mad at myself, nobody else. Pull over that chair, sit for a minute,' and Eve obeyed, giving Poppy a bright smile. She didn't know the child well. She was booked into the crèche for September, which meant that Eve would have just two months with her.

'I can't stay long,' she said. 'I'm due at the hotel.'

'Thanks for pitching in at such short notice. I forgot you were working there. How's it going?'

'It's alright, not too bad.' Susan must have told her, or someone else. News got around Roone, one way or another.

Another moment of silence. Eve heard the small sucking sounds that Poppy was making.

'And how are you feeling?'

Here we go, she thought. 'I'm OK. I'm fine.'

'Not queasy any more?'

'No.'

'And you're still keeping it?'

'I am.'

'You're quite sure it's what you want?'

'Yes ... Listen, I really should —'

'Eve,' Laura said, 'something's been bugging me.'

Eve curled her toes inside their shoes, instantly wary. 'What?'

'I don't think you've been completely honest with me.'

'What about?' But she knew what was coming. She sensed it. She should get out now, she should just get up and walk out, but she seemed rooted to the chair.

'About who the father is.'

There was no way she could know. No way. Fear crawled around in Eve's belly. 'I told you —'

'I know what you told me, but it doesn't add up. You're not the type to fall into bed with some stranger.'

'I was drunk, I *told* —'

'Really, Eve? Honestly? Is that really what happened? You met a man for the first time, and you got drunk and had sex with him?'

Her palms were damp. She pressed them to her thighs. 'Why do you find it so hard to believe? That kind of thing happens all the time.'

'Well, maybe not so much on Roone, but I take your point.' Laura looked down into her mug but didn't drink. 'I just, I don't know. It's not ringing true for me.'

Eve made no response. A voice inside her was screaming to get out, get out, but still she was unable to move.

Laura lifted her head. 'Won't you tell me who he is, Eve?'

'Don't ask,' she said, everything clenched so tightly inside her that she thought she might snap. 'It's better if you don't ask.'

'Are you protecting him? Is that it?'

Eve squeezed her hands into fists. She could feel

her face becoming hot. 'It's not that,' she said. 'Please stop asking about him. It's ... complicated.'

'Yes, you said that before. Eve, you don't have to do this alone. He needs to take responsibility.'

'He will. I'll let him know – I'm going to talk to him, but I have to— Look, I can't tell you, I just *can't*. You have to stop asking me.'

'So it's someone you know. It's someone on the island.'

Eve practically leapt to her feet, the sudden movement causing Poppy to start. 'I have to go, I'll be late.' She strode towards the door.

'I know who he is,' Laura said – and something in the words, something in the tone, *something* made Eve stop. She turned and stared.

She knew. She did know.

She'd guessed.

She couldn't have.

'Eve,' Laura said, steadily, quietly, 'he's with Tilly.'

Oh God. Oh God. Oh God. Eve felt the heat leave her face, felt a trembling in her legs. 'It's not him.' But even to her own ears, she didn't sound convincing.

'I think it is, Eve. I know it is.'

How? How could she have guessed? Had Eve let something slip in their conversation? Had she given it away?

'Look,' she said rapidly, 'it wasn't meant to happen, I swear to God. We didn't plan it, it just—' She broke off. She rubbed her face hard. 'I was drunk,' she said.

'That much is true. It was after Frog Hackett's party, his twenty-first. Look, I'd give anything to—' She stopped again. 'Please, Laura,' she said, 'don't say anything. Don't tell ... anyone. Please.'

Laura's face. So cold it had become. Looking at Eve as if she was a piece of dirt. 'You were drunk. Was he?'

'I – yes, he'd been drinking—'

'Was he drunk?'

'I don't know. He wasn't sober. Look, I have to go—'

'You must tell him,' Laura said.

Eve stopped again, her hand on the doorknob. 'I *will*. I've said I will. I'm waiting until Tilly leaves. Can't I wait till then? I'm trying to *protect* her – you must see that.'

'Protect her,' Laura repeated, and Eve heard how stupid it sounded. How ironic, or hypocritical, or whatever it was.

'Thank you for helping us out today,' Laura went on. Voice cold as stone. 'I'll get Gavin to drop over some money later.'

'I don't want money. I didn't do it for money.'

'I'd rather pay.'

She was angry. She was so angry. In her little bed Poppy sucked calmly on her soother, impervious, but Eve felt the anger leaking into the room, hanging between the clipped words. Colouring the silence.

'I'm sorry,' she said. 'I'm so sorry it happened, and I'm sorry I involved you. I shouldn't have.'

'No, you shouldn't,' Laura replied, in the same icy tone. 'You've put me in an impossible position. You're asking me to keep something from my sister, and from my best friend.'

'I know. I'm really sorry.'

'Tilly is crazy about him. This is going to break her heart. How could you have done it? How could you have been so cruel?'

'I keep *telling* you it wasn't deliberate. I wasn't trying to hurt anyone. And I'm not the only one to blame, it wasn't only me.'

'I'm well aware of that.'

Eve said nothing more. She could think of nothing else to say. She wished herself anywhere else but there in that room. She'd been a fool ever to open her mouth.

Laura lowered her mug to the floor. It was still practically full. She leant back and closed her eyes. 'I'm tired,' she said. 'I'd like you to leave.'

'You won't tell? Please don't tell, not yet.'

Laura made no response. When it became evident that none was coming, Eve left the room, closing the door quietly behind her. She made her way along the corridor and went downstairs, meeting nobody. She stood in the hall and listened to a burst of girlish squeals from the kitchen.

Laura wouldn't tell. She wouldn't want to upset Tilly or Nell. She'd leave it to Eve to do that.

She opened the front door as quietly as she could

and left the house – and with every step she took in the direction of the hotel, a chant beat like a drum inside her head.

What now?

What now?

What now?

Susan

IT WASN'T LONDON.

The city was every bit as vibrant and colourful and cosmopolitan as she remembered. It was the same melting pot of nationalities, bursting with culture and commerce and history and innovation. It was the same eccentric juxtaposition of ancient and modern, the same exotic and beautiful and dirty and characterful and edgy place as it had been on every one of her previous trips.

It wasn't London. It was her.

Each day she pushed Harry's buggy through crowded streets, weaving her way around sandwich boards and conversations and camera-toting tourists, past statues and fountains and galleries and mosques and museums, into little cafés and delis that sold alfalfa salads and tofu curries and falafels and wheatgrass shots.

In the week she'd been in London she'd emailed countless employment agencies and registered her details with them, and had been told that they'd be in touch if a suitable position presented itself. She'd signed up for an online computer course, and checked out a yoga studio close to Rosie and Ed's house, and called to three preschools in the locality to collect brochures and ask about their enrolment policies.

And some evenings, after Harry had fallen asleep, Rosie climbed the stairs and the two friends drank herbal tea or hot chocolate, and compared notes on what they knew about the continuing stories of girls they'd been to school with, and Rosie told Susan about her father's move to France with his second wife, ten years his senior, and about Ed's sister who owned a coffee plantation in Jamaica, and who'd flown the rest of their family – parents, brothers, in-laws, nieces – to Rosie and Ed's wedding, which had taken place in a Scottish castle.

And Luke Potter's name was never mentioned.

And in the middle of a city with over eight million inhabitants, Susan had never felt lonelier. It followed her around, the loneliness. It seeped into her days and ambushed her nights, and left her dispirited and fighting to stay positive. Ironic, given the loneliness she'd felt when she was with him, that she yearned for him now. But she'd left him, and she was here, and she was determined to stay here and give it every chance she could.

Rosie and Ed lived in a tall narrow red-brick terraced townhouse in Chelsea. The top floor – the house was three storey – comprised two fairly good-sized rooms, the front with two mismatched couches, an empty bookshelf set into an alcove, and a bay window; the rear, kitted out as a bedroom, overlooked a little paved courtyard. There was a small bathroom, with a shower but no bath, at the turn in the stairs.

You must use our kitchen, Rosie had said, but Susan had thanked her and declined, feeling that they were imposing enough as it was. She'd invested instead in a compact oven with two hob rings, an electric kettle and a miniature fridge, all of which she arranged on a trestle table that Ed had retrieved from the basement. By day she and Harry ate out, in one or other of the little cafés; in the evenings she cooked uncomplicated meals which they ate at a little folding table, scratched on top but otherwise sound, that she'd found in a nearby charity shop and positioned in the bay window.

Washing up involved filling the kettle at the bathroom sink and pouring the boiled water into a plastic basin. She tried not to think of her enormous Dublin kitchen, with every convenience and appliance and gadget she could possibly need, and several that she didn't.

But it wasn't all bad. Every day, Harry spoke a little more. There was still no chatter: his words were few and carefully chosen, but they were there. She was Mama, and yes was 'es'. No was still a shake of the head – but wonder of wonders, Toby, his beloved little blue elephant, was a perfect, precise Toby.

She helped him along. *Nose*, she would say, when she was showering him. *Eyes, mouth, ears*, touching each in turn with his small yellow sponge. He would listen silently – and later, when he was standing in his pyjamas at the window, or lying in bed after a story, she would hear them, or variations of them, echoed back. Softly, ruminatively. Trying them out. Getting a feel for them in his mouth.

He enchanted Rosie, who was on her second marriage, and whose two children were safely reared. *A man of few words is always good*, she said. *Nobody wants a chatterbox. Those eyes*, she said. *He'll break hearts with those eyes.*

Of course he would. He had his father's eyes.

Susan spoke often on the phone with Laura. The news of Poppy's tumble down the stairs had horrified her.

Do you need me? Do you want us to come back for a while? she'd asked, but she'd been assured that the patient was being pampered beyond all reason by everyone in the vicinity.

I'd rather hear your news, Laura told her. *What's happening?*

We're doing fine, Susan said, and told her about the tattooed, dreadlocked teen in the corner shop who gave Harry a solemn high-five whenever they called in, and Rosie's friend Claire who claimed to know half of London, and who'd promised to keep an eye out for a job for Susan, and the puppet show she and Harry had attended at a nearby theatre one rainy afternoon, and the little marmalade kitten that slept all day on a deckchair on the first-floor balcony of a house across the street. She pulled out the good things, and reported them.

Last evening, Laura had told her about Eve's pregnancy, and Andy's part in it. *I'm not breaking any promises*, she'd said. *You're not in a position to tell anyone, and I need to vent. I did tell Nell, before I knew it was Andy, and now I'm terrified I'll let it slip by accident that he's the father. I'm just so mad at them both. I can't stop thinking about Tilly, and what this will do to her – Nell and James too. I dread it, but it's got to come out eventually.*

The news of the pregnancy came as no surprise to Susan, having heard about it from Eve herself in the hotel garden – but the identity of the father did. She'd met Andy at Harry's christening on Roone, the summer before last. He'd struck her as a shy boy, with not a whole lot to say for himself, but Tilly, blushing and beaming, had seemed to have no complaints. Too bad if he'd been unfaithful to her – but that was the way of the world, wasn't it? Love wasn't to be trusted. Love let you down in all sorts of ways.

She finished the washing-up and emptied the water down the toilet, and flushed it away. She'd had Ed and Rosie to dinner, her first attempt at entertaining since their arrival in London. She'd bought a cooked chicken and accompanied it with roast potatoes and garden peas. For dessert she'd assembled a fruit salad. Where there was a will to thank friends for their kindness, there was usually a way.

She returned the crockery to the bookshelf, which

she'd pressed into service as a combination larder and dresser. The cutlery she stored on the shelf below, in the empty beans tin she'd rinsed and saved. The room still smelt of the drinks Ed had made for them after dinner, using some of his sister's excellent coffee and a bottle of Kahlúa they'd brought upstairs, and the remainder of the cream Susan had whipped for the fruit salad.

As she swept the wooden floor, her phone rang. She followed the sound and found it in the pocket of the jacket she'd hung on the back of the door. She pulled it out and saw Luke's name.

Her heart did a flip that was almost painful.

Something was wrong.

He was dead, and someone was using his phone to tell her.

She pressed the answer key – and found herself unable to speak. Seconds ticked by: she remained mute. A car passed in the street below. Her scalp prickled. Her face grew stiff with fear.

'Susan?'

His voice. Luke's voice. Luke, who wasn't dead.

'Yes.'

She heard his exhalation. 'Where are you?'

She hadn't been in touch with him since her missed call on the day they'd left Roone. She hadn't asked anyone yet to collect her things from the house. She'd wondered if she should text him her whereabouts as she'd promised, but she'd let the days pass by without doing it.

Three weeks since they'd spoken. Three weeks that seemed like decades to her.

'… London. We're in London.'

Another silence. She closed her eyes and pressed the phone to her ear and saw him, clear as anything. Hunched, frowning, stubbly, glasses halfway down his nose. The hair he'd woken up with, probably; he never thought to bother with a comb unless she reminded him. Paint-spotted shirt, trousers that sagged in the rear and bagged at the knee. Worn leather slippers.

'How is Harry?'

'He's fine. He's talking.'

'He's talking?'

'Yes. A little.'

Pause.

'Susan,' he said, 'will you come home? Will you both please come home?'

She squeezed her eyes more tightly shut, and gave no answer. Another car, more than one, sounded in the street. Somewhere, a door slammed. A siren became louder and then fainter.

'Will you?'

She shook her head. *I can't.* 'I can't,' she said. 'Not if you keep shutting me out.'

She heard a sound she couldn't identify. A rasp of his hand along his chin, or maybe a sharper, longer exhalation. 'Look,' he said, 'I'm no *good* at this, but—'

He broke off. She said nothing.

'I miss you,' he said. 'I *miss* you around the place. I want you to come home, both of you.'

It wasn't enough. She crossed the room and sat on the couch, and waited for more. He cleared his throat, she heard more muffled, jagged sounds – was he *crying*? She'd never known him to cry, ever.

And then there was a click that caused her to jump a little, and he was gone.

She set down her phone. She got to her feet and paced the floor. Four steps to the bay window, seven from there to the door, five across to the alcove and her makeshift kitchen, six back to the couch. Her world had shrunk to this. She'd come from him to this.

He missed her. He wanted her to come home.

It wasn't enough. He hadn't mentioned love. He'd made no promises.

She turned off the light and left the room, and went to the bedroom she shared with her son.

Laura

'HOW ARE YOU FEELING?' HE ASKED, TAKING her feet into his hands.

'I'm OK.'

She wasn't really. She was guilty and tired and preoccupied and fed up, and every time she saw Poppy's pink cast she wanted to scream at something, or someone.

Her youngest daughter's accident had shaken her. Every time she closed her eyes she lived through it again, the sudden heart-leap of fright as she heard the series of small thumps and slaps, and at the end of it, Poppy's wail. She'd raced from the boys' room and flown down the stairs to where Poppy lay, a tumbled little screeching bundle, her arm twisted terrifyingly beneath her. Thank God Gavin had been there.

She hardly remembered the drive to the clinic, Poppy roaring in her arms, and her own tears falling uncontrollably. Jack, when they'd pulled up outside the clinic, had probably not known which of them to treat first.

But life went on, and Poppy was bouncing back

the way children did, the cast seeming not to bother
her after the first day. In an effort to corral her for
a while, Laura had got Gavin to bring the playpen
out of storage. They'd parked it in its old spot in a
corner of the kitchen and Poppy had been installed in
it along with her many furry friends, and had giggled
at her sisters as they fed her raisins through the bars.
It wouldn't last, but it would give her mother some
peace of mind while it did.

Laura had also instructed Gavin to pay Eve for her
help. *Put twenty euro in an envelope and drop it through the
letterbox at the crèche next time you're out.*

That had surprised him. *I thought she was doing us a
favour.*

I asked her to come. We shouldn't take advantage. She
grudged every cent to that madam, but she wanted
no favours from her. The more she thought about it,
the angrier she became. How dare they? How dare
Eve make Laura her confidante, knowing full well the
pain she was going to inflict on Laura's sister when
the news got out? And how dare Andy do what he
had done, with Tilly's arrival just around the corner?

Tilly. Mooning around him like a calf, making
it obvious to everyone how she felt. He must have
seemed like something Heaven sent, after the
substitute teacher in Australia who'd taken advantage,
and then skedaddled without a backward glance
when his time was up, not knowing – nor caring, if
he *had* known – that he'd made her pregnant. This
new betrayal would destroy her.

'Do you want a cuppa, or a glass of wine?' Gavin asked.

She shook her head. It was late afternoon. Evie and Marian were playing next door. Tilly was selling ice-cream, Ben and Seamus were giving donkey rides in the field. Poppy had been released from the playpen and was now on the sitting room floor, building and knocking towers of wooden blocks. Laura was having her feet massaged by her husband, and wishing for the ability to turn back time so she could rewind it to two minutes before Poppy's fall.

Gavin worked his way along her soles, kneading with his thumbs. 'What'll we do for your birthday?'

Her thirty-second birthday, this day week. The last thing she wanted to think about. 'No party,' she said, although normally she adored one. Not up to it this year.

'What about a little dinner? Tilly and I could rustle up a menu.'

She thought about that, and decided it might work. A small quiet dinner party with lovely people could be just the lift she needed – although she and Tilly might handle the food. She was no great chef, but she was better than Gavin.

'I could ask that sweet Italian man, the one I told you about who's staying with Imelda.'

He shot her a look. 'Should I be worried?'

That drew a smile. 'He reminds me of Walter.'

'So you said. Who else?'

'Nell and James, Lelia and Pádraig. Imelda if she'll come.'

'And Tilly will want Andy.'

Of course she would. The thought of him sitting at her kitchen table made Laura want to call the thing off. 'I'd say he wouldn't be bothered.'

'He mightn't – but Tilly would want him.'

'He might have to work in Fitz's, fill in for James.'

Gavin pulled gently at each toe in turn. 'Has the young fellow annoyed you, by any chance?' Gav, who was normally immune to any kind of undercurrent. She mustn't make it so obvious.

'No, I just hope they're not getting too serious.'

He grinned. 'Hear you, Mother.'

'Well, I do feel responsible while she's here.'

Gavin deposited her feet on the couch. 'I should collect the two from next door: I'd say they might have outstayed their welcome.'

'Do.'

After he'd left, Laura sat on, relishing her rare night off from cooking dinner. 'Bring fish and chips when you're coming,' she'd said to Tilly. 'It's not often we treat ourselves.' And after dinner they were going to break into the Ben & Jerry's that was normally kept well hidden in the freezer for special occasions, because life was short, and you never knew what waited around the next corner.

She watched her little daughter, giggling delightedly as she sent yet another wooden tower crashing to the floor. She recalled the premonition that hadn't been about Eve after all. How quickly things could change. How abruptly lives could be transformed, for good or otherwise. Look at herself twelve years ago, a wife one day, a widow the next – and now it was Imelda's turn to have her happiness pulled away without warning, her turn to have to bear the unbearable.

For all Laura's current concerns, at least everyone was still alive – and Imelda, in all her grief, had phoned Tilly on the evening of the accident to see if there was anything she could do. Laura would call around to her sometime in the next few days, invite her and Italian Walter to the dinner party, bring her a box of eggs, or a little bar of soap from that pretty new craft shop across the street from Nell's salon. They didn't have to be bosom buddies, but a little kindness wouldn't go amiss.

Ten minutes later, as she was flicking through one of the magazines that Nell dropped in from time to time, the sitting room door opened.

'Hello,' she said. 'Are the rides finished?'

'Yeah.'

'How much did you make?'

'Thirty-six euro.'

'Not bad.' Three euro a ride, the price unchanged since they'd started up the business, the summer after their move to the island. A dozen customers on a sunny day wasn't great, but the sunshine sometimes acted against them and kept people on the beaches – and anyway poor old George could probably do with the break. They might think about cutting down his hours next summer, just do three days a week or something.

'Did you give the money to Dad?'

'Yeah.'

At the end of each season, the donkey-ride takings were divided in three. A third went into household expenses, another was set aside for a rainy day, and the rest was split between Ben and Seamus, who were saving up for a sailboat. Laura had googled *Boats for sale*, and was satisfied that they'd be at least twenty before they hit their target. Thanks to Nell's tuition they were strong swimmers, but still their mother quaked at the thought of them casting off and throwing themselves on the mercy of the capricious sea.

'Are the girls back?'

'No.'

Not surprising. Gavin would be chatting with James, the babysitter for the afternoon, while four small children wreaked their usual havoc. She hoped order would be restored before Nell got home from her day's work.

'So,' she said, 'anything else to report?'

Of course there was something else. They hadn't called in to enquire how she was, or to report on the donkey rides. She could read them like one of Nell's magazines, and they looked as guilty as sin. She prayed whatever confession she was about to hear wasn't serious. She'd had her fill of serious. Let it be a few broken eggs. Let it be something she could laugh off.

'We have something to tell you,' Seamus began.

'OK.'

'You're going to be cross,' Ben said.

She waited. The silence stretched. This was bigger than eggs.

'Tell me,' she said eventually – and out it all came in a rush, two voices butting into one another.

'We did it.'

'We threw the scarecrow off the cliff.'

'It was a joke. Jerry Malone bet us for a joke.'

'We thought it would just – we didn't know all the boats and stuff would come.'

The scarecrow.

The cliffs.

Dear God Almighty.

Laura took a long steadying breath. She set down her magazine and sat up straighter on the couch. She darted a glance at Poppy, who was curled on the floor now, babbling away to Rabbity and not paying them any heed at all. 'Let me get this right,' she said, keeping her voice even. 'You took the scarecrow from Michael Brown's field —'

'No, Jerry took it.'

She started again. 'Jerry took the scarecrow – he *stole* the scarecrow from Michael's field. Am I right so far? Did he steal it?'

Two shamefaced nods.

'And you two brought it to the cliffs – or did Jerry do that bit too?'

'All of us did.'

'We all did.'

They'd brought the scarecrow, which would probably have been awkward enough to transport, all the way to the cliffs. Somehow they'd avoided being seen – hid it in the ditch maybe, when they heard a car approach. Ducked out of sight when pedestrians or cyclists came into view. Then again, who'd have taken any notice of three boys carting an old scarecrow about?

'You brought it to the cliffs – and who threw it over?'

'Us two.'

A knot was forming in her chest, hard and tight. 'You two. Not Jerry.'

'No.'

'Don't mumble. So you climbed the safety fence.' Silence.

'Did you? Did you climb the safety fence?'

'Yes.'

'Yes.'

'Both of you climbed the safety fence, knowing that it was strictly forbidden ever to do that. *Ever*.'

Nothing.

'Am I right? Did you climb the safety fence, after being told thousands of times never, ever, to go near it?'

Two nods.

She tried not to see it in her mind's eye but there it was, clear as the sky on a fine day. Her sons on the cliff edge, inches from the void, manoeuvring the scarecrow over. One stumble, one crumbling piece of cliff, and they would have been lost to her for eternity.

'Did Jerry climb the fence?'

'No.'

'No. Of course he didn't. Jerry was sensible enough to send two clowns over instead.'

More silence. She looked at their woebegone faces, and didn't relent. 'So why are you telling me now?'

Seamus twitched a shoulder, darted a look at his sister on the floor. 'Cos … we think it's why Poppy fell down the stairs.'

It was unexpected. Poppy's head tipped up at the mention of her name. Laura frowned. 'What are you saying? You think it was some kind of … punishment for what you did?'

'Yeah,' Ben said. 'We did something bad, and then something bad happened to Poppy.'

Karma. Laura was reasonably certain that they didn't know the word, and here they were, blaming it for their sister's fall. And who was to say they were wrong? Who had the smallest idea how this convoluted universe worked?

'Well,' she said, 'it wasn't a very good punishment then, was it? Because a little girl was the one who got hurt, and she did nothing wrong.'

Seamus's chin began to wobble. 'We're sorry, Mum,' he said, his eyes filling.

'Yeah, we're really sorry, Mum. We didn't mean it. We didn't want her to get hurt.'

Both of them weeping now, tears rolling along

freckly cheeks. She'd have to talk to Gavin, who wasn't their father but who treated them like his sons. On the other hand, he was hopeless at disciplining them, urging leniency on Laura, whatever the offence. Gavin the pushover, the good cop to her bad.

No, she'd say nothing. He'd be no help. She'd tell him, but she'd wait until she'd dealt with it.

'You've done something very serious indeed,' she said, 'and very dangerous. You gave a terrible fright to that poor man who saw it. He could have had a heart attack – he could be dead now. And you two could have –'

She bit it off. Couldn't think it, couldn't say it.

'Listen,' she said. 'It's good that you're telling the truth now. I'm glad about that. But it doesn't excuse what you did. You're my oldest children, and you have three little sisters. Imagine if Evie and Marian knew it was you, and decided it sounded like fun, and wanted to do something like it. Imagine that.'

She stopped to let it sink in. She regarded them standing before her, scrubbing tears away, wiping wet fists on shorts. She took in the scabby knees, the ginger hair that never lay straight, the ears they hadn't quite grown into.

They were eleven. They were boys. Eleven-year-old boys got into trouble: it was part of their job description. Young boys were almost duty bound to cause their parents sleepless nights, and more than a few grey hairs. And eleven-year-old twins caused twice as much woe, so she was doubly cursed.

But occasionally, boys treated their mother to a pack of her favourite Maltesers on pocket-money day. And now and again they brought sheets in from the clothes line without being asked. And once in a while they could be persuaded to read bedtime stories to their sisters, so the adult readers would get a break.

And a few months earlier, on Valentine's Day, two boys had presented their mother with a bracelet made from colourful buttons that they'd strung onto elastic thread. It had snapped as Laura was taking it off that night: she'd gathered up the buttons and restrung them on a length of stouter elastic, and no one was any the wiser.

'I'll have to tell Sergeant Fox, because he's carrying out the investigation, and he needs to know so he can close the case. I'll ask him if he'll let you off, as it's your first offence. That's the best I can do.'

They'd already been punished, as guilt-laden as herself about Poppy's fall. And Tom Fox wouldn't be too hard on them. According to Nell, Tom's boy Alan, half a dozen years older than the twins, had caused his parents plenty of mortification growing up: skipping off from school, robbing orchards, moving early-morning milk bottles from one doorstep to another, borrowing the odd bicycle and depositing it elsewhere on the island. *Nothing too outrageous*, Nell had said, *but he was a right little scamp in his day.*

Settled down a while back – *He's going for the guards*, Tom had told Laura not so long ago when she'd met him on the street, his face full of pride – but the memory of his son's wayward youth might make Tom go easy on her lads.

Not too easy though. She'd ask him to call over and have a word when Gavin was out on his deliveries. Put the fear of God in them with talk of suspended sentences maybe, and juvenile detention centres. Keep them from carrying out any future nonsense.

'Now dry your eyes and go next door, and tell your dad to come home. And tomorrow I'll go with you to Michael Brown and you'll tell him you're very sorry for taking his scarecrow. We'll have to figure out how to replace it. And next time Jerry Malone wants you to do something really stupid and dangerous, tell him to do it himself.' She'd have her own word with the little thug, next time he crossed her path. She'd warn him that she was watching him. 'OK?'

'OK.'

'And give me a hug,' she said, because she was their mother, and they were eleven, and repentant.

When they'd left she rang Nell, disturbing her at the salon, which she rarely did, and asked her for Tom Fox's number. 'I'll fill you in later,' she said. 'Nothing to worry about, just some information he needs.'

'Tom,' she said, when he responded, 'I have a bit of news for you' – and when *that* conversation was over, and Tom had agreed that a serious chat with the young offenders would probably be enough of a sanction, Laura hung up and thought about Imelda's Italian visitor, and the fright he must have got when Michael Brown's scarecrow had plunged into the sea right in front of him. She hoped he'd take up her invitation to dinner: it would be some small recompense.

In due course Tilly arrived with their fish and chips, which were quickly disposed of. Laura regarded her family around the table as everyone ate. Still intact, despite all their catastrophes. Ben's bad tumble from his bike when he was five or six, four stitches to keep his chin together; Seamus's fall from one of the apple trees last year, a bump on his head the size of a golf ball; Gavin's acute appendicitis, which had caused him to miss Evie and Marian's birth. Her own breast cancer, diagnosed on the same day she heard she was carrying Poppy.

How to keep them all safe, that was the question. She wished there was a way, but of course there wasn't. When Death came to take you, like it had come for Walter, and Nell's mother Moira, and Hugh, it didn't leave empty-handed.

Afterwards, while Ben and Seamus were clearing things away, Tilly offered to put the girls to bed.

'You're not going out?' Laura asked. 'Two nights in a row? Not like you.'

'I'm tired,' Tilly said, 'and Andy's in the bar again tonight, so ...'

She'd been subdued through dinner. 'Everything OK?'

'Fine.'

She sat on the bench beneath the window, Evie on her lap, Marian tucked into her side. Her limbs were slender, her waist trim. She wasn't curvy, like Laura and Eve – no hips to speak of, and precious little on top. Boyish, you'd call her. She wouldn't be described as vivacious, or particularly funny, but there was a touching sense of vulnerability, a kind of charming puppyish eagerness, in her demeanour. She was gentle and generous, and the girls adored her.

It occurred to Laura – why had it never struck her before? – that she was pretty much the polar opposite to Eve, in both looks and personality. Eve was altogether more streetwise; there was more *bite* to her, good and bad – and yes, she could be very amusing. Had Andy deliberately chosen someone as different as he could find to replace the girl who'd broken his heart?

And following on from that question came another more disturbing one: what if he'd never got over Eve? What if their recent one-night stand was more than the accidental drunken encounter Eve was making it out to be? What if Tilly had never been more than a rebound romance until he could get back with Eve? She so wanted to ask Nell's opinion but instead she was forced to keep this wretched business to herself.

'Don't let them keep you up there too long,' she told Tilly. 'I'm putting on a batch of scones – we can have a cuppa while they're baking.' And maybe instead of a cuppa they'd break out the Ben & Jerry's that Laura had decided after all not to produce for dessert, given the boys' confession.

Gavin accompanied Poppy upstairs, Tilly following

with the other girls. Ben and Seamus took themselves into the sitting room. As Laura was assembling her scone ingredients, her phone rang.

'I have to know why you wanted Tom Fox's number,' Nell said.

'Sorry, forgot to get back to you.' She filled her in, one ear open for the sound of Gavin's return. 'Keep it to yourself,' she said. 'They've learnt their lesson – at least, they will once Tom's had a word with them.'

'The little pups. They could have been killed.'

'Stop – I can't go there. By the way, on a happier note, I'm having a dinner party for my birthday, and you and James are cordially invited.'

'Lovely – the night itself?'

'Yes, Wednesday.'

'I'll make sure James isn't working. And I assume we'll need a babysitter – Tilly will want her man there too.'

'I'm sure she will.' Laura would just have to force herself to smile, and have as little to do with him as possible. 'And I'm going to ask Imelda and her tenant.'

'Oh do – I still haven't met him. And how's my favourite patient?'

'Better than myself.'

Ten minutes later, as she was putting the scones into the oven, the door opened and Tilly reappeared.

'Perfect timing. Fancy some posh ice-cream – or are you all ice-creamed out?'

'Maybe a little. I rarely eat it in the van.'

'Wise woman.'

They settled at the table with two scoops each of salted caramel. 'How are you?' Laura asked, and Tilly ducked her head and stuck her spoon into her bowl.

'I'm fine,' she replied. 'I'm good.'

'Really?'

'Really.'

Silence fell. There was a sharp cry outside, a bird or an animal. They both ignored it.

'Listen,' Laura went on, 'I'm not poking my nose in, and I'm not looking for information. I just want to say that long distance relationships can be a bitch. I know I've said this to you before, but I'm saying it again because I think it bears repeating. When you're not with him you're wishing you were, and when you are, you're feeling this huge pressure for everything to be perfect, and nothing is ever perfect. It's not easy, is what I'm trying to say, so it's OK to get frustrated with the whole thing. It's perfectly understandable.'

What was she doing? She'd resolved to listen, and here she was, delivering a lecture. Worse, she was saying the wrong things. She should be preparing Tilly for a fall, because a fall was surely coming. Instead, she was saying hang in there, don't fret.

Tilly poked at her ice-cream, messing it about, yet to have a single taste. Eventually she spoke. 'Can I tell you something?'

'If you want.'

'I was going to ask him to marry me. This summer, while I was here.' She tried to smile, but couldn't.

It wasn't wholly unexpected, not entirely surprising – but not good either. 'You were going to? So you've changed your mind?'

'I think …' Tilly stopped, rubbed her nose. 'I get the feeling he's not quite there yet.' She let her spoon drop, pressed her palms to the table, studied her nails. 'I think he just needs more time, you know?'

Take care, Laura thought. Get this part right. 'Or,' she said, slowly, gently, 'the other thing is, he might not actually be the right one, Til. He might not be meant for you. It's just a possibility.'

Her sister nodded several times, quick little hops of her head. 'But I won't give up on him yet,' she said, with the same not-quite-there smile, and Laura saw the fight inside her not to crumple.

She pictured her flying to Ireland, hugging her resolution to herself. How brave of her, how foolishly wonderfully tragically brave of her to think of asking anyone to marry her, to run the risk of hearing the wrong answer.

Laura herself had popped the question to Gavin, but only after he'd already asked *her* three times, and been turned down three times, so she'd been reasonably confident of the outcome. And yes, men proposed all the time, and a share of women too – but for some reason, the idea of Tilly planning to do it seemed particularly valiant, and her subsequent decision not to, equally poignant.

I think he just needs more time. Suspecting, maybe, that he wasn't as in love as she was, but putting her trust in time to deepen his feelings towards her. The trouble with that was their separate lives on separate continents. The trouble was the thousands of miles that lay between them for eleven months of every year.

The trouble with trusting him to love her was that she couldn't trust him.

Laura reached for her sister's hand and squeezed it. 'Listen,' she said, 'do what feels right. It's what I always do. When it *feels* right, it usually *is* right. Now, we need to start planning the menu for my birthday dinner party – because I've decided to have one, and I'm useless at knowing what to serve. And eat that ice-cream, because it cost a bomb.'

They ate, and talked menus, and set the other aside.

Imelda

'TELL ME ABOUT YOUR RESTAURANT,' SHE said, and he took out his phone and found photos. Tosca, he said it was called, 'because is my favourite opera, and also is easy name for person to remember'.

He showed her a haphazardly paved courtyard bordered with orange and lemon trees in giant terracotta pots. Nestling between them were a dozen or so round tables of varying sizes, all topped with ochre cloths that toned pleasingly with the fruit on the trees.

One long rectangular table was placed behind the rest, covered with the same fabric. Imelda counted twenty-four chairs around it. 'For the big group,' Gualtiero explained. 'For the families, and the celebrations – and sometimes, if we are full, we put the different persons together at the big table, and they find new friends.'

A profusion of greenery studded with tiny white flowers – jasmine, he told her – spilt over first-floor balconies of the honey-coloured brick building to the rear, trailing almost to the ground. 'In the night,' he said, 'the perfume of the jasmine is strong.' Glass lanterns atop black poles stood sentry here and there between the tables. Fat red cushions sat on wicker chairs. A large blackboard was nailed to the wall of the rear building: he zoomed in and Imelda read *ravioli con ricotta e cannella al ragù di cinghiale*. 'The special for the day,' he told her. 'Every day we make new.'

'It looks beautiful,' she said. 'And you do the cooking?'

'Yes, with another chef.'

'And ... did your wife cook?' Wary of mentioning her, in case her memory, or the memory of her loss, cast a shadow on the conversation, but it didn't seem to upset him.

'Yes, sometime, and also she look after the tables.' He scrolled through his photos and said, 'Here is Dorotea,' and Imelda took in the curly dark hair and the high cheekbones, the slightly hooded eyes, the large nose, the wide smile.

'She looks happy.'

'Yes, she was 'appy woman.'

There was a short pause. 'When Hugh died,' Imelda said, her eyes still on Dorotea, 'his friends and neighbours, people he'd known all his life, sat up with him the whole night. It's a thing they do here. They never leave the dead alone until they're buried.'

'Is good thing,' he replied. 'After Dorotea die, the restaurant is closed for three week. On the night we open again, everyone in the village come for dinner. Everyone, everyone come, old person, young person, *bambini*, everyone. We must find more place for them, more and more place. Some person 'ave no chair, but still they come. Never before so many person on the same night. At the last, we 'ave no food.'

'People are good,' she said. 'There is a lot of kindness about.'

'Yes, Eemelda, is true. In Ireland, in *Italia*, everywhere there is kind person. When you are sad, is good to remember this.'

They sat on old wooden chairs beneath the shade of the horse chestnut tree at the bottom of the lawn, having just eaten the ham sandwiches she'd made for lunch. It was two days following the incident at the cliffs, and he had yet to resume his island meanderings.

Is OK, he'd asked, the morning after, *if I no go out today?* and she'd assured him that he was most welcome to stay around any day he chose, so he'd set up his easel in the garden. *Today I paint from my 'ead*, he'd said, and now it was the next day, and for the second time they'd eaten lunch together.

She'd been nervous of telling him about the scarecrow, when Nell had passed on the news. No doubt he'd be horribly embarrassed to have mistaken it for a human form, and to have instigated with his report the resultant extensive manhunt, but he had to be told.

He hadn't understood the word, so she'd taken a page from her writing pad and drawn a very poor scarecrow. *To keep the birds away*, she'd said, when he'd still looked puzzled. *To stop them eating the crops. Like a person, but not real* – and when it had finally hit him, far from showing signs of mortification, he'd shaken his head, smiling. *Eemelda*, he'd said, *when I go back to Italia I must say to my doctor of eyes that he must give me the better spectacles.*

Relief, she supposed, that nobody, after all, had fallen into the sea – and she in turn was relieved at his taking it so well.

They sat where she and Hugh had often passed a sunny afternoon. 'My husband's grandfather planted this tree,' she remarked. 'He built the house too, after he married' – and as Scooter gnawed on a ratty old tennis ball at their feet, she found herself telling him more.

'My husband owned a bar. It's called Fitz's – you might have seen it in the village. His niece's husband manages it. I haven't been able to call in since …

'We met here on the island six years ago, on one of the smaller beaches. I was on holidays with my sister and her husband. I went for a walk early on the first morning, and there he was. It was the last day of July, and we were married in December. It was a first marriage for both of us. I never imagined …

'I feel angry a lot of the time now. I'm sad, of course, I'm very, very sad, but I'm so angry too that we had such a short time together. Why couldn't we have met when we were younger, or why couldn't he have lived longer? I don't understand why things like that happen. It doesn't seem fair ...

'After he died I found myself looking at couples, people I knew who were happily married, and I felt – resentful of their happiness, jealous of what they had. I'm ashamed to say it. I'm still a bit ...'

He probably didn't understand much of what she said, and maybe it was just as well – and really, it didn't matter. He listened in silence as it emerged slowly from her. He allowed her to talk and didn't interrupt. She hadn't been able to speak like this to anyone, not to her sister, or Nell, or Eve. It was such a relief to give voice to all that was churning around in her head, to say it aloud to someone who demanded nothing of her, expected nothing of her.

When she ran out of words they sat in easy silence as birds flitted and fussed in the tree, as a breeze tapped leaves softly against one another, as the ferry horn sounded distantly. Imelda directed her gaze at the old house where she'd spent her happiest years, and wondered if she would ever feel such happiness again. It didn't seem remotely possible – but for the first time she acknowledged that maybe, one day, it might be.

Oh, not the happiness she'd known with Hugh, not the fierce bubbling excitement of their first weeks, when they were getting to know everything about one another, when love was sprouting and spreading and colouring all her days. Not the deeper joy they'd found later in the months and years of their marriage, not that, never that again – but maybe she'd find a gentler contentment. Maybe she'd be blessed with that, somewhere in the future.

She'd thought her life had ended, the morning she'd woken to find him gone – but only a part of it had ended. The happiest part, certainly, but the rest of it had gone on, was going on, whether she wanted it to or not. It would go on until it was her turn to die, and all she could hope for was that it would get easier to face each new day, easier to live with the absence of her soulmate.

Eventually she got to her feet, gathering plates and cups and apologising for talking so much, and he waved away her apology and resumed his painting. And for the rest of that day, as she baked new loaves of brown bread – he got through an astonishing amount of it each morning – and hung clothes on the line and brought them in again, and read a little more of her book, and finally found herself able to return to the crossword she and Hugh had been halfway through, as the day passed in this fashion, with the small tasks that used up the minutes and the hours, she felt a sort of calming within her, a small tamping down of her rage.

The following morning, as they breakfasted together – somewhere along the way, their separate morning schedules had dovetailed – as he was topping up their coffee from the cafetière, she gave voice to an idea that had come to her in the night. 'I was thinking,' she said, 'I could ask my niece – Hugh's niece – to dinner some evening this week, and you could meet her. I was wondering if you would like that.'

She was still wary of appearing in public with him, but Nell could come here, couldn't she? Nell, she knew, would like to meet him – and she'd be someone else for him to talk to. The thought of inviting anyone to dinner hadn't crossed her mind since Hugh's death, but Nell didn't really count. Nell was aware of the situation with Gualtiero, how Imelda had had little choice but to keep him. Nell wouldn't judge, wouldn't read anything into it that wasn't there. And James, she was sure, wouldn't mind being left out.

'I would like that,' he said, 'and I would be 'appy to cook for you, if you like.'

She opened her mouth to protest – he was the visitor – and then she thought how nice it would be to have a trained chef taking care of the menu. 'Something simple,' she said. 'Don't go to any trouble. And only if I can get the ingredients.'

It was nearly his last week. She couldn't believe how quickly his month had passed. It seemed like no time since she'd come home to find the green suitcase on the doorstep, and yet just eight days from now he was leaving.

After he'd departed for his day of painting, ready to resume his normal routine, she washed the dishes and swept the floor. As she did so, she found the restaurant courtyard returning to her mind's eye. She could imagine being there on a warm evening, the sky blazing with stars, the air redolent with jasmine, and aromas from the various dishes. Some aria playing in the background, maybe, given his taste for opera, and pleasant spatters of conversation drifting from nearby tables. She'd always considered Italian a beautifully lyrical language.

They should have travelled more, she and Hugh. They'd planned to – or at least they'd talked about it. Rome had been on their list, and the Cotswolds, and the Austrian Alps. They should have done it when he'd promoted James to pub manager a few years ago, and cut down on his own hours. They should have booked air tickets and hotels and just *gone*. They should have made so many memories.

At length she left the kitchen and wandered out to the patio, where Gualtiero's work from his two days in the garden, a small seascape, rested on the table, propped against Imelda's citronella candle. *Our place for 'oliday*, he'd told her, *when the boys are small. We go every year in the summer for two week. Is in* Toscana, *near to the island of Elba, where was put Napoleon.*

This painting was different from the others. This one was more structured, less chaotic, but every bit as colourful. There was a small sandy cove, seaweed-strewn and flanked by hills on which pretty pastel houses huddled together, as if holding one another up. Below a sky that was streaked with violet and yellow and orange and pink, the sun having presumably just slid out of sight, the sea was a darkening green, splashed with all the sunset shades, while Elba lay long and low on the horizon, putting Imelda in mind of how Roone looked from the mainland.

She'd miss him, no point in denying it. She'd miss his company, the sound of him cooking his evening meal in the kitchen, his scent left behind on the stairs, his green case sitting in the hall each evening. The house would feel emptier without him, particularly as there had been no further sign of Eve since her one and only encounter with him.

She wiped her hands and went to phone Nell.

AUGUST

Tilly

IT REMINDED HER OF HER FIRST, AND SO FAR only, Christmas Day on Roone. It put her in mind of the crowd gathered around the kitchen table for dinner, just enough space for them all. Laura and Gavin and the children, and Gavin's mother, who'd died just days after, and an American man, a refugee from the island hotel whose roof had been damaged in the storm of the day before, and Tilly, newly arrived from Australia. Ten of them if you counted Poppy, then just a baby on a lap.

This evening's gathering was different, of course. For one thing the children were missing, having been fed earlier. The three girls were in bed, the boys watching television in the sitting room. Around the table in their stead were Nell and James, and Lelia from the café and her husband who owned the ice-cream van, and whose name, Pádraig, Tilly avoided using, because it never sounded right when she said it.

There was also the Italian man from Imelda's

house, and a friendly Canadian couple who happened to be staying in the B&B, and whom Laura had invited on impulse that morning. Imelda had been invited too but she'd said no, which was probably just as well, because with Andy and Tilly it came to eleven around the table, which was definitely as many adults as would fit with any degree of comfort.

This wasn't remotely like Laura's birthday parties of the previous two years, which had taken place officially in the sitting room, but which had on both occasions overflowed into the hall and kitchen, and halfway up the stairs. B&B guests were invited so they couldn't complain about the noise, along with what looked like half of the Roone population. Baskets of cocktail sausages and chicken wings were circulated, wine glasses were kept filled. The cake was cut, the presents opened, and music and general merriment went on until the small hours. Laura's parties had gained a reputation, and invitations were coveted.

This was far more civilised, but none the less enjoyable, Tilly thought. Candles flickered; conversation was muted and easy. They'd eaten a starter of dates stuffed with feta and wrapped in bacon whose recipe Tilly had found online, and followed it with homemade pizza and a salad of lettuce, spinach and rocket from Gavin's garden, tossed in Laura's special dressing of mint and honey, lemon juice and wholegrain mustard.

The cake awaited, a coffee and walnut beauty that

Lelia had brought along as her gift. Tilly wondered if it was time to produce it. She looked to the top of the table where her sister sat, hoping to catch her eye – and was taken aback by the expression she caught on Laura's face.

Momentarily left unattended, the Italian man next to her having turned to address a remark to the Canadian wife, Gavin on her other side chatting to Lelia, Laura's mouth was set, her eyes narrowed and cold, as if what she was seeing greatly offended or repulsed her.

Tilly followed her line of sight, wondering what on earth could have prompted such a look – and arrived at Andy, seated directly across the table from her.

Andy? Could he really be the target? It certainly looked like Laura had him in her sights. Why, though? What could possibly have prompted such apparent ill feeling towards him? Could she be mad at him on Tilly's behalf, following their recent conversation? Could she resent him for falling short of Tilly's expectations? Surely not. She might be annoyed, but not angry. She wouldn't look at him as if she hated him.

Tilly shot another glance at Laura and saw her talking again with the Italian, her usual smile reinstated. She must have imagined the other, must have mistaken it for tiredness.

She turned back to Andy. 'How're you doing?'

'I'm having the craic,' he said, knowing the expression would make her smile.

It wasn't really his scene, this kind of gathering. He'd have more fun tomorrow night, at the big hotel birthday party. 'Thanks for coming,' she said. 'I'm glad you're here.'

'No worries, it's good. At least I'm getting well fed.'

She pushed back her chair. 'And there's more to come.'

In the scullery she lit the three candles they'd stuck into the cake and brought it back to the kitchen – and while Gavin was wondering aloud if it was time for the birthday bumps, and the Canadian husband was offering his help if needed, and Laura was threatening to evict him and his wife that very minute if he dared, Tilly stood by, waiting to distribute slices, and thought, *Three more days.*

Since the picnic she'd been taking things as they came. She hadn't suggested another afternoon or evening on their own, and neither had he. Laura clearly didn't hold out much hope for them, but Tilly knew she was mistaken. Laura was playing safe, not wanting Tilly to be hurt. It was understandable – but she was wrong.

She and Andy were still seeing one another every day, still spending a great deal of time together. It was all good, and really his friends were lovely, and she was determined to make the very most of what time she had left with him.

And then, the very next day, the row happened.

It came out of nowhere – or maybe it didn't. Maybe it arose from the disappointment that lay beneath her vow to remain cheerful and patient. Maybe it was a product of her frustration, and a quiet anxiety that she was doing her best to ignore. Maybe it didn't come out of nowhere at all; maybe it was more that she didn't see it coming.

It was the middle of the afternoon. They were in the van, dealing with the usual orders, chatting in the breaks between customers. Everything was fine until a girl appeared and asked for a 99.

Tilly knew her slightly. She was the younger sister of Frog Hackett, around Tilly's own age, but she didn't mix much with her brother's crowd. Curly dark hair, jade-green eyeliner. Denim shorts with frayed ends, exposing her rather hefty legs.

'Going to the party tonight?' she asked Andy, as he filled the cone, watching him turn it slowly under the feed so the ice-cream coiled in.

'Yeah, we'll be there.'

'Hardly be as good as Frog's, though.' This remark was accompanied by a wink, directed at Tilly. 'We all had a ball that night,' the girl told her. 'Some of us had a bit too much of a ball.'

Andy laughed. 'Ah now, Rachel, don't be trying to stir it.' He stuck a flake into the cone and passed it over. 'Two euro to you,' he said, although 99s were two fifty.

'Thanks Andy – see you later.'

The exchange left Tilly feeling mildly irritated. That party again. She watched Frog's sister vanish from sight. She yawned and rubbed her eyes.

'You should go home, have a lie-down,' he said – and for some reason, the remark only served to ignite her irritation. She'd go home if she felt like it, not when someone told her to.

She shifted weight from one hip to the other and folded her arms. 'So who exactly will be there tonight?'

He wiped the end of the ice-cream nozzle. He ran the tap in the van's little sink, held his cloth under the flow and squeezed it out. 'I told you, everyone. The whole island is invited.'

'No – I mean which of your friends? Which of the usual suspects?'

He gave her a quizzical smile. 'They'll all be there. Why wouldn't they?'

And that was where it stopped being just a casual conversation. That was where it all came pouring out, like the ice-cream.

'I *never* get you on your own,' she said, silencing the voice that urged her to be quiet, feeling the heat rise in her cheeks. 'You never seem to want us to be alone. I feel like I'm the only one who cares about us.'

He looked at her in what appeared to be genuine astonishment. 'I thought you liked my friends,' he said, which was all she needed to let fly, to round on him.

'That's not the point! That's not what I'm saying at all! Of *course* I like your friends. They're not the problem – *you* are! Have you any idea how much I miss you when we're apart, and how much I look forward to coming over here and seeing you again? And then when I get here, you don't seem to care that we're always, *always* surrounded by people – do you even *want* to keep going out with me?' she demanded, before she could stop herself – and of course just then another pair of customers arrived, and Andy turned away to serve them, giving her lots of time to cool down, which she tried to do.

It felt good, she realised, to let it out. She should have done it sooner. Her concerns needed to be stated, even if it meant a row. It would clear the air between them; it would make him realise that she deserved more of his attention.

Except it didn't quite work out that way.

'Tilly,' he said, when they were alone again, 'I don't know where this is coming from. I thought you were having a good time here. I don't see my friends too often when I'm away in college, so I like to catch up with them when I'm home.'

And that, unfortunately, was all she needed to blow up again. 'You don't see your *friends* too often? You don't see me at *all*! I'm on the other side of the bloody world, apart from a few weeks in the summer! I'm beginning to feel like you wish I hadn't come!'

'Oh, come on – you know that's not true. I've said often enough that I'm glad you're here.'

'Well then, why am I the only one who wants a bit of time on our own? I was the one who organised that picnic last week – no, two weeks ago. That's really the only time we haven't been surrounded by your friends or our families.'

'We had that walk the other day –'

'That walk? Whoop de doo, a whole half an hour to ourselves!'

'And that time we went to the beach –'

'Yes, and along came your ex, trying to cause trouble! That was a really lovely morning!'

And on they went, she attacking, he defending – and in the end, seeing a new group approach the van, Tilly stomped off, telling him she didn't want to go to the stupid party anyway, and he didn't call after her.

And of course she very much wanted to go to the stupid party, but two hours later he hadn't phoned, and it looked like she was stuck inside for the evening on her own, because the entire family, even Poppy, was going.

Laura had shown a disappointing lack of sympathy when Tilly had reported what had happened. 'I wouldn't worry about it; rows are part of any relationship. It's healthy to get things off your chest once in a while. You'll make up soon enough.'

'Soon enough? I'm going home in two days!'

'So you'll just have to make up before that.'

No sympathy at all. Glad, probably, that they'd fallen out. The more Tilly thought about it, the more she regretted her outburst. She replayed it in her head, and heard how needy and demanding she'd sounded – wasn't that a sure way to lose him?

At dinnertime she poked at her shepherd's pie, forcing down no more than a few mouthfuls. Afterwards she tidied up and mopped the kitchen floor, full of gloom, while everyone changed into party wear. Every so often she couldn't resist pulling out her phone and checking for a message that she knew wouldn't be there.

The party, now that she wasn't planning to attend it, took on a new significance. She'd seen the bunting, and the big white tent. It would probably be completely wonderful, and she'd miss it all.

At a quarter to seven, the others set off. 'You won't change your mind and come with us?' Laura asked, and Tilly said no, although it killed her. After they'd left she wandered dispiritedly through the downstairs rooms, finding a forgotten plate in the sitting room, tweaking a tablecloth straight in the breakfast room.

Laura was wrong: they wouldn't make up. Tilly had ruined everything. She imagined him at the party, chatting to other girls – girls he could see anytime he chose – and she wanted to cry. Seven o'clock came, and half past, and eight o'clock. The others would surely be home soon, the girls needing to be put to bed. From time to time she heard guests letting themselves in and going upstairs.

At one stage she turned on the TV. Ten minutes later she turned it off again, nothing grabbing her attention from the pathetic handful of channels available on Roone. In the kitchen she ate a leftover slice of birthday cake without appetite, and made tea but didn't drink it, just cradled the mug and stared disconsolately into the steam.

Twenty to nine. She rose abruptly to her feet. She couldn't stand this. She'd go to the party and find him, and tell him she was sorry. She'd put up with the way things were – it was better than losing him, wasn't it? Anything was better than losing him.

She poured the tea down the sink and left the mug on the draining board. Upstairs she changed quickly into her blue dress, and did her face and pinned her hair up as best she could. Laura made it look so easy when she did it for her.

She began to feel slightly better, more hopeful of not having made a mess of things. Laura was right: everyone rowed. It was perfectly normal. She and Andy would laugh about this tomorrow – and who knew? He might, he just might, take on board what she'd said. He might even organise a surprise farewell dinner for her last night, a table for two in the hotel. And next summer might be very different.

She hurried downstairs. She took one of Laura's scarves from the hallstand, a wispy grey one that she liked, and left the house. As she scurried down the road towards the hotel, she could feel her spirits rising with every step. It would be OK – of course it would. This was just their first proper row.

She thought of telling their children about it in years to come. *It was in an ice-cream van*, she'd say. *Your father was working there for the summer, and I was helping out. There was a big party that evening, but I was too mad to go with him. I went along later when I'd cooled down, and we made up.*

She smiled at her foolishness as she drew level with an elderly man. She glanced his way and he returned her smile – '*Signorina*' – lifting his straw hat an inch upwards. 'You were at dinner last night,' she said, falling into step with him. 'I'm Laura's sister, Tilly.' They hadn't spoken much, at opposite ends of the table.

'Yes, yes,' he agreed, his smile broadening. 'It was a very good night.'

'I'm going as far as the hotel,' she told him. 'There's a big party on there.' The pace was slower than she'd have liked, but they didn't have far to go.

'Another party,' he said. 'You are young, you can do this. Me, one party is enough. Tomorrow I go 'ome,' he added. 'Today my last day in Ireland.'

'I leave on Saturday, one day after you.' She felt a small tightness in her gut at the thought of leaving.

'You live … in Australia?'

'Yes, but soon I'll be moving to Ireland.' She could tell him anything: when would they meet again? 'My boyfriend lives here,' she said. 'We're getting married next year.'

'Ah – congratulation.'

'Thank you. I'm going to join him now, at the party.' They were approaching the hotel. Another minute or so and she'd see him.

Her companion inclined his head. 'I think you will 'ave dancing at this party,' he said.

'Oh yes, I should think so.'

'And much food.'

She laughed again. 'Yes, probably.' They reached the hotel gates and she put out her hand. 'It was nice to meet you again. Have a safe trip home tomorrow.'

They shook hands: he swept off his hat and dipped his head and shoulders. '*Incantata, signorina*. Enjoy the party.'

She hurried up the driveway, making for the tent. People were coming and going from it; others stood about in the landscaped gardens. Music played faintly; the bunting bobbed in a light breeze. There was laughter, and darting children, and an air of general festivity. It looked like pretty much the entire island population had shown up.

Tilly entered the tent, which was hot and noisy and crowded, and beautifully lit with what looked like millions of tiny white lights on strings that crisscrossed high above and trailed down the sides of the tent, like shooting stars. She was offered a glass of wine by a waitress who held a tray at the entrance; she accepted it and sipped.

She wove her way through the crowd, nodding at those she recognised but too shy to stop. Wafts of perfume and aftershave merged with savoury food scents. Hotel staff in black and white moved among the gathering with food offerings. Tilly took a little tartlet and tasted cheese and herbs, and chopped olives. The wine went down easily: she found another waitress, with another tray.

She did another round of the tent but there was no sign of Andy or any of his mates, and no Laura or her gang either: they must all be outside. She retraced her steps, fighting a dimming of her earlier optimism. What was the worst that could happen? He wasn't going to ignore her – he'd never do that. He might be a bit cool for a while, but he'd get over it. It would be fine.

'Tilly.'

Nell and James stood at the tent entrance, their sleepy little daughter in her father's arms. 'I didn't think you were coming,' Nell said. 'Andy told us you had a headache. You've just missed Laura and her lot. They left five minutes ago.'

Tilly decided she might as well be honest. 'Actually, Andy and I had a bit of a row and I got mad, but I've cooled down now.' Her fingers felt sticky; she wished she had a napkin. She was conscious of a small and not unpleasant buzz from the hastily drunk wine. 'Have you seen him?'

Nell gestured towards the rear garden. 'We were just with him. We're about to leave too, but we're waiting for our little man – he wasn't keen on going home, so we said he could have five more minutes with Andy.' She turned to James. 'I'll go back for him. See you at the car. Come with me, Tilly.'

They walked past knots of people, most of whom greeted Nell and smiled at Tilly. She knew faces but few names, and maybe they were unsure of hers too. Maybe they recognised her as Andy's Australian girlfriend, or

Laura's sister. Hard to remember someone who only showed up once a year for a few weeks.

Further on they encountered the party host, flushed and splendid in a formal black dinner suit, with an emerald-green cummerbund and matching bow-tie. He greeted Tilly warmly, saying he was delighted to see her, but not once using her name. Another person who knew her, but didn't really. She wished him a happy birthday: he thanked her graciously.

'I hope you're not leaving already,' he said to Nell.

'I'm afraid so, Henry – I have one very tired little girl, and a boy who needs his bed too, even if he doesn't realise it. I'm just chasing after him now.'

Beneath the babble of conversation Tilly heard again the music she'd caught on her arrival – and there they were, a quartet of women in black dresses and artfully arranged hair seated on wrought-iron chairs in the middle of the lawn, music stands before them, playing an assortment of stringed instruments. She wasn't particularly into classical music, but it seemed to suit the surroundings.

Where was Andy, though? She searched among the crowd and couldn't see him. She was half nervous, half eager at the prospect of meeting him, and willed the hotel owner to move on.

'There he is, the monkey!' Nell exclaimed. Tilly swung around and saw Tommy, careening towards them.

Nell caught him and swooped him up. 'What do you say to Mr Manning for the lovely party?'

'Thank you.'

'You're very welcome, young man.'

Nell scanned the crowd. 'Now where – oh yes, look, Andy's over there, to the left of that couple by the gazebo.'

Tilly looked, and finally spotted him. He stood, arms folded, in conversation with some girl, whose back was to Tilly. One of the waitresses, it looked like. Black dress, the white ties of an apron, an empty silver tray tucked underneath her arm. Red hair caught up in a tight bun.

Red hair.

Eve.

In the fading light Andy's expression was hard to fathom, but he didn't appear to be smiling. Were they arguing? Tilly couldn't hear them above the music.

And then, with a flourish, it stopped.

And in the silence that followed, Eve said clearly, loudly, 'I'm pregnant, and it's yours, Andy Baker.'

And everyone heard it.

Eve

NINE O'CLOCK, STILL HOURS TO GO. WHY on earth had she agreed to work this evening? She should have said no when her boss had asked if she was interested. She should have seen beyond the double-time money he was offering for the shift, and said no.

The older people weren't the problem. They smiled and called her dear when she approached them with her tray, and thanked her when they took what she was offering. And the parents she knew from the crèche were friendly too, asking how she was enjoying the summer, treating her like just another party guest. No, the problem was the teenagers, the fifteen- and sixteen- and seventeen-year-olds who sniggered behind her back, and snatched glasses of champagne from her tray, and dared her with their eyes to stop them, and never, ever said thank you. She tried to avoid them but they kept finding her, kept ambushing her with their silent mockery.

To add to her misery, her feet, in the only pair of

heels she possessed, were killing her. She'd been in them since five, and she hadn't sat down once. The black dress she'd been given to wear for the evening pulled uncomfortably across her front, and she'd been too embarrassed to ask for a larger size. The black tights – she *hated* tights – made her legs feel horribly hot, and she detested her hair tied up in a bun, but she'd had no choice.

Before everyone arrived they'd set up trestle tables and covered them with cloths, and polished what felt like a thousand glasses. They'd folded napkins and chopped strawberries and filled jugs with lemonade and water and hung balloons and put jellies and toys into party bags while the hotel owner had flapped around like a hen on acid, and kept reminding them to smile and look happy when the guests showed up, which was the last thing Eve had felt like doing.

Andy had arrived some time ago with Bugs and Frog and a few more, but without Tilly. Eve had kept them in her sights, and had managed to stay out of their orbit. The last thing she needed tonight was them looking pityingly at her – or worse, seeing her and pretending they hadn't, in a clumsy attempt not to embarrass her. Eventually, to her relief, she'd spotted them leaving the tent – and then, not five minutes later, Laura and Gavin and their children had shown up, and she'd been forced to give them a wide berth too.

She was still wondering how Laura could have

guessed the truth. The memory of their last encounter, when she'd been pretty much ordered out of the B&B, made her cross – after she'd juggled her hotel shift to help them out too. Talk about gratitude.

And what if she was wrong about Laura not revealing what she knew? Every day she waited for someone – Nell, James, Tilly – to come to the crèche and bang on the door. Mad at her, even though Andy was every bit as guilty. All the blame would attach to her. She was certain of it.

And what of Imelda? They hadn't met, hadn't spoken, in three weeks. Eve was torn about her, feelings of guilt and anger churning around in her head – but she didn't want Imelda to hear, not from Laura, not from anyone. Not until Eve was ready to tell her.

'Come along, dear – there are guests waiting for food.'

The hotel owner stood before her, pink in the face, looking pointedly at her empty tray.

'Sorry,' she muttered, moving towards the trestle tables, wincing inwardly at every step. Think of the money, she told herself.

'Do a few rounds outside, would you?' he called after her, so she loaded up her tray and left the marquee, where at least it was a bit cooler. She'd get rid of the food and then find a quiet corner where she could take her shoes off for a bit.

She made her way through the crowds, keeping an eye out for Andy and Laura. She spotted Bugs and

Frog with a couple of girls, but Andy wasn't with them. Had he left already? And where was Tilly? Why wasn't she here? Could the perfect couple have actually fallen out?

He hadn't left. A few minutes later, her tray empty again, Eve caught sight of him by the gazebo with Nell and James, and their two small children. She held back, shifting slightly so she was screened from them. James and Nell, she saw, were on the point of leaving – their little girl, in her father's arms, was drooping with sleep – but Tommy appeared to be protesting. She saw Nell make some remark to Andy, who bent to lift Tommy into his arms. She watched the others walking off, and Andy saying something to his little brother, who shook his head vehemently.

Tommy had been born while Eve was still with Andy. She'd loved seeing them together, seeing how gentle Andy was with his tiny new sibling. Now Tommy was four and must be due for school in September, a sturdy, quiet little boy who clearly adored his big brother. He hadn't attended the crèche, and there was no sign of the little girl's name on the new intake list.

She leant against a nearby wall, tray tucked under her arm. She wriggled her toes, trying to ease the ache in the balls of her feet – how did some women wear heels all day long, every day? A man brushed by her and murmured an apology; she didn't move. She was aware of music playing, but wasn't interested enough to look around and find its source.

She pushed off from the wall to walk towards them. She'd say hello to Tommy: nobody could object to that. Andy watched her thoughtfully as she approached. Remembering the day on the beach, she supposed. The last time they'd spoken, when she'd been a bit mischievous.

'Hey,' she said.

'Hey yourself.' She saw him taking in the black dress.

'Are you enjoying the party?'

'It's OK. I forgot you were working here.'

'Just for the summer, make a few extra bucks. Where's Tilly tonight?'

'She's got a headache,' he replied, which might well be the truth.

She turned to Tommy. 'Hello,' she said, smiling brightly. 'Remember me?' She often saw him around the place, but they didn't engage, and he showed no sign of recognition now.

'I'm Eve,' she said. 'I was Andy's special friend when you were a tiny baby.'

Still nothing. She gave up on him and turned back to Andy.

'Are you mad at me?' she asked, tipping her head to one side. Keeping her tone light for Tommy, who continued to study her impassively.

Andy gave a small smile. 'Sometimes you can be a bit much.'

'Because I brought up the party in front of Tilly? Wasn't planned, honest. It just came out.'

The smile was still playing on his lips. 'I wonder,' he said.

'Anyway, I only told the truth. I was grateful to you for …' She stopped. 'I had a good time,' she said, locking eyes with him. 'Didn't you?'

'Mum!' Tommy shouted suddenly, raising his hands. Andy turned.

'Let him off,' Eve said quickly. 'He wants to go.' This conversation wasn't over. The last thing she wanted was Nell descending on them.

He lowered his little brother to the ground, and off he scooted.

'Come on, Andy,' she said, 'it's me. It's Eve.' The music was beginning to get on her nerves: she wished she could shut it off. 'We're pals, remember? We have a history. Have you forgotten that?'

He sighed. He shoved hands into pockets. 'You were the one who put an end to it, Eve.'

'I know. It was —' She broke off, not knowing what she wanted to say.

'Look,' he said, 'I'm not trying to – I hope you didn't get the wrong idea.'

'The wrong idea?'

'I just wanted to make sure you got home safely, that was all.'

She stared at him. No, glared at him. She felt the simmering starting up again, felt her fingers tighten around her tray.

He gave a little puzzled tilt of his head. 'What? What's up?'

'What's *up*? How can you even ask me that?'

'Eve, I don't know —'

'That wasn't all, was it? You didn't just get me home safely, did you?' Her voice rising along with her anger.

'What are you saying?' His face full of frowning innocence. Letting on he hadn't a clue. 'What are you talking about?'

'In case you've forgotten,' she said tightly, 'you *slept* with me, the night of the party. In case you decided to wipe that little detail from your memory.'

His eyes widened. His mouth dropped open. '*What?*'

'You *slept* with me,' she repeated, louder. 'I'm pregnant, and it's yours, Andy Baker.'

And in the dead silence that followed, she realised that, somewhere along the way, the music had stopped.

Susan

'I GOT A JOB,' SHE SAID. 'I STARTED TODAY.'

'A job? Doing what?'

'… I'm in retail.'

Pause. 'You mean a *shop*?'

'Well, it's more a department store. I'm in the china section.'

Her mother's sigh floated clearly into Susan's ear. Her mother had perfected the art of the sigh while Susan was still at school. 'So you're a shop assistant now.'

'I'm earning a salary,' Susan said steadily. 'The work is pleasant and the money is fine. I'm perfectly happy with it.'

All of which was rather untrue. In due course the work might become pleasant, but today it had been somewhat of a trial, with Susan forbidden to conduct sales but commanded instead to observe Carol, her fellow worker, all eyelashes and nails and stilettos, and a good fifteen years younger than Susan.

Three times, while Carol was busy with a sale,

Susan had been approached by customers asking about specific china brands that meant nothing to her, forcing her to apologise and explain that she was new, and hover foolishly by Carol's side, waiting to pass on the enquiry.

The china department was vast, with gleaming glass cabinets and floor-to-ceiling brightly lit shelving, displaying what seemed like thousands of different patterns. In between observing Carol, Susan walked around, trying to familiarise herself with it all, but she couldn't imagine ever becoming knowledgeable enough to be able to locate a design on demand.

The money wasn't exactly fine either. The salary was only slightly higher than the wage she'd been earning as a school secretary before her marriage. Enough to buy the weekly necessities and occasional treat, and to offer an embarrassingly paltry sum to Rosie and Ed when she got paid – they'd demur; she'd insist – but nowhere near what she'd need, if she hoped to afford even a shared living space in London for her and Harry. She had Luke's generous monthly contribution, of course, but who knew how long that would continue? And even if it did, something felt not right about using it. She accepted that he was liable for his son's upkeep, but it still jarred to take money from a man she'd walked out on. *You're welcome here for as long as you need*, Rosie had told her. *You're not bothering us in the slightest* – but they couldn't impose on her and Ed for much longer.

'So you're going to stay there then,' her mother said.

'For the time being we will.'

'And how's Harry? Does he like living in London?'

'Oh yes, he's very happy here.'

Another not-quite-truth. It was hard to tell with her little boy of few words. He didn't seem particularly unhappy, but being cooped up in their two little rooms for a fair bit of the time was no life for him. In Dublin he'd had their big rear garden, and a nearby park where they'd go to feed the ducks, and a drop-in crèche in the local shopping centre, and a few little friends among Susan's circle. And even though they'd had just one room in the hotel on Roone, he'd had the beach five minutes away, and the hotel garden to run about in, and his little cousins to play with every now and again. Here he had nobody but her, and no park close enough for them to walk to.

The few times she'd taken the tube with him hadn't been a success. He'd clung to her, big-eyed and wary – and transporting him and his buggy through the crowds and up and down the escalators had been a challenge she didn't relish repeating too often.

'Who's looking after him while you're at work?'

'A neighbour, a friend of Rosie's.'

Angie lived three houses away, and was a carer for her invalid mother. Angie was from the West Indies, and friendly, and professed herself delighted to look after Harry, and wasn't charging a fortune to do it, but there were no other children in her house, and Harry had cried when she'd dropped him there this morning, and he'd been even quieter than usual when she'd collected him.

Angie might not last. Susan might have to think again, when she had time.

'You'll have heard the news,' her mother said.

'What news?'

'About Luke, about him retiring. There was something on the radio earlier.'

Retiring?

Luke retiring?

'I hadn't heard,' she said. She had no radio or television here, and she didn't buy a newspaper, preferring to let the outside world pass her by for the moment. 'What exactly – I mean, what was said?'

'There was a press conference or something, I didn't pay it too much attention. It won't affect you now anyway.'

A press conference? He avoided them like the plague. Luke retiring. It wasn't possible. Luke Potter, the great painter, no longer painting. She couldn't imagine it. Maybe her mother had got it wrong.

'I have to go,' she said. 'I can hear Harry calling me. Talk soon.'

After hanging up she went online – and there it was. She skimmed the article, with its *shock announcement* and its *eminent and renowned artist* and its *huge loss to the art world*. And in the middle of all the hyperbole and drama, she read, *In response to questions, the artist said, 'I have decided to do this in order to spend more time with my family.'*

She read the single sentence, and reread it, and then read it again. The artist said, not his agent or his manager or his anything. He himself had said it, so he must have been there in person.

I have decided to do this in order to spend more time with my family.

His family. The wife who'd walked out on him, taking their son with her. His family, now living in another country. And being Luke, being the infuriating contrary stubborn person he was, he hadn't picked up the phone to tell her what he'd done, like any normal person would. He wanted to spend more time with his family, but he'd omitted to let them know that. Instead he'd held a press conference, which he despised. He'd looked into the cameras and endured the flash photography and told reporters that he was retiring, and why.

He knew she'd hear about it. If someone didn't ring her to tell her, he knew she'd catch it on a news report, like her mother had, or she'd read about it in a newspaper. He knew she'd get word of it somehow. Luke Potter was big news, in Ireland and London and beyond.

I have decided to do this in order to spend more time with my family.

The arrogance of him, assuming she'd come running back just because he'd given up painting for her. For all she knew he was bluffing, just to get her to come home.

But he didn't do bluffing. What you saw with Luke was what you got. He was the most honest man she'd ever met, which was one of the things she loved about him.

She was pretty sure he'd cried on the phone to her last week. He'd asked her to go back to him, and he'd cried when she hadn't said yes.

I have decided to do this in order to spend more time with my family.

She clicked on the article to close it – and only then did she spot the missed-calls message. She'd felt her phone buzzing in her pocket while she was among all the china, but when she'd seen that the calls were from Dublin friends, rather than from Angie with a possible Harry emergency, she'd ignored them. She'd heard the ping of a voicemail message coming through after each call, and had resolved to play them on her way home from work, and had forgotten. She listened to them now, one after the other, and each told her of Luke's retirement.

She called Laura, but got only her voicemail. Had she heard the news about her father yet? She'd pretty much cut herself off from Luke a few years earlier. Might this new development, if it was genuine, change things now?

Would it last, Luke Potter no longer being an artist?

So many questions, so little information.

I have decided to do this in order to spend more time with my family.

She cracked open the bedroom door and heard the even breathing of her sleeping son. She tiptoed downstairs and tapped on Rosie and Ed's sitting room door.

'Come in,' Rosie called. She and Ed were on the couch, watching TV. Rosie reached for the remote control and muted the volume.

'Sorry to interrupt,' Susan said, 'but I was wondering if you'd heard anything about Luke.'

'You want tea?' Ed asked. 'Or something stronger?'

'Nothing, thanks.'

He knew. They both knew, or they would have said, *Luke? What about him? Did something happen? Is he OK?*

'It was on the news,' Rosie said. 'I wondered whether you knew.'

'My mother told me,' Susan replied. 'I just ... I wasn't sure that she'd picked it up right.'

'He's retiring,' Ed said. 'At least, that's what was reported.'

'That's what she said. It's ... unexpected.'

Had they heard the bit about wanting to spend more time with his family? If they had, they'd be wondering why he hadn't been in touch with Susan.

'So what now?' Rosie asked.

On the television screen a couple glided silently in tuxedo and long gown across a shining floor. So graceful they looked, her hand on his shoulder, his on the small of her back, her skirt billowing as they whirled and floated. So right they looked together, as if they belonged in one another's embrace.

'I don't know,' Susan replied. 'I don't know what now.'

That was the truth, wasn't it? She didn't know what to do. She didn't know if she could risk going back, if her heart and her soul could take another hammering if things didn't work out again. She didn't know what on earth to do.

She left them and returned upstairs. She sat for a while by the window in the darkness, looking out at the lights in the houses across the street.

She doubted that she'd ever be as proficient as Carol in the giant china department. She sensed that Angie wasn't the right fit to look after Harry. She couldn't expect Rosie and Ed, whatever they said, to put them up for more than another couple of weeks, but she balked at the thought of hunting for somewhere else to live. She imagined walking through strange rooms, trying to get a feel for them, trying to picture her and Harry there.

It was still early days, but she was beginning to suspect that London, for all its life, all its attractions, would never feel like home.

She thought of the man she'd married, twenty-three years her senior. Moody, talented, strong, irascible, generous, infuriating, compelling. The only man she'd truly loved, the only man with the power to ruin her, or make her happier than she'd ever been.

She thought of him this evening, having sent his message to her through a press conference.

Waiting for her response.

She looked at her phone, sitting on the folding table.

She couldn't do it.

She stayed by the window while the minutes ticked on. She remained there while the lights in the neighbouring houses winked out one by one, and the city of London surrendered slowly to the night.

Laura

'I HAVE TO ASK YOU,' NELL SAID, HER GREEN party frock still on, her hair caught up on one side with the diamanté clip that Laura had passed on to her when she'd admired it a few weeks earlier. 'Did you know about this?' she asked. The colour had washed from her face: in the moonlight she looked like a ghost. 'Did you know she was going to pin it on Andy? Did she tell you that?' Standing on the other side of the five-bar gate, making it a barrier between them. 'Did you know that, and say nothing?'

'I didn't know at the start,' Laura said, hating the tremor she could hear in her voice.

'At the start?'

'I didn't know when I told you.'

'So you found out eventually. She told you it was Andy, and you didn't think to come and say it to me.'

'She didn't tell me – at least, she only confirmed what I suspected when I challenged her.'

'You *suspected* him?' The disbelief in her tone, the awful grimace, as if the words tasted bad. 'Why would you think he'd do such a thing when he's going out with Tilly?'

'I – Nell, I wondered, I did wonder if it could be him ... Look, they had all that history, and she said there'd been drink taken – and I just thought it was a possibility. I had nothing to go on –'

'No, you hadn't, because there *was* nothing, and still you suspected him. And when Eve told you you were right, you kept it from me.'

'Nell, she asked me not to say anything. She begged me.'

'She *begged* you not to tell anyone she was pregnant too, and you told me.'

'I was wrong. I shouldn't have said anything. I'm sorry, Nell. I've handled it all wrong. I've messed up.'

In the ensuing silence, something rustled in the field. Near enough to ten o'clock, a big moon lighting the place up like Christmas. Tilly had burst into the kitchen earlier, in such a state as to be practically incoherent. Laura had taken one look at her and banished the gaping boys to the sitting room, thankful that Gavin had already gone up with the girls.

How could he? Tilly had wept. *I loved him – how could he do it to me?*

Laura had held her and pretended to be shocked at the news, and had agreed that it was terrible, and then Nell had texted, asking to meet her at the gate, so Laura had promised not to be long, and had come out to face the music.

'He didn't,' Nell said. 'Andy. He didn't sleep with her. He's told us he didn't, and we believe him. She's lying.'

'Nell, he was at Frog's party.'

'That doesn't—'

'And he walked her home.'

'He's not denying that. He says she needed looking after because she'd had a lot to drink. He says they both had. He's being truthful, not trying to get out of anything. He brought her home and went in and made coffee, and then he left.'

A car approached, its headlights whooshing ahead of it. A horn tooted as it passed: both of them ignored it.

'She's pregnant, Nell,' Laura said gently. 'That didn't happen by itself.'

'It still doesn't mean it was Andy. He's not lying to us, I know he's not. He wouldn't do that.'

'She can get a DNA test done. She can prove it's his.' Of course it was his. Of course Nell was having trouble believing that. 'Listen Nell, we're on the same side here. Of course I want to think the best of Andy, but the fact is, Eve is pregnant and she's saying it was him, and I have to look out for Tilly. Can you imagine what this has done to her?'

'Done to *her*?' Nell demanded. 'Andy's the one who's been accused, not Tilly – *we*'re the ones who'll suffer the fallout, not Tilly.'

'Nell, she's totally distraught. You were there, you saw her.'

A beat passed. 'She slapped his face,' Nell said. 'Did she tell you that?'

'... No.' Good for her.

'Well, she did, in front of everyone. She didn't even ask him if it was true. She should have more faith in him.'

Two more cars sped by. 'Has Eve been to see Jack?' Nell demanded.

'I don't know, she didn't mention—'

'He could put a date on it. He could tell if she's lying.'

Her logic was flawed. A doctor might be able to pinpoint the date of conception with a fair degree of accuracy, but that information wouldn't necessarily prove a lie. It wouldn't prove paternity, or rule it out. If Jack put the date a week before the party, say, or a week after – who was to say that Andy and Eve hadn't slept together then?

'He could say it happened while Andy was in college,' Nell went on. 'That would prove it wasn't him, wouldn't it?'

Clutching at straws, which was understandable – but in Laura's mind there wasn't an ounce of doubt. It all added up, it made sense. She wouldn't have expected it from him, he'd always seemed like an upfront lad, but the evidence was overwhelming. Only a fool, or a stepmother who couldn't face the reality of it, would try to protest his innocence.

'Nell, let's not fall out over this. Come on, it's not worth that. We can get past this.'

Nell's expression didn't alter. 'You still think he did it. You suspected him all along. You think he's lying. This is my *stepson* we're talking about. This is James's *son*.'

Laura tried again. 'Look, whatever I think, and whether Andy is responsible or not, we don't have to let it come between us.'

But even as she said it, she recognised the nonsense of it. Of course it was coming between them – how could it not? It was such a relief not to have to keep that secret any more but Lord, the way it had come out. The way Tilly had found out, right in the middle of Henry's party, in front of God knew how many witnesses. At least half of Roone must know about it by now, and the other half wouldn't be far behind. Of course it was driving a wedge between her and Nell, the closest friend she had.

'He wants to talk to her,' Nell said. 'Tilly. He wants to explain. He's tried ringing her, but she won't answer her phone. He's going to call around in the morning.'

'Nell, he's the last person she wants to see right now. Ask him to try phoning again tomorrow.'

Nell shook her head slowly. 'I can't believe it,' she said. 'You've decided he's guilty, without even hearing his side. I can understand that Tilly's upset and maybe not thinking straight, but I'm shocked that you of all people would be so quick to condemn him.' She turned abruptly and was gone. Laura looked after her in dismay. Was this the end of them? The thought of losing Nell's friendship was unconscionable.

Back in the kitchen she found Gavin reading the day's newspaper. 'Where's Tilly?'

'Upstairs, I presume: she scarpered as soon as she saw me. She looked in a bad way. What's going on, Laur?'

He knew nothing. He didn't know about Eve's pregnancy or Andy's part in it. All he'd seen was Tilly in tears. Laura filled him in quickly.

'Crikey,' he said, 'that's a bit of a mess.'

'You could call it that.'

'What's Nell saying?'

'She's in denial. Andy's insisting nothing happened, and she's taking his word for it.'

Gavin considered this. 'Maybe nothing *did* happen. You only have Eve's word for it that it did.'

'Gav, it happened. They were at a party together. They drank too much, he walked her home, and now she's pregnant. Doesn't take a rocket scientist to work it out.'

'Maybe it wasn't Andy. Could have been anyone.'

'Why would she say it was him if it wasn't?'

'Well, here's a thought. Maybe she's jealous of him and Tilly. Maybe she's trying to break them up.'

She shook her head. 'She might well be jealous – who knows? But the fact remains that Andy walked her home after a party, and now she's pregnant. Are you saying she just happened to have sex with someone else around the same time and decided to pin the pregnancy on Andy?'

'I'm just saying there's no proof it was Andy. And he's denying it, and he's a decent young fellow.' Gavin spread his hands. 'I'm saying don't jump to conclusions, that's all.'

Was that what she was doing? Was she wrong to believe Eve, and assume Andy was lying? She pressed her hands to her temples, trying to quiet her buzzing thoughts. What was true, what was not? How were they to know for sure, until a baby arrived and a DNA test was done? And in the meantime, fingers would point at Andy, and tongues would wag, and Nell and James would be caught in the middle. And thanks to Eve, Laura was caught up in it too.

'I could kill her,' she said. 'Eve. She told me she was pregnant a few weeks ago. She made me swear to keep quiet. I didn't know about Andy then; I only found that out later.'

Gavin took this in. 'You were good to her,' he said, 'when she was going through a lot. I'm not surprised she turned to you. Try not to be too hard on her.'

'Gav, look what this will do to Tilly. Look what it's doing to her. I know Eve went through some bad stuff, but it doesn't let her off the hook here. And now Nell is mad at me too, because I'm not protesting Andy's innocence with her.'

Poppy's birthday, she thought, in two days. Nell had promised to finish early at the salon and bring her two to the party. What were the chances of that happening now? Would she punish her children for Laura's mistake?

She'd worry about that when it came: there was other stuff to be sorted before then. 'I'd better go and find Tilly,' she said, feeling too tired for it. What in God's name could she say to her sister that would offer the smallest comfort?

'Hey,' he said, 'I nearly forgot. There was a bit about your father on the radio just now.'

Her father. Everything in her stood to attention. 'What was it?'

'Apparently he's retiring.'

Laura stared at him. 'Retiring? From what?'

'Painting, I assume. Only job he has, isn't it?'

Her father giving up painting? Couldn't be true.

And then she thought, yes it could.

Did Susan know? She had to be told. This would bring her home; this would bring her back to him. 'Where's my phone?'

'Behind you, on the worktop.'

She placed the call. Susan answered on the third ring.

'You've heard,' Laura said.

'Hi Laura. Yes, I've heard. I tried calling you earlier.'

'Has he been in touch?'

'No.'

'He's giving it up. He's doing what you want.'

Silence.

'You'll go back now, won't you?' No response. 'Susan?'

'It's not that straightforward.'

Laura opened her mouth – and closed it again. And opened it again. 'Susan, this is his way of showing you he loves you. He's giving up painting for you. This is the biggest thing he can do.'

'Laura, I need to think about this, and you need to let me.'

Laura had to tell her. She had to be told.

She couldn't tell her. She couldn't break her word again. He'd never forgive her – and suddenly, that mattered.

'I appreciate your concern,' Susan said. 'I do, honestly. But this is between Luke and me. I'll let you know what happens.'

And she had to be content with that, because Susan was right, it wasn't her business. Except that she *was* involved: he'd involved her. After hanging up she dialled her father's number. Quickly, before she could think better of it. She counted the rings until she heard his voicemail message. 'This is me. I need to talk to you, it's important. Will you ring me back as soon as you get this?'

Would he? She wasn't hopeful.

She slipped her phone into her pocket. 'Right. Tilly, and then bed. See you in a bit.'

'I'll be up soon,' he said.

She checked the sitting room and found it empty. She climbed the stairs and stood on the landing. The door to the room Tilly shared with the twins was ajar, but its light was off. She pushed it open a little wider and slipped quietly in, and waited for her eyes to adjust.

There were the silent little humps of her daughters, asleep in their bunks behind the door – and there was Tilly on the far side of the room, at the chest of drawers. Laura glanced at the single bed and saw the open suitcase.

'Tilly,' she whispered, 'what are you doing?'

Tilly lifted clothing from a drawer and placed it in the case. 'I'm packing.'

'Well, I can see that, but—'

'I'm leaving on the first ferry.'

'What? Tomorrow? You can't.'

'I have to,' Tilly whispered fiercely. 'How can I stay here, with him living next door?' A sob caught in her throat, caused a hiccup in her breath.

Laura moved closer. 'Tilly, please, this is crazy. Your flight isn't until Saturday. Where will you go if you leave tomorrow?'

'I don't care. Away from here.'

'Look, we'll talk about it in the morning, OK?'

'I'm going. You can't stop me.'

'But you don't know anyone off the island. I can't let you leave like this. Please don't.'

Tilly lifted the case and set it on the floor by the end of the bed. Without a word, she left the room. Laura waited until she returned with her toilet bag and dropped it with a small soft thump into the case. Even in the near darkness, the misery on her face was plain to see.

'This is crazy,' Laura repeated. 'I can't let you go.'

'You must.' She sat on the bed and pulled off her shoes. She turned back the duvet and climbed in, still fully clothed, and rolled over to face the wall.

Laura remained where she was. How could Tilly leave a day early? How could Laura let her go?

How could she stop her? At nineteen, Tilly was an adult, not a minor in Laura's care – and with Andy living in such close proximity, could she blame the girl for wanting to flee? But the idea of her heading off on her own was unnerving. What if something happened to her? What if her parents, her adoptive parents, got in touch on Monday to say she'd never arrived home?

The first ferry left at eight in the morning. Laura would somehow have to persuade her to stay before that.

'Goodnight,' she whispered – and when there was no reaction she left the room and pulled the door closed. She checked on the boys and found them in bed reading comics.

Poppy was asleep in her parents' room, in the fold-up bed they hauled out of storage whenever Tilly was due. Laura regarded her daughter's sleeping face in the soft light of the little minion lamp that Poppy insisted be left on at bedtime – a present last Christmas from her godmother Nell.

Would Nell cut off contact with them all now? Would she look the other way when they encountered one another on the road? Would she forbid her children to play with Laura's?

Laura couldn't think about it, couldn't countenance it. Instead she feasted on the sight of Poppy's half-open mouth, the flush in her plump cheeks, the trusting, defenceless look of her. Three years old on Saturday, her ice-cream cake already bought and waiting in the freezer.

In the en suite Laura washed her face and brushed her teeth. She slipped off her clothes, leaving them where they fell, and pulled on Gavin's old grey T-shirt that served her as a nightie. She climbed into bed and closed her eyes and tried not to think about the morning, and what might lie ahead for all of them.

Imelda

'WE'D BETTER GO,' SHE SAID.

It was a quarter to eight. Her body felt sluggish
with tiredness. She'd had one of her bad nights,
drifting in and out of sleep, her subconscious, when
it took over, throwing up muddied unconnected
images: Hugh on a ladder, smiling down at her;
her brother-in-law bent over a crossword puzzle;
her sister in a navy suit, standing on the steps of
Roone's church; Imelda herself piping white icing
onto a cake.

In her waking moments, when her clock-radio was
showing one and two in the morning, she'd heard
more than a few cars passing outside. They'd puzzled
her – where could they be going at that time? – until
she remembered the big party at the hotel. She hoped
it had gone well. She was fond of Henry, who'd been
so welcoming in her early days on Roone. *Looks like
Hugh held out for the best*, he'd said once. Such a lovely
remark to make.

Trying to return to sleep, her thoughts had drifted
towards Eve, as they often had of late. She missed her.

She hoped she was eating properly. Her last sighting of her had been from Nell's salon, two weeks earlier: in the act of putting on her jacket, she'd glanced out of the window and seen Eve about to enter the fish shop across the street. She'd lifted a hand to rap on the window and had lowered it again, afraid she might be seen, and ignored.

She might return to Imelda, once she heard Gualtiero had gone home.

'I wish to thank you very much, Eemelda,' he said. 'Is very sad time for you, but you were very kind for me.'

'I was glad to be able to do it,' Imelda replied. 'It was good to have someone in the house.' They were driving to the ferry. They passed the little white gate that led to the holy well. She approached a bend, and slowed. 'I'm sorry you never met Hugh. I think – I know you would have liked him.'

'Yes, I am sure.'

She drove by Fennessy's, with a clothes-line full of billowing sheets at the side of the house. Clancy's, Regan's, a field of sheep, another of cattle. The primary school, where Nell's father had worked for years as principal, a basketball hoop, just one, in the front yard. It always struck her as a shame that they didn't have two, so the children could have a proper game.

'Tomorrow,' Gualtiero said, 'I will be in my restaurant again.'

'Yes. I'm sure you'll be happy to be back.'

She pictured him in the lovely courtyard, stopping by tables to talk to his customers; or maybe in the kitchen, surrounded by pots and pans. A light mist began to fall, settling silently on the windscreen, the first rain they'd had in weeks. He'd been so blessed with the weather.

'How long,' she asked, 'before your paintings arrive?' He'd brought the bulk of them to the island post office a few days earlier, over a dozen, and arranged to have them shipped back to Italy.

He shrugged. 'One month, maybe more. Is not important when they come: I 'ave everything inside.' He tapped his chest.

She understood. When she'd left Roone after her first holiday there, the island had remained with her. It wasn't just that she could close her eyes and picture the village street, the little pebble beach, the coast road edged with bushes of drooping fuchsia and slanting sheaves of montbretia. It was more than that. It was almost as if she could feel the fine mist of salt spray carried on every breeze, could inhale the clean briny air that permeated every nook of the island. The low musical song of the sea in the bay was the undercurrent to her thoughts, the sharp cries of the gulls overhead dipping into her empty moments. Once it got under your skin, Roone was a hard place to forget. *Roone picks its people*, Hugh had said to her once – and she believed it, and felt like she had been picked.

'You might come back,' she said lightly. 'I'd be

happy for you to stay again, if you wanted.' Glancing his way, seeing the smile her remark generated.

'*Grazie*, Eemelda. I would like very much to return. And perhaps you will come to see my restaurant some day.'

'That would be lovely. You're an excellent cook.'

He'd presented them with a fish stew, four nights ago when Nell had come to dinner. Chunks of sea bass, monkfish and sole in a rich sauce of red wine, tomatoes, garlic and chilli, poured over slices of bread that he'd rubbed with more garlic. They'd had seconds.

'So,' she said, as the pier hove into view, 'who will collect you at the airport in Rome?'

'Collect?'

'Who will come for you?'

'I will take the train, and then the bus,' he declared. 'Paolo will be busy in the restaurant.'

He'd be on home turf in Rome, easily able to navigate from the airport, but still she felt sad at the thought of nobody meeting him. It was no mean feat getting from Roone to Dublin airport without a car: a bus from the mainland to Tralee, a train from there to Mallow, another to Dublin, a second bus from the station to the airport. He'd be worn out before he left Ireland.

'If you come back,' she said, 'you must fly to Kerry airport, from Dublin or London. It would make it easier for you.'

'Yes,' he agreed. 'I will do that.'

It was a friendship, no more. She didn't expect or

want anything more. But a little trip to Italy, maybe a long weekend, was certainly appealing. She wouldn't rule it out in a year or two, when she wasn't so broken. It might help her to heal. It might go some way towards fixing her heart.

As she pulled in at the pier, she saw Gavin's white van parked a short way down the road. Dropping guests maybe, or collecting an early arrival. The ferry was docked, about to make its first trip of the day.

She halted by the ice-cream van, its shutters down until later. 'I won't wait,' she told Gualtiero. 'You don't mind?' Conscious still of wagging tongues, even at this early hour. Hating goodbyes anyway, always wanting them over as quickly as possible.

'Of course.' He took his case from the boot as she opened her door and stood by it, shielded from the short line of vehicles waiting to board. He came to her and placed his hands on her arms and kissed her on both cheeks, bringing his scent with him. 'Eemelda, thank you for all. *Grazie mille per tutti*, Eemelda. *Arrivederci.*'

'Goodbye,' she said. 'Safe trip, and thank you, Gualtiero,' stupidly feeling yet again the threat of tears. These days, anything at all could set her off. She climbed back into the car and pressed the heels of her hands briefly to her eye sockets. She watched him walk towards the boat, pulling the case behind him, his straw hat, a little more battered now, held in his free hand.

When he had passed out of sight she turned the

car around and drove home, sadness settling heavily around her again. In the kitchen she turned on the radio and washed their breakfast dishes as a female singer sang about the wonder of a first kiss, the heaven of a first night. She opened the fridge to return the milk and butter, and she saw the olives and cheese and sundried tomatoes and anchovies that she hadn't bought, and the remains of the streaky bacon she'd cooked for his last evening on Roone.

She left the dishes to drain and went into the sitting room to open the curtains and check for forgotten cups – and there, lying on the coffee table, she found his gift.

To Imelda, he had written in the accompanying folded note, *to say thank you from your friend Gualtiero*.

It was the scene he'd painted in her back garden of the little Tuscan beach where he and his family used to holiday, and the island of Elba sitting out on the horizon, squat and long and black. It was on canvas, about eighteen inches wide and a foot high.

She picked it up. She sat on the couch and held it at arm's length and gazed at it. She brought it closer and traced the bumps where he'd loaded up the paint for the wave crests, and the black boulders that rose from the sea. She'd talk to James about getting a frame for it. She'd hang it in the hall, so it would be the first thing visitors saw.

And just then she heard the sound of the kitchen door opening, and someone entering the hall.

She froze. The back door was unlocked, like

it always was during the day. Crime was rare on Roone, but not unheard of. She waited, gripping the painting, for whoever it was to find her.

'Imelda?'

Eve: thank God. 'In here,' she said, and Eve's face appeared.

'You gave me a fright,' Imelda said, setting the painting aside, getting to her feet. 'I wasn't expecting anyone so early.' Not moving towards her, not yet – but she would forgive, of course, even if no apology was offered.

'Sorry. I figured you'd be up.' She hovered in the doorway. She was very pale; the skin beneath her eyes was tinged with grey. Her face was bare of makeup, her hair pulled into a ponytail that draped over a shoulder. 'Is the man ... still here?'

The man. 'No – I just dropped him to the ferry. Have you eaten, dear? Have you had breakfast?'

'Imelda,' Eve said, a hand going up to clutch the end of her ponytail. 'Imelda,' she said again, mouth trembling, the colour rising quickly in her cheeks, washing away the white. 'I – I have something – there's something I have to – to tell you.'

Bad news, it had to be. Imelda felt goose pimples rising on her arms. 'What is it, Eve? What's wrong?'

'I – Imelda, I'm so sorry,' she said, eyes brimming. 'I didn't mean it to happen, honest to God, I swear I didn't do it on purpose,' the words galloping out as fast as the tears that were spilling over now and racing down her cheeks.

'Eve, please, you must tell me. What's happened? What have you done?' Possibilities raced through her head – something illegal, drugs, something that had caused injury, or worse, to another person. 'Tell me,' she repeated, and Eve cried out that she was pregnant, and that she was so sorry, and that she'd give anything for it not to be true.

Pregnant.

Eve was pregnant.

Imelda resumed her seat, slowly and carefully. 'Well,' she said, and couldn't think of another thing.

Eve, pregnant. Eve, storming out of the house not once but twice. Being inexplicably rude to Gualtiero. Avoiding Imelda, ignoring her calls. It began to make some kind of sense. Pregnant and afraid, and keeping her distance or lashing out, because it was easier than voicing her fears.

'Sit down,' she said, shifting the painting to the coffee table to make room – but instead Eve took Hugh's armchair by the empty fireplace. She sat all huddled together on the edge of it, head bowed, shoulders hunched, hands gripping her knees. Waiting, Imelda knew, for her reaction.

She looked again at Gualtiero's beautiful gift, the sandy cove and the colourful houses, the sea and the island. She thought about the man who had created it, who should be on the bus by now that would take him to Tralee, and on a plane a few hours later that would carry him back to his life in Italy.

That was the thing about time, she thought. It

kept moving forward, kept pulling everyone along with it, regardless of circumstances. A person might lose a job, another a house, another a beloved child or partner: none of it mattered a jot to Time. *Come along*, it said. *Keep up*. Forever moving things forward, putting more and more distance between people and the sorrows that had been visited upon them – which, when you thought about it, was probably the kindest thing it could do.

And after having the worst possible thing already happen to her, after managing to cling on to the impossible, but ultimately essential, assembly line that Time insisted on, Imelda wondered if anything else, *anything* else, really mattered all that much. Before Hugh's death, this news would have seemed like the end of the world – but now that she'd been brought to that very place, or to within a stone's throw of it at least, this was … what? A shock, certainly – but nowhere near the end of the world. Miles and miles from the end of the world.

And this was Eve, whose mother had failed her, who'd been abused within the family she'd been entrusted to. This was Eve, the closest thing to a daughter that she and Hugh had been given, whom they'd both grown to love. This was Eve, who'd baked her very first cake for Imelda's birthday, a few months after she'd moved in with them, *Happy Bday* she'd written in wobbly lettering on the top, because she'd run out of space.

This was Eve, who had held Imelda's hand all

through the first endless night without Hugh, when they'd sat up with the other islanders to look after what remained of him. This was Eve, in tears and in trouble now, looking to Imelda for forgiveness and help. How could she turn her back, even if she wanted to? Hugh wouldn't have done that: she was certain of it. He'd have been disappointed, of course, but he'd have been there for Eve, like he'd always been there for her. Like they both had.

'Come and sit over here,' she said, patting the couch beside her, and Eve obeyed. Imelda put an arm around her shoulders and Eve rested her head on Imelda's chest and went on crying as Imelda told her that she wasn't alone, that they'd cope. 'You can move back here if you want,' she said, 'and we'll go from there. How does that sound?'

She had no idea what she was taking on. She didn't know the ins and outs of it yet, but she'd hear soon enough. She didn't think there was a steady boyfriend: Eve would surely have mentioned him. She hoped to God he wasn't someone else's partner – but if he was, they'd cope with that too. Having survived the unbearable, she could bear everything else.

People would talk, once the news got out. If Eve wanted to keep the baby – let her want to keep it: the alternative was abhorrent to Imelda – people would have plenty to talk about. Let them say what they wanted.

A baby in the house. A grandson or granddaughter

for Imelda, or as near to it as made no difference. Once he'd got used to the idea, Hugh would have loved it, would have doted on it. Look how wonderful he'd been with Nell's little two.

She was about to suggest tea when the doorbell rang. She felt Eve instantly stiffen. 'Stay here,' Imelda said, getting up. 'It's probably a neighbour. I'll get rid of them.'

Eve sat up, swiping beneath her eyes, dabbing at them again with a sleeve. 'Imelda,' she said quickly, 'I have to tell you —'

A hammering on the door interrupted her. A voice. 'Eve? Are you in there?' A woman's voice.

Nell, it sounded like.

'God,' Eve whispered, dipping her head into her palms.

More hammering, followed by repeated short bursts of the doorbell. 'Eve!'

'I'll handle it,' Imelda said. She left the room, pulling the door closed. 'Coming!' she called. What now? Nell was clearly not happy – and it could only, she thought, have something to do with Eve's news.

Andy. The name flew into her head as she opened the door. 'Nell,' she said.

'Imelda, is she here?' Nell demanded, her face pinched with anger, her words clipped. 'I've been to the apartment and there's no sign of her.'

'Nell, what's going on? Eve is here, yes, but —'

'I have to talk to her.' She moved forward, forcing Imelda to step aside and allow her entry.

'Nell, please, calm down—'

'Where is she? I need to talk to her, Imelda. Where is she?' Her eyes darting around the hall, as if she might find a clue. 'Is she in there?' Pointing at the sitting room door.

'Look, she's told me—'

'Please just get her, or bring me to her. Don't make me search the house.'

'Nell, for goodness' sake, please get a—'

'I'm here.'

Imelda swung around, and there she was, standing in the doorway, her hand on the jamb. Looking at Imelda, not Nell.

At the sight of her, Nell strode forward. '*You!*' she snapped. 'How *dare* you accuse Andy? How *dare* you? You know as well as I do that he had *nothing* to do with it!'

Andy, Imelda thought. Andy, who was going out with Laura's sister. Could it be true?

'It *was* him,' Eve said, and Imelda heard the wobble in her voice. 'He's the father, he knows he—'

'Shut up!' Nell shouted, her face darkening, her hands in fists by her sides. 'Shut up with your lies! Just stop it!'

Imelda was horrified. Was this really Hugh's smiling, cheerful niece? She'd never seen her in such a state. 'Please,' she said, taking a step towards them, 'please Nell, it's obvious you're upset, but—'

'I *am* upset,' Nell shot back. 'Of course I'm upset! I'm sorry, Imelda, I didn't mean you to be involved—'

'Well, it's too late for that,' Imelda said, trying to sound calmer than she felt. 'Eve has come to me for help, and I have to stand by her. I *will* stand by her.'

'Imelda, she's *lying!*' Nell insisted. 'She's saying Andy made her pregnant, and it's a *lie!* She's a pathetic, jealous *liar*, and she—'

'I'm *not* lying!' Eve cried. 'I'm not! It *was* Andy!'

Nell swung back to her. 'You're jealous of Tilly!' she snapped. 'You broke his heart, and now you can't bear to see him happy again – it's pathetic! God knows how many men you've had, but you're determined to pin this on Andy!'

Imelda attempted again to intervene. 'Nell, please, there's no need for—'

'Imelda,' Nell said urgently, 'you must believe me. Whatever she's told you, whatever she says, it's a pack of lies. Andy was *not* involved in this.'

Imelda felt pulled in two, wanting to believe both – but both couldn't be right.

'She lied last night, for all the world to hear,' Nell went on. 'Did she tell you that? She accused him, at Henry's party, in front of everyone – in front of Tilly too – and now the whole island thinks he did it.'

Imelda couldn't imagine it. 'Is this true?' she asked Eve. 'Did you do that?'

'Yes, but I wasn't planning to. I wanted to—'

'Whether she planned it or not, it's a lie!' Nell repeated. 'He swears he didn't, and we believe him. *She*'s the liar,' jabbing a finger at Eve, '*she*'s the one—'

Imelda had had enough. 'Nell!' she cried. 'I need

you to stop this! If you can't calm down, you have to leave right now! You're in my house and I won't have it! This is a house of *grief* – shame on you!'

She wasn't given to outbursts. This one made her face flame, her heart bang in her ears, her legs turn suddenly to rubber. In the pause that followed it she was conscious of her loud, ragged breathing, and the awful shrillness that had been in her voice. She put out a hand and clutched a banister, needing something to hold on to.

'You believe her,' Nell said dully. 'You actually believe what she's saying.'

'Nell, I honestly don't know what to believe. You're giving contradictory accounts. I can't possibly tell—'

Nell's face hardened. 'You're against him too. I should have known you'd take her side.'

'Nell, that's not fair,' Imelda protested. 'I'm not against anyone. This isn't about taking sides – but I must listen to Eve's point of view too. You have to see that.'

'Oh, I see that,' Nell said grimly. 'I see it clearly. She comes to cry on your shoulder, and you want to save her all over again.'

'Oh, that is so—'

'I just wish you could see what this is doing to Andy, and to Tilly. Try to remember that when you're listening to her point of view.'

What was Imelda to do? What was she to say to that? Before she could find a response, Nell wheeled and left the hall, striding through the open front door and on down the path to the gate. Imelda looked at Eve, who regarded her mutely.

No. They couldn't leave it like that. She hurried outside. 'Nell, please wait, please let's try to sort this out.'

But Nell didn't wait. She climbed into her car and slammed the door and drove off too quickly, without another look in Imelda's direction. Imelda remained on the path, shocked and upset, waiting for her racing heart to slow down. Nell falling out with her was absolutely the last thing she needed.

She returned to the house. She closed the front door and leant against it. Eve stood unmoving, arms folded across her chest now, face pale, eyes glittering.

'Will you tell me the truth, Eve?' Imelda asked quietly. 'On Hugh's grave, will you tell me the truth of what happened?'

Eve flinched at the words. Her chin trembled. 'Imelda, don't say that.'

'On his grave,' she repeated. 'I need to know, Eve. I really need you to be honest with me now.'

Eve looked at the floor, drew in a deep breath. 'Andy walked me home from a party,' she said, so quietly that Imelda had to strain to hear her. 'It – wasn't long after Hugh. I was in bits, you know that. I wasn't going to go to the party, but my friends … they said it might do me good, let me forget for a while. I – I had too much to drink, and Andy brought me home. He came in, and –'

She broke off. Imelda waited. Not wanting to hear,

but forced to listen. Owing it to Nell, to Andy, to James, to Tilly, to get at the right version.

'Eve, I need the truth. Was it Andy?'

'... Yes. He ... was there.'

Imelda frowned. 'He was *there*? You mean in the apartment?'

'Yes. He was the only one. It had to be him.'

'Eve, you don't sound very sure. How can you not be sure? Either it was or it wasn't Andy.'

'I *am* sure. It *was* him. There was nobody else. I just—' She broke off, pressed her hands to her cheeks, inhaled deeply. 'I just can't remember that part.'

She stopped again, chewed at her bottom lip. 'Imelda,' she said earnestly, 'it *had* to be him – I haven't been with anyone else. You *must* believe me. It's true, I swear it.'

Distasteful as the story was, Imelda wanted to believe it was the truth. 'Did others see you going home with him?'

'Yes – we left in a group. Bugs was there and ... a few others.'

'But Andy was the one who brought you home. You're absolutely certain of this.'

'Yes. *Yes*. The others dropped away one by one. It was just the two of us by the time we got to my place. He came in, and one of us made coffee – the mugs were there the next morning.'

'And Andy?'

'... He was gone.'

'Have you spoken with him since?'

She shook her head. 'No – at least, not about this, not until last night. We met a few times, but I thought – I didn't think he'd want me to bring it up. I thought he must have … regretted it.'

'And when you found out you were pregnant?'

'I decided I should wait – till Tilly was gone back, I mean – before I told him.'

'But instead you told him last night. At the party, in front of everyone.'

Eve grimaced. 'I didn't mean to. I met him, and he – tried to make little of it, acted like it was just a bit of fun, and it made me mad to think he could just dismiss it like that, when I was going through— well, and it all just came out. I wasn't going to say anything, honestly I wasn't. I knew I'd have to tell him after Tilly left, but … I was going to wait. And when I told him, I shouted it because I was angry, and … people heard.'

'What did he say?'

'He didn't say anything. He – he looked completely shocked. It was like he'd forgotten it or something. And then – I went away, I left, because I was embarrassed, with everyone looking at us.'

'And Tilly heard.'

'She must have. I didn't know she was there.'

Imelda closed her eyes briefly. 'And Nell was there too.'

'… She must have been. I didn't see them.'

Imelda could imagine it. The row that had sprung up, the angry words clearly heard, the stir in the crowd. And oh, poor Tilly to witness such a thing, to be there when Eve had dropped her bombshell.

Eve's account sounded genuine. It had the ring of truth about it – but how could she be sure of anything, if she'd drunk too much to remember it properly? And Nell had seemed so certain, so convinced of Andy's innocence.

What would Hugh do, faced with this impossible situation? He'd be torn, like Imelda was, with his niece saying one thing and his former foster daughter another. What was the answer? How was Imelda to arrive at the truth of it?

'Were you thinking,' she asked, 'of telling me at all?'

Eve's face flushed instantly. 'I – I wanted to tell you, but – I was afraid. I knew it would be a shock, and you wouldn't like it, and especially not now, after ...'

After Hugh.

'I had decided to leave the island. I didn't want to ... embarrass you. I was going to write to you, when I was gone.'

She had planned it all, and Imelda had known nothing.

'I'm really sorry, Imelda. I've let you down and I have no excuse. But everything I'm telling you is the truth, I swear it.'

It was the truth. Imelda was sure of it. Or she was telling a version of the truth, as she remembered it. She was telling *her* truth.

'So the party was the end of May?'

' Yes, the twenty-fourth.'

And this was the first week of August. She totted up the weeks and arrived at eleven, give or take. 'Have you seen Dr Jack?'

'No.'

'But you've done a test.'

'... Well, no, but I've missed two periods, and earlier I felt sick, and I was throwing up. I'm definitely pregnant.'

'Will you come with me to the doctor, Eve? Will you let him check you out?'

Eve nodded. 'If you want me to, I will.'

It was all she could think of, a visit to Dr Jack. It probably wouldn't help a lot – it wouldn't come at the truth they needed, but she'd have to see a doctor at some stage, and Jack was sensitive, and tactful.

'Will you come back to this house?' Imelda asked. 'Will you move in here again?' Because this was her home, not some dreary little collection of rooms above a crèche with no companions, no neighbours.

'I'd like that,' Eve whispered.

'Let's go and pack up your things now so. Let's get you moved back, and we can go to the surgery after lunch.'

She didn't want to think about the next few months, and the challenges they'd bring. She couldn't dwell on the awful things Nell had said, or the way she'd looked at Imelda just before she'd left the house. She couldn't face the thought of the whispers this scandal would cause.

All she could do, all they could do, was get through today, and take it from there.

Tilly

IN THE END, TILLY HAVING GIVEN HER NO other choice, Laura had to let her go. 'Get off the bus in Cahersiveen,' she instructed, 'and call this number.' She handed Tilly a small cream card. *Sycamore House Bed & Breakfast*, the card read. *Joshua and Mary Finnerty. Free WiFi. Organic eggs. All rooms ensuite.*

'Mary is a niece of Maisie Kiely's,' Laura told her. 'I met her at Maisie's eightieth party last year. She's lovely. She'll put you up, or she'll find you somewhere else if she's full. Give me a ring when you're sorted.'

Cahersiveen, half an hour or so from the ferry terminal. Tilly had passed through it on every one of her journeys to and from Roone, but had never paid it much heed. A long main street – a petrol station, a library, a church – was all she could remember.

'Gav will pick you up tomorrow,' Laura went on. 'I'll be in the middle of Poppy's party but he'll come and bring you to the airport,' and Tilly said nothing to that, although she knew it wasn't going to happen. She had no intention of getting off the bus in Cahersiveen. She wasn't going to call Mary or Joshua

Finnerty with their free WiFi and their organic eggs. She was staying on the bus until it pulled into Tralee bus station, and from there she was travelling on to Dublin.

She'd crept downstairs when everyone was asleep, and planned her trip using Gavin's computer. She wanted to get as far from Roone as she possibly could, and Dublin seemed like the most logical place to aim for. She'd been scheduled to travel through there anyway on her way home. Kerry to Dublin to Dubai to Singapore to Brisbane: now she would have only three flights to endure.

And as long as she was going to Dublin, she figured she might as well look up her father. Why not? She had nothing to lose. She still had his address: she'd held on to it, even after he'd ignored the letter she'd written to him. She'd find his house –she'd figure it out.

He's not child friendly, Laura had said – but Tilly wasn't a child now, she was an adult. Susan had left him, and so had Laura and Tilly's mother, so clearly he wasn't wife friendly either, but Tilly didn't care about any of that. She didn't give a damn how it turned out. *I don't want anything from you*, she'd say. *I just need a place to stay for one night. You won't have to do anything. You don't even have to talk to me if you don't want to.* Worst case scenario, he'd tell her to get lost. If he did, she'd find a hostel.

Try as she might, the ugly little scene in the hotel garden insisted on replaying itself over and over in her head, every detail still cruelly intact. Her appalled disbelief as the angry words that had burst from Eve had sunk in. The feel of Nell's hand suddenly on her arm, the dead silence from all the people who had heard Eve's pronouncement too. An odd sort of ringing in her head as she'd watched Eve turn and hurry off.

And then, without thinking about it, she'd found herself pulling out of Nell's grip and marching towards him. *Tilly*, Nell had called – but she'd kept going. Something, some instinct, had propelled her in his direction. Something she couldn't control had made her lift an arm and slap him across the face, hard enough to create a hot sting in her palm. She'd had no thought then of Nell witnessing it, with Tommy still in her arms. God, the thought of Tommy seeing that, seeing her hit his big brother, made her want to bawl all over again.

Immediately afterwards she'd whipped around and blundered away through the crowd, and Andy had rushed after her. *Tilly*, he'd shouted, *wait* – but she hadn't waited, she'd kept going, her palm still smarting, shocked and appalled by what she'd heard, what she'd done. She couldn't think beyond getting away, getting back to Laura.

He'd caught up with her before she'd reached the gates – she couldn't outrun him in her party shoes. He'd caught her arm to halt her, and she'd rounded on him and screamed: *Go away! Let me go! Leave me alone!* Loud, harsh screams that had hurt her throat.

She'd had a sense of more heads swinging around to stare at them, and he'd dropped her arm then and let her go.

She'd rushed back along the coast road, her head reeling, unable to process properly the implications of what had just occurred. She'd made her way back to Walter's Place, stumbling along in her heels, careful to avoid eye contact with the few people she passed.

She'd expected Nell and James and the children to catch up with her. They'd been about to leave: unless they made a big detour they'd have to come this way. And what if Andy had opted to go with them, determined to try to talk to her again? She'd steeled herself for another encounter – but they must have taken the long way home, because there was no sign of them, or of him.

She couldn't bear the thought of the news flying excitedly around at the party. *You'll never guess what I just heard! You won't believe it!* She imagined the pity they'd all feel for her, Andy Baker's innocent girlfriend who'd come all the way from Australia to discover he'd been cheating on her. Her only consolation was that she wouldn't be there for the fallout, for the accusations and the protestations, for whatever further ugliness this horrible situation would throw up when word spread throughout the island.

She could never come back to Roone after this. Never, ever, ever. If she wanted to see Laura and the others again, they'd have to meet somewhere else. The thought of having to abandon the island that she'd hoped to make her home was unbearable, almost as awful as her other loss. So much had changed in an instant, all her dreams wiped out, her future as good as obliterated.

He says it wasn't him, Laura had told her when morning had finally come, when Tilly was cradling a cup of tea and shaking her head at anything more. *He admits he walked her home from a party because she'd had a lot to drink, but he swears nothing happened.*

I got horribly drunk, and he looked after me, Eve had said, that morning they'd met her on the beach. He walked her home. *Like old times*, she'd said. Reminding him of what had happened, what they'd done, right in front of Tilly. Getting a kick out of it, probably.

Do you believe him? she'd asked Laura, and her sister had turned back to the frying pan without replying, because guests were waiting for breakfast, and because it gave her something to do when she couldn't give Tilly the right answer. Clearly she didn't believe him, and neither did Tilly.

She'd been such a fool to trust him, to imagine that she'd found someone who truly loved her. In the end, he'd turned out no better than John Smith.

How could he? How could he have slept with his old girlfriend, knowing how Tilly felt about him? Oh, she hated him. She despised him for breaking her heart so cruelly and denying her a future on Roone, with or without him.

'I think you need to make a move,' Gavin said. 'I mean, if you're still determined to go.'

His voice pulled her back to the present. He'd insisted on driving her to the pier, and now the ferry was loading up, and she must at all costs avoid looking across to where the ice-cream van was parked, even though she'd have to pass within ten yards of it to reach the boat.

'I have to go,' she told him. 'I have no choice.'

He didn't argue. He took her case from the back and wheeled it onto the ferry. 'Listen,' he said, in the green T-shirt with a koala bear on the front that had been her gift to him last year, 'nothing has been proven, that's all I want to say. It's her word against his, so let's wait and see, OK? The truth will come out, Tilly.'

It was cold comfort. Nothing had been proven: this much was true, but every cell in her body knew that Eve had spoken the truth. Still, he was doing his best to make her feel better. She hugged him tightly and told him goodbye, and he hugged her back and kissed her cheek. 'See you tomorrow,' he said, but he wouldn't see her tomorrow: he might never see her again. She watched him returning to his white van, needing to get back to start his morning deliveries.

She recalled his many kindnesses. Welcoming her into the family when she'd first arrived; leaving his vegetable patch to help her anytime she went out to take bed linen from the clothes-line; bringing her little chocolate gifts like he brought to Laura. *She's so chuffed*, he'd told her, *to find she has a sister. You have no idea*. A pushover with his children; the most loving father on the planet. Biggish front teeth, lending to his many smiles an endearing childlike quality. The fondness she felt for him, as close to her as any brother could be.

Last evening she'd turned off her phone, after Andy's first attempt to call her. This morning there had been eight missed calls from him, along with three voicemail messages that she'd deleted without playing them. She'd phone Laura from Dublin – maybe from their father's house – and let her know that Gavin didn't have to cross to the mainland tomorrow.

Keep strong, Laura had whispered, as she was saying goodbye. *Don't let this break you* – but Tilly, feeling utterly broken, could give nothing in reply. They'd been standing on the road by Gavin's van, and Tilly had been terrified that Andy would appear from the house next door, but he hadn't – which had stupidly made her feel worse.

She became aware that it was raining. Not heavy rain, this was the soft gentle kind, tiny whispery drops so you hardly needed an umbrella. She avoided the steps to the rail, where she and Andy had stood on the day she'd arrived. She still refused to look in the direction of the van they'd spent so many afternoons in together. Would he continue working there now, knowing that all of Roone must be whispering about him? Oh, let him do what he liked. Let him go back to Eve if that was what he wanted: she was welcome to him.

She hauled her case over to a space under the top deck where another, large and lime green, already stood. A little further along, seated on a bench, she spotted the Italian man she'd met last evening on her way to the hotel. Straw hat covering the head that was tilted slightly forward, hands folded together in his lap.

She'd told him that she and Andy were getting married. Next year, she'd said. Serve her right for lying. Serve her right for believing they had a future together. Serve her right for being a stupid innocent dreamer.

She could avoid the man. She could cross to the other side of the boat for the duration of the short journey – but she found she didn't want to. She found herself walking towards him, not away.

He turned at the sound of her steps. His face lit up in recognition. '*Signorina*,' he said, rising to his feet, sweeping off his hat, '*Buon giorno*.'

'Hello.' She indicated the bench. 'Can I sit with you?'

'*Certo, certo*, you sit, please.' When she was settled he resumed his own seat, returned the hat to his head. 'The rain, she comes again,' he said.

She shrugged. 'I don't mind the rain.' It could rain till Doomsday – it could pelt down for all she cared.

Leo the ferryman arrived then, the worn strap of his leather bag crossing his yellow oilskin. He took money from them and pulled tickets from his book. 'You enjoyed your holiday?' he enquired of

Tilly, and she said yes, it was lovely, praying he wouldn't mention Andy, and he didn't. Seeing in her face, maybe, that things hadn't gone according to plan. 'Safe journey home,' he told her. 'See you next summer, please God.'

When he'd moved on, her companion tilted his head at her. 'You have nice party in the 'otel? There was dancing?'

She shook her head, not having the heart to keep pretending. 'Not really. I ... finished with my boyfriend.' He didn't need details. 'That's why I'm leaving today.'

His smile faded and died. '*Signorina*, I am very sorry to 'ear. You go back to Australia?'

'Yes, tomorrow. I'm going to Dublin now.' She hesitated. 'My father lives there.'

'Ah.' He nodded. 'I too go to Dublin, to the airport. Perhaps we go together.'

'How are you travelling?'

'I take first the bus, and after the train, and then another train.'

'I'm going by bus all the way,' she said. 'There's a direct one to Dublin from Tralee. It's a bit slower, but it's cheaper too.' After an hour on Gavin's computer, checking out all her options, she was an expert.

'Then, if I 'ave enough time for my aeroplane, I too will take the bus,' he declared, 'if you are 'appy that we will travel together.'

'I'd like that,' she said. There was something likeable about him, something open and honest about his face, and talking to him might keep her mind off Roone and everything associated with it.

'Your name, please,' he said, 'I forget it' – and she told him Tilly, short for Mathilde. 'And you are Mr Conti.'

'Gualtiero,' said.

She repeated it uncertainly. 'I might not remember.'

'Then,' he said, 'I will say it again,' and he gave one of his sweet smiles.

'Tell me about Italy,' she said, as they left Roone behind them, as tiny droplets of water continued to fall on them.

Time passed. The ferry docked and they boarded the waiting bus that took them to Tralee, and from there they found the one for Dublin, and as they moved further from the island, as they crossed the country from west to east, he spoke of his restaurant and the village where he lived, where bakeries opened at dawn and closed at midday, and meals could last for hours, and the setting sun was a glory to see on a spring evening.

He seemed to sense that she wanted him to go on talking. He told her of his lost wife, and his two sons, and the little dark-eyed granddaughter with her grandmother's smile who called him Nonno, and a nephew who'd returned from a holiday on Roone with his wife last summer – *They stay with Laura, where you stay* – and who'd thought that Gualtiero might like to paint the sea there.

When he finally ran out of things to tell her, she

spoke of the parents she'd thought were hers until she'd found out, almost by accident, that they weren't, and the little brother and sister whom she loved, but who had no blood connection to her. She told him of the Indonesian restaurant where she'd begun working at weekends while she was still at school, and the owners who felt like family at this stage, and who held her job open for her each time she travelled to Ireland. She told him of her best friend Lien, whose grandparents had moved to Australia from China in the 1950s.

She recounted meeting her birth mother, and how they hadn't connected at all, and of her journey a few months later in search of the sister she'd been told about who lived on a small island off the Irish coast, and how she'd found a brother-in-law and a clutch of nieces and nephews too.

She didn't tell him about John Smith. She made no further mention of Andy. A few times he'd wander into her head, and then she'd have to stop talking and look out of the window of the bus, blinking, until she could breathe him away. When this happened, her companion sat back and remained silent, and gave no sign at all that he'd noticed anything amiss.

They said goodbye on a busy street in the middle of Dublin. The further east they'd travelled, the heavier the rain had become: now it was pouring down, but she didn't care. 'I wish for you 'appiness,' he said, kissing her on both cheeks, and Tilly watched him climb into a taxi, and tried to remember what happiness felt like.

After Roone, Dublin was a shock. So crowded and noisy, so many people scurrying past, toting umbrellas or with hoods pulled up, all looking as if they knew exactly where they were going. Nobody catching her eye, nobody saying hello like everyone did on Roone, no smiles that she noticed. The roads were clogged with every type of vehicle, cars and vans, buses and trams, and cyclists whose lives seemed to be in imminent danger as they swerved around the puddles and wove through the lanes of traffic.

She crossed a street with a wave of other pedestrians as the waiting vehicles growled at them. She bought two sausage rolls in a bakery and sat on wide stone steps to eat them, rain dripping from the ends of her hair as she watched Dublin rush by. She saw a man walk past who reminded her of Andy – something in his stride, in the tilt of his shoulders – and she swallowed a giant lump in her throat and tasted the saltiness of more tears, and forbade them to come out.

She wheeled her case across a bridge and saw people sitting on the ground with damp paper cups placed in front of them. One held an opened newspaper over his head; others seemed impervious to the rain as it streamed down on them. A little dog huddled quietly beside its owner on a sheet of soggy-looking cardboard, head resting on forepaws. It reminded her of Charlie, the dog at Walter's Place, and Captain, his brother, living in the house next door. She smothered a swoop of despair.

Outside a building with enormous stone columns she spotted a policeman. She showed him her father's address and he directed her to a nearby street and told her to take a bus from there. 'Not sure which number you need,' he said. 'Anyone will tell you.'

'Hop on,' the driver of the first bus told her. 'Stay close. I'll tell you when to get off.' His accent reminded her of Andy's and James's. She sat on the seat right behind him, next to a man with a young boy on his lap. The boy, who looked about Tommy's age, pulled absently at the gold-coloured bracelet on his father's watch as the bus trundled out of the city centre. Tilly peered through steamed-up windows as they crossed a different bridge, as they passed a park and a cinema and a church and more shops, and long terraces of red-brick houses.

The journey seemed to take ages. The floor of the bus was dotted with small puddles. Giant windscreen wipers swept across the glass, making her eyelids heavy. The man and the boy got off. She wondered if the driver had forgotten about her, but just as she was about to ask him, he called out the name of her father's street. She got hastily to her feet, almost losing her balance as the bus braked sharply. 'First left,' he told her, pointing, and she thanked him and manoeuvred her case carefully down the step.

The gate was unexpected. Not in itself – every house on the beautiful tree-lined road had gates – but this one was more like a shop shutter, a solid metal expanse that completely blocked any view of the house behind it, apart from its black-slated roof into which a large skylight was set.

An intercom was mounted on the wall. She could press the button and talk to her father. She peered at the gate again. So forbidding it looked. She checked the house number, hoping she'd got it wrong, hoping his house was one of the others, with normal gates and manicured lawns behind them, but she hadn't got it wrong.

She sneezed. She was wet through. Water trickled from her hair down the back of her neck. What if he sent her away – what if he refused even to let her in? She'd thought she could handle it, but now she was unsure. Another rejection, on top of last night? And really, what were the chances that he'd want to see her, in the face of his complete indifference to her up to this? Did she need further confirmation that he didn't want to know?

Maybe not.

As she deliberated, a silver car approached and pulled up at the gate. The windows were blacked out. She remained where she was, feeling exposed, and oddly guilty. The driver's window slid down, and a man looked out.

His face was familiar. She'd seen it online enough times to know it. He looked older though, and thinner.

'I'm Tilly,' she said, because he wasn't saying anything. 'I'm your daughter.' She sneezed again. 'I need a bed for the night,' she said.

They stared at one another for what felt like a

long time. He didn't blink, or smile; neither did she. Eventually he did something in his car that made the big metal gate rumble aside.

'You'd better come in,' he told her. He slid his window up and drove on, and she pulled her case after him, the wet making her feel cold, although the day was mild.

The house was big and built with bricks in varying shades of orange and red. Three steps led to the front door, which was glossy black and panelled, with lots of glass around it. Gravel the colour of sand, a tiered flowerbed running along one side. A giant rust-coloured pot by the door had something green and white trailing from it.

Tilly hauled her case up the three steps. She watched him get out of his car and shut his door and press his key fob. Locks clicked, lights blinked.

He walked across the gravel to where she waited. He was taller than her by a few inches, but he stooped a little. His hair was unkempt; he hadn't shaved in a while. Nell could have tidied him up. His eyes were the same colour as Tilly's, the same colour as his little son's. He opened the front door without comment, and stood back to allow her to enter.

She stepped in. The hall was spacious, with small black and white tiles on the floor. Walls covered with paintings. Fancy chairs with striped padded seats. A sculpture of a man's head and shoulders on a wooden stand, bronze it looked like. Presumably someone famous, but she didn't recognise him. She thought it odd to have something like that in a private house. White doors opened into other rooms. Stairs swept upwards in a curve.

'Here,' he said, reaching for her case, so she let him. It felt surreal, to be standing there with her father. He pushed in the handle she'd extended and lifted the case easily. 'Follow me.'

He led her into a bedroom on the ground floor, with a double bed that was covered with a pink blanket. 'Bathroom,' he said, indicating a door that faced the bed. 'Hot water if you want a shower. I'll get towels' – and he was gone.

Just like that, she was staying. He hadn't told her to get lost. She supposed he could hardly have refused to let her in, with the rain still so heavy and her so drenched. She was lucky he'd returned to the house when he had.

She peeled off her jacket and looked for somewhere to put it. She didn't want it to drip in the wardrobe, so she took a hanger and hung it in the shower. She stood uncertainly by the bed, wondering how the rest of the day would go. Just after four o'clock by her watch. She'd have to ring Laura and tell her where she was.

Laura would be shocked to hear he'd taken her in.

'Towels.' He was back, handing her a white bale, neatly folded. 'There's a tumble-dryer,' he added, 'off the kitchen.'

No emotion that she could discern in his voice. He'd just met his daughter for the first time, and he spoke as if she were a random stranger he happened to be putting up for the night.

'I'm glad to meet you,' she said. 'I wasn't sure ... you'd be here.' *I wasn't sure you'd want to see me*, she'd been about to say, but her courage failed her. *Did you get my letter?* she wanted to ask, but that stayed inside too. She felt a shyness in his company.

He acknowledged her comments with a minuscule tilt of his head. He didn't look dismayed to see her, she told herself. Maybe solemn was his default expression. Maybe he just had trouble communicating. Maybe that was all.

'I left Roone a day early,' she found herself saying, feeling he deserved some kind of explanation. 'That's why I'm here. I got the bus. I'm flying home tomorrow.' Let him fill in the blanks himself. Let him think she'd come especially to see him, if he wanted.

Another tiny nod.

'I won't disturb you,' she said. 'You can pretend I'm not here.'

There was a moment of silence. 'You must,' he said, 'have heard terrible things about me.' No change of expression, no hint of a smile.

'No—' Flustered now, feeling her face becoming hot. Not sure if she'd put her foot in it. 'Well, I just – didn't know. Arriving unannounced like this, I mean.'

'Plenty of room,' he said, 'as you can see.'

He didn't know. He couldn't know that she knew about Susan and Harry leaving him. She wouldn't mention them; she'd play safe. 'Thank you,' she said, suddenly remembering. 'For the money, I mean. The cheque you gave to Laura.'

He made no response to that. 'You'll want dinner.' It wasn't a question.

'I can do my own thing,' she said quickly. 'You don't have to feed me.' The idea of sitting across a table from him, trying to make conversation in this stilted way while they ate, was intimidating. She could go out, walk around until she found a deli, or a supermarket. She wondered if it would be presumptuous to ask him for a key.

'There's food in the fridge. You're welcome to help yourself.'

'… Thank you,' she said, wondering what *he* intended doing for dinner. Keeping out of her way maybe. Waiting until he heard her returning to her room.

'Well,' he said, and nothing more. She stood where she was, listening to the sound of his retreating footsteps. Off to do some painting, she imagined. She must look properly at the ones hanging in the hall, find out if any were his. After seeing so many of them on the internet, she thought she'd recognise his style, even if they were unsigned.

She undressed and turned on the water, stepping in before she remembered her soap and shampoo, still packed in her case. No matter. She stood under the warm, powerful flow, eyes closed, mouth open, trying to think of nothing at all.

Afterwards, wrapped in a towel, her hair damp and uncombed, she phoned Laura. 'I'm in Dublin,' she said without preamble.

'*What?* Tilly, what brought you to Dublin? Where will you stay?'

And when Tilly told her, Laura's voice rose again. 'You went to his house – and he actually came to the *door*? He let you in?'

'He drove up,' Tilly said, 'while I was at the gate.'

'... How is he?'

'He's – OK. Not what you'd call overly friendly, but he's fine.'

'Is he with you now?'

'No. I think he went upstairs. He put me in a downstairs bedroom.'

Pause. 'And how are you?'

'I'm ...' Tilly stopped, her unhappiness rising up. 'I'm here,' she said, because that was the best she could manage.

'Andy called around,' Laura said. 'I was just finishing the breakfasts. I told him you were gone.'

The sound of his name conjured up his face, which sent a fresh wave of despondency through her. 'Did he – ?' She cut the question off. It didn't matter.

'Tilly, sweetheart, I'm so sorry this happened. So desperately sorry.'

'You looked at him,' she said then, suddenly remembering. 'The night of your dinner party. I caught you looking at him, and it –'

She stopped. Things slotted into place.

'You knew,' she said. 'Didn't you? You knew about him and Eve.'

No response.

'Hello?'

'I'm here,' Laura said.

Tilly waited, but no more came. 'How did you know?'

'Eve told me. Not about Andy, just that she was ... pregnant.'

'And how did you find out it was him?'

'Tilly, there's no point —'

'How did you find out?'

'I – asked her, and she admitted it.'

'You *asked* her?' She stood at the window, seeing but not really seeing the perfect sweep of lawn, the trees, the sandpit. 'You mean you suspected him, without her saying anything?'

'Tilly, it wasn't that I thought he'd have set out to be unfaithful, but because they had history, I had to consider the possibility that he was involved. I had no proof, so I asked. Of course I was hoping she'd say no, but ...'

He might not actually be the right one, she'd said to Tilly. *He might not be meant for you*. Knowing then that he'd fathered a child with his ex, *knowing* it. 'How could you have found that out and not told me?'

'Tilly, I couldn't tell you. I couldn't do it to you. I'm really sorry.'

It felt like another betrayal. By Laura, whom she'd felt she could trust absolutely.

'Sweetheart, I messed up, I know I did. I didn't want to hurt you, but I see now that I should have told you. I hate what he's done to you: I told him that this morning.'

She could imagine it. Her sister had a scary tongue on her when she wanted to. But Laura was also kind and generous and funny, and the worst she'd done here, the very worst, was keeping something to herself out of a desire not to cause hurt. How could Tilly fault that, even if the hurt had just been deferred, even if her heart had been broken anyway?

'Thank you,' she said.

A few seconds passed. 'For what?' Laura asked. Suspecting sarcasm, maybe. Waiting for the tirade.

'For everything. For all you've done.'

Another pause. 'You're not mad at me?'

'Well, I am a bit. I think you should have told me, but I know you meant well. I'm not going to hold it against you.'

'… I wish you hadn't left.'

There was nothing to say to that. She felt a yawn rise within her. She raised a hand to cover her gaping mouth, even though nobody was there to see. She'd sleep tonight. 'Your house is very fancy.'

'I suppose it is. Can't say it ever really felt like home, though.'

'I'll email Gavin,' she said, 'when I get home.'

'Do – and I'll write, end of the week. I'll make up news if there isn't any.'

'Don't tell me,' she said, 'anything about … him,' and Laura promised not to.

'Safe trip. Hope all the flights are on time.'

'Bye.'

She dressed in dry clothing. She bundled up her wet things and found the kitchen, and the tumble-dryer in the room beyond it. The house was still, no sign or sound of her father. She wondered if she'd meet him again before she left in the morning.

She returned to the bedroom while her clothes were tumbling about. She lay on the bed and closed her eyes. Within a minute, she was asleep.

Eve

SHE KNEW.

She worked in the fish shop. Eve didn't know her name. She glanced up from her magazine when Eve and Imelda walked into the waiting room. She nodded at them, her eyes settling on Eve for several seconds until Eve met and held her gaze, forcing the woman to drop hers.

She knew, for sure. *Guess who I saw at the doctor's*, she'd say later, to her husband, or to her friends, or to whoever she felt like saying it to.

They sat in silence while the clock on the wall ticked the minutes away. Imelda made no move towards the magazines on the low table to their left, and neither did Eve. She hoped fervently that nobody else would come in.

The walls of the waiting room were a putrid shade of green. She wondered who could possibly have thought it attractive. A small radio on the windowsill was plugged into a socket below, but not turned on. A smell of sour milk crept up from under the air-freshener that someone had tried to banish it with.

The last time Eve had been here was two weeks before Christmas, when she'd got a chest infection that had refused to leave of its own accord. That time the room had been full of people coughing and snuffling, and a tiny baby who had screamed non-stop in its apologetic mother's arms.

After what felt like an eternity, the door opened and Dr Jack's secretary put her head in. 'Now, Julie,' she said, and the fish-shop woman got up and walked out without another look at them.

Eve felt wretched. Could it have been this time yesterday that she'd been making party preparations at the hotel? It felt like a month ago. Her prospects then had been bleak, her future uncertain to say the least, but she'd had a plan. She'd had a course of action all mapped out, and she'd been prepared to follow it and hope for the best. Now, because she'd lost her cool and revealed in anger what she'd meant to keep for later, everything was up in the air.

The worse part, the very worst part, was his reaction. She kept seeing his face, and the look of utter bafflement on it. As if she was speaking in a language he didn't understand, as if what had happened between them was so unimportant he'd wiped it from his memory. He'd had no right to look at her like that – and now he was denying it entirely. He was making her out to be a liar.

And Nell this morning, arriving at Imelda's in such a state. Looking like she wanted to kill Eve, like it would have taken very little for her to raise her closed fist and strike a blow. If Imelda hadn't been there, it might well have happened. Nell, of course, believed Andy without question.

So now what? She was still trying to get her head around the fact that Imelda hadn't hit the roof when she'd heard the news. On the contrary, she was being brilliant. Eve was back in the house with her, installed in her old room again. But could she remain on Roone as things were, with Andy having abandoned her, and Nell, and probably James too, gunning for her? And Laura was mad on Tilly's account, which probably meant Gavin would turn against her too.

She'd made enemies, and they all lived a stone's throw from Imelda. Could she really stay in such a situation – and was it fair to Imelda, who'd said she didn't want to take sides? How could she not be seen to be taking sides, with Eve living in her house? Already it had caused trouble between Nell and Imelda, and it would only get worse as time went on.

She would go; she had no choice. She would stick to her original plan and leave the island. She'd manage without Andy Baker's help; she wouldn't beg. She wouldn't do a DNA test either – what was the point, if he didn't want to know? She had her pride. But she'd tell her child, when the time came, who its father was. Every child deserved to know that.

And in the meantime, her summer job was finished. After the scene with Andy she'd gone straight to the staff locker room and changed out of her black dress, and taken a back way out of the hotel without saying anything to anyone. She figured the owner would hear soon enough what had happened; no way would he want her back. She felt bad leaving things like that, but she'd lacked the courage to ring him this morning and apologise. Another person she'd have to avoid until she left.

She sighed. Imelda looked at her. 'Alright?'

She shook her head. 'I've messed up, Imelda. I've been so stupid – and I've put you in a horrible position with Nell. You don't need this, not now.'

'No,' Imelda agreed. 'I don't need it.' She paused. 'On the other hand—' She stopped again, started again. 'You know,' she said, 'when you came to us first, and you were so unhappy, and so ... closed off from us, I really thought we'd never be able to connect with you. I felt like a real failure as a foster parent, and I know Hugh did too, although he wouldn't admit it. And then you opened up, and we were able to help you, and I loved seeing the change in you. You blossomed, you really did, and we took some of the credit for that.'

'It was all down to you,' Eve said, 'you and Hugh' – but Imelda carried on as if she hadn't spoken.

'And then you did the childcare course, and you got the job in the crèche, and we were so proud at how you were turning out.'

Eve bit her lip. They *had* been proud of her. They'd told her that, when she'd got her qualification. They'd taken her and Keith out for dinner to celebrate. They'd given her a bottle of her favourite perfume.

'What I'm saying,' Imelda continued, 'is that you're a good person, Eve. And good people make mistakes, just like everyone else, but it doesn't make them bad. Try not to be too hard on yourself. We'll cope with this. It might be tough, you might get people saying nasty things. If you do, you'll need to be strong – and I'll be here for you.'

'Thank you. I don't deserve it.'

'You do. Everyone deserves to be helped.'

They sat on until the receptionist returned. 'Do you want me to come in?' Imelda asked her, and Eve said yes, so they went together.

'Imelda,' Dr Jack said, shaking her hand, 'and Eve. Good to see you both.'

Danny, his first grandchild, had attended the crèche the year before, when Eve was still Avril's assistant. She liked the doctor. He gave you time when you visited, he let you talk if you needed to. Imelda had brought her to him when she couldn't sleep, around the time she'd finally told them about Derek Garvey, and he'd given her a week's worth of pills that had got her back on track, more or less. He'd been the one to recommend counselling, but she didn't blame him when it hadn't helped.

Now he sat behind his desk and rested his forearms on it. 'What can I do for you?' he asked, looking from one to the other.

He didn't show surprise when Eve told him. Like everyone else he'd already heard it, or else his training would have taught him not to react to news like that. He asked if she knew how far gone she was, and she gave him the date of Frog's party.

He tapped buttons on his computer. 'Have you done a home pregnancy test?'

'No. I don't need to,' Eve told him. 'I know I'm pregnant. I've missed two periods, and for the first few weeks I was throwing up a lot, and my stomach felt sick all the time. I'm just here to get advice, to know what I should and shouldn't do.'

'Sure,' he said. 'I understand that. I still need to check you out though, do my own diagnosis. Call me a fusspot.' Smiling at her, opening a drawer in his desk. 'Could you pass water for me?'

She could hardly refuse, although it seemed like a waste of time. He gave her a little plastic container and sent her to the toilet off the waiting room. She wondered, as she hunkered over the bowl, what he and Imelda were talking about. Maybe nothing at all to do with her. Maybe Imelda was asking after his family; maybe he was enquiring as to how she was coping as a widow.

She returned to the surgery and gave him the sample. 'This will take a couple of days,' he said. 'I have to send it off for analysis. If you want to do a home test in the meantime, go ahead – they're very accurate now, and you'll get an instant result, particularly as this much time has passed.'

Eve smothered her irritation. Hadn't he been listening? Maybe he wasn't as good a doctor as she'd given him credit for. 'I'll wait,' she said stiffly.

If he noticed her annoyance, he didn't show it. 'No problem. I'll be in touch as soon as I hear.'

Back in the car, Imelda didn't immediately turn on the engine. 'Eve,' she said, 'I think you should take a home test.'

Eve stared at her. 'Why? Don't you believe me?'

'Of course I do. But wouldn't you like to know for sure?'

'I *do* know for sure.'

A beat passed. Rain began again, splattering onto the windscreen, harder than before. 'How about,' Imelda said, 'you take it to keep me happy then?'

Eve bit back a retort. She owed Imelda, her only ally, so much. It wouldn't kill her to take a test. 'OK,' she said, 'if you really want me to.'

They stopped outside the chemist in the village. 'I'll go in,' Eve said – but to her relief Imelda said no, so she waited in the car, careful not to catch the eye of anyone who passed. Imelda returned with a two-pack of tests, and Eve took them both early the following morning, before breakfast, like the instruction leaflet recommended.

And both gave a negative result.

Laura

'THIS IS RIDICULOUS,' SHE SAID.

Nobody answered, because nobody was there. Poppy was napping in the playpen, which had become her daybed. Marian and Evie were spending the afternoon at the home of their pal Nuala White. Gav had taken the boys to a matinee at the drive-in cinema, after the donkey rides were cancelled on account of George being a bit poorly. Her B&B guests had checked out, or disappeared for the day.

It was Monday. Four days had passed since the party at the hotel, since Laura and Nell's last conversation, standing at the field gate in the near dark. Three days since Tilly's departure, and Andy's appearance at the back door a few hours later. Laura had heard a tap and gone out, thinking Nell, hoping Nell, but it hadn't been Nell.

How could you? she'd demanded. *How could you do it to her?* and he'd shaken his head and said it wasn't true. Still sticking to his guns, still denying what everyone knew. *She's left*, Laura had told him. *You've driven her away* – and he'd turned then and walked off, and Laura had imagined him reporting the conversation to Nell.

And Tilly. Tilly was a whole other headache.

Where is she? Marian and Evie had asked, when they'd woken on Friday morning to find her gone, and Laura had told them that there had been an emergency, and Tilly had had to leave early, and she was very, very sorry she couldn't say goodbye. Another half-truth, but they were at least ten years too young for the full story.

And with Gav all set to pick her up in Cahersiveen and bring her to the airport, Tilly had sprung another surprise. Without a word to anyone, she'd made her way to Dublin and pitched up, of all places, at their father's house – and wonder of wonders, he'd agreed to her staying the night.

And she'd guessed. From an unguarded moment on Laura's part she'd figured it out. To think of it made Laura wince with shame. *How could you have found that out and not told me?* she'd asked, her voice filled with bewilderment, and Laura's reasons had sounded more like excuses.

She'd be landing in Brisbane around now, if she wasn't there already. Her father – her adoptive father – would collect her, like he always did. A six-hour round trip to the airport: clearly, she was loved. How much had she told them about Andy? And what would she tell them now? Laura would write before the week was out, and fill at least one page with apologies, and slip a bar of her favourite Galaxy into the envelope.

Would she ever come back to Roone? Had Eve lost her a sister, along with everything else? Only time would tell – but Laura would do what she could to make sure Tilly returned to the island, and Andy Baker could just bugger off.

Today was Monday, with Nell's salon closed. She'd probably have called to the mobile library in the morning, like she did most Mondays. She'd more than likely be at home now with her two: the day, grey and dreary and threatening rain since midday, wouldn't tempt anyone out.

Poppy's party on Saturday had come and gone, with no sign of the neighbouring children. *When are they coming?* Poppy had asked – they saw one another all the time when things were normal – and Laura had told her that Nell was too busy to bring them over. All the stories mothers told their children to keep the hurtful truth at bay.

She didn't envy Nell and James the next few months. She didn't envy James, having to go to work in Fitz's, having to serve drink to people who'd heard that his son had fathered a child, and was denying it. Or Nell, working in the hair salon above the bar, cutting and colouring hair as she tried to talk about anything else.

The doorbell rang. Too early for her next lot of guests, who'd told her they'd be here around six. She went to answer it, and found Imelda on the doorstep under a red umbrella, the rain having finally arrived.

'Laura, may I talk to you for a minute please?'

She looked tired. She never called on Laura – and Laura's resolve to call on her with a little gift had never materialised, had turned into a phone call instead to invite her and Walter to dinner, and only Walter had come.

'Come in,' Laura replied, wondering if she was in for a lecture. No end to the fallout.

Imelda folded her umbrella closed and propped it against the wall before wiping her shoes on the mat and entering the hall. In the kitchen she perched on the edge of a chair, tension coming from her like heat, making no move to take off her jacket. She reminded Laura of Eve, the night she'd come with the news of her pregnancy.

'Tea or coffee?' Laura asked.

'Nothing, thank you.' She ran her tongue quickly over her lips. 'Laura, I felt I should tell you, in the light of – your involvement in the whole business – well, I mean Tilly's involvement, I suppose. You know what I'm talking about.'

'I do.' Laura took a seat, and went on looking polite.

'It's Eve,' Imelda said. 'The thing is … she's not pregnant.'

Not pregnant.

Not pregnant?

Laura stared at her. 'What? You mean – she's had a miscarriage?'

Imelda shook her head. 'No. I mean she was never – she thought she was, but it turns out she had, she *has*, what's called a false pregnancy. Dr Jack had another name for it, a proper name – I've just spoken with him on the phone – but I don't remember it now.'

'Phantom,' Laura said faintly. 'I've heard of it. But—' She broke off, still trying to puzzle it out. 'She told me she'd done a test.'

Imelda frowned. 'Eve told you that? You knew about this?'

'I did. She came to me a while ago – but only because she didn't want to upset you. She just needed someone to tell.'

'And you didn't think to pass it on.' Said entirely without accusation, presented as a simple comment, but still Laura felt the sting of it.

'Imelda, she asked me not to.' And still I told Nell. 'To be honest, I wish she'd never involved me. But she definitely said she'd done a test. I remember her saying that.'

'I see.' Imelda's gaze slid to the big old dresser behind Laura, with its stacks of mismatched plates and mugs, and plastic tubs of broken crayons, and bundle of old newspapers, and everything else that had no place on a dresser. 'I'm afraid that wasn't true,' Imelda said. Hating to have to admit that Eve had lied, you could see that. Proud of what she and Hugh had achieved with her, no doubt. Taking this as a personal failure maybe, even though no blame at all could be attached to her.

'So you brought her to see Dr Jack.'

'I did – and she also did two home tests. There's definitely no pregnancy, and there never was.'

The clock on the wall ticked loudly in the silence that followed. Had it always been that loud? 'So she and Andy ...'

'Nothing happened,' Imelda said. 'Or I'm assuming nothing happened.' She hesitated. 'Eve – doesn't remember.'

But Andy did. Andy had sworn it wasn't true. Laura hadn't believed him, and neither had Tilly.

Dr Jack was calling it a phantom pregnancy, which meant that Eve had genuinely believed herself to be pregnant. She'd believed it to the extent that her body had been fooled into displaying the symptoms of pregnancy: the missed periods, the nausea, the works. She hadn't lied about anything, except taking the pregnancy test.

Laura recalled practically throwing the girl out of the house, the day she'd revealed the identity of the man she'd slept with. Allegedly slept with. Laura remembered how angry she'd been at the confirmation of her suspicions about Andy – when in fact nothing at all had happened. No sex, no pregnancy.

'How is she?'

Imelda's face seemed to collapse a little. 'Not good. She's pretty devastated, actually. She's ashamed and embarrassed, and ...' she let the sentence drift away, looking thoroughly miserable.

'What will happen now?'

'Well, Dr Jack has recommended counselling for her. He feels that this, all of this, might have been prompted by her upbringing, and by what happened to her afterwards in the foster home. He thinks it's still ... unresolved, and she won't be happy until it is. We brought her for counselling before, and she didn't take to it, and foolishly we didn't pursue it, but now I might try and persuade her to give it another go.'

Laura felt enormous sympathy for her. Here she was, trying to handle this complicated situation, trying to sort out this mess, when clearly she was still deeply grieving. 'Let me know if I can do anything,' she said. 'I'm not sure what, but I'm here, and I'd be more than happy to help.'

Imelda summoned a smile. 'Thank you, Laura. I do appreciate that. I haven't forgotten how helpful you were when she first came to us.' She got to her feet, and Laura rose too.

'Have you told Nell about this?'

Imelda dipped her head, buttoned her jacket. 'Yes, I've just come from there. She's glad, and very relieved. They all are.'

So things would blow over. Life would return to something resembling normality, and hopefully Andy and Tilly would manage to get past this. Should she get in touch with Tilly, let her know the outcome? No, she decided, better if it came from Andy. Better for both Laura and Nell to stay out of it now, let them work it out together if they could.

And, in the meantime, there was something else she had to do. Well, two somethings.

As soon as she'd seen Imelda off, she placed a call. She waited, drumming her fingers on the kitchen table, until she heard the beep.

'It's me again,' she said. 'I need to speak to you. If you ignore this call like you ignored my last one I'm going to contact Susan and tell her what I know. You have half an hour.'

She hung up and made a cup of tea. She sat at the table and drank it. Was half an hour enough? She should have given him longer. She should have said by the end of the day. Ten minutes passed, and ten more. As she was steeling herself to call him back, her phone rang.

'I was in the toilet,' he said crossly.

'How was I to know? You never answer your phone.'

Silence. She'd forgotten how he was. To get a response you had to ask him a question.

'How are you feeling?'

He took so long to answer she thought he wouldn't, but then he did. 'Up and down. Tired.'

'Are you eating?'

'I am.'

A mine of information. She changed tack. 'You gave Tilly a bed for the night. She told me.'

Nothing.

'I was glad you met her. She's very sweet.' Had

Tilly told him what had happened with Andy? She couldn't imagine it. He didn't encourage heart-to-hearts.

She shifted ground again. 'I hear you're giving up painting.'

Silence. The man was impossible.

'Have you spoken with Susan? Did you ring her to tell her you're giving up?'

'I fail to see—'

'Isn't that why you're doing it, so she'll come back to you?'

'Laura—'

She ignored the warning tone. What could he do but hang up? And if he did that, he ran the risk of her telling Susan what he'd asked her not to tell.

'Look,' she said, 'I know you think it's not my business, but I'm going to have my say anyway, so you may as well listen. I'm not sure if you know that Susan came here to Roone when she left Dublin. She and Harry spent two weeks at the hotel before they went to London. I don't know if you rang her while she was here, because I didn't ask. I didn't want to upset her by asking, in case you hadn't rung. I did ask her something else, though. I asked her if she loved you, and she said she did.'

She halted. 'Are you listening?' she demanded.

'I didn't think I had a choice.'

'She loves you, Luke. She told me she loves you. She knows you're retiring, because I've spoken with her about it. She's waiting to hear it from you. And she needs to hear everything. She does. You can't go on keeping it from her.'

She paused. Go on. Say it.

'The thing is, you can't put it all on me. It's not fair to tell me you're dying and ask me not to tell anyone else. I don't mind being your emergency person, but it's too much to expect me to keep it to myself. It's too big. And Susan has a right to know. You must tell her.'

Was he still there?

'Are you still there?'

'I'm still here.'

'I'm asking you to ring her, and tell her. I can't remember the last time I asked you for anything, and I swear I'll never ask you for another thing. Just do this. Just do it, please.'

Five years, he'd told her. Five years he'd been given. Cancer, he'd said, while they walked around the field that had George the donkey and Caesar the pig and all the hens in it. *I need to give someone's name in case of emergency*, he'd said. *I was wondering if I could give yours* – and what could she say but yes? He was her father, even if he'd made a pretty poor job of it. He was the man who'd started her. She hadn't had it in her to refuse what he was asking, not when he was down to five years.

'There's another thing,' she said. 'You mightn't remember, but the last time I met you in Dublin, when I called to tell you about Tilly, I said – well, I told you you'd die alone. I was mad when I said it, because you were being so – well, it doesn't matter. What matters is I said it, and I'm sorry. I shouldn't have, and I don't want you to. Die alone, I mean.'

She stopped for breath. She closed her eyes.

'I don't want you to die,' she said. 'I don't want my father to die, but it looks like it's going to happen, so if it is, I don't want you to be *alone*. I'm going to come and see you, whether you want me to or not. I'm going to come as often as I can, but I can't be there all the time. You need Susan.'

She came to another stop. She listened to the silence. She wondered if what she was saying meant anything at all to him.

'I think that's it,' she said. 'I'm hanging up now. Please ring Susan. Please do it for me.'

She hung up, forgetting to say goodbye. She set down her phone and looked at it. He was an impossible man to love, but Susan loved him – and Laura supposed she must too, in some way, because the news that he was dying really hadn't gone down well with her at all.

She'd go to see him at the end of the season, as soon as the last of the guests had departed the B&B. She'd bring him a book or something; she'd have to think about that. They'd sit down somewhere, just the two of them, and she'd attempt to cover some of the distance between them, although she had no idea in the world how she might do that.

He's dying, she'd told Gualtiero, the day she'd met

him sitting on the stone wall, remembering whoever he was remembering. *He's dying and I don't know how I feel about it* – and Gualtiero said, in his gentle, Walter-ish way, that maybe she should go and see him. *Go,* he'd said, *and tell 'im what is in your 'eart, even if it is difficult.*

It had seemed like sound advice to her. She thought it was worth a try.

'Next,' she said aloud. She clattered about the kitchen until Poppy stirred and opened her eyes.

'Oh good – you're awake.' Laura scooped her up. 'Let's go to Nell's.' There was method in her madness: Nell could hardly turn away a child with a cast on her arm, however much she might feel like slamming the door in Laura's face.

They got into raincoats, Poppy with just one sleeve on. They went out the front way to avoid the wet grass in the field. They walked the short distance to the house next door and went down the side passage to the back, the way they always did.

Laura tapped on the door, holding tightly to Poppy's hand. What if she'd judged it wrong, and Nell refused to let them both in? Or what if Andy answered? How would he greet her, after her sharp words to him a few days ago?

The door opened and there was Nell, a striped apron over a red sweater and jeans. Flour on the apron, and on her cheek.

'Imelda told me,' Laura said quickly. 'She's just left.'

Nell looked at her for what seemed a long time –
it was probably all of three seconds – and then she
crouched and addressed Poppy. 'You want to go in
and watch cartoons with Tommy and Berry?'

'Yes!' She pulled off her raincoat and shoved it at
her mother before trotting through to the hall. The
confidence of small children, the certainty that they
would be well received wherever they went, until
time made them grow up and snatched the self-
esteem away from them.

'Sit if you want,' Nell said, turning back to the
table.

Laura saw a baking sheet, and rolled-out cookie
dough, and a cutter. At least she was being allowed to
stay. She shrugged off her raincoat and hung it with
Poppy's on the back of the door, and took a seat at the
table.

Nell worked quickly and in silence, cutting circles
and transferring them to the baking sheet. Laura
watched, framing sentences in her head and discarding
them, wanting whatever she said to come out right.

Nell got there first. 'He was telling the truth.'

'Yes. I'm sorry, Nell. I shouldn't have rushed to
judgement.'

The baking sheet was full. Nell slid it into the oven
and got another. She gathered the leftover dough
into a ball and rolled it out again, her movements
practised and confident.

'I'm really sorry,' Laura repeated.

More circles, three of them, before Nell lifted her

gaze and trained it on Laura. 'You had no reason to doubt her.'

'No, but … I should have trusted Andy, like you did. I should have known he wouldn't lie.'

Nell went on cutting. 'You had Tilly to think of,' she said. 'I can't blame you.' Her cookies were legendary. These were bumpy with chocolate chips.

'How is he? How's Andy?'

'He's … he was very upset. He'll be OK, now that the truth's come out.'

Laura thought about how mad she'd been at him, how she'd almost hated him. How would she ever make amends? And James, who might also know that she'd wronged his son. James, who would have every right to resent her, to look the other way the next time they met.

'You weren't the only one who doubted him,' Nell said, sliding the second sheet into the oven. 'Imelda thought he'd done it too. She believed Eve as well.'

She closed the oven door and straightened up, and leant against the worktop. 'I called over there, the morning after the party. I went looking for Eve, and she wasn't in the apartment, so I kept going to Imelda's and found her there.' Long pause, nibbling her bottom lip. 'I … wasn't very nice to her, to either of them.' She broke off to scrub a hand across her mouth, and Laura saw how close to tears she was.

'Nell, don't beat yourself up. You were overwrought, they'd have seen that.'

She shook her head sharply. 'I was *mean* to Imelda.

How could I be mean to her, when she's so—' She broke off, coughed away the threatening tears. She lifted a cloth from the sink and squeezed it out. 'I'm not without fault here, is what I'm saying. I believed Andy because I had to, because he's James's son, and my stepson. I – I *told* myself I believed him.' Her voice still full of wobble, wiping down the draining board, which didn't need it. 'I *wanted* to believe him, but – I had no proof. How could I be sure that he hadn't … done what she said? I couldn't be *sure*, that was the thing. I'd lie awake beside James, and it would be running around and around in my head, and it *tormented* me. I felt so disloyal.'

The woebegone expression on her face made Laura want very badly to hug her, but it might be too soon for a hug. Instead she cleared the table and ran water into the sink and added washing-up liquid. She rolled up her sleeves and pulled on Nell's yellow rubber gloves and washed what needed washing, and Nell took a tea towel and dried it.

The kettle was boiled, and tea made. Mugs were set out, cookies taken from the oven. They didn't say much. They tiptoed around one another. They were careful with words, but Laura knew it was going to be alright.

They drank tea and ate warm cookies. Little by little they inched closer. Bit by bit they forgave, and were forgiven.

Susan

HER PHONE RANG. IT WAS MONDAY EVENING, an hour after Harry's bedtime, and four days after the news of Luke's retirement had broken. She was reading a book Rosie had passed on, a romance set in small-town America of the fifties. She was engrossed in prom dances and Dairy Queens and jukeboxes and station wagons, and rolled-up newspapers landing with a thump on porch steps.

'It's me,' he said, his voice pulling her back to the second millennium. 'How are you?'

'I'm alright.' She made no mention of the job.

'How's Harry?' he asked.

'He's doing OK.'

He wasn't really. In the last few days he'd begun to suck his thumb again, something he hadn't done in over a year. *He's a quiet little fellow, isn't he?* Angie had said when Susan had picked him up earlier. *I wonder if he needs to be around other kiddies.*

'You'll have heard,' he said.

'Yes.'

'I've retired.'

'Yes.' She played with the corner of her bookmark. 'Is it what you want?'

An infinitesimal pause, which she didn't miss. 'What I want is for you to come back. You and Harry.'

I have decided to do this in order to spend more time with my family.

'I'm just afraid you'll regret it, and resent me because of it.'

His sigh was heavy. 'Susan,' he said, 'I've never been good with words, you know that. I'm better with paint – but I'll try. I thought I could live without you and Harry, but it would appear that I can't. I thought that as long as I could paint, it was all I needed, but I was wrong. Without you, it's not coming out right. It means nothing. It's all nonsense.'

'But if I –'

'Hang on,' he said. 'Let me get to the end of this, because if I stop I mightn't be able to pick it up again. I'm not doing this just because you left. I'm doing it because it's time I gave up. It's time I sorted the nonsense from what matters. I want you to come home, Susan. I love you and I need you, and I need our son, because it's also time I learnt how to be a father. I mightn't be much good at it – Laura would tell you I was lousy at it, and she'd be right – but I'll see what I can do. I'll try and do better, for you and for him.'

With every word she felt an unravelling within her, an easing of the tightness she hadn't realised was there, until it began to loosen.

'There's another reason,' he said. 'I'll tell you when I see you.'

'Can't you tell me now?'

'I'd rather not.'

She thought about that. She remembered him telling her he had things on his mind, the day she'd left him and taken Harry with her. It felt like he might finally be ready to let her in. It felt like that.

'How does that sound?' he asked.

'It sounds ... hopeful. It sounds promising.'

She'd have to hand in her notice, so soon after starting in the china department. No, she wouldn't hand in her notice: she'd bring Harry in with her in the morning, and she'd tell them she had to quit, right then. She would imply some kind of family emergency, which wasn't far from the truth. *I can't go into it*, she'd say, *but I must attend to it right away.* They'd probably be put out: she'd take it. They might say she'd have to forfeit her earnings in return for leaving them so abruptly. She'd do her best to look disappointed.

Her mother wouldn't be pleased at this development. Her mother would have to lump it.

Rosie and Ed would get their top floor back. She'd send them something lovely from Dublin.

'Are you still there?' he asked.

'I'm still here.'

'Do you believe me? Do you understand what I'm saying?'

'... I do.'

She'd said *I do* to him before, the day she'd taken him as her lawful wedded husband. It hadn't gone according to plan, not according to her plan, not the way she'd envisaged it going – but he was trying to make amends now. Was he softening as he got older, or had it taken her absence, like he said, to make him realise what mattered?

And what was he going to tell her when he saw her? What was it that had driven a wedge between them and forced her away? So many questions that still needed answers.

'Will you please come home?' he asked.

'No,' she said.

Imelda

EVE. WHAT WAS TO BE DONE WITH EVE?

I was so sure, she'd sobbed. *I really thought I was pregnant, Imelda. I wasn't lying, I wasn't trying to get him into trouble, or to come between him and Tilly. You must believe me* – and Imelda had promised her she did, and it was the truth.

It drove me crazy, she'd wept. *I was still trying to get my head around Hugh, and it was like another thing crashing down on me. I felt like I was on the brink of exploding, all the time. I said things, I did things – I was so awful to you, so awful,* and Imelda had held her and told her it was all forgiven and forgotten, all in the past.

I know she tried counselling before, Dr Jack had said, when he'd phoned to tell them what they already knew, *but I really do think it's what she needs. A false pregnancy is often a reaction to a psychological trauma, and I think she's deeply unhappy because of all she's gone through. Until she learns to acknowledge and confront it, she can't put it behind her, can't get better. It won't be easy, but she'll have to give it another go.*

So this all came about because of her past?

Well, without investigating it, without her opening up, it's hard to say exactly what caused it. He'd paused. *Hugh's death may have been a contributing factor – that would have been traumatic for her. They were close, weren't they?*

They were, yes.

It was a relief, of course, to find out that there was no pregnancy, no baby on the way. Eve must see that. On some level she must see it, or she would eventually – but for now she was inconsolable. She hadn't left the house since she'd taken the tests Imelda had bought, since they'd seen the evidence for themselves. She hadn't got dressed since *not pregnant* had appeared in the little window, twice.

It was almost, Imelda thought, as if she'd lost a baby.

Going to see Nell, once they'd had confirmation from Jack, had been something Imelda had dreaded, but a phone call had seemed cowardly, so she'd taken her courage in both hands and driven over. And thankfully, Nell had made it easy.

I'm sorry, she'd said immediately. *I'm so sorry, Imelda. I had no right to speak to you like I did.*

No, you were upset, I understand perfectly –

And when they'd got past that part, and Imelda had delivered the news, Nell had gone straight to Andy's room to tell him, and right after that she'd phoned James, who was at work, while Imelda had moved on to Laura's house. And now that they all knew, word would spread, and soon everyone would stop talking about it, and in time people would forget that Eve Mulqueen had thought herself pregnant one summer, and had named Andy Baker as the father.

But in the meantime Imelda must talk to her, and convince her that counselling was necessary. She'd tell her that they could try someone new, that they could keep trying someone new until Eve found the right person. It would take time, and it would surely be costly, but the money was there, thanks to Hugh's careful planning.

'I could use your help,' she told him now. 'I'm not at all sure I can handle this on my own' – but Hugh was gone and couldn't help. She heard a scratch at the kitchen door and opened it to let in Scooter, who went straight for her food bowl.

'Good idea,' Imelda said. She took two salmon cutlets from the fridge and wrapped them in oiled tinfoil with salt and pepper. She scrubbed and pricked four potatoes that had come from Gavin's garden and put them into the microwave. She switched on her computer while she waited for the oven to heat up, and found a message from Gualtiero.

Hello Imelda

Here is Gualtiero, home after my holiday in Ireland, so I write to say once again thank you very much for your good kindness to me. The restaurant is OK, and my customer happy to see me again, and in Italy the sun is shining and the sky is blue, and the jasmine is many. I would like very much if you will come to see it. I will

look forward to it when you have the time, and when
you are ready.
Be happy!
Your friend
Gualtiero

When the potatoes were half cooked she took them
from the microwave and put them into the oven
along with the salmon, an idea beginning to form in
her mind. She set the table and filled a small saucepan
with water, and cut florets from a head of cauliflower.
She went upstairs and tapped on Eve's door.

'Come in.'

She lay in bed with the curtains drawn. She'd put
in a brief appearance for a toast-and-tea breakfast and
skipped lunch, like she'd done for the past three days,
despite Imelda's coaxing. She rose again each evening
for dinner – but only, Imelda suspected, to keep her
happy. The air in the room was what Imelda's sister
Marian would have called whiffy.

Imelda took the chair by the bed. 'Dinner won't be
long,' she said. 'Ten minutes or so.'

'Thanks.'

She remained where she was. The room wasn't
dark. The curtains, chosen by Eve a few months after
her arrival on Roone, were tangerine with splashes
of navy. They were no good at all at blocking out the
light, but Eve had said that was precisely why she'd
chosen them. *I don't like the dark,* she'd admitted, and
Imelda could well understand that – but now she

guessed that Eve would prefer to shut everything out, including the daylight.

'I've had an idea,' Imelda said, leaning forward a little in her chair. 'I haven't really thought it through yet, but I wanted to run it past you, to see what you think.'

No response.

'I was wondering,' Imelda went on, picking her words carefully, 'if we should … take a little trip. Just the two of us, just for a week or so.'

Still no reply – but she wasn't saying no. It was enough to be going on with.

'I thought we might go to Italy.'

Eve remained quite still, but Imelda sensed a new alertness in her, a more attentive quality to her listening.

'We could fly to Rome, my treat. I've always wanted to visit Rome. You could look online and find somewhere nice for us to stay.'

'Rome,' Eve murmured.

'It looks so beautiful in photos, and there's so much to see – and I've heard the food is just wonderful.' She let a beat pass. 'You can blame Mr Conti, my visitor, for putting the idea into my head. When he spoke about Italy, I mean.'

'I wasn't nice to him,' Eve said. 'I was rude. I didn't like that you had to put him up. I thought he should have left when he heard about Hugh. I thought it wasn't fair on you.'

'Oh, sweetheart, I didn't mind – well, of course I

got a bit of a land when he turned up. He did offer to leave, after I told him about Hugh, and I tried to find him somewhere else on the island but every place was full, so I decided it wouldn't be the end of the world if he stayed. And he was a nice man, and he was company for me.'

Eve was silent for a while. Imelda was about to rise when she spoke again.

'The thing is, I didn't want you to have company. I wanted you to ... need me. I felt – left out when he was here.' She paused. 'God, that makes me sound so selfish, doesn't it?'

Imelda reached across to rest a hand on the girl's shoulder. 'Eve, love, please don't be too hard on yourself. This is a horrible time for both of us. I'm sure Gualtiero – Mr Conti – didn't even notice if you were a bit ... short with him.'

How completely alone she must have felt. Pregnant as she thought she was, still grieving for Hugh – and Imelda, mired in her own sadness, and preoccupied with Gualtiero's presence in the house, hadn't sensed her trouble, hadn't seen the crisis that she was living with. How abandoned she must have felt, first by Hugh, and then by Imelda. Little wonder she'd turned to Laura.

'So what do you think about Rome?'

'... I'd like it. I haven't been there.'

She hadn't been anywhere. Her mother, by the sound of it, had never been in any state to take her and Keith on a holiday – and the Garveys had gone away each summer and dumped Eve with whoever would take her in, which was how Imelda and Hugh had got her. Twelve weeks of respite fostering on Roone that had turned into a permanent thing, or at least until her eighteenth birthday two years ago, when she'd officially stopped being the responsibility of the social welfare system.

Considered an adult at eighteen. Assumed to be able to lead an independent life, when the truth was that she was still all over the place, still with so much bottled-in, unresolved emotion. Fooling everyone into believing that she was fine, even those who should have noticed.

Imelda got to her feet. 'Get dressed so and come down. We can make plans over dinner.'

It wasn't the way she'd thought it would go. Certainly not nearly as soon as this – and not with Eve, or with anyone. She'd imagined slipping away in the springtime: maybe not next spring, maybe the one after. A small quiet place in the mountains, in Gualtiero's village or in another one.

She'd imagined booking into a little family-run hotel, somewhere with a nice garden where she could sit in the shade and read her book and listen to birdsong. Ideally it would be close to a forest where she could walk now and again, to breathe in the pure oxygen-rich wood-scented air, different from the clean saltiness that surrounded them on Roone, but just as nourishing for the soul.

This wasn't the plan at all. This was nothing like

she'd imagined. But Eve needed something to pull her out of the darkness in her head – and Rome, with its fountains and statues and art galleries that she'd seen only in pictures, might do. Rome, with its Colosseum and its Vatican, with its dazzling culture and its rich history and its wonderful food, might just do it.

And there was a chance that they'd take a bus or a train to Gualtiero's village on one of the days. It might or might not happen; she'd play that bit of it by ear – but however the trip went, Imelda would broach the subject of counselling when the time felt right, and Eve might be open to giving it another try.

And maybe, after all, Imelda *did* need Eve. Maybe she needed her, like she'd needed Gualtiero, to take her mind, even temporarily, off her great grief.

Ten minutes later Eve appeared in the kitchen, her hair damp from the shower, her laptop tucked under an arm.

And over dinner, they began to plan.

Tilly

'I DON'T BELIEVE IT,' LIEN REPEATED. 'YOU must be devastated.'

'I am.' Tilly pulled clothes from her case and threw them into a pile on the floor. 'But I'm glad to be home.' She was. She felt she'd never truly appreciated it till this day, but now it was the only place she wanted to be.

'Fancy heading out somewhere?' For her eighteenth birthday last year Lien's parents had presented her with a new silver Hyundai Getz. 'We could go to the mall.'

The mall, with its crowds and bright lights and jolly piped music. Usually Tilly loved it: she and Lien would dip in and out of their favourite places, and finish up in a coffee shop with skinny lattes or flat whites – but today she wasn't in the mood.

'I'm still a bit jetlagged,' she said, although she wasn't. She'd slept from Dublin to Dubai, and again from Singapore to Brisbane, and she hadn't done too badly last night either, her first night home. She sat on the edge of the bed that had been hers since childhood, recalling the bigger, softer one she'd been given in her father's house.

She'd woken from her nap around six. In his big kitchen she'd found eggs and cheese and made an omelette. She'd eaten it at the counter, taking in the shining surfaces, the absence of dishes in the sink, the tiled floor that hadn't a mark on it. Either he was a pretty impressive housekeeper, or he had someone coming in.

Afterwards she'd studied the paintings on the walls in the hall, and found none that she thought might be his own. She'd peered into the other ground-floor rooms, and come upon a small sitting room with a television. She'd watched a black and white film set in a travel agency, her mind not really on it, alert all the time for a step outside the door that she'd left ajar, but he hadn't reappeared. She'd gone to bed early, sure she'd sleep, but sleep hadn't come. Instead she'd found herself back in the hotel garden, listening to her future falling apart, over and over again.

In the morning, as soon as it got light, she'd made toast and drunk milk, not wanting to mess up the fancy coffee machine, and unable to find instant. She'd torn a page from her diary and written him a note, and left it on the kitchen counter.

Thank you for letting me stay. I'm glad we met. I'll write from Australia, and I would love if you wrote back.

Tilly, she signed it, and added two kisses, because she'd be gone when he saw them.

Maybe he would write back, next time she sent him a letter. The world had a way of surprising you.

'I'll call you tomorrow after work,' Lien promised. 'We'll get together at the weekend. Try not to think about it.'

Easier said than done. She wished she'd never set eyes on the island, or anyone living there. She'd survived fine without Laura, before discovering she had a sister. If only she'd never learnt that she was adopted, never gone looking for her birth mother.

If she could rewind it all, if she could go back to a time before she'd walked past a house and seen a blue-eyed Irish boy shovelling snow from the path outside it. But there was no rewinding, just pushing on. Probably just as well, or everyone would be fixing mistakes and changing course, and things would get mighty complicated.

'Tilly!' Robbie's high-pitched voice hollered up at her from the bottom of the stairs. 'Supper's ready!'

She went down and ate what she could of the meat pie, and fielded the careful questions that came across the table at her. They knew something was up, of course they did. She hadn't told them about Andy – at least, they'd known a boy was on the scene, she'd felt obliged to let Ma in on that much, but they hadn't got the full story. They didn't know she'd fallen in love, they didn't know she'd planned to—

Stop. Don't.

Back in her room she brushed her teeth and changed into pyjamas and opened her laptop. She'd watch Netflix, take her mind off everything with a movie until she got tired enough for bed. She was starting back in the restaurant tomorrow afternoon, which she was glad of, but she'd need a proper night's sleep before she could pretend, for eight hours, to be happy.

She logged on. *New message* pinged onto her screen. She opened her inbox and saw it was from Andy.

She sank her head into her hands.

She couldn't.

She couldn't not. She had to.

She sat up. She clicked on the message and it sprang onto her screen.

Tilly

I'm not sure if this will come out right, but I hope it will. I hope you'll read it too, but that's up to you.

You know I've tried to call you loads of times over the past few days, and you haven't picked up. Well, now I'm thinking it was probably just as well, because it gave us both time to really get our heads around everything, and to figure out what it means for us.

Let me start by telling you what happened – on the night of Frog's party, I mean. A few of us left together, but by the time we got to Eve's apartment the others had gone off in different directions, and it was just the two of us. We'd both had a fair bit to drink, but I remember everything. We went in and I made coffee, although she said she didn't want any. She was crying about Hugh, and already half asleep by the time I left.

I didn't see much of her after that. She wasn't around a lot. I figured she was still cut up about Hugh – and anytime we did meet, there were always others there. To be honest, I'd completely forgotten about that night by the time you arrived.

Now here's the thing. Yesterday Imelda called – Eve's old foster mother – and she told us that Eve isn't pregnant, and never was. She had a false pregnancy or something. It sounds totally weird and I don't understand it, but it's a thing. I looked it up and it does exist.

I tried to tell you nothing happened, but you didn't listen. In a way I don't blame you, because often when a woman accuses a man of making her pregnant, it's true. It's just that it wasn't true in this case.

I'm sorry you left Roone before you were supposed to. I'm sorry you went away hating me, but at least now you know the truth. Maybe I shouldn't have walked Eve home, but she meant a lot to me once, and she was still a friend, and I thought she needed someone to look after her that night. Not that I was in a much better state than her, but I was a bit more sober.

It would have been nice if you'd trusted me more. It hurt that you didn't give me a chance to tell you my side, but like I say, I do understand. I think part of the reason you believed her was because you weren't sure how I felt about you, or whether I felt enough. I get it, and now that all of this has happened, it's time to tell the truth about that too.

I really like you, I think you know that, but I don't love you the way I loved Eve. I'm sorry to hurt you like this. I've been a coward. I knew how you felt about me, and I wanted to feel the same but I didn't, and I didn't know how to tell you, so I avoided it. I knew you wanted more time on our own this summer, but I kept bringing you out with my friends, because I thought you might ask questions I couldn't answer if we were alone. That time we went on the picnic I waited for you to say something, to ask me how I really felt about you, and I was relieved when you didn't.

I'm really sorry. I'm sorry it took something as awful as Thursday night to get me to say what I should have said ages ago. I'm sorry I couldn't be what you wanted me to be. I'm sorry I let it go on so long.

I hope you can forgive me, but I'll understand if I don't hear from you again. I hope you won't let it stop you coming back to Roone. I would like us to stay friends, and I know Laura and her family would hate for you not to come back. And whether you believe it or not, I did enjoy the time we spent together. You're a cool person.

Andy xx

Long after she had finished reading it, she remained staring at the screen, too numb to move. Trying to take it all in, trying to sort it out in her head.

Eve wasn't pregnant.

He hadn't been unfaithful.

She'd wronged him: she hadn't given him a chance to deny the charge. Not that it mattered, now that they were over.

They were over.

They were really over.

Tears poured down her face, and she let them. They were hot and bitter, full of the hurt and the pain and the humiliation that had been festering inside her since Thursday evening.

At least now she knew where she stood. It didn't help much; it didn't really help at all. Knowing where she stood didn't lessen the pain, all it stopped was the uncertainty. She'd never be Mrs Andy Baker, never have a van selling hot food, or cold food, or any kind of food, at the end of the village street. She'd never write her book looking out at the sea that washed around the island.

It was finished. All of that was finished.

I don't love you the way I loved Eve – God, how that stung, how that sliced into her like a sharpened knife. *I would like us to stay friends*. No chance. That wasn't going to happen. Next summer she'd stay at home, or maybe take a trip with Lien, who was always saying she'd love to visit New Zealand.

But she *would* go back to Roone sometime. She wouldn't allow him to deny her that. She'd go back, maybe the year after next, and stay again at Walter's Place. She'd say hello when they met, and move on. She wouldn't be his friend. That wouldn't happen.

She selected all of his emails and deleted them, and removed him from her contact list. She wiped his number from her phone, and binned his WhatsApp and text messages. She tore her photos of him, and her photos of them, into tiny squares and dropped them into her wastepaper basket. She erased as much of him as she could, crying all the way.

She'd get over it. The logical side of her brain knew that. She wasn't twenty yet: time was on her side. She'd throw herself into work, and she'd go back to cycling in the mornings, and on her days off. She used to love cycling. She'd fill her head with new stuff to replace him. There would come a day when it didn't hurt any more, or not anything like it hurt now.

When nothing of him was left she blotted her face dry and opened Netflix, and began the business of forgetting him.

Eve

LYING IN BED, WATCHING DAYS TURN TO nights and back again, she'd figured out a lot of things.

She'd wanted the pregnancy to be real. She hadn't realised how badly she'd wanted that. She'd wanted to be carrying Andy Baker's child because she was still in love with Andy Baker.

She'd finished with him because of Derek Garvey, who had damaged her in a way that made her feel she wasn't worthy of being loved. She'd convinced herself that she wasn't good enough for Andy. She'd been frightened of her feelings for him, frightened he'd discover how worthless she was, and leave her, and break her, so she'd called a halt to their relationship before any of that could happen.

She hadn't stopped loving him. Not for a minute.

She still didn't understand how she could have believed herself to be pregnant when she wasn't. It had felt so real. All the signs had been there. How could the entire thing have been in her head? Dr Jack, when Imelda had handed her the phone, had been gentle – and pretty useless. *We're not entirely sure why it happens*, he'd said, *but it can often be as a result of some trauma* – and Eve had known he was talking about Derek, and yes, maybe Mam too. Maybe Mam had played her part.

Come and talk to me when you feel able, he'd said, *and we can discuss it further*, whatever that meant. *When will my periods come back?* she'd asked, and he'd said it would depend on how quickly she recovered, which had told her nothing much either.

So now she had to try to recover – and to help that along, Imelda was taking her to Italy.

She didn't deserve it. The last thing she deserved was a holiday, but all the same they'd booked flights and a hotel, and this time tomorrow they'd be there. She could put all this aside, even if it was only for six days.

It wasn't over. It was far from over. Earlier her phone had rung, and she'd seen *Veronica D* on the display, and her heart had sunk. Veronica Delaney was head of the island committee, and the call wasn't unexpected – Eve had wondered why they hadn't been in touch before now – but it was certainly unwelcome.

Hello?

Is that Eve? The brusque tone. Pure Veronica.

Yes.

Eve, it's Veronica. I'm sure you know why I'm ringing. We're very disturbed by what we're hearing. We need to have a word with you as soon as possible.

Eve had explained that she was going away, and

a date had been arranged for the following week. She'd be hauled before them and cross-examined – or maybe they'd skip the questioning and sack her on the spot. She prayed that wouldn't happen: she loved working at the crèche. She hoped they'd give her a chance to explain, and feel some sympathy for her, but the hope was faint. She'd got drunk enough not to remember the events of an evening, and then she'd conjured up a pregnancy. She suspected it wouldn't end with them handing her tea and a biscuit, and telling her all was forgiven.

There was one thing at least that she'd done, or tried to do, to make some kind of amends. Right after the call from Veronica, before she could lose her nerve, she'd pressed the number for the hotel, and held her breath until the phone had been picked up.

Manning's Hotel, good afternoon, Betty speaking. How may I help?

Betty, whom she didn't know well: a small blessing. *Um, could I speak with Mr Manning please?*

He'd kill her. He'd give her a right tongue lashing, and she'd just have to take it.

But there had been no tongue lashing.

I'm afraid Mr Manning is away on leave. May I take a message?

She'd said no and hung up, forgetting to ask when he'd be back. She'd have to ring again when they got home from Italy. It would have to be done. It was the right thing to do. She'd apologise, if he gave her a chance. She'd do that much.

She pulled on her jeans and slipped her feet into sneakers. She'd bring Scooter for a walk. She'd avoid the village, take the quieter road to the lighthouse. If she met anyone she knew, she'd look them in the eye. She had no idea if the latest news had got around, but she couldn't stay holed up. She'd face whatever there was to be faced.

As she buttoned her shirt, there was a tap on the door.

'Andy is downstairs,' Imelda said. 'He'd like to talk to you. You don't have to if you don't want to.'

Andy. The name caused a great burst within her. He was either here to kill her, or forgive her. 'I'll come down. Give me a sec.'

'He's in the sitting room.'

She stroked on mascara and lipstick. She brushed blusher onto pale cheekbones. She still looked crap, but there was no time for more.

He stood by the window, hands in jeans pockets. The sight of him. She closed the door and leant against it, and they regarded one another for what seemed like an age. She wondered if he could hear the pounding inside her. He didn't look angry. He didn't look anything. Finally, she found the courage to speak.

'I don't blame you if you hate me.'

'I don't hate you – although you did land me in it.'

'I'm so sorry. I honestly believed what I said was true.'

'I know you did.'

'I wasn't going to say anything until Tilly was gone home. It was just … when you said …' She stopped, floundering, unwilling and unable to rehash it all. 'I'm sorry,' she repeated. 'I hope you can fix things with her.'

He continued to regard her. She forced herself to return his gaze, although it killed her to be in the same room as him, to be so close to him, knowing she'd thrown him away when she shouldn't have. Knowing he would never again be hers.

'Actually,' he said, 'Tilly and I have … separated.'

It took a few seconds for that to sink in. She'd broken them up. She could think of nothing at all to say in response.

'It's not your fault,' he went on. 'It's not because of what happened. It wasn't working out, that's all.'

'I'm sorry,' she said, because she did feel responsible, whatever he said.

'How about you?' he asked. 'How are you doing?'

She tried to smile. It didn't happen. 'I – think I probably need to … talk to someone.' She'd never imagined she'd say that, not after the last time. But there were other counsellors – or maybe she was more ready to listen to them now, more open to the idea. She'd ask Imelda what she thought about that, if the right time came in Italy.

He nodded. 'I think that might be good for you. Anyway, I just wanted to come and … see you. See that you were OK.'

His concern, so ill-earned, so unexpected, caused tears to spring to her eyes. She'd accused him wrongly in front of half the island. He'd been publicly humiliated, and his relationship was finished. And yet here he was, bearing her no grudge, calling to see that she was OK.

She squeezed her eyes shut. 'Thank you,' she whispered – and then he was beside her, putting his arms around her, telling her not to cry, telling her it would be OK, it would all be forgotten in no time. Telling her he hoped they could still be friends.

At first she held back, terrified to submit to his embrace. She resisted but he stayed put, and in the end she gave in and rested her head against his chest and allowed herself to be held as the tears flowed. And it felt good; it felt better than it should. They fitted together like they'd always fitted together.

It didn't mean anything; she knew that. He was offering comfort, no more – but she accepted it gratefully.

Eventually they drew apart. She fished for a tissue and found none, and ruined her shirt sleeve instead.

'Imelda says you're going to Italy.'

'Yes, tomorrow.'

'I'll give a shout when you're home,' he said, 'if that's OK.'

She nodded. *It means nothing. It means nothing.* 'Yes,' she said, still nodding, nodding far more than she needed to, unable to stop nodding. She saw him to the front door and closed it after him, and returned upstairs before Imelda reappeared and asked questions she wouldn't be able to answer.

She washed her face. She dabbed concealer beneath her swollen eyes and redid her lipstick. She left the bedroom and went to find Scooter, and all the time she told herself it was over between them. It had been over for a long time, and after what had happened there was certainly no chance of them getting back together.

But he was giving her a shout when she got back from Italy. He still wanted them to be friends.

She held on to that. She held on tightly.

Susan

'SEE THE BIRD?' SHE POINTED TO A THRUSH that had just alighted on a nearby branch.

He looked, and saw. He laughed. 'Bird,' he said.

'Bird,' she agreed.

The park was small, and very pretty. Roughly triangular in shape, and bordered by ornate white railings. Inside were a row of trees with slender silver trunks, and flowers in rectangular beds framing patches of neatly trimmed grass, and a rose garden still in full bloom running along the park's shortest side.

A paved path wove its way around the place, with wooden benches positioned alongside it at intervals. Attached to the back of the bench where Susan and Harry sat was a little brass plaque that read: *For Edith, who loved this place.* Susan imagined Edith – tiny, grey-haired, tweed-coated, smiling – coming to the park each day, a little paper bag of seeds or breadcrumbs in her pocket for the birds.

The morning was fine, a sky of deep blue

interrupted only by the wispiest of clouds. Susan lifted her face to let it bask in the warmth of the sun, and she felt determined to be happy.

A man entered the park. He wore a navy pinstripe suit over a white shirt, and his black shoes were very shiny. His hair was silver and sparse; he walked slowly, back curved into a stoop, his right hand clasping the bulbous head of a stout wooden stick. She wondered if he was Edith's husband, and if they were sitting on the bench he always chose, but he gave no sign that he was put out. He nodded as he passed her, and said 'Nice day,' and she said it was, beautiful.

They were in Kensington, staying in a Georgian townhouse across the street from the park, less than three miles as the crow flew from Rosie and Ed's house. She'd found the place on Airbnb, and taken it for a week. It was bright and airy and spotless, with high ceilings and big windows. There was a full kitchen with black and white floor tiles, like in their hall at home, and three bedrooms, and a wonderful claw-footed bath in the larger of the two bathrooms. The place was far bigger than they needed, but after their cramped conditions at Rosie and Ed's, Susan had craved lots of space.

A second man entered the park. She watched as he drew closer, a newspaper tucked under one arm, a cardboard cup in each hand. He wore a dark grey fleece, and jeans that had seen better days, and soft brown shoes. Even with his glasses on she could see the pockets of skin beneath his blue-green eyes. His hair – the darkness washing out of it, particularly at the temples and sides – could do with a cut.

He wasn't really, she thought, a man you'd pay too much attention to. Not really a man worthy of a second glance, unless you were his wife, and loved him.

He handed her one of the cups, and she caught a waft of the nuttiness of freshly brewed coffee. He dropped the newspaper onto the bench and pulled open the pocket of his fleece. 'Put your hand in,' he said to Harry, 'and see what you can find' – and Harry drew out a cookie studded with Smarties, or maybe M&Ms, and a carton of apple juice.

'Mama,' he said, passing it to his mother, who poked the accompanying straw into its designated space and handed it back to him.

'What do you say to Daddy?'

'Ta ta,' he said, looking up at his father.

They sat on the bench, their child between them. Susan and Harry had taken possession of the townhouse the previous afternoon, and Luke had caught a flight from Dublin in time to join them for an early pasta dinner. Her idea, the neutral territory where the three of them could reunite, a week of settling back with one another before resuming their life in Dublin.

The doorbell had given her a start, keyed up as she'd been about seeing him again. *Wait here*, she'd told Harry, *and I'll bring Daddy in*.

You found us, she'd said, wearing the new turquoise dress that Rosie had complimented when she'd put it on for her.

He carried the weekend bag she'd bought him a few birthdays ago. His raincoat was slung over an arm. In the four weeks they'd been apart he seemed to have lost weight. Was it only four weeks? It felt like months. She ached to put her arms around him, but held back.

My God, he'd said, *I'd forgotten how beautiful you are.*

He sounded tired. Maybe he hadn't slept well, without her beside him.

Come in, she'd said, tucking the compliment away safely – and stepping over the threshold he'd stumbled, and she'd put out a hand to steady him, and he'd let his bag and coat go then, just let them fall to the floor, and they'd found themselves pressed into one another, his hand cradling her head, rocking her against him, saying her name, his mouth against her face, his breath warm on her cheek, *Susan, Susan*, he'd said, and she'd wrapped her arms around his waist and clung on, and thought maybe this time they'd get it right.

And later, much later, after Harry had been tucked up in bed with Toby, and they were finishing off the bottle of red Luke had bought in Duty Free, he'd told her the news he'd been given in February.

Five years, he'd said, holding tightly to her hand, never once letting his eyes move from hers. *I swear I'll make the best of them. I'll make it up to you, and to Harry.*

He was dying. Her husband was dying. It was unthinkable. She'd felt everything collapse inside her.

Are you sure? How can you be sure?

I've had tests, he'd said. *I've had a battery of tests, and several opinions. I'm sure.*

But there must be trials, there must be something —

Not for me, he'd said. *Too far gone.*

He'd gone through all that, and she'd had no idea. *When were you going to tell me?*

I was going to wait until I had no choice. I was being a coward.

You're not a coward. You're the bravest man I know. Are you in pain now?

No.

He would never see his son grow to manhood. Before Susan was fifty, she'd be a widow. It was too much. It was too sad. Her heart wasn't able to take it in.

Let's try to enjoy what's left, he'd said, and in the midst of her immense shock she could see, she could understand, that that was their only choice. Impossible as it seemed, she would have to find ways to push the future away, to live in the moment with her husband and son.

They'd sat close together, their talk sporadic, the news settling into her, filling her, leaving room for nothing else.

Let's go to bed, he'd said finally, and they'd left the wine unfinished and gone upstairs, and rediscovered one another in an unfamiliar, but very comfortable, king-size bed. She'd lain in his arms afterwards, her face tight with the salt of the tears that their lovemaking had released, and she'd listened to his sleeping breaths and determined, by whatever means, to meet this new chapter, this terrible unexpected episode, head on.

They might travel a little, before Harry started school, and while his father was able. They might move out of the big house, find tenants for it and rent a smaller one in the countryside, or near the sea, or both. Close enough to Dublin, and to hospitals, and to whatever might lie ahead for him.

They might get a dog. A dog might be a comfort. Dogs loved so unconditionally. Yes, she thought, they needed a dog.

He might paint a little. If that was what he wanted, she wouldn't object.

And now it was the morning after, and the three of them were on a park bench, and at some stage during the week they would take a train to Windsor to see what Harry made of Legoland – or maybe they wouldn't. They were going to have a week of taking each day as it came, of not planning ahead. They were just going to be in the moment, like she would try to do for all the moments, until they ran out.

For now all she wanted was to drink coffee, and sit in the sunshine with her husband and child, and take what happiness she could from wherever she found it.

HENRY MANNING, PROPRIETOR OF ROONE'S only hotel, was taking stock.

Seventy years on this earth as of today, eight years more than his brother had got. Ten to go until he passed out his father, fifteen for his mother – and with Henry's death, the Manning family would be no more.

It was a sobering thought. It was perhaps not one best suited to the little pavement café where he currently sat, with its view, albeit distant, of the Eiffel Tower, and its more immediate distractions in the shape of the immaculately dressed businessmen who didn't sit down to drink their swift espressos, and who vanished as fast as they had appeared, while Henry lingered over his second *café au lait*.

He turned his attention to his recent party, which hadn't exactly gone to plan. It had started promisingly enough, with a turnout of pretty much everyone he'd been expecting, and precisely the ones he'd thought might give it a miss staying away, which was for the best. Live and let live, et cetera.

For the first few hours there had been a gratifying buzz about the place. Food and drink going down nicely, an embarrassing number of gifts presented, which were accepted and quietly removed to be unwrapped later. His speech had been well received, and only interrupted once by the wailing of an overtired infant, who had been whisked away promptly. The cake, all five generous tiers, had been admired and cut and sampled.

And just as he'd begun to congratulate himself on a well-orchestrated and successful event, and was enjoying his first glass of champagne, now that the speech was safely behind him, it had happened. He'd missed it, having just returned to the marquee at the time, where Maisie Kiely was getting into the party spirit and threatening to dance.

They'd gradually become aware of a stir among the assembly, a new excitement, a nudging relay of news that had spread through the marquee like licking flames. *Has something happened?* Maisie had wondered – and Henry, feeling it incumbent on him as host to find out if something had indeed happened, had set aside his glass and made enquiries, and been told.

Out he'd gone in search of Eve Mulqueen, his newest chambermaid, and one of his waitresses for the evening – but his search had proved fruitless. She wasn't to be found, so he hunted down the other names he'd heard mentioned, Andy Baker and his stepmother Nell, whom he'd known her entire life, and with whom he'd been chatting only minutes earlier, and Andy's unfortunate girlfriend, who must now, if the reports were true, be in a bit of a state.

But here again he drew blanks. Nell, he was told, had left – and Andy, it was assumed, had gone with her. As for the girlfriend, whose name he couldn't recall, nobody could tell him what had become of her.

He'd done what he could to salvage the night. He'd scurried about, issuing orders for glasses to be refilled, food trays replenished, more of the cake cut and passed around. And it *had* been salvaged, to an extent – the chat had resumed, the noise level gradually cranked up to its previous volume – but he'd fancied that the atmosphere about the place had altered.

The incident, not surprisingly, had remained the topic of the evening. Passing groups of merrymakers, he'd heard frequent mentions of Eve and Andy's names. Some heads had shaken in disapproval; others seemed to find it all very amusing and diverting. His party, he'd realised, had been hijacked by the girl he'd taken in largely out of pity, because he'd heard her story from Nell, and because she'd recently lost Hugh, who'd been like a father to her.

Her work had been good. He'd checked it out discreetly, as he checked out the efforts of all his staff – well, he had standards to uphold – and apart from the occasional stray hair that she missed, he'd found no fault. She'd been pleasant and polite in manner whenever they'd encountered one another in the course of her duties. There had been no indication, no warning, of what was to come.

She hadn't returned to the hotel after the night of the party. She'd missed her shift the following day, and his manager reported, when Henry enquired, that there had been no further sighting of her. It hadn't surprised Henry all that much. He knew how the island tongues could wag: who could blame the girl for wanting to hide from them now?

She should have let him know, of course. She should have been in touch to tell him she couldn't face the aftermath. That would have been the right thing to do. He'd felt hard done by, put out by her lack of consideration – but then he'd heard, just yesterday, and also via his manager, that the pregnancy she'd revealed on the night of the party was an imaginary one, a figment of a troubled mind, and it had prompted a measure of sympathy towards her.

Treat others as you would like to be treated: someone had advised Henry of that as a boy – his mother, it might have been – and he'd tried, all his life, to live by it. He would listen to the girl, he decided, if she made any contact on his return, and he would show kindness if he felt it was called for. He'd take her back, if she wanted to come back. Some might call him a fool, and they were perfectly entitled to their opinions.

He sat alone in dusky pink cotton shirt and navy linen trousers, and the grey calfskin loafers, deliciously comfortable, that he'd splurged on during a little shopping trip to Milan in the spring. With each lift of his cup he experienced a pleasant waft of the bergamot and citrus notes of the Tom Ford eau de toilette he'd applied to his pulse points before dressing. Treating others kindly was all very well, but being kind to oneself was also to be recommended.

He'd strolled to the café this morning from his hotel in the Marais, after a leisurely breakfast and a long bath, and he intended to spend the day ambling from museum to gallery, with regular intermissions such as this one. He had yet to decide on a restaurant for dinner, but was reasonably confident that a suitable one would present itself in the course of his perambulations.

'*Monsieur?*'

He glanced up to see his rather delectable waiter at his elbow. '*Encore?*' the waiter asked, indicating Henry's almost empty cup, giving Henry the opportunity to admire his impeccably manicured nails.

'Actually,' Henry replied, 'I'd prefer a cognac, *s'il vous plaît.*'

A few minutes shy of noon, but to hell with it. Not every day a man turned seventy.

Acknowledgements

HEARTFELT THANKS AS EVER TO EVERYONE who helped to get this one over the finish line. All at Hachette Books Ireland, agent Sallyanne, obliging research contributors Geraldine Exton, Philip Gleeson and Nicky Quinn.

Thanks to my family for their constant support and encouragement.

Thanks to the dedicated book bloggers who play such vita roles. You know who you are.

Sincere thanks to my faithful readers (and welcome to the new arrivals). You are truly appreciated.

Roisin x

www.roisinmeaney.com

@roisinmeaney

'If you like
Maeve Binchy,
this will be a treat'
Stellar

*One
Summer*
Roisin
Meaney
NUMBER ONE BESTSELLER

Nell Mulcahy grew up on the island – playing in the shallows and fishing with her father in his old red boat in the harbour. So when the stone cottage by the edge of the sea comes up for sale, the decision to move back from Dublin is easy. And where better to hold her upcoming wedding to Tim than on the island, surrounded by family and friends?

But when Nell decides to rent out her cottage for the summer to help finance the wedding, she sets in motion an unexpected series of events.

As deeply buried feelings rise to the surface, Nell's carefully laid plans for her wedding start to go awry and she is forced to make some tough decisions.

One thing's for sure, it's a summer on the island that nobody will ever forget.

Revisit the island of Roone in
After the Wedding *and* I'll Be Home for Christmas

Also available as an ebook and audiobook

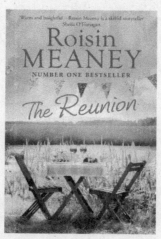

It's their twenty-year school reunion but the Plunkett sisters have their own reasons for not wanting to attend ...

Caroline, now a successful knitwear designer, spends her time flying between her business in England and her lover in Italy. As far as she's concerned, her school days, and what happened to her the year she left, should stay in the past.

Eleanor, meanwhile, is unrecognisable from the fun-loving girl she was in school. With a son who is barely speaking to her, and a husband keeping a secret from her, revisiting the past is the last thing on her mind.

But when an unexpected letter arrives for Caroline in the weeks before the reunion, memories are stirred.

Will the sisters find the courage to return to the town where they grew up and face what they've been running from all these years?

Also available as an ebook

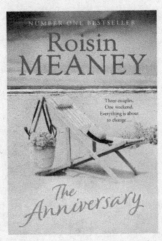

It's the Bank Holiday weekend and the Cunningham family are escaping to their holiday home by the sea, as they've done every summer for many years.

Except that now, parents Lily and Charlie are waiting for their divorce papers to come through – and have their new partners in tow.

Their daughter Poll is there with her boyfriend and is determined to make known her feelings for Chloë, her father's new love. While her brother Thomas also has feelings for Chloë – of a very different nature...

And amid all the drama, everyone has forgotten that this weekend also happens to be Lily and Charlie's wedding anniversary.

Will any of the couples survive the weekend intact?

Also available as an ebook and audiobook

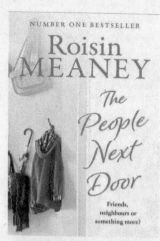

NUMBER ONE BESTSELLER

**Roisin
MEANEY**

*The
People
Next
Door*

Friends,
neighbours or
something more?

When Yvonne in number 7 joins a dating website, she's looking for something more than friendship – but gives up after a series of disastrous encounters. Is she shutting out her only chance of finding love?

Meanwhile next door Dan, still reeling from his wife's desertion, signs up for a cookery course. As his lemon soufflé rises, so does his interest in someone close to home ...

Further along, Kathryn is struggling to keep her marriage together despite her interfering mother-in-law's best efforts. As tension grows between the two women, Kathryn wonders if Grainne will finally succeed, as she realises that she may never give her husband Justin what he wants.

As the drama unfolds along Millers Avenue, its residents learn that the things you most yearn for can often be found on your own doorstep.

Also available as an ebook and audiobook

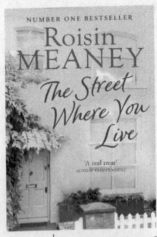

When a heatwave coincides with rehearsals for an end-of-summer concert, temperatures soar - so too do the small-town scandals ...

It turns out that some members of the choir have secrets they are desperate to keep hidden.

Christopher, the handsome and talented director, is embroiled in a steamy affair with someone who is strictly off-limits; Molly has become obsessed with a young boy whom she's convinced is her grandson; while Emily has just fallen in love - with the wrong man.

As opening night approaches, it becomes clear that there are some tough decisions to be made. But until the curtain falls, you never know what might happen on *The Street Where You Live*.

Also available as an ebook